The critics on Victoria Clayton

'A delicious teasing love story' Elizabeth Buchan

'Told with tremendous affection and care, this is an engrossing yarn that encompasses a range of endearing, sometimes eccentric characters and a not entirely predictable ending' *Ideal Home*

'Delightful humour which overlays a beady observation and perception' *Mail on Sunday*

'The writing is assured . . . plenty of hardcore wine-and-roses romance' *Sunday Times*

'An excellent story told with dash and verve; and the characters leap out of the page to greet one . . . a lovely summer read' *Publishing News*

'The charm and vivacity with which the author presents her scenario and the precision with which she describes character and setting make this a very enjoyable read. Social comedy is a difficult thing to do well, but Clayton shows herself an adept practitioner' *The Times*

'Clayton is unsentimental, and there is nothing sugary about her account of love, sex, friendship and manipulation' *Times Literary Supplement*

Victoria Clayton published two children's novels when in her early twenties. She then read English at Cambridge as a mature undergraduate, married and had two children before returning to writing fiction.

By the same author

Out of Love
Past Mischief

DANCE WITH ME

Victoria Clayton

ORION

An Orion Paperback
First published in Great Britain in 1999 by Orion
This paperback edition published in 2000 by
Orion Books Ltd,
Orion House, 5 Upper St Martin's Lane,
London WC2H 9EA

A CIP catalogue record for this book
is available from the British Library.

Typeset at The Spartan Press Ltd,
Lymington, Hants
Printed in Great Britain by
Clays Ltd, St Ives plc

CHAPTER I

'Y ou'd better take Viola with you.'
Pierce, who had just spoken, looked at me with a mixture of amusement and malice. We were seated round the boardroom table in the offices of SCAB, the Society for the Conservation of Ancient Buildings. It was a brilliant, freezing morning in late April. Our headquarters occupied the very top floor of a former gentlemen's club just off Pall Mall. Flocks of white, grey and dun-coloured pigeons promenaded on the balcony, which ran the length of the office, eating the scraps I had just put out for them. A ray of sunlight shot through a dusty window-pane, lit Pierce's sleek fair head and touched the shabby, claret-coloured leather of the buttoned armchairs with crimson. Giles, the third party in this conversation, frowned. Of course, Pierce knew that Giles would very much prefer to go without me.

'I shouldn't think I'd be much use . . .' I began.

'It would be a pity to take Viola away from the filing . . .' said Giles, at the same moment.

'Nonsense. The filing's been in a mess for the last six months. One more day will make no difference.' Pierce picked up the telephone and began to dial a number. It was one of his manoeuvres for ending a conversation he found inconvenient or tedious. Having been his girlfriend for the three months preceding this conversation, the techniques were familiar to me.

Pierce called me his 'doxy'. I looked it up and it means a beggar's trull. I looked *that* up and found that 'trull' means a low prostitute. I hardly think the occasional taxi fare Pierce gave me when he couldn't be bothered to drive all the way out to E1 qualified me to be called 'a woman who is devoted to indiscriminate sexual intercourse esp. for hire', low or not. That's how the OED defines a prostitute. I have to look up words a lot, being a girl of meagre education, though that isn't my fault. Also I like to know exactly what words mean.

Pierce was my first real lover and as I was, at the time of this narration, nearly twenty-one years old, the strictest guardian of morals could not accuse me of being undiscriminating.

SCAB, whose workforce consisted of Pierce, Giles and me, was a mongrel organisation, a cross between the National Trust and the Distressed Gentlefolk's Aid Association. Its aim was to help owners of historic houses to carry on living in them without resorting to exotic livestock or giving tea to 'the beast with many heads'. Pierce taught me this expression. It is Shakespearean for the general public. I *think* I see what it means.

To be considered for SCAB's assistance the house must have been in the same family for three generations. Giles wanted to change this stipulation for a more rigorous five as he thought that anything constructed this century was probably better torn down but Pierce's mother, who was the chief fund-raiser for SCAB, lived with Pierce's father in a huge baronial castle in Wester Ross, built in 1910. She spent a great deal of time in her flat in London, happily raising money for SCAB as, she told us frequently, she disliked rain, cold, whisky, sermons and heather, and had a particular antipathy to tartan.

The office consisted of four rooms – the large, graceful room in which we were sitting, which had good cornices and big windows, a tiny kitchen, a lavatory and a small conservatory, which was really just a glassed-in bit of the balcony. I was delighted by the conservatory, and one or two of the pelargonium cuttings I was attempting to grow had actually put out little white roots, though Giles told me that by digging them up every day I was bound to kill them. By a superhuman effort I had managed at the time the above conversation took place not to interfere with them for three whole days.

'Well, if you really think it's necessary,' said Giles, compressing his lips and shooting me a glance of annoyance.

'I do. Most certainly I do.' Pierce put down the telephone without making the call, having gained his point. 'Now, I'd better go and see my godfather about that bequest to SCAB. Lunch at Simpson's. Got to keep the old coelacanth rising to the fly. What sacrifices I make for the preservation of the upper classes!'

Giles leaned back in his chair, just the faintest suspicion of contempt in his eyes. We all knew that Pierce would enjoy a leisurely lunch at his godfather's expense, then be obliged by the quantity of champagne, burgundy and brandy he had drunk to go home and sleep it off.

Ten years ago Giles and Pierce had been at Oxford together. When it had occurred to Pierce that an organisation that combined visits to interesting country houses and partying with the rich and philanthropic in London might be constructed so as to pay him a reasonable salary he had lost no time in recruiting Giles. Giles had read History of Art at Balliol and since then had worked in museums in Paris and Rome, and at the V and A. He was, Pierce told me, simply the best. He had an immense knowledge of domestic architecture, antiques and antiquities and was exactly the partner Pierce needed to ensure that they selected only the worthiest recipients for SCAB's charitable outlays.

'It's all a question of organising people into doing for a salary what they would naturally do anyway,' Pierce had explained to me the first time I met him, at a private view in the art gallery where I was then working. 'I like making contacts and setting up deals, my mother likes giving parties, and Giles likes looking at old things.'

I reminded him of the conversation a week later when he telephoned me to ask if I would be his secretary. 'No one could say it's what I'd naturally be doing. For one thing I can't type or do shorthand. I'm dreadfully untidy and disorganised and I've only kept this job because the man who owns the gallery is a friend of my aunt.'

Pierce had laughed and said that I was unusually and disarmingly honest, which made me a very suitable employee. This was not at all what Caspar Phipps, the gallery owner, said when I told him I was leaving to go and work for Pierce. He said that I was more of a liability than a receptionist and I needn't stay to work out my notice as it would be cheaper to hire someone else straight away who could begin to work out the muddle I had got his books into. I went down to the basement to get my coat and bag and to say goodbye to Paws, the darling tabby cat I had grown so fond of during my six months at the gallery. When Caspar came downstairs and found me in tears, with Paws on my knee, he said he was sorry he had been so rough with me and that he didn't mean it. Then he tried to kiss me. It is odd that men can never think of anything else to do in a crisis.

No sooner had I got myself out of the clutches of Caspar Phipps than I fell into those of Pierce. I was quite pleased about this. Well, very pleased, really. Pierce was extremely attractive and my most onerous task as his secretary turned out to be putting off all his ex-girlfriends who rang up and called round, begging him to come back to them. I saw at once the mistake they were making and though, as I said, I have hardly any proper education and the great rivers of the world are a watery blank to me, I can learn quickly.

So I was stern with myself about never showing Pierce any particular mark of my favour. Whenever he asked me out I was offhand with my acceptance and during dinner or drinks or dancing I schooled myself to be indifferent to the point of rudeness. This meant that Pierce had so far remained interested and intrigued. When we went to bed the first time I made the mistake of putting my arms round him and kissing him but I sensed at once that his amorousness had suffered a check so after that I was as apathetic as a large, warm doll.

'What about a cup of coffee?' I asked Giles after Pierce had left, in an attempt to lighten the atmosphere.

'Thank you, but I'll make it myself.'

I knew he was remembering all my unsuccessful attempts to produce the only kind of coffee he approved of – madly strong and scorchingly hot and silted up with bitter black grounds. Giles was a tremendous aesthete and everything that came into his path, including what he ate and drank,

4

was subjected to penetrating analysis and carefully chosen. I drank water from the tap in a Bugs Bunny mug, given to me by Bolter, the office caretaker, who was an absolute pet. Giles had cases of Perrier sent in which he drank from a special engraved glass which, he warned me, was eighteenth century and quite irreplaceable.

On his arrival at SCAB Giles had installed a complicated coffee machine, which took up nearly all the kitchen. It had fiddly parts that had to be washed after use and were quite impossible to put back together and several times I had burned my hand on sudden jets of scalding steam. Pierce refused to touch it. He had nicknamed it Phlegethon which, he explained to me, was the burning river surrounding Tartarus, the region of Hades where the most wicked people of all were sent. Pierce had read classics at Oxford and he knew a great many things. That was one of the reasons why I wanted to go on being his girlfriend despite the hard work of being cold and unaffectionate. Most of the men I met were rather dim and conversation with them was hard work of another, far worse, kind.

I was getting better at managing Phlegethon, though Giles never acknowledged any improvement in anything I did. Nor did he ever tell me anything interesting if he could possibly help it. A few days after I came to work for SCAB I was potting up my cuttings in the conservatory when I heard him say to Pierce that he didn't think that SCAB was sufficiently prosperous to support feather-brained debutantes in need of pin money, however decorative. I was extremely hurt by this, though pleased to hear that he thought me decorative for he always treated me with a high disdain as though I was ugly enough to turn milk sour. For a whole week after overhearing this wounding remark I didn't go out at all in the evening but stayed at home and read a canto of *The Faerie Queen* and three of Ben Jonson's plays. There was a lot of it I didn't understand and I got fearful headaches as my landlord did not allow electric light in his house but it must have done me some good.

Nor can I help being impractical. Being brought up by my aunt, who kept a cook, a butler, three housemaids and a dresser, meant that I had never so much as washed my own stockings before the age of twenty, when my aunt decided that I must go out in the world and begin to take care of myself. She had assured me that she was thinking solely of my welfare. I knew that my darling aunt would have shaved off her beautiful hair and walked the length of St James's naked and bald if it would have done me any good.

'Don't forget to push down the little thingummy that stops the water boiling over.' I meant to be helpful but I could see from the set of Giles's nostrils that I had only annoyed him more.

'What's that horrible mess on the balcony? It looks like a dead pigeon.'

'That's only the jam from my landlord's Bakewell pudding. He's the most wonderful cook. I can't cook at all. When he saw me – the first week I moved in – eating those little triangles of processed cheese on toast for supper he threw them into the fire. I really like convenience food but he says it upsets him to have it in the house. So now he always cooks for two. He's an absolute lamb, really, though madly eccentric and most of the time in a rage –'

'Why don't you do some dusting?' Giles interrupted. I could see that my talking annoyed him but I wasn't sure why. Giles was much harder to understand than Pierce whose own immediate satisfaction was the sole purpose of anything he said or did. 'The table, for one thing,' Giles continued, very cold and sarcastic. 'As a medium for writing *billets-doux* I realise that it's economical, even picturesque, but I hardly think that visitors to SCAB will be impressed to know that you are Pierce's little *cocotte* and that you are to meet him for dalliance in a box at the Shaftesbury. Plus a rather off-colour pun.'

Pierce always left messages for me in the dust on the boardroom table. Giles was rather fussy about things like hygiene and cleanliness. Pierce said he thought Giles was a closet homosexual but I thought it was his good yeoman stock coming out. Apparently Giles's mother – a widow – lived in Worthing in a small villa called The Poplars. Pierce was sneering about Giles's efforts to rise above this kind of thing but I have always thought it admirable to aspire to something else . . . I suppose because I wanted so desperately to be different from what I was. Giles so nearly got it right but he always slightly overdid it. His clothes were beautiful but just a bit too smart, his shoes too new. His vowels were so clipped that people often asked him to say it again, which made him very cross. Pierce sometimes looked very scruffy and his accent was a lot more relaxed, besides being peppered with swear-words. He didn't care what people thought of him. He said Giles was a dandy and that this would always exclude him from being mistaken for a member of the upper classes. When I said to Pierce that this kind of thing wasn't important he told me that I was a baby and I'd learn.

Through my aunt, Pierce and I knew a lot of the same people but if Giles felt left out of this charmed circle he was careful not to let it show. On that spring morning when this whole story begins Pierce had been showing us a letter he had received from Sir James Inskip, informing us of his willingness to consider financial aid from SCAB to repair the tattered seat that was Inskip Park.

'Do you know these people, Viola, my duck?'

Pierce was looking unusually spruce, no doubt because of the impending lunch with the godparent whose coffers were about to be ransacked. His pinstriped suit was a model of conservatism, though he wore it with a bright pink shirt and a tie, which had been a present from a former girlfriend, depicting a nude woman with impossibly large breasts. His hair, very fair, was swept back from a high, intelligent brow above a nose that was large and sharp. His eyes were blue and mocking. I had never seen in them an expression that could be described as tender or even reflective. One could not call him handsome at all, his chin and mouth were too small and his face too long and thin, but his appearance, like a playful shark, was extraordinarily attractive to women. Perhaps it was the suggestion that he might bite that excited them.

'I was briefly at school with Arabella Inskip.'

It was then that Pierce had decreed that Giles had better

take me with him on a preliminary visit to survey the Inskip demesne.

While Giles made the coffee I tripped off into the conservatory to look at my cuttings. I had only very recently been seized by burning longings to grow things so I was thrilled when I saw a chartreuse frill, the size of a baby's fingernail, clinging to the thick white stem of one of the plants. I picked up the flowerpot and ran back to tell Giles. As I was crossing the boardroom, pregnant with good tidings, I heard a yelp from the kitchen followed by swearing so I knew that, despite my warning, Giles had forgotten to push the lever down. My aunt has always said that tact is the most valuable asset a woman can acquire. I think this is putting it a little too high but I do try to please her as I am conscious that I owe her everything. So I fumbled in the drawer for the feather duster and wrote my name very large in the dust on the table to give Giles time to calm himself. When he came out a few moments later I could see an angry-looking pink patch on his hand but, remembering my aunt's directive, I said nothing.

He put the two cups down on the letter V and frowned.

'Isn't it glorious?' I said, pointing to the infant leaf.

Giles's frown deepened to disgust as he picked two oval cigarette stubs from the compost.

'Those are Pierce's.' I recognised the brand – Passing Clouds – which he always smoked. 'He had to hide in the conservatory when Julia Sempill-Smith fought her way in here yesterday. She was furious, I don't know what about. She gave me a terrific lecture for allowing Pierce to be out of the office.'

'Pierce was going to marry her.' This was news to me but I thought it more dignified not to let this be apparent so I pretended to hunt for a biscuit though I knew the tin was empty, having eaten the last one myself half an hour before. 'They had a big party on New Year's Eve at the Sempill-Smiths' house in Gloucestershire to announce it and her father made a very generous contribution to SCAB funds. Then it was all off when Julia's mother found Pierce in bed with Julia's aunt the next day.'

'That *was* rather discouraging. For Julia, I mean.'

'Apparently Julia was perfectly willing to forgive him in return for a promise of future good behaviour but her mother wouldn't hear of it. Pierce's idea is that Mrs Sempill-Smith is in love with him herself and that's why she couldn't forgive the defection in favour of her sister.'

Giles looked amused despite himself. It was the first time he had actually allowed himself to be chatty with me.

'Julia did talk rather a lot about money. She seems to think that she's made an investment in him. She kept calling me "girl" as in "Good God, girl", which I didn't like particularly.'

'She'd have called you something much worse if she'd known you were Pierce's current mistress.'

I didn't like that very much either. Neither the 'current', which suggested that my expulsion into obscurity was merely a matter of time, nor 'mistress', into which Giles put something of a sneer. I felt less sorry than I would normally have done when he knocked his burnt hand against his hot coffee cup and winced with pain.

'Anyway, Pierce's love life isn't my concern, thank God. Why don't you ring up Inskip Park and make an appointment for us to visit the place?'

I did as I was told. Out of the corner of my eye, as I heard the telephone ringing far away in darkest Nottinghamshire, I saw Giles screwing up his face and blowing on the burnt patch. 'Why don't you put it in a bowl of cold water?' I suggested.

'I beg your pardon? Who is this speaking?' said a voice, very wheezy, at the other end.

'Oh – this is Viola Otway, speaking on behalf of the Society for the Conservation of Ancient Buildings. I want to make an appointment to see Sir James.'

'This is Sir James's steward speaking.' There was a pause for heavy panting. 'If that's the lady from Harrington's Sir James wishes me to say that the last lot of port was quite inferior and he'd like a discount in acknowledgement.'

'No, it isn't. I want to come and see Sir James.'

'A letter will be sufficient for the purpose. If that's all I'll thank you to end this call. The draught is very bad to stand in when you've arthuritus like mine.'

I tried very hard to get the message across but he was determined not to understand me. At last Giles snatched the receiver from me and asked to be put on to Sir James. There was a long pause during which Giles pointed to the coffee cups and then towards the kitchen. I wished he wouldn't treat me like a maid. By the time I had finished this lowly chore and made efforts to clean the sink with the last few grains of Vim that remained and a dark-grey, holey dish-cloth, Giles had put the receiver down. 'Lunch tomorrow. Not exactly convenient. No suggestion that we might stay the night. It must be all of four hours to drive to Inskip Park from London. He was as ungracious as it's possible to be. Hardly the right attitude if you want to squeeze money out of people to keep your ancestral acres. Can you make an early start?'

'I could stay the night at my aunt's house in Richmond. That's more in the right direction.'

'You live in some impenetrable part of the East End, don't you? All right, give me your aunt's address.' I gave him directions as well. He wrote them down with difficulty due to the pen having to rest on the burnt bit between his thumb and forefinger. 'I'm going out now. I shan't be back today. Don't forget that table. It looks worse now you've stirred it up. And do something about the kitchen sink.'

'I've tried but there isn't anything to clean it with, only that dirty old rag.'

Giles sighed. 'Really, Viola. You seem to be absolutely helpless. God knows why I agreed to take you with me tomorrow!' I knew exactly why he had agreed. Pierce made things so unpleasant if you didn't fall in with his plans that it was only worth the row over really important things. 'Go and ask Bolter for whatever you need. Eight thirty, don't forget.'

He went without saying goodbye. I looked at the table. The mahogany top was at least fourteen feet long and was mounted on sturdy Victorian legs. Ever since I had started working for SCAB I had longed to dance on it. Dancing was one of my few accomplishments. Now I come to think of it, at that time it was my only accomplishment.

Every winter, when R.D. was still alive, my aunt had spent a month with him at the Hôtel Majestique in Monte Carlo. When I reached the age of twelve I was considered sufficiently grown-up to accompany the small group of intimates who made up R.D.'s circle. This was thought to be a great treat for me but the truth was that these were the unhappiest weeks of the year.

From eleven o'clock onwards, when my aunt's hair, face and figure had been respectively curled, powdered and dressed by her maid, she went to stroll about the town with R.D. before coming back to the hotel for an elaborate lunch. Then she lay on her bed for an hour before some amusement – golf, yachting or driving along the coast to visit the villas of friends – took her out again until six o'clock, which was the hour for drinks. Dinner was a long, formal affair, sometimes accompanied by dancing. Then at eleven o'clock, the real purpose of the holiday began when they left for the casino to gamble until two or three o'clock in the morning.

To all these amusements I was superfluous, and after the tedium of lunch, which was not at all the sort of food I enjoyed and invariably had on the menu something tricky to eat like artichokes or *écrevisses*, I was left in the care of Agnes, my aunt's maid, who was devoted to my aunt to the point of obsession but who felt very differently about me. She wanted me to be silent and invisible every minute, even when we sat alone together in the sitting room set aside for my aunt's use. While she made beautiful silk underwear for my aunt and from time to time fell asleep, I read. I liked reading, which was lucky because it probably saved me from a decline into dribbling madness. But after four hours' reading my head would ache and I longed to go down and walk on the beach and stroke the noses of the donkeys who were hired out for rides to those children who were, in the general view, held to be so much less fortunate than I. Agnes had nothing but contempt for such plebeian occupations and I was forbidden to set foot outside the hotel by myself.

Any girl in the adventure stories I read would have defied this rule and sneaked out on her own. She would have fallen at once into the hands of diamond thieves or smugglers, brought the criminals to justice and received the grateful thanks and veneration of the populace. But I was a compliant child.

Besides, I was always conscious of how difficult Aunt Pussy's life was if anything in my behaviour brought me to the notice of R.D. In his presence I never spoke except in a whisper in answer to a question and I kept my replies as brief as possible. Even the careless swinging of a leg or the humming of a tune could turn his great red whiskery face with its long brown teeth in my direction, suggestive as these acts were of independent and, therefore, seditious thought. R.D. wore a monocle and as a small child I had been terrified of it. In my imagination God was very like R.D. but larger. God also had a monocle and through this glittering, magnifying window He was able to penetrate the thickest clouds to scrutinise the hearts and minds of His human creations.

In the third week of my second visit to Monte Carlo, when wretched to the point of despair with dullness and inactivity, I was thrilled to make friends with the man who was paid by the hotel to dance with the rich old widows and spinsters.

His name was Antonio and he was Italian. He had lovely, wistful brown eyes and black hair so oily that it shone like my aunt's cook's jet brooch. We met in the staff lift, which I always used when I could, because pressing the buttons and working it myself were about the most exciting things I did all day. Sometimes I would travel several times from the basement to the attics in order to while away a few minutes. On this occasion I was returning to my room after lunch, which had begun with a *bouillon* with noodles, very difficult to eat tidily and without sucking noises. R.D. had guzzled and slurped like a buffalo at a water-hole but if anyone else made the tiniest sound his monocle, with its deadly rays, was bent on them at lightning speed.

He was sad, Antonio told me that afternoon as we

whirred upwards, because he felt that his job was a disgrace to *la Tersicore* who, he explained, was the muse of dancing. 'It is one of the great arts, to make beautiful movements with the body but men call me these terrible things . . . a lounge liz-zard . . . worse, a poo-dle-faker. I see insults in their eyes. As for the women . . . Oh! it is horrible to have their heavy bodies in my arms, like steering a cow. I must eat, I must have somewhere to sleep, I must put by money to buy my ticket to Hollywood. But by the time I have done this I shall be too old to dance. My joints will be stiff, my hair grey.'

'You could dye it. Fred Astaire looks absolutely ancient! Honestly, quite a bit older than you.' I had not at this stage quite mastered tact.

'Ah, the sweet child! How little she knows of life! However, with you it would be a pleasure to dance. You have the graceful figure and the small feet.'

We both looked gravely down at my size threes in neat black kid pumps. At this point we arrived at the top of the hotel because I had been too interested to stop at my own floor.

'*La signorina* would like to listen to a little music on the gramophone, perhaps?'

The invitation was irresistible. Lunch was an occasion of elastic length depending on how much R.D. was amused by the talk of his companions so Agnes would not miss me. Antonio guided me to his room, a mean servant's chamber.

'We shall observe the proprieties. *La signorina* will stay outside.' So I stood in the dusty corridor while Antonio put on a record. 'You do me the honour?' Antonio bowed before me, his hand turned gracefully on his breast. He took me in his arms and we began to waltz. I had been to dancing classes in London and knew a few steps but this was quite unlike plodding over parquet trying to avoid contact with the huge, soft bosom of Mrs Peel.

We seemed to be moving in a different element from ordinary air. We were gliding, floating, flying. I felt weight-less, cradled within the framework of his arms, poised, perfectly controlled though he held me away from him, one hand just lightly touching my waist, the other supporting my small hot one at the level of my ear. The minute I stopped thinking about it, my feet knew at once where they ought to go.

I have danced with scores of men since but I have never found anyone with whom I could repeat this symbiosis. Some men dance as though they are stepping out the croquet lawn at the beginning of the season. Some bob on the spot as though their feet are bare and the floor red-hot. Others clasp you to them with demonic grip. Their body temperature shoots to 110 degrees and they rub you over their fronts as though you are a bar of soap and they are trying to work up a good lather. Dancing with Antonio was on a par with being smiled at by R.D.'s beautiful groom who was called, smitingly, Gervase de Valence and with whom, at the age of thirteen, I was in love.

'You have a natural talent, mees, a feeling for the phrasings. Now, one minute, I change the record. I teach you how to foxtrot.'

After that Antonio and I met every afternoon after lunch and danced until tea-time. He said he liked teaching me and that it was a pleasure for him to dance with someone fleet of foot. It did not occur to me at the time that he was a kind-hearted man, taking pity on my obvious loneliness. I told Agnes about the dancing lessons in such a way as to suggest that they had official sanction. It wasn't until my aunt came looking for me one afternoon to take me out to tea that the deception was laid bare.

Agnes was angry with me but my aunt's wrath was turned on poor Antonio. She accused him of trying to take advantage of my youth and innocence.

'But, Madame,' said Antonio mournfully, 'I am not of the persuasion which would permit me to take advantage of any young lady's innocence. Alas! If I could take up only half of the kind offers made to me by the female guests with whom I dance, I should soon be able to earn enough money to go to Hollywood.'

I had no idea what he meant by this. I begged my aunt not to stop my dancing lessons and I made Antonio take me through some of the steps he had taught me so that she could see how beautiful our dancing was and how profitably I was spending my time. Dear Aunt Pussy seemed amazed by my progress when she saw us twirling in graceful unison. She said that she would make enquiries and speak to Antonio the next day when she had made up her mind what was to be done.

Whatever Antonio's mysterious secret was, it convinced my aunt that I would be safe in his hands. I was allowed to dance with him in our sitting room, with Agnes present for the sake of decorum, each afternoon for the remainder of our stay.

'Your aunt, she is a generous woman,' said Antonio, at the end of the four weeks when I went to say goodbye to him. 'Be good, my little Miss Viola, and be sure to come back next winter when I shall find you a pair of shoes with the metal under the toes.'

I longed for winter to come again and I tried to persuade my aunt to promise that we would go back to the Hôtel Majestique. She said she would see what she could do but I must understand that she was not in a position to do just as she wanted. I did understand. I could not remember a time when Aunt Pussy was not subject to the whim and exigencies of R.D.

My cup of happiness was full as, the following January, the train pulled out from Victoria station and the labels on our luggage read 'Monte Carlo – Hôtel Majestique'. Antonio was as good as his word and had found me some black strap shoes with a small metal plate nailed to the sole. I think my aunt must have had a word with the management for that year an empty upstairs room with a wooden floor was provided for our use. Dancing on a proper floor wearing shoes with taps on was like skimming over ice after the squashy resistance of carpet.

Antonio and I had our moment of triumph the year I was sixteen. We were practising, one morning, a long, complicated sequence of steps that Antonio had adapted from *Top Hat*, which was, not very surprisingly, his favourite film. It involved a great deal of flying apart and coming together, and ended in a dramatic flourish with me bending backwards over Antonio's arm until my hair touched the floor. Without warning the door opened and my aunt came in accompanied by R.D. himself. Everyone in Monte Carlo, including the man who gave donkey rides on the beach, knew who R.D. was, of course. We stopped at once and Antonio did a beautiful bow while I did my usual little bob. Agnes got into a fluster, pricked herself quite badly and let blood all over the peach silk camisole she was making. I thought R.D. would be furious but Aunt Pussy had obviously prepared him for he merely waved his cigar and said, 'Go on . . . go on.'

So we danced our best routine to the tune of 'Cheek To Cheek'. When we had finished R.D. waved his cigar at us again and Aunt Pussy winked at me and looked commiseration at Agnes, who was clutching her finger and stifling expressions of pain, and they left without saying anything. That evening after dinner the band began to play 'Cheek To Cheek' and Antonio came up to me and asked me to dance. My aunt smiled and nodded encouragement. I was astonished as I had always imagined that R.D.'s dignity, which was more awful than you can possibly imagine if you did not know him, would have been impiously besmirched by anyone connected with him actually dancing in public with a hireling.

It was heaven to be gliding across the floor beneath the glittering chandeliers to the music of a real band. My one regret was that I was not wearing my proper dancing shoes but only satin slippers dyed pale-pink to match my dress. It wasn't quite like in films when everyone drifts to the side of the dance floor to watch with undisguised envy and admiration the spectacular skills of the hero and heroine but I knew that people were looking and when we spun to a sensational close the applause was terrific. R.D. didn't clap but he smiled graciously to left and right as though he were some sort of impresario, responsible for the fine display.

This was the one and only occasion in my life that I have been resplendent in the public gaze. We left for England the next day and six months later R.D. had a stroke. He died three days afterwards and Aunt Pussy's life, and mine necessarily too, were changed for ever.

CHAPTER 2

At about five o'clock on the day Giles was dragooned into agreeing to take me with him to Inskip Park, I caught the bus home to Tolgate Square. A slip of moon swam in the sky, which was icy blue at the top, descending to lilac and becoming a grubby yellow at the rooftops. The further east I travelled, the more the scene reminded me of a scene from one of my favourite novels, *Phineas Finn* perhaps or *Our Mutual Friend* – latent with mystery, brooding with poetry – less brutally 1976.

I was in the front seat on the top deck of the number 23 bus for Liverpool Street station and Spitalfields. I didn't read as I usually do but looked out of the window and thought about going to Nottinghamshire and how furious Giles had been when he came back to the office unexpectedly, just as I was doing a spectacular shuffle, hop, spring and toe-tap, which brought me right to the end of the table. 'Serves you right if you fall off and hurt yourself. You'll scratch the table and it's not ours. Sometimes, Viola, I wonder if you are quite sane.'

I debated this as we picked up speed along the Embankment past the sparkling, shivering river. The Thames looked very clean and the river traffic was orderly but I would give anything to have seen it when the Elizabethans held markets and built fires on the ice or even when it was a black, stinking sludge heaving with typhus. What is sanity, anyway? I asked myself this in much the same defensive spirit as Pontius Pilate asked what truth was, not expecting a sensible answer. I think that truth and sanity must be the same thing, or very nearly. I was so engrossed in an imaginary argument with Giles, in the process of which I dazzled him with the complexity and brilliance of my reasoning, that I almost missed my stop.

This was something I had become accustomed to doing. Because I wasn't used to taking responsibility for myself, it had taken me some time to master the fickle ploys of London Transport. Until I was sixteen I had travelled everywhere in Aunt Pussy's car driven by Bert (Bertram to my aunt), who was the kindest man you could hope to meet and who always had a tin of yellow-and-brown humbugs striped like bumble bees, and a clean handkerchief which he would lend if I had lost mine. I nearly always had. When I underwent the first great ordeal of my young life he was a true friend.

My aunt had decided to send me to the local county primary school. She felt my upbringing was so unlike that of other children that I would become odd if I didn't 'mix'. On my first day at school Bert parked round the corner and contrary to all the rules took off his cap and left it in the car. He said that it would be better and, though it seemed odd, I was too well trained to question a grown-up. He held my hand and took me to the headmistress's office. Her name was Miss Cherry and I had already taken a dislike to her. When my aunt had interviewed her she had been syrupy, assuring Aunt Pussy that little Vee-o-la – she pronounced my name like the musical instrument instead of like the flower – would be happy in her little nest and that she was attempting to bring up the standards of the school in order to attract a more genteel sort of child. This ought to have been warning enough but my aunt was busy admiring fat robins on the Christmas frieze and didn't notice. When Bert presented me on the first morning of term Miss Cherry conducted me personally to my classroom. Twenty curious faces stared at me as I was given a desk, an inkwell, a dip pen and a new exercise book. When told to write my name on the cover I had to confess that I did not know how, and the titters of the other children made me grow hot with shame. This was nothing to what followed.

At break an interested party of girls gathered round me.

'You a princess or sumfink?' asked the boldest, fingering

my smocked lawn dress with white Peter Pan collar. 'Why jer 'ave your hair like that?'

I saw that she, like the other little girls, was wearing a skirt and jersey. Beneath her skirt showed layers of stiff net petticoat. Her shoes were white satin, rather grubby and had little heels, which contrasted daringly with her luminous pink ankle socks. Her hair was fastened in bunches high above her ears, which were pierced. Her nails were polished red. Agnes always plaited my hair tightly into two braids which she fastened with bows to match my dress.

'You're pretty enough to be a princess,' said another, when I strenuously denied any blue blood. 'You wanna play tag?'

'What's that?'

'She doesn't know what tag is,' they exclaimed wonderingly. 'Don't she talk funny?'

They took me into the playground and taught me the rules and treated me with deference. I thought it was going to be all right.

'What've you got for dinner?' asked one, when the bell rang for midday break. I saw that they all had plastic boxes or brown paper bags. My own lunch-box was a tiny wicker hamper.

'I don't know.'

'Well, let's have a look, then.' They gathered round my lunch-box, which my aunt's cook had packed for me. 'Coo! What's this pink stuff, then?'

'Smoked salmon, I think.'

'Cooer! Look at this shiny knife and fork. They got letters on them. And a glass with leaves on. Ent it pretty? And a serviette, look, made out of cloth! Hey! Little tarts! Grapes. Blimey!'

It was round the class in a flash that I had brought a banquet. The boys began to show interest.

'Give us one of yer sandwiches, then,' said the largest boy, called Mick, who sat behind me in class.

I politely offered him the box, which he snatched from me and handed round to the other boys.

'Eugh! Stinks,' they all said, and spat them out. 'Let's have the cakes to try.'

These were more popular. The girls protested that the boys had eaten all my food but the boys just laughed. One of them tied my napkin pirate fashion round his head and they kicked the glass around the room until it broke. I never saw the knife and fork again.

'She's ever so stuck up, ent she?' said Mick, seeing me cowering in a corner. 'Come 'ere, and let's play a game. Woon't it be ever so naice?'

Mick was evidently the wit of the class. Emboldened by this satire the boys took hold of me and tied my napkin over my eyes. They spun me round until I fell over. They all made noises like pigs honking, in fits of laughter. When the bell rang for afternoon lessons, my dress was dirty and missing its sash, and the ribbons had been torn from my plaits.

'How did it go?' asked Bert. When he saw my face he put his arm round me and said, 'Never mind, it'll be better tomorrow.'

But it was not. Agnes was very angry with me that first afternoon when she saw my dishevelled state. She thought I was inventing my history of persecution. Bettina, the cook, was cross about the lunch-box. By the time Aunt Pussy saw me I had been tidied up and as she was going to the theatre I had no opportunity to tell her how wretched the day had been.

It was difficult to let go of Bert's hand the next morning. The girls, seeing that the boys considered me a figure of fun, were disinclined to take my part. The glamour of my outlandish appearance had worn thin and now they sniggered at my Start-rite bar shoes and knee-length socks. I stood in a corner at break surrounded by my jeering classmates. Bert had told me that whatever happened I must not cry and that I had to learn to stick up for myself. So when Mick came towards me bearing something in his cupped hands which he said was a spider, which he was going to put down my neck, I screwed up my courage and said, as Bert had instructed, 'Yar! You're just a stupid fat bully. Piss off!'

Miss Cherry's window, below which we were gathered,

was open and in no time her head was sticking out of it and I was told to report at once.

'I'm very disappointed, Vee-o-la. I expected you to set an example to the others. I shall send a letter home to your aunt and you'll have to spend the lunch-break alone in the classroom as punishment.'

I was so relieved to hear this that I didn't mind the ticking off at all. The lunch-break was an oasis of peace even though the boys crowded round the classroom window and made hideous faces at me. But in the afternoon I was the target of ink pellets, rubbers, and chewing-gum, and I got flustered and upset the inkwell over the row of As I was painstakingly copying into my book. The form mistress, a chinless stork of a woman called Miss Rasp, who smelt of peppermints, was severe with me. Miss Cherry had told her in my hearing to watch me closely lest I was a corrupting influence. Miss Rasp ripped out the blotted page and told me to stand up with my hands on my head. As she walked back to her desk I heard whispered giggles and found Mick lying on the floor trying to see up my dress to my knickers.

Just before the four o'clock bell, which would release me from my purgatory, Miss Rasp told me to sit down. I sat rubbing my arms, which were tingling with pins and needles, and counting the minutes to freedom. A sharp pain made me cry out as one of my plaits was pulled hard. The class was convulsed with laughter. Mick had leaned over my chair and, with the scissors he had stolen from Miss Rasp's drawer, cut off one of my plaits at the level of my ear. I knew Bert would be disappointed with me but I couldn't help it. Huge tears dripped down my nose and ran into the grooves on my desk. Miss Rasp gave a shriek when she saw my plait lying on the floor like a small brown snake.

'You bad little girl!' she cried, gripping me by the shoulder and shaking me. 'What a naughty thing to do! What *will* your aunt say?'

I sat and sniffed back the tears and felt hot with misery until the bell went. Then I walked very fast out of the room and ran across the playground into Bert's arms. I expect I looked funny with one side of my hair short like a boy's and the other long and braided but Bert didn't laugh.

'I'm going to speak to Madam about it,' was all he said. He allowed me to sit in the front next to him and stopped at the corner shop for a bar of chocolate, which had a marvellously drying effect on my tears. But he did not need to speak for Miss Rasp had put the severed plait into my lunch-box and Bettina, when she found it, screamed the house down, thinking that I had been kidnapped and this was the precursor to a ransom note.

I told Aunt Pussy what had happened. She hugged me and cried and said how sorry she was. It was the end of her experiment with 'mixing'. The next week I attended a small school in Kensington where my daringly short hair was envied by the other little girls, who were all wearing virtually identical smocked dresses and plaits or Alice bands. We used to spend our break times inventing ways to persuade our parents to let us have our ears pierced and our fingernails painted.

After R.D.'s death, Aunt Pussy said that she had been to enough parties, balls, races, dinners, receptions, lunches and soirées for several lifetimes. She wanted to stay in bed and read books and let her hair go out of curl. (This last threat she never carried out.) Now that she left home so rarely it was much simpler to order a taxi. So Bert, who was over seventy by then anyway and getting a bit shaky, left us and bought a nice little house in Barnes where he lived with his wife and grew dahlias. I never forgot what a good friend he had been in my hour of need. Looking back, the experience of my first school was seminal. It gave me a small insight into what it feels like to be persecuted, and planted in me a sympathy for the underdog which, for good or – more usually, I must say – ill, has remained a fundamental part of my character.

Even taxis were too elevated a form of travel once I had left home and was trying to live on what I earned. I had a bank account funded by my aunt but it was a matter of honour with me to save it for emergencies. When I had left myself enough time I walked, and when I was in a rush, which was generally the case, I got to grips with the whimsical ways of public transport.

Last autumn – it was October, actually – I had caught the bus, intending to go to have tea with my cousin Miranda at the Ritz. I was reading *Vanity Fair* and I was so captivated by Becky Sharp's extraordinary wickedness that I went a long way in the wrong direction. I got off the bus as soon as I could and found myself in an unfamiliar part of London.

At first sight it was grimy and bleak but as I walked the length of Tolgate Square, hoping to find someone who could put me on the right path for Piccadilly, I couldn't help noticing how beautiful the houses were beneath their dirt, with well-built brick fronts and sash windows looking just as they were intended to, without Victorian additions or gentrification of any kind. I stopped before one that had a particularly beautiful fanlight. Its delicate bars, like linked ears of wheat, were thrown into silhouette by a soft glow from within. I was standing looking at the house, admiring its probity, when the front door opened unexpectedly to reveal a very odd-looking man.

What had seemed at first, in the deepening light, like a grotesquely large head was in fact a head of ordinary dimensions with a monkey embracing it. It sat on its master's shoulder, one delicate paw clasping his brow. The other paw held something small, which it put to its mouth and sucked. The man's eyes were fierce and his expression was almost a scowl but I was reassured by the devoted way in which the monkey clung to him. Pierce would have mocked this as a piece of specious sentiment but the monkey looked so wise that I trusted its judgement. It wore a little red coat against the cold and this was reassuring, too. Its master wore a dark suit of an old-fashioned kind, with high lapels and long tails. He was tall and stooped. A Paisley shawl was draped around his shoulders against the cold. He stared at me without smiling and I was about to walk away quickly before he could accuse me of loitering when he spoke to me. 'Are you looking for lodgings?'

'Yes.'

I was surprised by my answer. I had been sharing Stella

Partington's flat in Kensington since leaving home and not liking it very much. Stella was the same age as me but she seemed centuries older. She was very wise about men and very mercenary. Although I had known her off and on all my life we had almost nothing to say to each other. Luckily she went out a lot. It had not occurred to me until that moment, as I stood in the chilly dusk outside number 46, that I might do something to change this unsatisfactory state of affairs.

'There are not many rules but they must be adhered to.' My future landlord's tone was uncompromising. His English was good, his accent unmistakably foreign. 'No dogs, no transistor radios. There is no electricity in this house so there can be no gramophones, hairdryers, television sets, or vacuum cleaners. There is no central heating or running water in the bedrooms. Young ladies are not encouraged to entertain gentlemen in their rooms.'

'That's all right. I don't own any of those things and I haven't got a dog. Or a gentleman.' This was before I knew Pierce but anyway he had not, in the three months we had been lovers, set foot inside my bedroom. He had a flat in Rutland Gate, which was much more convenient for making love. For him anyway.

'Very good.' The owner of the house appeared to look at me more kindly. 'Come in.'

When he closed the front door I was enveloped in a soupy gloom, which smelt wonderful. First there was the smell of cooking – bacon, garlic, coffee, all mixed together. As well, I identified woodsmoke, wax and lavender. He took a lighted chamber-stick from a table and held it high so that I could see my way in the hall. Then I smelt candle-smoke and a whiff of something sharp, like lemons, which seemed to come from the folds of his coat. As my eyes grew accustomed to the dimness I saw that the ticking in my ear came from a long-case clock. Otherwise the house was quiet and all the agitations of the day – the noise of traffic, the beastly accounts at the art gallery which wouldn't add up, Stella's shrieking little laugh which had no humour in it – all these things drew away from me and diminished to pinpoints as the presence of the house revealed itself. Pierce would have said that houses are only bricks and mortar but I know that isn't true. You can feel things about a house the minute you step inside it. All right, perhaps it's what you see, a question of proportions and colours and furnishings, but there's something else as well. This house was dignified and elegant and, at the same time, friendly.

My prospective landlord lighted the way up a flight of uncarpeted stairs. 'This is the room.' He opened the door and disappeared into darkness.

At first I had to feel my way through the blackness with my toes but when the shutters were opened I saw that the room was large and that the bed was a four-poster. What a bed it was! Silky red damask curtains, tied with gilded tasselled ropes, hung in swags to the floor and the mattress was so high that I would have to run to jump into it. There was a chest of drawers and a washstand with a white pitcher and ewer. A knee-hole desk, a stool with a needlework cover and a wing chair upholstered in green velvet by the fireplace were the other furnishings. There was not a right angle in the room for the plain scrubbed floor sloped in wooden billows down to the window and the bowed ceiling curved up in each corner. The chair was patched, the blue-and-white tiles in the fireplace were cracked, the only carpet was a small threadbare rug before the hearth, but the room was affectingly beautiful.

'It's perfectly lovely! Can I have it?'

He bowed and the monkey jumped from his shoulder on to the wing chair, curling up its tail into the letter O and looking from its master's face to mine as though trying to plumb the meaning of our words.

'For ten guineas a week it is yours. My name is Daniel Fogg.'

'I'm Viola Otway. How do you do? I've forgotten. How much is a guinea?'

As soon as I got back to Kensington, after a very late tea with Miranda, who was always angelically good about things like my maddening inability to be anywhere on time, I broke the news to Stella that I would be moving out the next day. She was rather cold about it until I gave her a month's rent instead of notice. I was sad to draw so soon on Aunt Pussy's emergency fund but I knew it was only fair. Stella thawed instantly and asked me to have lunch with her at Harrods the following week. I was so glad that she was being friendly again that I said yes. I could have kicked myself afterwards. It was the sort of stupid thing I was always doing because I so disliked moods and rows. Anyway, I hoped that something might intervene to make it impossible. I always hope this when I have agreed out of cowardice or laziness to do something I absolutely don't want to do but of course the appointment unfailingly rolls round with sickening promptness. I packed my things and then, after Stella had gone out, I telephoned my aunt.

I described my new room to her. I don't think I managed to convey the beauty of it for instead of being delighted she sounded rather worried.

'No electricity, darling? He must be a very peculiar sort of man.'

'I think he is but I did like him. And he has the most wonderful monkey.'

'That hardly seems an important qualification for a landlord.'

'Well, no . . . but you can tell that the monkey – her name's Josephine and she loves sugared almonds but he has to ration them because of her teeth – loves him passionately and I don't think a monkey would love someone who was cruel.'

'But, my darling Viola, you are thinking in extremes! I dare say the number of cruel landlords in London is quite small but they may, on the other hand, be dishonest or idle or lecherous . . . any number of very undesirable things.'

'Ten pounds fifty isn't a lot. If he were dishonest he'd charge much more. It's the most wonderful room! There's a fireplace and he says he'll have a fire lit for me first thing tomorrow so that the room is warm and aired before I get there.'

'Tomorrow? Aren't you being rather impetuous? Oughtn't I to come and look at the house first?'

'You did say I was to learn to be properly independent. And he was pleased by my wanting to move in at once. I could see that he was touched by my liking his house so much. I don't want to offend him by seeming to have second thoughts. As to his being idle, I don't think that matters even if he is. I don't want him to do anything for me, just let me live there. I can assure you that he isn't lecherous.'

'How can you possibly know?'

'I think one does know . . . more or less at once. Lecherous men take so much more trouble to be nice.'

'Darling, this sounds worse and worse. Do you mean he is rude?'

'Well, no. Perhaps reserved is the word. Anyway, I met the woman who cleans and brings up hot water and things. Her name is Mrs Shilling. I can't imagine her staying five minutes in a house that wasn't what she'd call respectable. She's worked for Mr Fogg for twenty years.'

'That is a good sign,' Aunt Pussy conceded. 'Spitalfields, you say. I don't think I know it. And no telephone? That's very inconvenient.'

In the end I conquered my aunt's objections by gentle persistence. Having got the morning off from Mr Phipps, who sounded relieved that I wasn't coming in, I set out the next day, full of happy anticipation, for my new lodgings.

The house looked just as wonderful by daylight, though it was raining hard and water was coming out in a spout from a broken gutter and running in torrents into the area by the front steps. Mrs Shilling answered the door and helped me carry up my things. She had a long face with a tiny pursed mouth and perpetually raised eyebrows. She reminded me of Frankie Howerd, who had been R.D.'s favourite comedian. R.D. liked jokes to be smutty. He hated satire and I don't think he was capable of recognising irony. He always flew into a rage when he came across what he called 'this modern craze for debunking everything that's made this country what it is'. He thought satire had been invented in the sixties with *Beyond the Fringe*. When I told him once that *Gulliver's Travels*, which he had given me for Christmas when I was a child, was satire in just the same way, he had started breathing hard in the way he did when he suspected impertinence and Aunt Pussy had given me that look of hers – a sort of winking frown that meant 'Shut up, Viola darling' – so I had, at once. It's obviously very bad for people always to be given in to. It means that they can make absolute fools of themselves and no one will tell them. Unpleasant though it is to be told – and I should know – at least one has some hope of improving.

Mrs Shilling had laid a good fire in my room and I could see by the morning light that the walls were panelled and painted a pale cucumber green. Above the fireplace was a painting of a lion in a forest in a battered gilt frame. There were no curtains but wooden shutters above a window-seat. I was too ignorant to know it then but the bedroom was a textbook example of early Georgian furnishing. I unpacked my suitcase and put my clothes away in the drawers. There was no wardrobe so I imagined that I was going to look rather crumpled all the time as without electricity there could be no iron. I didn't care. New candles stood in the pair of mirrored sconces either side of the fireplace and in the silver chamber-stick by my bed.

For a while I just wandered about looking at things and touching them in a sort of reverie of happiness. It was so beautiful after Stella's shiny, smart flat. Then it occurred to me that I would need quite soon to go to the lavatory. What could the arrangements be? Perhaps a bucket in the garden? I went downstairs and stood irresolute in the hall. By day, light came into the hall from a window overlooking the square and I saw that the panelling was painted a rich ivory and there were pale blue, shell-backed niches either side of the fireplace in which were displayed a pretty pink-and-green dessert service. Apart from the long-case clock and table on which stood a row of candlesticks the only other piece of furniture was a looking-glass with a beautiful frame, garlanded with gilded flowers. I looked at myself in the speckly, rippled mirror. My skin, generally pale when not blushing, looked greenish and my eyes, which are dark grey, looked large and solemn.

A burst of singing from the basement encouraged me to

venture further down. Mrs Shilling was filling a large cauldron at the sink from a single giant brass tap. 'Give us a hand, dear. One of these days my back will go and then where will we be, I'd like to know?'

I took one side of the handle and together we staggered with it over to a black range in which a fire was burning. 'Isn't this lovely?' I said, looking round at the dresser with its blue-and-white meat plates and the flat stone sink surrounded by green tiles. The ceiling was a glistening black with two hundred years of grease and smoke. A bare scrubbed table took up most of the space. 'Am I allowed down here?'

'Of course you are, dear. You live here now. How're you going to cook your supper if you can't come into the kitchen?'

It hadn't occurred to me that I was going to have to cook for myself. When I lived with Stella I had gone to eat at the cheap and friendly café on the corner. Stella was generally out with a boyfriend. She lived, so she told me, on caviar and lobster or whatever was the most expensive thing on the menu. Stella's fridge never had anything in it but ice cubes and jars of olives and her mink coat.

I had seen nothing remotely like a café in Tolgate Square. Anyway, I was rather cheered by the idea of learning to cook. I imagined myself producing voluptuous soufflés and sole Véronique for Pierce while beautiful babies with golden hair played about my feet.

The rain continued to make a waterfall past the basement window. While Mrs Shilling told me where she lived (just round the corner), what Mr Shilling had died of (a stroke), and how Noreen, her daughter, was due for her fourth, the cauldron got up a good head of steam so that soon everything in the kitchen began to drip as though in sympathy with the rain, including Mrs Shilling's nose and cheeks, which trickled with sweat as she poked the fire and ladled the hot water into buckets. I explained to Mrs Shilling that I had no idea where the lavatory was. I was half disappointed and half relieved to be shown a room next to the kitchen with a proper flushing lav, very decorative with maroon flowers on white porcelain. There was a bath as well, which was sad as I had hoped to have a slipper bath in front of my bedroom fire.

Mrs Shilling offered me a cup of tea, which I accepted. I tried to remember how she made it. It was fiercely orange in colour and very strong and I thought it tasted quite horrible but I got it down somehow. Mrs Shilling put the packet of tea back into a brown pot on the shelf above the range. 'That's my own tea, that is,' she declared in a voice of triumph. 'Fogg has this stuff he keeps in that silver caddy there. Pooh! Nasty thin stuff with leaves the size of a hanky, comes out like babies' piddle. How are you settling in, dear?'

I told her very well and thanked her for making such a good fire. Then I asked her about the other lodgers, of whom I had seen nothing so far.

'Well, you won't have yet because they're out to work. On the first floor opposite you there's Tiffany Tredgold. That's her stage name. Real name's May Wattles. I like May better meself but Tiffany says it's old-fashioned. She's trying to be an actress. Been trying for the last six years . . . you gotta admire her pluck. Miss Barlam has the room at the top. She works for one of them illustrated books. Magazine, she calls it. Paints a treat. You should see her flower pictures. You could almost pick 'em. A very ladylike person – quiet and ever so well-mannered, and everything she should be. Sews very nicely, too. She made a dress for my Noreen's third. She's like that, thoughtful – too good, really. The world takes advantage of someone like that. I said to Noreen it was worth getting Baby christened just to show it off but her Alf don't hold with church. What I say is that it can't do no harm if it's all a fairy-tale but what if it ain't? Where will the likes of Alf be then, I'd like to know?' Mrs Shilling clutched the bib of her apron, pursed her small mouth and rolled her eyes. 'I go regular every Sunday and I won't say as I don't have forty winks during the sermon but where's the harm in that? But Alf – he wants me to call him Alfred but I think it's unfriendly – he's always got to know better than other folk. That's men for you all over.'

Mrs Shilling waggled her eyebrows, expressing exasperation. We had an interesting talk about men, which was rather one-sided as I knew so little about them. R.D. was hardly a useful role model and I had always thought that my father was quite different from other men. Certainly Mrs Shilling's strictures did not apply to him. She felt a contemptuous affection for the male sex and was convinced that none of them had an atom of common sense. Afterwards I learned that this is an opinion almost universally held by women but I heard it now for the first time. 'Silly vain things, always play-acting – that's what a man's world is about. Wars and football and fighting each other to be top dog. And don't they make a mess of it! If men had the babies and women ran things, then you'd see something! It's true what they say, men are interested in only one thing. If they can get enough how's-your-father they don't bother about anythink else. Course they has to work but it's my belief if they was let they'd never get outa bed. My Ernie now, when he'd had a drop you'd think he was Clark Gable the way he used to carry on. "Get away with you," I used to say. "What with your great belly and red nose – I've got better things to do than canoodle with you." Not that I don't miss him sometimes for all he were a fool. You get fond of 'em.'

'I can't imagine Mr Fogg canoodling.'

'Fogg, now, he's another kettle of fish. I dare say he's got red blood in him, same as the others, but he's been dealt a bad blow by life and it's winded him, see? He's a man what's crippled and it weren't his fault, the poor dear. No, he ain't like other men. In some ways he's superior, you might say. He don't go about making a fool of himself. Knows everything there is to know and read every book what was ever writ, too. But what's the use if it don't make you happy? I don't hold with too much book-learning. I don't see the point.'

'Well, I suppose you could use your knowledge for the benefit of others.'

'Uh-huh. There's something in that, I'll grant. But Fogg don't like the human race much. He wouldn't do anyone harm but he's a strange cantankulous man what keeps himself to himself.'

'What does he do?'

'Buys and sells that old furniture he's so fond of. If he loves anything in the world it's this house and what's in it. Cupboards and drawers, bits of chiny and carpets, anythink that's old. Soon as I gets used to something the next day it's gone and there's somethink else to dust and polish. Funny way to carry on, *I* think.'

'Does he have a shop?'

'No. He wouldn't like that. He's that wayward in his temper he chafes at ordinary folk. He deals with other men in the same trade. Out all day but I don't know where. I've seen him bring 'em home for a glass of wine a few times. But in general he keeps himself to himself. Says he ain't fit company for others. Not but what he could be if he chose. He's got a sharp wit. Often he says things really aggravating and I fly up and then I see him looking at me in such a way that I knows it's been said to prowoke me.' Mrs Shilling pronounced her Vs as Ws just like a character in Dickens. 'And the ladies now, for all he don't chase after them, they go for him. Perhaps that's why.'

'Really?' I was very surprised. Mr Fogg had seemed quite old to me.

'Ah, that's taken you back a bit, I can tell. But he's got a little way with him that you don't just forget.' Mrs Shilling glanced towards the door and then lowered her voice. 'It's gossip but you'll know soon or later anyway. Poor dear Miss Barlam has broke her heart over him. Been going on a year now. Off her food something chronic. She shuts herself away in her room on her days off and Saturdays but when *he* comes in she's down here like a streak of lightning. I try to encourage her to have a square meal but she just sits and picks. Once I caught her down here sniffing at his coat what he'd left. Rubbing her face in it, she was. I wouldn't be surprised if – well, there's no telling what folks'll do. But,' Mrs Shilling leaned forward, supporting her generous breasts on the tabletop and spoke confidentially, 'don't say I didn't warn you. That poor girl'll do something daft one of these days. There was that other one, a Mrs McPhee what used to buy things from him, she was always coming round to see him, all hours. It's my belief she spent a fortune trying to catch him. And then there was Lady Clara something or other – bold as brass, all hair and eyes, you know the sort – she used to drive up in her smart car and toot the horn. He hated that. Can't abide noise. In the end he was very firm with her. Not rude, mind, but he didn't mince his words. Not that I was listening particular but I happened to be doing the stairs at the time. She went off crying fit to bust. Oh, yes, the girls like him all right! It's because he ain't like other men. Must have been a handsome man when he was young. Very handsome.' Mrs Shilling sighed and it struck me that she was more than a little in love with her employer herself. I was delighted to think that I was moving into such an interesting household. She got up, fetched a saucepan and began to peel potatoes. I offered to help and she gave me a knife, but snatched it back when she saw how I did it.

'You *are* unhandy, my duck. There'll be nobbut a marble left at that rate. How old are you now?'

'Nearly twenty-one.'

'You don't say! I've have put you at eighteen at the most. Your mum's spoilt you, I dare say. We all do it.'

'I suppose Mr Fogg doesn't return Miss Barlam's feelings?' I didn't want to tell her about my aunt's grand establishment in case it impaired the cosy rapport I felt we were establishing. 'Isn't there something else I could do to help?'

'That's good of you dear. You can rub up that silver if you've a mind. No, and you can tell he doesn't like it though he does his best not to be unkind. That's what I mean about Fogg. Most men would take advantage of a lady's susceptibilities – you know what I mean, dear, they takes their pleasures where they can and never mind the consequences. But he don't do that. If anything he keeps out of her way. Poor soul! I feel ever so sorry for her. Ah, well, we come weeping into the world and weeping we go out of it.'

Mrs Shilling had a fund of philosophical sayings by which she steered her course. As I got to know her, I admired her spirit more and more. From what she said about her life it seemed to have been a very hard one but she was a stoic and always cheerful. What was more, she had all the common sense she denied to men. That was the first of many conversations, all of which were for me like a discourse on the human condition.

That evening, when I got back to Tolgate Square from an afternoon of helping Mr Phipps hang a new exhibition – which involved losing the hammer and upsetting the tin with the hooks at least every five minutes, which made him quite unreasonably cross with me though he did it just as often – I was conscious, the moment I set foot on the steps leading up to the front door, of an instant revival of spirits. As I closed the door and stood for a moment savouring the comfort and beauty of my surroundings, I noticed that there was a new smell – patchouli – mingling with the other odours of the hall.

'Hello? Is that Miss Otway?' said a trilling voice, and a head crowned with a chestnut plait popped up from the basement staircase. It was followed by a slender body, clad in something purple and flowing – what Aunt Pussy would have called 'arty'. Tiffany Tredgold stood before me. She must have been six foot in her stockinged feet, which were very large, I couldn't help noticing. She was not actually pretty but I thought her face very interesting. A scarf of black chiffon trailed from her neck to the floor.

'How do you do?' She extended her hand covered with silver rings. 'I'm so glad you've come to live here. You'll love it, I expect. I do.' Tiffany's voice managed to be breathy and ringing at the same time. I felt at once as though we were on a stage in a Noël Coward play . . . *Hay Fever*, perhaps. 'You poor darling! You're soaked through!' I was very wet as it was still raining and I'd run out of money and had to walk the last bit back to number 46. 'Come downstairs and I'll make you some of my rum grog. It will stop you catching cold.'

I had to accept such a kindly given invitation though spirits always taste like poison to me. Luckily Tiffany put a great deal of honey into it as well as a frightening amount of dark brown rum so I was just able to get it down though it remained burning in my throat and chest for an hour afterwards. While I drank it Tiffany talked all the time. She asked me how old I was and what my job was and did I like it and what did I really *long* to do? This last question I couldn't answer truthfully as I thought she would despise me if I said I wanted to get married and have babies and live in the country with cats and dogs and rabbits and chickens. So I said that I wanted to be a writer.

'I knew it!' Her long amber and silver earrings seesawed violently as she flung back her head. 'When we shook hands in the hall, a voice in my head said, "This girl is a fellow artist."'

It was jolly well lying, then, I thought. Aunt Pussy had a cupboard full of coil pots, wooden book troughs, Christmas cards and cross-stitched table mats all made by me and there wasn't one thing that showed an ounce of talent. Also she kept all my exercise books of poems and compositions. At the bottom of every one a teacher had written something along the lines of 'Viola writes with verve and imagination but must learn to spell/ punctuate/ organise her ideas/ remember to have a MAIN VERB!!!' No enthusiasm could survive this sort of thing.

'I am,' continued Tiffany, with a toss of her head, 'for good or ill devoted to the stage . . .

> ' "the well-trod stage anon,
> If Jonson's learned sock be on,
> Or sweetest Shakespeare, Fancy's child,
> Warble his native wood-notes wild . . ." '

'Sock?'

'Yes, sock. It's Milton. "L'Allegro". I don't think he means something in grey wool.' Tiffany giggled. I joined in and couldn't stop. I'm not used to drinking large amounts of liquor.

'You two seem to be enjoying yourselves.' Daniel Fogg, who had come in quietly, picked up Tiffany's mug and sniffed it. 'You'll be an alcoholic when you make your name. Only poverty keeps you on the straight and narrow.'

'Thank you for saying "when". Despair has no part in the makeup of the Tredgold nature but sometimes I feel just the teensiest bit doubtful about my future. If only Fate would send that hateful Bebe Ballantine a sick headache, then I'd show them!'

The monkey, Josephine, jumped from his shoulder on to Tiffany's, unfastened her plait and pulled on it as though it were a bell-rope until Tiffany cried out for her to stop. Mr Fogg stood with his arms folded across his chest, watching. His skin was swarthy – perhaps olive would be more polite – and his eyes were so dark as to appear black. His hair must once have been black, too, but now was mostly grey. He looked as though he 'lived on his nerves', as Agnes would have said. Frequently he contracted the corners of his mouth and pressed his lips together. I saw him close his eyes for a few seconds then open them wide with an expression of weary resignation. The wrists that stuck out from the sleeves of his coat were as thin as a girl's. I thought he looked poetic and interesting in a consumptive way. Swiftly he turned his head and caught me staring at him. He returned my look. Then he lifted one eyebrow and a shadow of amusement passed rapidly across his eyes. The effect was startling. I saw at once why poor Miss Barlam was off her food.

'If you don't stop, Josephine, I shall pull your tail and see how you like it,' protested Tiffany.

'Would she – do you think – come to me?' I asked, in an agony of longing.

'Offer her one of these,' said Mr Fogg, taking from his pocket a pink sugared almond.

I held it out to her and said her name in winning tones. She stared at me and at the almond doubtfully. Then she sprang on to my knee and up on to my shoulder, grabbing the almond as she did so. I felt her little paw slide round my head and fasten on to my ear. I stroked her warm soft body very gently and tried to stop myself grinning idiotically. 'I'm going to love it here,' I said.

CHAPTER 3

Tolgate Square fulfilled its promise of happiness. Tiffany and I became the best of friends. She was older than me by seven years and vastly my superior in worldly knowledge but she never made me feel ignorant or dull. We fell very quickly into the habit of daily meetings in her room or mine where we gossiped endlessly about our trials, our triumphs, our loves and our dreams. She had a most flexible, liberal mind and expanded Mrs Shilling's theory of Christianity to include absolutely every possible belief on the grounds that you never knew. She was superstitious, like all theatre people, and black cats, ladders, spilt salt, cracked pavements and broken mirrors all exacted their toll in evasion tactics. She was addicted to fortune-telling and we regularly threw coins for the I Ching or laid out Tarot cards or searched for enlightenment by other more arcane methods, the most fun being something called ceromancy – a simple method of prophecy that involved dropping melted wax (of which we naturally had a plentiful supply) into cold water. Tiffany was endlessly resourceful in her interpretations of the amorphous little lumps that bobbed to the surface. 'Look! Definitely a train! Like the *Flying Scotsman* with wings on the front. And this bit's a bridge. This blob's one of those South American countries – Uruguay, I think.' I was admiring, my knowledge of geography being hazy and consisting of not much more than the counties of England of which I had once had a jigsaw puzzle. 'I know!' Tiffany continued. 'It isn't that you're going on a railway journey but you're going to build one! You're going to be a famous engineer in South America. A female Isambard Kingdom Brunel.'

Though the idea was dismaying I tried to look pleased. Because she was kind-hearted Tiffany could only forecast the rosiest of futures. Had I been in the least danger of believing her I should have stepped into the path of express trains and placed every penny I had on the sorriest nag with a limp in each leg for I was destined to live for ever and find gratification for every desire.

Mrs Shilling, who was a great believer in tea-leaves, was much less sanguine in her foretelling. 'Into every life some rain must fall, my duck. I see some disappointment ahead . . . Look, see, that speck like a bowler hat? The man you love will be unfaithful sure as eggs is eggs. But don't you be downhearted, Miss Viola, dear, that leaf like a seagull says that you'll marry him in the end.'

'Ought I to, though?' I said, doubtfully. 'It doesn't sound like a very good idea if he's going to run after other women.'

'I'm sure he won't,' said Tiffany, who was in the kitchen with us when the prediction was being made. She had caught a glimpse of Pierce – who had just come into my life at this point – from her bedroom window when he had brought me home and had been deeply impressed by his bold looks and dashing manner. 'He must know he couldn't do better than you, Viola, and anyway if he did, everyone adulterates these days, after all. We've left the dark ages of grim, sexless trials of loyalty and endurance that our parents thought were right and proper.'

As a description of my own parents' relationship it could hardly have been more inaccurate but I didn't say so because of my promise to Aunt Pussy always to be discreet.

On Sunday evenings when there was no performance in the theatre where she worked Tiffany would sometimes ask me to share her supper. It was extremely good of her as she was earning little more than I was and had no kind aunt to supply her lavishly with food at weekends. She was a vegan and her cooking was inventive though not always successful – things like okra and banana stew (very slippery) and lettuce and carageen mousse (like a rubber quoit) but I now knew how very difficult cooking was so I was not disposed to be critical.

Tiffany had been understudying the part of Mrs Erlynne in *Lady Windermere's Fan* at the Arena Playhouse for the last year. It was enjoying a good run and Tiffany said it was a brilliant production but the actress whose part she was understudying enjoyed the rudest health, which was maddening. Tiffany left the house at six o'clock every evening to sit in a dull dressing room by herself for four hours. Luckily she liked sewing and had recently taken to making cushion covers and quilts and even a pair of curtains for her room.

She had a friend who was a theatrical costume designer and she gave Tiffany all her leftover scraps of fabric and trimmings. They were, predictably, flaunting in colour and frequently glittery. Tiffany stitched them into crazy-paving patchwork then appliquéd curious alembic shapes on the top, ornamented with beads and sequins for extra drama. She gave me a tablecloth she had made soon after I moved in and, though I thought it was rather hideous, I treasured it because I was so fond of her.

Daniel, as I was permitted to call him after a polite interval, begged her not to give him any examples of her needlework as, he said, it was just the kind of thing he most disliked. 'There was a period in English culture par-*tic*-ularly unfortunate in the first half of this century when one or two associates had the talent to write and paint, and anyone who had once blacked their boots was elevated to the status of fellow artist.' I loved it when Daniel was disapproving. Then he looked like the most important grade of mandarin, the ones that wore a ruby button in their caps as opposed to the lowly ninth-grade silver. Daniel would pull down the corners of his mouth and stab the air with his elegant bony fingers in the direction of his audience. His eyes would narrow to dark chinks of animosity in the long oval of his face. 'The Bloomsbury Group. Faugh! I abhor crude swirling shapes in harsh, jarring colours. This century has covered the earth with ugly things. It has been the aesthetic ruination of the human race as well as the culmination of moral degeneracy.'

I tried to look penitent as Daniel seemed to be aiming his disapproval chiefly at me.

'Perhaps the hopeless members of the Bloomsbury Gang knew they weren't any good,' I said. 'They couldn't help it if they had a few famous and talented friends. Perhaps they did it just for fun and other people made them out to be serious writers and painters.'

Daniel stared at me with his eyebrows practically vertical with annoyance before he began to laugh. It was part of his peculiar charm that his emotions were so volatile. His presence was charged with uncertainty, which I enjoyed.

'Quite right, Viola. They may well have been shy violets forced to blush in public. But, you know, the Bloomsbury *Gang* were eighteenth-century Whigs, adhering to the Duke of Bedford, something a little different from the *Group*.'

I visualised something white and powdered before I realised he was talking about politicians. What a curse it is to be benighted by ignorance.

Miss Barlam accepted a cushion of Tiffany's making with strong expressions of gratitude though the vermilion and gold velvet trapezoid looked strangely at odds with her pretty, elegantly furnished room.

Miss Barlam, I guessed, was somewhere in her mid-thirties. She was small and slender with soft rusty hair and faintly freckled skin. She had an indeterminate face and one would be in danger of forgetting it if it were not for her eyes, which were large, gentle and luminous. Sometimes, when she was talking about something that pleased her, they were quite beautiful. I think she liked me, for once she had discovered my regrettable and childish love of sweet things she used to buy cakes and invite me to have tea with her. One could never be quite certain of her preferences for individuals because she behaved in exactly the same way to everyone, even the tramp who often lay drunk and cursing at the corner of the square. She was polite, deferential and gravely considerate of one's least sensible remark.

She had two suits, one navy and the other grey, and a number of blouses in Liberty lawn. When she went to church, which she did every Sunday for she was a good Catholic, she wore a hat with a spotted veil. It had once been chic but now it looked sadly *passé*. Her eyes behind it reminded me of captive animals, nervously padding around their cage.

The first time I went to tea she was anxious and diffident and fussed about sitting me in the warmest place out of draughts. She apologised with every sentence. The light was too bright in my eyes, the chair too hard, her conversation too dull. She explained that she never went anywhere but to the occasional lunchtime concert and had no existence outside her job and her life at number 46. Her shyness clearly made it difficult for her to feel comfortable in the company of another human being but after I had told her about working for SCAB and what my life had been like before coming to Tolgate Square (with the usual excisions), during which she laughed a lot, we became quite confidential with each other. She told me about her childhood.

'I was six when I was sent to England. Daddy had a tea plantation. Granny – my maternal grandmother – didn't approve of the marriage and when he took Mummy away to India she predicted that no good would come of it. They were killed in a plane crash near Rajpur when I was eight. I shall never forget the look on Granny's face when she came to tell me about it. She stood in the headmistress's study of my horrid, cold, unfriendly boarding-school and there was an expression of perfect triumph in her eyes. After that the girls were even less friendly and I was even more of an outcast.'

'I can hardly bear to think of you so lonely in a hateful school with your darling parents dead! However did you stand it?'

'I suppose I lost myself in the world of books. I read in every available moment. People like Frances Hodgson Burnett, whose heroines were lonely, parentless misfits. It helped quite a bit. The holidays were worse, though. At school I got enough to eat and I was left alone. At Granny's house there were only the two of us. She had a nice daily help called Mrs Tugwell, I remember. I liked going to her house because it was warm. Granny didn't approve of central heating, or fires after March or before November. I couldn't get used to the cold. Granny didn't like self-indulgence so we always had the nastiest food possible. To this day I cannot look cold tongue in the face especially accompanied by pickled beetroot. Granny was a good woman. I should be misleading you if I gave the impression that she was cruel or neglectful. She was a staunch Roman

Catholic and had a tender conscience. Every night we said our prayers together and she'd pray for fortitude to bear the responsibility of looking after me. "Oh, Lord," she would pray, "let me not stumble beneath the weight of this heavy burden."' Miss Barlam laughed. 'Funny, isn't it, what one minds as a child? Now I see she meant to square up to doing the best she could. But at the time it wounded me terribly to feel that my existence was nothing but a nuisance.'

'How I sympathise with that!' I exclaimed. 'Not that my aunt was ever anything but lavishly affectionate but I did feel that I was a trouble and a pest, however often she told me that I was the person she loved most in the world. Did it get better as you got older?'

'In some ways it did. Granny liked me more when I could do the cooking and save the expense of employing a cook. When my grandmother died I realised what a pitiable life she'd led. The only people at the funeral besides me were her solicitor, a woman from the Catholic Women's Guild – who made it clear that she was doing nothing more than her duty in attending the obsequies – Mrs Tugwell and the gardener. It was dreadful to see how unlamented her passing was. I've always felt guilty about not being able to love her. She had no family but me and not a single friend. Well, there is actually a niece still alive but she lives in an institution in Devon and is, poor thing, quite demented. She writes me long incomprehensible letters in the person of Mary, Queen of Scots.'

'Oh dear, it all sounds so sad. What did you do then, after she died?'

'The hardest thing of all was to face up to the emptiness of my own life. I was twenty-two. All I had in the world was a small, ugly house, which I had always hated, three hundred pounds that Granny had left me in her will – the rest going to build a home for retired priests – and two slight friendships left over from school. One girl had married and gone to live in Scotland and the other worked in New York so even they were more or less out of my life. But I was young and still hopeful. I answered advertisements in *The Times* and after six months I got a job, sold the house and came to London. I took a room in a boarding-house in Muswell Hill. It was dingy and poky but it was all my own and I had left Dunstable for ever!'

When I tried to imagine what it must have felt like to be Miss Barlam, I was astonished by her courage. The idea of being so utterly alone in the world filled me with sorrow and fear. In Aunt Pussy's circle everyone had friends by the score or they would simply not have been in it. They were popular either because they had social cachet or because they were charming, talented, and amusing. I was appalled to discover how lonely and bereft of friendship it was possible to be. Afterwards I talked about it with Tiffany and she agreed with me that we neither of us had any excuse ever to be less than radiantly cheerful.

Miss Barlam worked for a magazine called the *Lady's Companion* for which she did illustrations. Its heyday was past and its circulation in England was derisory but it was kept going by subscriptions from old ladies living abroad in the last lingering beams of what had been the bright sun of the Empire. Her particular accomplishment was botanical painting and the walls of her room were hung with examples that were, to my untutored eye anyway, really beautiful. She was fanatically neat and fastidious in all she did. We always had China tea with lemon from her own precious New Hall cups, little silver forks for our cakes and we caught the crumbs on our knees with embroidered napkins. The only untidy element in her life was her love for Daniel.

The third time Miss Barlam asked me to tea it was already December and the weather was foggy and freezing. There was perhaps an additional warmth in the blaze of the fire and a brighter gleam to the candlelight in contrast to the dark sky beyond the dormer windows, which encouraged her to be even more confiding. It always happened that after playing with a forkful of her custard *millefeuilles* or mandarin tart she would confess that, after all, she was not hungry and could I possibly manage two? I always could. 'I hope, Viola, that you'll go on enjoying the good things of life. They are God's gifts, so Father Declan always says, and He doesn't like his bounty to be spurned. From the particular shade of red of Father Declan's nose I think he's piously sacrificing himself in the interests of gratitude and appreciation.'

Miss Barlam – or Veronica, as she had asked me to call her – made a face at her own joke, raising her eyebrows and folding her lips together, so that I should understand that no real malice was intended.

'I shall never have any trouble doing my duty in that direction.' I took a huge bite of custard. 'Do you like Father Declan?'

'I've known him ever since I first came to London. I'd say I'm used to him, nothing more than that. Neither he nor I have a talent for making friends. Do you know, I really think it is the greatest gift of all? When I left Dunstable I imagined a whirl of shopping, theatres, little dinners and lunches. I thought that because London was so big and crammed with people I should have no difficulty in finding the sort of life I wanted.'

'Wasn't it like that?' I asked, when she paused.

'No. I must admit it was painfully disillusioning. I was awkward, self-conscious . . . I tried too hard to make people like me, I think. I was too pressing with invitations. And everyone I met seemed to have their own lives already completed. I suppose the truth is they thought me too dull.'

'You aren't in the least bit dull, not the very smallest bit!' I said, moved almost to tears by this saddest of confessions.

Veronica shook her head and smiled. 'There were times, particularly long, wet, winter weekends, when I would have given anything to hear Granny's sharp voice telling me that there was too much salt in the stew and to hurry early to bed so that I could trim her toenails – not my favourite job, as you can imagine. But I was so lonely that I would have kissed those wrinkled yellow feet all over if only it meant hearing the sound of another voice. That was before I came to number 46, of course.'

'Wasn't there anybody at the *Lady's Companion* to be friends with?'

'Well – everyone's very polite. But the younger girls are

busy with boyfriends and clothes and parties and things. I expect they pity me for being plain and spinsterish. And the women my age are married with children. It's all they talk about. I haven't much to contribute. There *was* someone. I suppose I can talk about it now – how strange that it doesn't seem to matter very much any more. I did meet a man who seemed to like me. It was about six months after I moved to London. He was the accountant for the *Lady's Companion* and used to come into the office from time to time. He told me at once that he was married but that his wife had had a terrible car accident and couldn't speak or move. She lived permanently in a nursing home. I was so sorry for him. His name was Gregory Vince. After I'd known him a few weeks – we met every Thursday for lunch – I used to imagine what it would be like to be called Veronica Vince. V.V. I even embroidered it on to the corner of a tablecloth. It looked very neat. Then I unpicked it because I felt guilty about his poor wife – it seemed to be wishing for her death.

'We used to go to a little restaurant in Shepherd's Bush. It was called the Golden Gondola. The waiters' gondolier hats were plastic and the murals of Venice were terrible. But the cooking was good. Gregory would hold my hand and tell me stories about his life at school and, later on, in the army and what it was like starting out as an accountant. He used to make me laugh so much. Once he told me that my eyes were so beautiful and kind that whenever he looked into them he forgot about being miserable. I longed to make him happy. I wanted to take care of him. It didn't matter that we couldn't be married. Then he became . . . he wanted . . .' Veronica blushed. 'You know what men are. And, of course, it's quite natural. These days, people think nothing of making love outside marriage. I know I'm old-fashioned. But I couldn't let him make love to me without confessing to Father Declan. And the very idea was an agony of embarrassment. How could Father Declan and I share Nescafé and digestive biscuits in the vestry afterwards? I would have had to give up going to St Mary's altogether. Gregory couldn't understand how I felt. He asked me if I was more in love with Father Declan than him but of course it wasn't that.'

'I think I would have skipped telling Father Declan if I felt like that.'

Veronica smiled. 'That's because you aren't a Catholic. It would have been as impossible to commit such a sin as adultery and not confess as to . . . Oh, I don't know, ill-treat an animal or go out without any underwear.'

'Quite often in hot weather . . .' I began, but stopped as I saw that Veronica looked shocked, 'I wish I hadn't got any on,' I finished lamely.

'One day, about three months after we met, Gregory told me that the worst thing for him, apart from feeling sad for his wife, of course, was that he had these sexual fantasies and they seemed to be getting out of hand and he was afraid that frustration might make him do something he would later regret. He was almost weeping. I realised how selfish I was being. Wasn't my embarrassment, however acute, less to bear than what he was going through? So I . . . gave myself to him. It was only a few days later that someone in the office told me that they were having a "whip-round" for Gregory Vince, who was getting married and leaving the firm. It seemed that all the women considered it a great joke that he had been caught at last as he was always such a one for the girls. Apparently he always told them that he was married so that they wouldn't expect him to get "involved".'

'The mean rat!' I felt so sorry as I looked at Miss Barlam's gentle face, cast down at the memory of this early betrayal.

'As you say. It was a long time before I could even think of it without shuddering. It ruined whatever small confidence I had in myself. I made the decision – very sensibly, I now think – that I was better off without men since I clearly had no ability to judge them.'

'Oh, but what a shame! Everyone makes mistakes. And men do too.'

'I suppose so. But anyway, the time for all that's past. I'm an old maid. I'm not fitted for romance and that's all there is to it.'

'But surely –' I stopped, not daring to speak of Daniel first. 'This house is romantic, isn't it?' I went on.

'When I tell people at work that there's no electricity they think I'm making it up. They don't know how beautiful it is . . . such a haven from the nasty ugly modern world. Sometimes I pretend I'm a character in a book, Clarissa, perhaps, or Anne Elliot.'

Veronica and I had already discussed our favourite writers, which included Richardson and Jane Austen, Dickens and the Brontës.

'But Daniel isn't in the least like Captain Wentworth. He's much more like Mr Rochester.'

'I see him more as Monsieur Paul Emanuel.' Veronica blushed a fiery red, and for a moment her secret shone out from her eyes like the beam from an opened lantern, before she lowered her eyelids and extinguished it.

'Yes, I see what you mean. Fiery and sarcastic. Impossibly high standards for everything. But Monsieur Paul was little and ugly, wasn't he? I think Daniel's quite beautiful in an ascetic, refined sort of way – like a painting of Christ.'

'Yes! He has that look of inward suffering. He is so good!'

I thought of all the times Daniel was impatient and angry and unreasonable. When Tiffany had left a pair of tights in the bathroom a few days before, he had lost his temper completely and raged at the top of his voice, which frightened Josephine so much that she had jumped from his shoulder on to the top of the dresser and it had taken him nearly an hour to coax her down. He had a horror of what he called 'female esotery'. I looked it up in the *OED* and it means 'secret lore'. It was then true that love is not only blind but deaf as well.

His shouts could have been heard on the other side of the square when Mrs Shilling threw away his ripe Camembert because it had run off the plate and made a mess in the pantry. And there was the time when Tiffany and I had been singing an accompaniment to the zither for which she had paid fifty pence in a junk shop. She had bought it, she explained, in a rush of nostalgia for the days of her childhood when Shirley Abicair and her zither were all the rage. It proved almost impossible to play but we were enjoying strumming and singing our way inaccurately through a two-part version of 'Greensleeves' when Daniel rushed in, threw up the sash, and hurled the zither into the street. He and Tiffany made it up the next day when both were calmer but he said if we ever made such a hideous noise again, like a hundred cats having their ears and tails pulled simultaneously, he would throw *us* out of the window. One of Mrs Shilling's favourite sayings was that the bee sucks honey from the bitterest flowers and the good thing that came out of this was that when he was in a friendly mood Daniel would ask us to his sitting room in which there was a Steinway piano and play Mozart and Haydn to us so that we would know what music was.

Daniel had black moods that sometimes lasted for days, during which his face reminded me of the picture of Bloody-bones the hobgoblin in one of my storybooks, which had frightened me very much as a child, but these were dispersed as soon as something happened to make him laugh. He seemed to find me particularly amusing but I never knew why. While I am delighted to be a source of cheer to my fellow men, naturally it is annoying to be considered a figure of fun. He never laughed at Veronica, whom he always called Miss Barlam with great punctilio, though I am sure she would not have objected in the least. He treated her with an impatient kindness, which had more than a tinge of irritation in it on the occasions when he caught her staring at him with a melting look of love on her transparently guileless face.

When Daniel was in a good mood his face was most romantically sinister, like a Mogul warrior prince, with its long aquiline nose, dark complexion and black eyes that seemed to shoot out arrows of light, either benevolent or mocking. He very quickly took up an attitude towards me that was tutelary. On that first day in October when I had discovered that I would be expected to cook for myself I had forgotten to buy anything to eat and would have gone to bed hungry if Tiffany had not given me one of her swede and nut chops.

The second day I went out in my lunch-hour to shop. Mr Phipps's art gallery was in Belgravia and I could have bought anything in the world except food. Finally, after walking for ages, I found a fishmonger. The counter had rows of exotic fish, most of which I didn't recognise. There were live blue lobsters with waving feelers, which I couldn't bear to look at for pity, oysters – also alive, of course, but less obviously miserable – and a swordfish with an angry look in its dead eye. It must have been a shop that supplied local restaurants for all the customers were men, buying in huge quantities. I felt more and more doubtful as I stared at the scaly, silvery bodies and tried to imagine what I could do with them. In the end I asked the fishmonger, who was very abrupt and unfriendly, which was his nicest fish. I expect he thought I was sadly deranged but that didn't prevent him from taking the opportunity to sell me a baby sturgeon. It sounded rather sweet and I hoped it would turn out to be one of those pretty little iridescent fish at the front but it was the biggest thing on the counter, virtually. When he had wrapped it up I asked him how much it cost. The price was very nearly my week's wage. I was by now much too embarrassed to refuse it. I consoled myself with the thought that fish is good for the brain, which was obviously my most deficient organ, and that there would be enough sturgeon to feed me for a week. Its long tapering snout worked its way out of the parcel on the bus as I was going home and I was beginning to get some odd looks.

Daniel found me down in the kitchen later that evening, struggling to fit the sturgeon into the largest saucepan. It was horribly spiny and I began to entertain the deepest hatred for it. I could see that he thought it funny but for once, after looking at my tear-filled eyes and my hot face, he refrained from teasing remarks. He skinned and sliced the sturgeon expertly, insisting that I watch what he was doing. I didn't at all like seeing its head being cut off. Then he cooked a fillet briefly in butter and parsley until it was crisp and brown and delicious.

When I attempted the same thing myself the next evening something went very wrong for it was greasy with bitter-tasting black specks all over it. Mrs Shilling took the rest of the sturgeon home for her cat. It was a pity that Tibby couldn't know that he was dining, so Daniel told me, on the much prized source of caviar and isinglass.

When Daniel discovered what vast gaps there were in my knowledge and experience he took pains to teach me things. He gave me books to read and tried to structure my education so that I had some idea of what made the earth go round the sun and who St Thomas Aquinas was and what the Thirty-nine Articles were. And when he had cooked something delicious he always made me eat some so that my palate would be educated. As he gave me generous quantities my cooking skills remained non-existent during that first part of my life at number 46.

Our only serious disagreement was over Charles Dickens. He is far and away my favourite writer and I had a complete set of his novels in my room, along with *The Princess and Curdie*, *Jane Eyre*, and *Anna Karenina*. Daniel despised Dickens as a hack. Not for nothing, he said, had Trollope called Dickens 'Mr Popular Sentiment'. We argued for a long time about whether popularity implied mediocrity. I loved this kind of empirical conversation. Pierce only wanted me to shut up and get into bed. Daniel conceded that there was something remarkably fine in passages of *Our Mutual Friend* and *Bleak House*, but *The Old Curiosity Shop* aroused his most virulent hatred and he said that it would have been a service to mankind if Little Nell had been drowned in a vat of syrup on the first page. This was the first time in my life that anyone had taken the trouble to cross swords with me about something as serious and intellectual as literature in such a way as to suggest that my opinion was worthy of consideration. I was deeply – though mutely – appreciative.

CHAPTER 4

My life in Tolgate Square was so different from anything I had known before that, for a long time, it absorbed nearly all my thoughts. It became clear almost at once that Daniel was the centre of everything that happened at number 46. We were all, I think, very conscious of his comings and goings, his humours, his pleasures and his pains. I could not decide if this was because he was the owner of the house, or because he was one man among several women, or whether it was because his character was the strongest. He did not attempt to monopolise anyone's attention – on the contrary he was frequently silent and reclusive. There would be days when I scarcely saw him and only knew he was there because I heard him coughing. When his chest was particularly bad it seemed that he coughed incessantly all night. It must have been a torment to him but though he was vociferous about anything else that annoyed him he never spoke about his own health or lack of it.

'Bed not slept in again,' Mrs Shilling said, one Saturday morning just before Christmas. Saturday mornings were our opportunity for a good long gossip when Tiffany and I, and occasionally Veronica, would gather in the kitchen and drink Mrs Shilling's pumpkin-coloured tea. 'He's been up all night in his chair. It's that east wind. I said to him, "Fogg," I said, "you'll wrap up that chest of yours before you go out if you've half a loaf," and he turned round, quick as wink, and told me to mind my own business. He looked that bilious, yellow as a cat's eye, so I knew he was bad. But he never goes to the doctor's or nothink. I think he's afraid of hospitals. It's hinstitutions he can't abide and who can blame him? "Well," I said, "I suppose you'll look to me to order the flowers for your funeral." "Shilling," he said, "I won't even trouble you to attend. I know a busy woman like you has better things to do." Then he gives me a look like Old Nick scowling from the Oven of Hell and goes out with nothing but that old jacket on.'

Mrs Shilling chuckled. It was marvellous how tolerant she was of Daniel's shortness of temper. I think she would have cut off her arm for him.

I went to Richmond for Christmas where my aunt had shaken herself from her customary sloth and gathered a large party. Tiffany went to her parents in Yeovil. I thought of asking Veronica to come to Richmond with me but I guessed that she would rather be in the house alone with Daniel. When I got back to number 46 I saw that something had happened to Veronica. She had hope.

She told me later that she had returned from Mass on Christmas morning with the intention of cooking a chicken wing and heating up some mince pies. Daniel had met her in the hall and asked her if she would join him in his sitting room and share his own version of Christmas lunch. A table was laid for two in the window with Daniel's beautiful English Delft plates, eighteenth-century silver and glass. He had cooked grouse and dumplings and red cabbage and made little marzipan cakes, which he said had been his favourite as a boy in Bavaria.

'I never heard him speak of his childhood before.' Veronica's eyes were soft with love. 'He didn't say much about it. Just that the cook's name was Minna and that he used to fasten her apron strings to the knobs on the kitchen dresser and put slugs in her bed. When he was laughing about it I could see him quite clearly as a naughty little boy. Sometimes his eyes are so wicked – almost frightening – but then one remembers how tenderly he rescues spiders and beetles.' Veronica gave a little sigh. 'After lunch we played duets. Just simple things. My technique isn't up to his but I can sight-read quite well. We played some little Schubert pieces.'

'Goodness, how clever! I had no idea you could play the piano.'

'Granny considered it a suitable accomplishment so I was made to practise for hours. Daniel was very encouraging about my playing. He said I had a sensitive touch. I'm thinking about taking a few lessons. When I said I'd better go – not wanting to outstay my welcome – he bowed and kissed my hand and thanked me for helping him to enjoy what was usually one of the most depressing days of the year.' Veronica sighed again, unconsciously cradling her right hand with her left as though to protect the sacred place. 'One wishes one could do more. Only I'm afraid of intruding. This morning when I met him in the hall he looked at me as though he didn't know who I was. Other people are quite baffling, aren't they?'

'Baffling,' I agreed, with absolute sincerity. 'Daniel, perhaps, more than anyone. I suppose that's part of his attraction.'

I had spoken without thinking. Veronica put both her hands, palms outwards, in front of her in repudiation of the idea.

'Of course, it's nothing to me. He and I are relative strangers, just happening to live in the same house. Hardly even friends. I don't in the least mind if Daniel prefers to keep it like that. We're both used to living our lives alone and we respect each other for that, I hope. It's just that if one can help one's fellow man – well, it seems a pity to miss the opportunity.' She laughed unconvincingly. 'Well, now, let's talk about something more interesting. What did *you* do on Christmas Day?'

But I saw as I talked that, though she appeared to be listening, part of her mind was elsewhere. I wondered if Daniel had not made a mistake with that brief moment of Christmas conviviality. Was it possible that he might be able to return Veronica's passion? It seemed unlikely some- how but, then, what made people fall in love with each other? I was simply too inexperienced to know.

The trouble with having had such an odd and, in a way protected, childhood was that I had little to offer either in practical advice or worldly wisdom. And I always seemed to be the youngest of any group to which I belonged. At best I could be a novice assistant, at worst a hanger-on, who had to be looked after and considered and included in plans, but who was pretty nearly useless. At home it had been just the same. My aunt loved me, I knew, but there was never anything I could do for her except try not to be more of a nuisance than I could help. I longed to be able to do good to someone. I was terrifically flattered therefore when, one day in March, when the trees in Tolgate Square were brushed with green and the birds were full of boisterous song, Mrs Shilling came up to me as I stood in the hall peeling off my coat – it was army surplus, very cheap and hard-wearing but so thick and stiff that I felt like a dragonfly clambering out of its pupa-case every time I took it off – and said, 'Miss Tiffany's been home an age, shut in her room and crying fit to bust. She won't let me in when I knock. I thought to myself, If anyone can help it's Miss Viola. Seeing as how you're such friends and that.'

I picked up Josephine, who now had the thoroughly endearing habit of holding up her long arms to greet me when I arrived home. She put up admirably with the kisses I gave her instead of sugared almonds, which I had forgotten to buy. She clung round my neck as we went upstairs, shrinking close to me as sobbing became audible from Tiffany's room. I knocked at the door. 'It's me. Viola. Can I do anything to help you, Tiffany dear?'

There was a silence. I was about to go away when I heard Tiffany say, 'You can come in.'

Tiffany was lying on her bed, her handkerchief up to her eyes. When she lowered it I saw that her face was the kind of flaring scarlet true redheads go when angry or upset. 'It's all over! I don't care whether I live or die! He's going to marry that woman!'

That woman could only mean one person – the actress Tiffany was understudying. 'Not Bebe Ballantine!'

'Yes!' Tiffany turned on to her side and drew up her knees almost to her chin. 'I really thought . . . I really thought . . . it was me he was fond of.'

'Oh, Tiffany, I'm so sorry.'

I sat on the bed beside her and stroked her beautiful hair. I knew that Tiffany had considered herself in love with Montague Browse, the director of *Lady Windermere's Fan*. Only a week ago she had come back from the theatre in a state of high excitement because they had made love on the

Snow Queen's sledge in one of the property rooms beneath the stage. The time before it had been on the stage on the sofa of the Windermeres' drawing room after all the cast had gone home. Once they had made love in the royal box, actually during a rehearsal. The fact that he had never asked her to meet him outside the theatre, he explained, was because his producer's wife was madly in love with him and, though he had not given her the least encouragement, he was afraid she might damage his career if she got to hear of another attachment. Monty, according to Tiffany, had a stammer and the sweetest way of brushing his hair back from his face with both hands and huffing out through his lips when he was anxious. She had described him so well that I almost felt I knew him.

'Are you quite sure? You're always saying that everyone gossips so much . . .'

Tiffany held out a piece of paper. It was an invitation to the whole cast to attend a drinks party after the show that evening to celebrate the engagement. Tiffany worked during the day as a waitress at a vegan café in Camden Town and had found the note when she got home that afternoon.

'Only last week he said what rotten luck it was that Bebe was so healthy and that I never had a chance to show what I could do. Then he said that I'd better keep that remark under my hat as Bebe would tear his eyes out if she got to hear of it. He looked so vulnerable when he said that. Defenceless men *always* turn my knees to water. The absolute bastard! To think I nearly asked him to go away with me for a clandestine weekend but didn't because I thought I might frighten him off! Men are often intimidated by me because I'm bigger than most of them.'

'It seems very strange that you didn't notice that there was anything going on between them.'

'Not really. Now that Bebe's a star she never spends time in the theatre except when she's acting. She's too proud to mingle with the cast. Oh, I hate her so!'

After a while Tiffany stopped crying long enough to sip a tumbler of sherry while I went to the telephone box in the next street and rang the theatre to tell them that Tiffany wasn't well enough to come in that evening. We sat up very late, talking about Montague and love and life and, to comfort her, I told her something I had never told anyone else . . . about the only man I had ever been in love with and how it had pretty nearly spoilt my life between the ages of fifteen and twenty.

When I was a child and Aunt Pussy had to go away with R.D. to grand parties where children would have been in the way, I often used to stay with my cousin Miranda. She is much older than me and has three children, the eldest, James, being about my age. She lives in the most beautiful moated manor house, centuries old, by the sea in Kent. We used to have great fun in the garden and on the beach, swimming and making camps and things. It was my only experience of real family life and some of my best memories come from those days. Miranda's husband, Jack, was away a lot but when he was there he added something else . . . an element of excitement. He was a tremendous tease and would make a fool of you if he could. James always hated that. Once Jack told him that he'd had a note from the headmaster to say that James had failed all his exams and was going to be asked to leave the school. Poor James was miserable for hours until Miranda came home and found out about it. Of course it wasn't true. Jack said that James was gullible and it was ridiculous to cry about having to leave school. Anyone with any guts would have been delighted. Jack was cruel. I knew that, but he was so strong – you couldn't think about anyone else when he was in the room.

One summer holiday when I was fifteen Miranda gave a party. We children kept out of the way and took a picnic supper to the field where Elizabeth's pony was kept, on the other side of the moat. I offered to fetch the ice-cream. I was standing in the pantry, scrabbling about in the deep-freeze, when Jack came in. He said he was looking for ice cubes. I asked him if the party was going well. He said, 'Actually I'm bored stiff. Perhaps I'll come and join you kids and let them get on without me.'

I said, wouldn't it be unkind to Miranda to do that? Otherwise, of course, we'd love to have him. He laughed very much when I said that. I didn't know why. Then he said, 'You've always been a taking little thing. And now you're growing into a beauty.' He touched my face then ran his hand down the back of my neck. All my skin came out in goose-bumps. He put his arm right round me and started to breathe very hard. Then he kissed me. My blood fizzed like the ginger beer we'd been drinking. I felt terribly sick in a delicious kind of way, excited and horrified all at once.

'My darling Viola,' he stopped kissing me long enough to say, 'you are the most wonderful creature. You could make me do something really wicked.' He kissed me again and this time I kissed him back. I shouldn't have done, I know. Then we heard someone coming. Jack said, 'Fuck!' which surprised me as none of the men I knew ever said that, only boys wanting to seem grown-up. 'I'll have to go, darling. I'll find a way to see you alone later. My God, you're quite delicious. Heaven help me if I don't –' Then Rose, who used to be Miranda's nurse and still lived with them, came in. She said she wanted to take some dog meat out of the deep-freeze. I noticed she looked at me very hard and in a way I didn't like. I ran back to the others with the ice-cream.

Those two kisses made everything seem different. I suppose it was I who was different. For the first time I saw how lush and green the field was, speckled with brilliant blue speedwell and purple vetches and white moon daisies I hadn't noticed before. Now their colours seemed to throb with brightness. The moat was black with silvery rings where the carp leaped for flies. The clouds passing across the setting sun, just turning vermilion, were so beautiful that I was moved to tears.

All evening I was in a sort of trance of happiness, astonished to have been noticed by him, thrilled by the possibility of being kissed like that again. I went to sleep that night in a daze of expectation. But in the morning I woke feeling quite different. Miranda had been so kind to me and I loved her. I must have been mad to think of doing something that would hurt her so much. I felt miserable with guilt.

I saw Jack at breakfast. He read the newspaper and didn't look at me once. I was certain of that because I could hardly drag my eyes away from him, though all the time I felt worse and worse about my behaviour. I imagined that he felt guilty too, and I was relieved as well as painfully disappointed when he didn't come back from London that evening or the next. I was due to join Aunt Pussy in Nice after that so we didn't see each other again.

I was certain that he had stayed away because he was afraid of behaving badly. The awful thing about that was that it made me fall in love with him. He was not only the most attractive man I had ever seen but desperately honourable as well. I relived those two kisses over and over again and each time my stomach would turn over and I would start to feel sick. I decided that my loving him would not harm Miranda as long as Jack and I didn't see each other any more. So I made excuses not to stay with her. Aunt Pussy asked me if I had quarrelled with James and I said that something had happened that made me feel it was wiser not to go there for a bit. I knew she thought that James had tried to flirt with me and that was what I wanted her to think.

Because I felt so treacherous I made much more of those two kisses than there was. I decided it was only *not* despicable if Jack and I were truly in love. I imagined him thinking of me night after night, longing for me, sadly, hopelessly, writing me letters and tearing them up in frustration. For ages I used to wait every morning for the postman with my heart thumping in case there was a letter from Jack, asking me to run away with him.

I wasn't at all interested in boys my age after that. Aunt Pussy was always finding suitable young men for me but I felt that I belonged to Jack and I owed it to our love not to have anything to do with them. Anyway, they seemed silly and dull by comparison. I don't know what I thought was going to happen . . . perhaps that Miranda might fall in love with someone else and then Jack and I could legitimately be lovers.

When Aunt Pussy got the news of Jack's death, in a shooting accident, she was appalled by my reaction. I tried to pretend it was flu but I think she knew it was *crise de nerfs*, which was what she called any upset of an emotional kind. I was too ill to go to his funeral and Aunt Pussy didn't go either. She tried very hard to get me to talk to her but I felt more than ever that I owed my darling, dead Jack the loyalty of silence.

About six months after Jack's death Miranda asked me to meet her for lunch in London. I was so pleased to see her after five years' absence and so sorry to think of how unhappy she must be that when I walked into Bertolino's and saw her sitting there looking just the same, with waving hair the colour of primroses and that lovely, slightly quizzical smile, I felt my face flame and tears rush into my eyes. Miranda hugged me and said she was on the point of crying too because it had been so long, which was nice of her.

We ordered oysters and champagne to celebrate our reunion. I asked Miranda about herself and everyone at Westray Manor but I couldn't bring myself to say Jack's name.

'Everything's just the same,' said Miranda, when she had talked about the children, the house, the garden, the pony and the dog, 'but of course all the time there's the difficulty of accepting that Jack is dead. He was away a lot in the last few years so it isn't unusual not to have him in the house but it still seems quite impossible that we shall none of us ever see him again.'

'You must feel desolate.' I took hold of her hand, wishing that my heart wouldn't beat so fast just to hear him talked about.

'I *am* sad but not probably in the way you think. I feel grief-stricken for the children. And I'm wretched that our marriage was such a failure.' Seeing my expression of incredulity Miranda smiled rather forlornly. 'Oh, I know it all looked idyllic to outsiders. We *were* very happy – well, *I* was anyway – for the first few years until just after Elizabeth was born. Then I found out that Jack had been having an affair with one of my best friends. That was only the beginning. After a while I gave up trying to keep track of Jack's women. And I stopped loving him.'

Miranda went on talking about Jack's infidelities and her reaction to them while I stared at the empty oyster shells on my plate. A sensation of soreness grew as though I had been punched in the soft part just beneath my ribcage. I imagined Jack smiling down at me as I had conjured him up so many times before but now I had to excise the image for the wave of nausea it induced. Jack had tired of his affairs the moment he began them. Sometimes he had had two lovers at the same time and delighted in making them known to each other. What he had liked best was to lull them into a feeling of security and then break off the affair without warning. As Miranda talked a feeling of hatred swelled inside me until I could not make even a pretence of eating. I hated Jack for having made Miranda so unhappy and for having amused himself with me. But, most of all, I was sickened to the heart by a fierce self-disgust.

When the waiter brought our *raie au beurre noir* I dared to look briefly at Miranda. Her huge, dark eyes were filled with a sort of tender anxiety and then I knew that she and Aunt Pussy had put two and two together and made four. 'So you see,' Miranda finished, 'while I was distraught for a time and hopelessly at sea, struggling with emotions like guilt and anger and grief, his death was not as intolerable as if I had loved him. I hope that doesn't sound cruel. I have to be truthful. I wish he weren't dead, I wish he were able to go on doing all the things that he once enjoyed, I wish above all that the children still had their father. But in a way Jack's death has meant that now I'm just beginning to live again properly. I'd had to stop myself feeling anything to bear it, you see.'

I could have howled at that. The idea that Miranda had been so miserable and brave while I had been fantasising about betraying her made me feel monstrously guilty. But one cannot howl when out to lunch. Miranda changed the subject and asked me about what I was doing and I made an attempt to be expansive and amusing. We parted with a long embrace and promises to meet again soon. For several days I walked around in a kind of dream of despair. Then Aunt Pussy suggested that I should think about leaving home and being independent. It was exactly the right thing. I found my heart wasn't broken, after all. The bruised feeling started to get better and I got excited about the idea of making my own way in the world. I think Aunt Pussy guessed a great deal of what was going on but she didn't try to force my confidence.

About three months later, after I had moved in with Stella Partington, I had lunch with Miranda again and she told me that she was in love with someone and was going to marry him. She looked extraordinarily happy. I really was pleased, though shocked too, in a way, because I couldn't imagine her with anyone other than Jack. That's it then, I said to myself. Miranda has got over Jack after having been married to him for goodness knows how many years, so you can get over two kisses. But I made up my mind that I would never allow myself to forget, because I had learned one very valuable thing: that up to that point I had been an ignorant, romantic little fool, ripe for deception, and the deceiver I had most to beware of was myself. Now my eyes were opened.

CHAPTER 5

'Am spending night at Richmond. Off to Nottingham-shire in morning to look at SCAB house. Back latish tomorrow night. Remains of chicken sandwich in larder for Tibby. Can I keep lipstick till then? Kiss for Josephine.'

I left the note on the hall table at number 46. Daniel had been very angry with me when I stayed all night at Pierce's flat the first time. He wouldn't say why he was angry or even

61

admit that he was, but it wasn't hard to tell what mood he was in. Anger made his face much older – he was actually forty-eight – and his eyes unseeing, sort of blank with rage as though he had withdrawn from you in every way but bodily. Tiffany said that as it got late, Daniel had started to pace about the house and stare out of his drawing-room window, which looks out on to the street, saying what a child I was and capable of any folly.

Of course I was annoyed by this. I was supposed to be grown-up and taking care of myself and there was Daniel behaving like the strictest nanny. But I didn't want to make him anxious so after that I always left a note, not addressed to anyone in particular but just to say where I was going and how long I would be away.

Daniel had met Pierce once by chance. He was coming out of the house as Pierce was dropping me home in his two-seater MGB. The hood of the car was down. I introduced them. Pierce gave an offhand wave and Daniel gnashed his teeth and went straight back into the house. After that I never mentioned Pierce except to Tiffany, who was avid for all details, her own love life being, she said, as featureless as a salt flat.

It turned out that several female members of the cast of *Lady Windermere's Fan* were nursing severe disappointments over the engagement of Montague Browse and Bebe Ballantine. Tiffany vowed that in future she would have nothing to do with flirtatious men. But how was one to know – short of grilling all the other women with whom he had anything to do – if a man's interest in one was just an indication of his seductive temperament or something more genuine, sparked by one's unique charms?

Aunt Pussy was thrilled to see me. I hadn't let her know partly because our local call-box had been vandalised again and partly because Aunt Pussy led such a cosy, stay-at-home existence that there was never any danger of her not being there. She spent all day in bed and only got up in time for tea. Her most intimate friends visited her in the morning. Her bedroom was enchantingly pretty, the bed a *lit à la polonaise* hung with white silk painted with flowers and butterflies. The room had french windows and a balcony from which you could see the Italian garden . . . a graceful arrangement of hedges, canals, statues and fountains. Often you would hear gales of laughter as her friends brought her the latest gossip. Aunt Pussy was never unkind but she loved to know what was going on in the world in which she had once been such a bright and particular star, though, she insisted, she had not the smallest desire to be part of it now she didn't have to.

Aunt Pussy was the elder by five years of the two dashing Otway sisters who had come over from Ireland to entrance and shock London society in about equal measure with their beauty and unconventional manners. Aunt Pussy – her real name was Adeline but she was called Pussy by everyone – was fair-haired with translucent skin and eyes of delphinium-blue. Her younger sister Constantia, my mother, had dark curls and eyes of a smoky colour. People said I looked exactly like my mother. I couldn't tell. I so rarely saw her that I might have passed her in the street and not recognised her.

Both the Otway girls had had plenty of suitors from the faster set but Aunt Pussy was more popular because her nature was sweeter and jollier. I only know this from what people said, forgetting that I was behind the curtains reading or sitting on the floor under the table, playing with my dolls. Aunt Pussy was the most easy-going person in the world, which virtue made her peculiarly suited to her role in life.

R.D. was a duke. Not just any old duke either. For twenty-one years my aunt was his mistress. Even now, four years after his death, saying that makes me feel nervous for discretion was the hallmark of my childhood and R.D.'s relationship with my aunt, though known to the entire world, including the Duchess, was never *ever* referred to publicly by anyone.

My aunt called him Roddy as Roderick was his favourite of the half-dozen names with which he had been baptised. As a child I thought she was calling him R.D., being short for royal duke, and I never managed to think of him as anything else. To his face, I called him 'sir'. I usually tried to get out of talking to him at all. He was dreadfully unpredictable and I never got over my infant dislike of his wet yellow moustaches and being barked at when anything upset him. Innumerable things did and unfortunately one of the things that never failed to put him in a temper was the Duchess. She was a dull woman and everyone was fearfully bored by her. She had eyes very close together above a large bony nose. R.D. called her the Timber Wolf behind her back but I never heard my aunt be unkind about her.

Over the years there grew up an understanding between Aunt Pussy and the Duchess, who could not help but see that my aunt's presence always soothed her irascible husband. Once or twice it was only my aunt's intervention that prevented R.D. banishing the Duchess altogether. According to my aunt, when R.D. lay dying, partially paralysed and unable to speak, the Duchess knelt by his bedside, her face buried in the bedclothes, practically roaring with grief. R.D. couldn't bear women to cry. I don't think he approved of other people having feelings. Apparently R.D.'s eyes were bulging with rage. The Duchess asked R.D. to give her a sign that he had loved her, even if only a little. Aunt Pussy who was standing on the other side of the bed, leaned over and lifted his hand from the sheet, put it on the Duchess's bowed head and held it there. It was, she said, the only time she had thwarted him, and for some time after his death she had been haunted by the baleful glare in his eyes before he closed them for ever.

When I asked Aunt Pussy if she had loved R.D. she said that she had loved him very much when he was younger and not so unreasonable. He had been charming then and absolutely besotted with her. No woman in the world could have resisted such devotion. Later on, when he got testy and perverse, she felt sorry for him. Most old men, my aunt warned me, were cross and selfish and difficult and dukes more so, having been spoiled like babies all their lives.

R.D. left Aunt Pussy the house in Richmond in his will,

and a generous allowance as well, so she was able to do just as she pleased. All her friends, including the Duchess, came to call. Men and women who knew her less well and were denied the intimacy of bedroom chats would come for tea or dinner but even this was becoming too much of an effort for my aunt, though she was not yet fifty. She said that living with R.D., even when he was being nice, was like being the captain of an ocean-going liner with impossibly demanding passengers, wildly unpredictable weather, constant engine trouble and a mutinous crew and she was worn out by years of superhuman vigilance.

'Tell me about Giles, darling,' said Aunt Pussy, as we sat down to shrimps with anchovy butter. Pooh Bah, my aunt's Pekinese, had his own dish of shrimps. He hoovered them up in two seconds flat and then sat watching and staring up at me with soulful, popping eyes. 'You never seem to talk about him.'

'That's because I don't know anything about him.'

'Well, who are his people? Do I know his mother?'

'Oh, I shouldn't think so. His name is Fordyce. He was at Oxford with Pierce. His mother lives alone in Worthing. She's a widow.'

'Dear, dear. Poor thing! It *does* sound dull. Is he a nice boy?'

'He's a man. Thirty, I should think.'

'I keep forgetting, darling, what an ancient old thing you are now. And Pierce is the same age, then? Do shut up, Pooh Bah.'

'Mm.'

I had tripped myself up there, having allowed my aunt to think in earlier conversations about Pierce that he was roughly my own age. I gave Pooh Bah my last shrimp, which he ate very fast and then took up his former pose, pressing his reproachful face against my leg.

My aunt had an absurdly out-of-date and – considering her own career – quite unreasonable expectation that I was going to sprint up the aisle as soon as possible, clothed in virginal white, to throw myself chastely into the arms of some pillar of the establishment. That conventional men would be unlikely to approve of my background and origins did not seem to have occurred to her. Therefore I had let her think that Pierce was an inexperienced youth with damp palms and spots and that quite probably we only held hands and fumbled with experimental kisses at the end of the evening. Because she knew his mother she was reassured that he was suitable.

If she could have known how violent Pierce's love-making was she would have had the gravest doubts. As he was my first lover I had no standard of comparison but after our last sexual encounter I had had to borrow Tiffany's dark red lipstick to conceal the bite on my mouth. Tiffany had been horrified when I showed her. I said nothing of the scratches and bruises in other more intimate places. It had been agony to sit down all morning. All in all it was better to keep Aunt Pussy in complete ignorance.

'You're so young, darling,' said Aunt Pussy, 'and, bless you, in many ways rather innocent.' I knew at once she was thinking of my passion for Jack. If *only* one were allowed to forget past *bêtises*. 'You must be very careful. Perhaps I ought to meet Giles before you go off with him into the blue.'

'There's really no need. We're only going for lunch tomorrow. He'll have to drive like anything to get there in time and I suppose he won't try to ravish me among the cold cuts on the dining-table at Inskip Park. Besides, you'd have to get up so early. He's picking me up at half past eight.'

One or all of these arguments seemed to convince Aunt Pussy. 'Take Pooh Bah away and give him his supper, would you?' she said as Tilda, the maid, brought in our *suprêmes de volaille* in a cream sauce.

'He's just had it, madam. And he's eaten the cat's.'

'Oh. What was I saying? Ah, yes. Giles. I hope he's a careful driver.'

'Bound to be. He's a very strait-laced person . . . rather severe, really, and fussy about things.'

'Good-looking?' Aunt Pussy helped herself to sauté potatoes and buttered peas.

'Well . . . not bad, actually. Come to think of it, quite a

dish. Dark hair and a nice nose. I can't remember what colour his eyes are. But you don't notice it because he's so disapproving. Quite the most disapproving person I've ever met.' I could see Aunt Pussy was warming to Giles by the minute. 'And he's terribly clever.'

'Is he? My goodness, he sounds rather divine.' Aunt Pussy adored clever men. R.D. had been terribly stupid, if the truth be told. Aunt Pussy was so bewitching that the stiffest, most withered sage became a lady-killer under her influence and she loved intelligent conversation. Although she couldn't understand a lot of it, she said she knew that it did her good, like vitamins and sea-bathing.

Tilda brought in a glass of syllabub for each of us with some *langue de chat* biscuits.

'Heavens, Aunt Pussy!' I took a spoonful. 'Blissful food as always but you don't think just a little rich?'

'I read recently that a high-fat diet is good for the skin. Prevents wrinkles, you know.'

'I expect because one's skin is stretched to snapping point over mountains of flesh.'

'I have put on a few pounds since I started this diet,' Aunt Pussy admitted. 'It would be just the thing for Marie-Louise.' Marie-Louise was R.D.'s duchess. 'She's as thin as a pencil and having another *crise de nerfs*. Her companion's leaving. The usual thing.'

'Not expecting a baby? That's the third in a row.'

'I think it's Percival.' Percival was Marie-Louise's second son. 'She really will have to put him in the navy. It's the only thing that answers for these libidinous boys. Now, my angel, we must find you something lovely to wear. You can't go to the Inskips in that garment, amusing though it is.' I was wearing a black velvet dress of Tiffany's, which almost reached the ground on me, and a beaded headband round my brow, Red Indian fashion, which I knew was old hat and sixties but it concealed a small bruise above my eyebrow, given me by Pierce at the height of his passion, that Aunt Pussy would have been sure to ask about. 'Let's go upstairs and see what we can find.'

We left Pooh Bah with his front feet on the table licking

out the syllabub glasses. Aunt Pussy's dressing room smelt of Joy by Patou, which was the scent she always wore. Agnes looked after my aunt's dresses with tender dedication, though Aunt Pussy rarely bothered to put on anything but the simplest things these days. She said she had spent too many years in clothes that demanded 'wearing' and constant surveillance to avoid the least crumple.

'I remember this.' She picked out a grey coat and skirt. 'Feel how soft it is. Alpaca. I wore it for a trip to Paris with a hat trimmed with chinchilla. I think there was a chinchilla scarf as well. But it's too old for you.' Aunt Pussy adored giving me her clothes but generally I had to refuse them as they were wholly unsuitable for my way of life. 'Oh, this dress!' She shuddered as she held out a stiff tube of white moiré embroidered with silver thread. 'So fagging to wear. It was made much too tight. I could hardly breathe. Then I got caught on one of Roddy's dress studs – we were at a ball somewhere, Rome was it? – and he burned the loop of thread with his cigar. I spent the rest of the evening with a black mark on my bosom. He *was* an irritating man in many ways. Look, Agnes has mended it but you can just see. Anyway, it won't do for lunch. Now what about this?'

We went through two rows of clothes before Aunt Pussy declared that a charming dress of palest aquamarine, like a thrush's egg, was exactly right. 'Silk and cashmere. Light as a whisker and terribly chic. Now, you must have a warm coat. Millicent Inskip is the most impractical woman in the world. If not mad. Her house is probably very badly run. Dirty and cold, I suspect.'

She chose a beautiful black mink coat.

'Won't I be rather overdressed?'

'Nonsense. You will be warm and smart. Nothing spoils one's looks more than a red, dripping nose. Where are the shoes that go with that dress?'

Eventually she found them. They were aquamarine suede and had four-inch heels.

'Gosh! I really think, darling Aunt, that the Inskips will be somewhat overwhelmed by my gorgeous appearance. You don't think a tweed skirt and jersey . . . ?'

'I do not!' My aunt was emphatic. 'I can't have my niece going round looking like a beggar. Won't you try the dress on, darling?'

'If I do I won't have time to see Jenkins. You know how early he goes to bed.' I didn't want to have to remove the headband.

'Run along then, my poppet. I'll ask Agnes to take these things to your room. I'll be in bed when you get back so I'll say goodbye now. Tell Giles to drive very, very slowly and make sure you have a good breakfast before you go. Porridge and bacon and eggs. I'll speak to Bettina.'

I managed to get out of the porridge but Aunt Pussy was firm on the matter of the bacon and eggs. Not wanting to waste time arguing, for it was already nearly ten o'clock, I kissed her goodbye and ran downstairs to let myself out by the side door. It was fairly dark but I was familiar with the paths through the formal gardens and down to the orchard. At the lowest part of the garden stood the cottage *orné* where Jenkins, my aunt's gardener, lived.

I opened the little pointed Gothic door. Jenkins was sitting in his favourite armchair by a good fire, his feet upon a stool, his head nodding a little as he slumbered. The smell of earth and plants and tobacco was deliciously familiar and better than the most expensive scent. The table was spread with newspapers on which stood trays of seedlings, brought in to protect them from the frost. The flowered cretonne curtains were drawn back, revealing boxes of seed potatoes spread out on the sills for chitting. When I closed the door behind me Jenkins opened his eyes with a start. 'Viola! My duckling! Light of my life!'

He stood up, smiling, and held wide his arms. I threw myself into them. 'Hello, Dad! How are you, you darling dormouse? You were fast asleep, and it isn't ten o'clock yet.'

Jenkins – my father – pushed me gently into his warm chair and got out his silver pocket watch. It began to chime as he looked at it. 'There you are! This watch is never wrong. I closed my eyes a minute seeing as how I've been making the new asparagus bed this arternoon and it's warm work. I must've dozed off. Well, well! How's my lovely one? Shall I get you a cuppa now?'

While Jenkins put the kettle on the stove and warmed the teapot by the fire I told him what I'd been doing this last week. Though his hair was touched with grey and there were broken veins across his cheeks and the bridge of his nose, befitting one who worked outside in all weathers, he was a handsome man, tall and trim with big strong hands and long legs in corduroys with string tied round the knees. His face was broad and his nose thin. I loved his eyes, which were bright blue and honest. He gave me a bourbon biscuit from the tin with robins on that he kept on the shelf by his chair. I was bloated with butter and cream but I ate it so as not to hurt his feelings.

'You're looking thin, pet. Have another.'

'No, really, thanks. I couldn't. A new asparagus bed? What was the matter with the old one?'

'Your aunt wants a pineapple pit. I told her it in't the right climate for them but you can't budge her when her mind's made up. So I gotta make a cold frame with manure stacked against it for the warmth and th'old asparagus bed was in the hottest place. It's a downright terrible family for whims and fancies.'

He didn't smile but I could hear affection in his voice as he said this. He had perhaps more right than most to complain of the Otways' erratic behaviour. When my mother, Constantia, had fallen in love with Jenkins, who had been at the time a dazzlingly good-looking youth of eighteen, four years younger than she and the newest of Aunt Pussy's under-gardeners, she had seduced him without a second thought. It had not occurred to her that she might be pregnant until it was too late to do anything about it. So she had been obliged, much to her fury, to give birth to me.

Aunt Pussy had appointed herself my guardian. She said that as my mother was incapable even of running her own bath and never could keep a servant beyond three weeks she might find a baby more than she could manage. My aunt stipulated that my father's identity was to be kept secret. I

70

think that she was anxious that no scandal should reach R.D.'s ears. Though his own behaviour was erratic to the point of eccentricity, he disliked anything that looked like wilfulness in others. I suspected that my aunt would have liked to keep the knowledge of my paternity even from me but she was a fair woman and understood that Jenkins was not entirely to blame for the fiasco and it would be wrong to deprive him of his child. I was allowed to spend many blissful hours with him while he dug and hoed and planted and watered. My aunt's friends used to comment on our attachment. 'Too adorable, Pussy, to see that little mite and Jenkins together. He's almost like one of the family. Madly loyal to you, darling.' My aunt's friends had good reason to know this as they had all of them at some time tried to poach Jenkins's services for no one could grow sweet peas or roses as he could, and the vegetables he provided for the table were the envy of all her circle.

'Jenkins is a good man. Obstinate, not to say pig-headed, but thoroughly sound at bottom,' my aunt would reply.

Jenkins – his first name was Jonas but he preferred to be called Jenkins without the Mr – was desperately in love with my mother and wanted to marry her but she only laughed at the idea. He told me this himself, calmly and without rancour. 'Your mother's got spirit. Stands to reason she won't want to settle down yet. I'll wait.'

He was still waiting. Now she was forty-two and had been married three times, too briefly to give me the brother or sister I longed for, but Jenkins was still optimistic. 'She'll come back when she's ready. She's the only woman for me. And I'm the only man that'll tame her. The day'll come when she'll quit flitting and then we'll be man and wife as we ought.'

Privately I thought Jenkins was much too good for my mother. 'How's them that you live with now?' he said, stirring his tea as he did everything with careful deliberation. 'What about the big girl with red hair as wants to be in pantomime? Toffee, was it?'

'Tiffany. Actually, I think it's serious acting she wants to do. I've never had the chance to see her in anything but I bet she'd be good. Her romantic hopes have been badly dashed, though.'

I told Jenkins all about Montague Browse and Jenkins was properly sympathetic. He loved hearing about my life and was a source of encouragement, comfort and good advice . . . whatever was needed. 'And this Pierce now? Funny name, though I suppose a Jonas ain't got no room to be particler. Are you sweet on him still?'

'Yes, pretty sweet.'

'Aha?'

'Well, the only thing is he's rather . . . rough.'

'Aha.' Jenkins filled his pipe. Strings of onions and bunches of lavender made lumpy shadows against the limewashed wall behind his chair. 'Roughness from a man towards a woman has a deal to do with passion but it ain't got much to do with love. I'd say it was more to do with hate . . . hating yourself, that is. It's the thing, I'm told, these days, to go all the way when you're courting. And I remember what it was like with your mother. So I'm not going to wag me finger. But what I know now is that you lay yourself open for hurting. That's all I'm going to say. You just be careful, young Viola.'

I was very interested in his theory about Pierce. Pierce had frightful nightmares and was noisy in his sleep, shouting incomprehensible curses and grinding his teeth. Perhaps there was a troubling undercurrent of dark complexity beneath the *soigné* manner. I felt intrigued and much more inclined to be in love.

When Jenkins's watch chimed the half-hour I got up to go. Despite my protests that I would be quite all right by myself he insisted on bringing his torch to see me to the garden door. The moon was free from the clouds at the moment and poured chilly light on to the patterns of box and the trembling water in the canals. 'Heard anything from your mother?' He always asked me this when we met and ninety times out of a hundred, as on this occasion, I had to say no. 'Ah, well. There's time enough. Now, my chick, don't do anything silly. Eat your vegetables, like a good girl, and do as your aunt tells you.' He gave me a kiss and a biscuit to have by my bed in case I felt hungry in the night.

Certainly, I reflected, as I went up to my room, there was no danger of my wasting away or wandering into error for lack of guidance. I knew it was all sheer kindness but I would welcome being treated with a little more respect, considering my age and general *savoir-faire* which, though patchy, I considered quite extensive.

I was woken the next morning by knocking on my bedroom door.

'Eight o'clock, Miss Viola. Hadn't you better be getting up?'

Agnes's yellow face appeared round the door. I leaped from the sheets. While I splashed briefly in the bath and brushed my teeth, Agnes arranged my clothes on a chair with the same care that she gave to the organisation of my aunt's clothes. Even my rather grey M&S knickers and bra were laid out with immaculate artistry, as though for display in the window of Harvey Nichols. My black tights with the hole in them had disappeared, replaced by a suspender belt and a pair of Aunt Pussy's finest stockings. I hate suspender belts. Those little rubber knobs are always just where you want to sit down but who can argue with someone who is kindly doing things for you? I flew downstairs. Tilda brought me scalding coffee and a plate brimful with bacon, eggs, mushrooms, tomatoes and sausages. I burned my tongue on the coffee and gobbled the food so quickly that it gave me a pain in my chest. Pooh Bah for once in his life did something useful by eating both sausages before Tilda noticed. I grabbed my bag and Aunt Pussy's fur coat, took the clean handkerchief Agnes held out to me as she had since I was a small child, and ran out as fast as I could teeter in my impossibly high heels to the front gate.

A silver Bentley, elegantly ancient, was parked outside. Giles was sitting in it, looking at his watch.

'I'm terribly sorry,' I gasped, as I clambered in.

'I did say eight thirty on the dot. It's ten to nine and we'll have to step on it.'

Giles engaged the clutch before I had closed the door. I

fought to get my coat inside while hanging on to my bag as we swung round the corner of the lane. Well, it was a refreshing change from people doing things for me. The interior of the car was warm. I sat and sweltered in my coat, which I had had no time to take off, and relished this neglect. 'Lovely car.'

Giles grunted and accelerated hard, as though to emphasise my selfishness in being late.

'Have you had it long? What year is it?'

'Nineteen forty-nine. No. I bought it a couple of weeks ago.'

'She's really lovely. I like the walnut dash. Does she absolutely sozzle petrol?'

This was the sort of thing that Pierce said and I hoped that this masculine talk would placate Giles.

'Yes, rather.' He looked anything but placated. I noticed that he was wearing an immensely smart three-piece greenish brown suit, the sort of thing you might wear when marching about on moors. It looked very tweedy and itchy.

'Are you going to give her a name? What about something rather exotic? Ianthe, perhaps, or Scheherazade. Did you ever read the *Arabian Nights*? Imagine having to make up a thousand and one stories . . . I'm sure I couldn't think of more than a week's worth. Perhaps not even one with the strain of being strangled in the morning hanging over me . . .'

'I detest the practice of giving cars whimsical names.' Giles had forgotten, probably, that Pierce called his MGB Pasiphae, who, he said, had been a woman of easy virtue in Greece long ago, with a partiality for bulls. 'Now, if you wouldn't mind, I like to concentrate when I'm driving.'

I shut up. I wasn't offended. I closed my eyes and enjoyed the feeling of total irresponsibility and not having anything to do. I reviewed my life. Hardly anything that could be called an achievement so far but I was managing to keep myself, more or less. And I lived in a beautiful house with people who were interesting and of whom I was very fond. Then there was Pierce. I yawned. Odd that though we were lovers there was nothing between us that might have been described as friendship. Perhaps the one precluded the other. The Bentley had a deep purr like a plump panther after a hearty supper. Sleep was relaxing my thoughts and they began to caper in untoward directions. A magic carpet undulated beneath me like a giant manta ray as I flew over St Paul's Cathedral in the company of a fast-talking princess in tweed harem trousers, who changed, to my great delight, into Mrs Shilling's cat, Tibby.

CHAPTER 6

'Viola Otway speaking. I'm afraid we're going to be late for lunch. Our car's broken down.'
The garage doors through which I had steered the Bentley, with Giles pushing behind, honed the keen wind into a bayonet that stabbed my neck and ankles. I clutched my coat around me and tried to keep my beautiful shoes out of the puddles of oil which were everywhere on the floor.

'Will you kindly speak up, madam? There's a crackle like a knife through my head on this telephone.'

'The car has broken down! We won't be able to get there in time for lunch!'

'Sir James has guests for lunch,' said the voice severely. 'If you require a donation please apply in writing.'

'Us! We're the guests! And we can't get there until later. We hope to be with you by tea-time.'

'Yes, you may telephone Sir James tomorrow. Goodbye.'

There was a click and a buzzing sound. I picked my way across the garage floor to where Giles stood with his hands in his pockets staring into the open bonnet of the Bentley. His expression was stormy.

'I'm terribly sorry about the hedge.' I was anxious to show Giles that I bore no malice about the hard things he had said.

'You don't want to worry, miss,' said the mechanic, from

the depths of the engine. 'No damage but what a lick of paint will hide.'

Giles pressed his lips together and refused to catch my eye.

'Is there anywhere we could have lunch?' I addressed the mechanic's bottom. He withdrew himself from the engine.

'There's a nice hotel up the hill.' He winked at Giles. 'Go on, guv. Take the missus away for a bite to eat and we'll fit you up while you're enjoying yourselves.'

'I prefer to stay, thank you.' Giles's tone was bitter in repudiation. 'Miss Otway can go if she wants to.'

'Suit yourself, guv. The Black Swan in the main street, miss. It's only a step.'

The interior of the Black Swan was draughty and unflinchingly Tudor. Hard chairs and sofas the colour of dried blood stood in grim confrontation with each other on a carpet of mottled brown. Shiny black beams criss-crossing above made one's head swim. In the chill inglenook, lit by a flickering neon tube, stood a life-size leather pig. Its button eyes expressed surprise at finding itself embowered with horse-brasses, dimpled copper warming-pans and miniature straw hats entwined with dried flowers. Everything smelt of cabbage and gravy.

Thanks to Aunt Pussy's coat, only my extremities were cold. I found a chair near a radiator and took out the volume of stories by Saki which I had in my bag. Soon I was enjoying myself, despite the unfriendliness of the only waiter, who refused to catch my eye. At last he responded to my request to see the menu with a repelling hauteur R.D. might have envied. During lunch – the gravy and cabbage tasted better than they smelt – I tried to suppress outward shows of amusement but when I got to the story of 'The Unrest-Cure' I was overcome by laughter. Looking up I saw, through streaming eyes, that the other guests in the dining room were staring at me resentfully. 'Do you know these stories?' I held up my book to show a grumpy old man with a purple nose and a monocle who was at the next table. 'They're terrifically funny.'

'Certainly not!' He spoke with shocked emphasis as

though I had accused him of something iniquitous like spitting into babies' prams.

The waiter approached and inclined himself stiffly to murmur, 'The garage has just telephoned. Madam's car is ready.'

When Giles drove up to the door in the Bentley, the waiter permitted himself an obsequious smile.

'Such an odd place,' I said, as we drove away, forgetting the embargo on conversation. 'Pigs in the fireplace and the pudding was Peach Surprise . . . I think the surprise was that there weren't any peaches in it. Only marshmallow lumps in custard. The chicken was okay but the gravy was rather thick and wrinkly. Cabbage and horrible big khaki peas but the roast potatoes weren't bad. Did you get anything to eat?'

'No.'

'Oh. Poor you! How boring cars are when they break down.'

'I wasn't particularly bored. A man came to see me about the hole you made in his hedge. Some of his sheep got out. He was on the point of calling the police. It took me some time to convince him that we were not hooligans bent on the destruction of the countryside.'

'It was only a small hole, after all.'

'It cost me five pounds nevertheless.'

'Oh dear. You must let me pay you.' I opened my bag, then remembered that I had only a pound left after paying for my lunch.

'It doesn't matter.' Giles's tone was unconvincing. 'Let's just concentrate on getting there. The mechanic said not to go above fifty in case the fan-belt flies off. It isn't a very good fit, apparently. What a bloody awful day this is turning out to be.'

I nearly said that I could think of thousands of much worse things that might happen but I remembered that I was full of lunch and that nothing affects one's temper more than chirpy remarks from other people when you are hungry and fed up, so I kept quiet.

We drove for at least an hour without mishap. The

countryside changed and, instead of being dully agricultural, became dramatic with stands of windswept trees and huge rocky outcrops. Great flocks of birds reeled in swirling formations among the pearly clouds. I knew very little about the countryside. Aunt Pussy had always lived in London and although as a child I had accompanied her to weekend house parties there was never any freedom to explore but instead an oppressive emphasis on being sociable with the other inhabitants of the nursery. R.D. only liked things that were tailored to his moods and convenience. He grumbled constantly about spots of mud and drips of rain. Bird droppings on a garden seat invoked his most bilious rage. It was just this unrestrained, unpredictable quality about Nature that always filled me with romantic awe. I longed to be tossed about in a boat or lost in a forest or wuthered on a moor. It was a pity that there would be no opportunity to take even a step into anything like proper countryside before being rushed back to London.

About twenty miles from Inskip Park there was a clunk and the radiator began to puff clouds of steam. Fortunately we were approaching a small village.

'Oh, isn't that lucky! What a heavenly cottage! And a pond with ducks! Look, and two men to help you push. I promise to be more careful this time only I wasn't expecting a hill and I got muddled as to which was the brake –'

'Would you be quiet for one minute?' Giles almost shouted, which I thought rather unfair as I had maintained the strictest silence during the last hour, though I had seen plenty of things I had longed to point out. He stuck his head out of the window and asked for the nearest garage.

'Garidge? There baint be no garidge here.'

The men seemed to think the very idea extremely funny. I could see that Giles was getting upset so I leaned across and said, with a smile I hoped was winning, 'Do help us, please. We've come absolutely miles and we're desperate to get to Inskip Park before dinner.'

'Well,' one of the men rubbed his chin, 'there baint be no garidge for ten mile or so but Barney, as lives over the shop, is champion wi' cars.'

Barney turned out to be a boy of about fourteen with a dribbling nose and a piece of gum which he rolled round his jaws with sickening noises. Giles let him loose on his precious car with visible reluctance but it soon became obvious that Barney knew what he was doing. I went into the shop to wait. The woman sitting knitting behind the counter was friendly and we enjoyed a good long talk about suitable colours of wool for babies – she favoured 'lemon' as suitable for either sex – and the progress of her daughter's pregnancy, which seemed to have been attended by every possible trouble, including sickness, high blood pressure, iron deficiency, flatulence and a few days ago the final blow: the baby's father had run off with the girl from the mobile library van.

By the time Giles came in to fetch me nearly an hour later, Mrs Gorringe – that was the shopkeeper's name – and I were sitting cosily next to the stove behind the counter with cups of tea and pieces of very good home-made cake, discussing Aunt Pussy's cure for insomnia, which was to arrange to be woken by telephone, every hour throughout the night, on the principle that the mind and body generally work in contrary ways to each other.

Barney had mended the car by replacing the fan-belt with a pair of tights, which luckily Mrs Gorringe sold in the shop. This would, he assured us, get us as far as Inskip Park. I paid for the tights and spent the rest of my pound on chocolate and biscuits by way of a thank-you to Mrs Gorringe for the tea.

'That was a stroke of luck, wasn't it? Finding Barney, I mean. Poor Mrs Gorringe's daughter. What brutes men are sometimes. Gorgeous cake. She made me eat two huge slices. I can hardly bend in the middle.' I noticed that Giles looked tired and realised that he must be extremely hungry. 'Do have a biscuit. I bought custard creams. Or there's some fruit-and-nut chocolate if you'd prefer it?'

'Thank you. I never eat in the car.' His face looked very pale in the dying light and his ears were pink with cold. After a while he said, very grumpily, 'I think I will have some of that chocolate.'

I broke him off bits and fed them to him, glad to think that at last I was of some use. I imagine the chocolate did him some good for after five minutes he said, much more cheerfully, 'Not far now. Let's pray that the tights hold out.'

And when I said what a lovely car it was to be driven about in, regardless of broken fan-belts, he actually smiled.

We got on at a slow but steady pace. I watched the trees losing their shape in the gathering gloom and the pale stream of the road winding through the woods. Rabbits paused in front of us, frightened by our headlights, but Giles managed not to run them over. Everything was delightfully harmonious. It was entirely my fault that this did not last.

'Why didn't you go at the shop?'

'I didn't want to go then. It's all the tea I drank.'

'You'll have to go in the bushes. I don't think there's another village until we get to Little Whiddon. Couldn't you wait until then?'

'I don't think I can.'

Giles found a gateway into the wood and drew off the road. I plunged off on foot into the darkness. Luckily the ground was dry though treacherously brambly. I tore my stockings. 'Damn!' I said aloud. My voice sounded shrill in the quietness. I listened. The purr of the Bentley was out of earshot. There was a scraping and pattering of leaves in the wind and an occasional squawk or whistle from the inhabitants of the wood as they prepared themselves for the night. I found a discreet corner and crouched down, my knickers stretched to snapping point in order to save my beautiful shoes.

A high-pitched scream, a few yards to my right, made me spring upright and nearly fall over. My heart thundered in my chest as I pulled down my dress and peered anxiously about for the source. All was quiet again but there was an almost palpable tension as though the ears of all animal life were straining to listen. I longed to run away but common sense made me stand still. Then the cry came again from the same place, a patch of dark undergrowth, between two round bushes. I ran back to the car.

'There's something hurt in there but I can't see.' I reached into the back of the car for my bag. I always carry cigarettes and, more important on this occasion, a lighter, though I don't much like smoking. Pierce says it looks sexy.

'Oh, nonsense, Viola! Get in, for God's sake. We're late enough!'

'I don't care! There *is* something. It was a dreadful scream. I need my lighter. Damn! Oh, here it is.'

'You'll only set the place on fire and that'll be more expensive than the hedge. There's a torch in the glove compartment.'

I glared at him. 'I've said I was sorry! I'll give you back your beastly five pounds when we get back to London. It's mean of you to keep on when I can't do anything about it!'

'So it is,' said Giles unexpectedly. 'Oh, come on. Show me where you thought you heard this scream. I expect it was an owl.'

'You must think I'm a complete dope if I can't tell the difference between an owl and something in pain!'

Giles did not answer. He strode a little ahead of me, shining the torch on to the ground so that we could avoid the brambles. I saw the two rounded bushes looming up on our right. 'There! Shine the light on that dark patch.'

The large clump of stinging nettles looked uninviting.

'There's nothing there.' Giles's voice was exasperated. 'Now do let's get on . . .' He stopped as the high thin cry sounded very loud, almost at our feet.

'Stop clutching me!' Giles struggled to free himself. 'I'm trying to look!'

He parted the nettles with his toe and then we saw it. A rabbit lay on its side, its eye wide in the torchlight. I could see its flanks heaving with terror. Something glinted beside it.

'It's a snare! Hold the torch.' Giles bent down. 'Not there, you idiot! Here! Oh, bugger these nettles!'

I tried to keep the light trained on his hands and to be calm but the rabbit squealed in fright the minute Giles touched it and struggled so hard to get away from the metal thing that was biting deep into its fur that there was a lump like an egg in my throat. I stayed quiet and thought curses on the head of whoever had done this vile thing. If only one of them worked he would be a broken man.

'Okay. I see how it opens. Just a minute . . . That's it.' Giles drew the snare away from the rabbit and tugged at the chain that pegged it to the ground. 'What shall we do with it?'

'Let's bury it. Otherwise whichever brute put it there will use it again.'

'If we had a spade that might be a sensible suggestion. You're only frightening the poor thing. Leave it alone now.'

I was stroking its fur. It lay still and stared at me with its one upward-facing eye as though fathoming my soul. 'We can't leave it. A fox will eat it at once. Perhaps its back is broken. It doesn't seem to be able to move.'

'If that's the case the kindest thing would be to leave it to the fox.'

'How like a man to suggest that! We'll have to take it with us. Have you got any kind of box in the car?'

'Viola, I absolutely forbid you to bring that rabbit into my car!'

It was only after heated words had been exchanged and a few tears shed that I was allowed to pick it up. I stumbled after Giles back to the gate. He walked ahead very fast (he had the torch) trailing the snare from his hand and I knew that he was angry. I didn't care.

In the car the rabbit lay on my lap so quietly that I began to wonder if it was dead. Only the occasional twitch revived my hopes. Perhaps the warmth and softness of my fur coat comforted it. Remembering that mink is a predator of rabbit I trusted that after twenty years or so the pelts would have lost their natural savage smell. I kept stroking the rabbit's head with my finger and making low and, I hope, reassuring noises to it, ignoring Giles's sighs of annoyance.

The sign for Little Whiddon loomed up suddenly in the headlights.

'Would you mind getting out the map?' Giles switched on the interior light.

My eyes met Giles's defiantly. 'I'm afraid of frightening the rabbit if I move.'

Giles leaned over and got it out himself. 'Two miles beyond the village, turn left opposite something marked "gyp. quarry". Well, it seems that we are nearing our journey's end.' He yawned. 'I suppose there isn't any of that chocolate left?'

'Have a custard cream.' I was delighted that he was talking to me again. 'I hope they'll give us a drink. Perhaps they won't ask us to stay for dinner. In that case we'll have to find a pub. This really has turned out to be an adventure, hasn't it? Let's hope the natives are friendly. My aunt didn't seem to care for Lady Inskip very much.'

'I hardly think that arriving seven hours late for lunch with a rabbit dripping blood everywhere will endear us to our hosts.'

'It's they who want to endear themselves to us, anyway. We're the ones with the dosh.'

I could see Giles was impressed by the force of my argument.

'How *is* the rabbit?' he said, in quite the friendliest tone he had used all day.

'Not panting quite so much.' Then, reluctantly, because I was sorry to have to spoil the more cheerful note we had struck, I went on, 'Is that fog coming up or is the radiator boiling over again?'

By the time we reached the bottom of the drive to Inskip Park the light from the headlamps had dwindled to two sullen yellow spots. A light drizzle defeated the windscreen wipers. We drove beneath the arch of a gatehouse, which was little more than a deeper shadow in the darkness. As we rounded a bend the Bentley gave a tubercular cough and the engine died. Giles clutched his head and swore, in a muffled but violent way. I rubbed a clear patch in the misted windscreen.

'I saw some lights through those trees. I don't think the house can be far. You take the torch and I'll carry the rabbit. Honestly, I never thought anything so dull as lunch in the country could turn out to be so exciting!'

My enthusiasm was quelled more than a little by the bitter coldness of the night wind. A spray of rain dampened my face. I tripped on a branch that lay on the drive and the rabbit responded to my convulsive clutch with a jerk.

'Do be careful, Viola!'

'I can't help it. If you shone the torch a bit more in front of me I might be able to see where I was going.'

'Sorry. Look out! There's a huge trunk across the drive there. My God, that would have played havoc with the suspension! These woods are in need of drastic coppicing. The trees are spindly from lack of light and top-heavy with ivy.'

'I can't see if you shine the torch upwards. Ow! Now I've laddered my stockings again.'

Giles took my arm and we got on rather better after that. All around us branches creaked and rasped against each other and the moon cast baffling shadows of the wind-rocked trees on the gravel. My feet were protesting about having been crushed all day into narrow points. Aunt Pussy's were fractionally smaller than mine. I remembered the story of the little mermaid whose penalty for loving a mortal was to feel that every step she took was like walking on knives. When I mentioned this to Giles he said wasn't she the one who had been struck dumb as part of the ordeal? There was something ironic in his tone that rather annoyed me.

By the time we reached the house my pioneering spirit was but a rush-light in comparison with the blazing torch it had begun as. The moon rushed briefly from behind a cloud to show us a façade that would have made Palladio faint.

'Look at those domes! Like the Brighton Pavilion. What do you call this sort of architecture?'

Giles was turning his head from left to right to see what he could before clouds obscured the moon and we were left in darkness. 'I call it perfectly hideous. Oh, my God! What's that?'

He shone the torch on something looming to our left. A pair of eyes, blood-red, glowered above us. I screamed. I

84

really couldn't help it. The rabbit struggled to flee the sanctuary of my arms.

'You nearly deafened me! For heaven's sake, give some warning next time you try to hit top C. It's only a statue. Get a grip on yourself, Viola!'

My hair had blown into my eyes and was making them water. My feet were agony and I had barked my shin painfully on a branch. Rain was dripping on to the top of my head. 'Do let's go in,' I said, which I felt, as a demonstration of self-control could hardly be bettered.

'There's a bell-pull here, I think.'

'Give it a tug, then. My nose is itching like mad and I haven't got a hand free.' I heard a distant tolling but there was no response. 'Pull it harder, for heaven's sake!'

'See what you made me do!'

'Well, I call that low, blaming *me*!'

At last there was a sound of bolts being withdrawn and the door opened to reveal a very old man with thick white upstanding hair, framed in welcome light.

'You'll pardon the delay, sir and madam,' he said, sucking in whooping breaths and tugging at his stiff white collar, 'but it takes me a while to reach the front door from the kitchen on account of its being a long way and my feet play up till I can't hardly bear to put weight on 'em.'

We glanced down at his feet. He was wearing the traditional black coat and striped trousers of a manservant but his feet were shod in stout brown boots, thickly encrusted with mud and straw. There was an unmistakable farmyard odour. I felt rather guilty at having made the poor old thing rush. So, I think, did Giles for he presented him with the handle of the bell with something of a propitiatory smile. 'I'm sorry. Obviously I must have pulled it too hard.'

The old man examined it very carefully for some time, turning it over several times between his hands as though he were on the panel of the Brains Trust and had been asked to identify a mystery object. 'Thank you, sir,' he said at last, in a mournful voice. 'Very nice. Perhaps you'll step inside and let me have your coats and I'll tell Sir James you're here.'

We followed him into the hall. I am afraid we both forgot

our manners and stared rudely. I had never seen anything like it. To our left a staircase ran up into deep shadow. To our right a thrice-lifesize statue of a woman was seated cross-legged in a large niche. She was green all over, with an Oriental face and a conceited expression, despite having many more than the usual complement of arms. Ahead of us was a long table of the kind Aunt Pussy would have described as 'colonial', which meant that she hated it, along with tribal carvings, furry shields between crossed spears, reproduction lacquer cabinets and all the things people drag back from across the waters to remind them in retirement of their former days of power and glory. The table was inlaid with a rash of bits of brass and ivory as though in the acute stage of a cruel disease. On it stood a stuffed peacock with two remaining tail feathers and a crest that dropped crazily over one eye. I could have gone on looking for hours at this exciting and novel taste in interior decoration but that I became aware that the old man was urging me to give up my coat. 'I'm afraid I can't take mine off because of the rabbit.'

'I'm a little hard of hearing, madam, if you'll kindly speak up.'

'I've got a rabbit,' I said loudly.

'It *is* sharp, madam, for the time of year. My rheumatics don't like this wind, I can tell you. But there's a fire in the drawing room.' He laid hold of my coat and grappled with surprising strength for one so old and infirm as I hung on to it. Finally, he gave a discouraged sigh and let go. 'Perhaps you'll give me your names, sir and madam.'

'Miss Viola Otway and Mr Giles Fordyce,' I said, as loudly as I could without actually shouting.

The old man inclined his head towards me and cupped his hand behind his ear. Giles spoke slowly and clearly and evidently with more success. The old man set off across the hall with Giles's coat and the bell-pull and we tripped after him. The wallpaper looked very interesting, a panorama of temples and bridges and rivers in gold on crimson but much of it was obscured by great black bruises of damp. Several buckets were placed about the hall.

'Watch for the drips, madam, if you will. They play havoc with the neck. Many's the time I've had my head screwed on lop-sided for weeks with stiffness. Handsome, aren't they, sir?' he added, seeing that Giles had stopped to look at a pair of plaster blackamoors waving tall golden fans. Their complexions were strangely leprous and dappled. 'It's the damp has made their faces grey. Watch that fan, madam. It's loose and apt to come tumbling down when you ain't expecting it.'

In front of us was a pair of half-glazed double doors but instead of glass they held cracked pieces of mirror. I caught sight of myself. My hair looked like one of those balls of tumbleweed that roll around the desert in westerns. There was a streak of blood down the front of my lovely dress. My makeup had more or less worn off and the purple bruise on my mouth made me look frighteningly wild.

The manservant threw the doors wide, drew himself upright and said in ringing tones, 'Mr Charles Fortress and Miss Valerie Hotwee.'

A tall, strikingly attractive girl, one of the three occupants of a room the size of King's Cross station, stood up and came towards us. A three-headed thing, like something out of a dictionary of Greek mythology, undulated on the rug in front of the fire. A grizzled Great Dane and two black-and-white border collies separated themselves and started to follow the girl, growling. I held the rabbit tightly and began to retreat.

'Lie down, you pests! Daddy, do control those brutes! Why, if it isn't darling Viola! What an absolutely heavenly surprise!'

CHAPTER 7

'Hello, Lalla. How lovely! I had no idea you'd be here. Do be careful of the rabbit.' Lalla had kissed me, which made the rabbit struggle frantically. The dogs, on receiving a sharp reprimand from one of the men, went back to their rug. 'This is Giles Fordyce. Arabella Inskip. I'm afraid . . .' I rolled my eyes in the steward's direction and whispered '. . . he didn't hear our names properly.'

'Rubbish!' Lalla's lovely voice, slightly husky and deep, was impatient. 'Huddle can hear perfectly well. He's seen all these films about decaying country houses with deaf butlers and it's just his way of getting attention. How do you do?' Lalla put her hand for a second into Giles's. 'But what on earth are you doing here? I'm thrilled to see you, darling, but I couldn't be more surprised. Ugh! What's that thing you're holding?'

'We're here on behalf of SCAB. You know . . . to look at the house. We were supposed to come to lunch but the car broke down. We found this poor rabbit caught in a trap when we stopped in a wood.'

Lalla laughed, showing perfect teeth. 'How like you, darling! We mustn't let the dogs see it. They'll want to crunch it up at once. Fancy you having a job, Viola! How marvellously funny! And to think Jeremy was saying you were bound to be a couple of grimly earnest aesthetes. We were rather relieved, actually, that you couldn't make lunch. We were planning to dispatch you to the Dog and Bone but now, of course, you *must* stay.'

'Well, that's very kind . . .'

'Don't be polite. It's too boring. Daddy, come and meet Viola. She was at Danbury House when I was there. She's a perfect lamb. Viola, my father. And this is . . . Sorry, I've forgotten.'

'Giles Fordyce,' said Giles.

It was obvious at once that Lalla and Jeremy, her brother who came prowling towards us like a large sleepy leopard, had not inherited their looks from their father. Sir James was a short man, very upright, with a barrel chest encased in stained tweeds. His head was small in proportion to his body, and his ears, like his nose and cheeks, were large and crimson. His nose, in fact, was the nearest thing to a snout that I had ever seen on a human being, very broad and turned up with large nostrils. He had a fringe of ginger hair, a ginger moustache, and all over he seemed to be red. Even his little peering eyes were bloodshot, either from ferocity or indigestion.

He offered me his hand and then, seeing that I was mysteriously encumbered, shook Giles's and turned back to the fire without saying a word. He tucked his hands beneath the tail of his coat, placed his feet well apart and stared at the heap of sparking ashes in the grate with all the gloomy fatalism of Napoleon musing at St Helena.

Lalla and Jeremy were sleek and handsome. They were both nearly six feet in height with long rangy limbs and elegant bony faces. A severe critic might have thought Lalla's mouth too small and her chin too large but her eyes were fascinating, large and hazel and slanting upwards like a water pixie's. She was wearing a dark red woollen dress that, frankly, had seen better days and her hair was fastened back with a rubber band, but she was undeniably magnetic.

Jeremy, who was eyeing me with a measuring expression, which was slightly disconcerting, looked so much like her that I thought they must be twins. He had the same fair straight hair, so smooth and slippery it reminded me of sweets I used to love as a child, called Satin Cushions. His lips were fuller than his sister's and his chin in perfect proportion. 'Hello,' he said, taking my hand and holding on to it. 'This is a turn-up for the books. Lalla's right. I thought you were going to have big hips squeezed into a hand-loomed skirt and a moustache.'

He smiled and I noticed his only imperfection: his front teeth were slightly crossed. I thought it was rather sexy.

'You must be freezing.' Lalla took hold of my elbow and drew me towards the fire. 'It's an appalling night. Huddle, where's the sherry? I hate sherry but there's never anything else and it does pep up the circulation.'

'Shall I bring the sherry now, sir?' Huddle inclined towards Sir James, who nodded without looking up.

'Remind Lady Inskip of the time. And tell the cook to get a move on. Lunch was late again. That's the third day running. She'll have to be got rid of if this goes on.' Sir

James's voice echoed mournfully in his nose like a breeze in a sepulchre.

'If it comes to that, sir, I don't think she's likely to stop. Bowser's been aggravating her over the vegetables. He won't let her have the leeks at any price.'

'Why ever not?' Sir James turned his head and fixed his irritated gaze on his steward.

'He wants them for the horticultural show on account of the Giant Vegetable Cup.'

'All right. I'll speak to him.' Sir James took a packet of cigarettes from his breast pocket, lit one and returned the packet to its place of lodging without offering them to anyone.

'Shall I bring the sherry now, sir?'

'For goodness sake, yes! Why everyone has to consult me about the smallest domestic detail I don't know!'

'Probably because you kick up such an awful row if they don't,' said Lalla, with a cool disrespect that shocked me, conditioned as I was to treat my elders, however wildly unreasonable, with deference. 'Last week when Mrs Pim called about the cricket match in aid of the Scout hut you told Huddle he wasn't to offer sherry to every Tom, Dick and Harry who called as though we were a public house. She heard you and was very upset. Particularly after Huddle had announced her as Mrs Pig.' Lalla and Jeremy caught each other's eye and began to laugh.

If anyone had spoken to R.D. in such a way extensive empires would have fallen. The two men were autocratic and self-consequential in just the same style but while everyone quaked at R.D.'s wrath, it seemed that Sir James's children, at least, were unimpressed. Sir James examined the glowing tip of his cigarette for a few seconds, then followed his steward from the room without a word.

While Jeremy and Lalla continued to giggle and Giles tried discreetly, with fierce looks and threatening gestures, to discourage one of the dogs from sniffing his trousers, I did a quick examination of the drawing room. I'm no good at estimating distances but I would have guessed that the roof was something like thirty feet above our heads in the highest part. On the other side, at right angles to the wall that contained the fireplace, ran a sort of colonnade with a series of shuttered french windows beyond. The tops of the columns were made to look like palm trees. Much of the gilding had worn away, exposing grey stone, so the effect was of a petrified forest. The chimneypiece was supported by two caryatids of Asiatic features who strained beneath an imposing temple-like structure. Chandeliers hung with yellow glass lustres dripped from the ceiling like bunches of dessert grapes. The walls were panelled and painted blue and gold. There were some grand chairs and tables in the eastern manner. I particularly liked the gilded elephant stools with velvet cushions strapped to their backs like howdahs. They contrasted oddly with the pair of very ordinary sofas in William Morris stretch covers on either side of the fire and a round leather thing of the kind that my aunt's cook favoured and which she called a pouffe. A pair of monkey bookends enclosed a single volume of the *Reader's Digest* and on the Benares brass table by the fire was the board game called solitaire, with half the marbles replaced by cherry stones, a single glove and a jar of murky water in which something small swam. It was the sort of eccentric mixture I enjoyed. Giles's nostrils were pinched with Proustian sensibility so I guessed that he didn't like it. When he wasn't looking at Lalla he stared round the room with an expression of wonder.

'Sit here, darling, next to me.' Lalla patted the sofa invitingly causing a puff of dust to rise. 'Why didn't you give Huddle your coat? Madly gorgeous mink. You're looking quite stunningly elegant. They must pay you an enormous salary. Jeremy, chuck some wood on the fire. Poor Viola's freezing to death.'

'Oh, no, it isn't that!' I was cold though. A breeze shot from under the sofa and tried to saw through my ankles. There seemed to be rocks beneath the sofa cushions. 'I think my coat's having a calming effect on the rabbit. Have you got a box or something I can put it in? Its leg is cut quite badly.'

'Jeremy, go and find something. So,' she gave Giles who was attempting to stand near the fire without treading on the dogs, a dazzling smile, 'you poor things have been all day in the car having the most wretched time.'

'Yes,' said Giles.

'No,' I said, at the same moment.

Lalla laughed. I had forgotten Lalla's laugh. It was smoky and seductive. 'I hope you didn't quarrel.' She shot me a glance from her samphire-green eyes. 'Is that how you got that cut lip?'

'Certainly not,' Giles said emphatically.

I was eager to exonerate him. 'Oh, no. I got that a few days ago. Poor Giles hasn't had anything to eat all day. He had to look after the car and it was horrible in the garage – cold and oily and smelling of petrol. I had a huge lunch and an enormous tea. Besides, I could enjoy looking at the countryside while Giles had to concentrate on driving.'

'You'd better have these,' said Lalla, taking a silver dish of tiny salted biscuits from the tray Huddle had brought in and giving them to Giles. 'I expect they're stale. Our cook hoards everything until it's as hard as a brick and growing a beard.'

I noticed that Giles responded with a much more ready and charming smile than anything he had ever given me. He took the biscuits and ate several in quick succession, watching Lalla as she went on talking. I drank my glass of sherry quickly, to get rid of it. I always think sherry tastes like paraffin smells. Pierce said I had the palate of a child and I expect he was right. The cushion on which I sat felt damp as well as lumpy. The fire began to consume the extra logs Jeremy had thrown on and the mirror above misted over like a frosting pond.

'I couldn't be more glad to see you.' Lalla offered me a cigarette but I declined as I needed both hands for the rabbit. 'We were in line for the most poisonously dull evening. My uncle Francis and my cousin Susan usually come for dinner but he's got gout. Not that they aren't both absolutely frightful in their way but at least it takes the pressure off Jeremy and me looking after Mummy. Daddy never says a word. You wouldn't think that he was once a diplomat, having to be nice to people all the time. As for Mummy . . . Ah, here you both are,' she said, in a different tone as Jeremy came back, accompanied by a woman whose appearance would have made me stare had I not been smacked for it as a child.

It was easy to see that she had once been a beauty, perhaps even lovelier than Lalla. But now she wore a startling quantity of makeup. A plum-coloured mouth and cheeks with circles of pink looked hectic on a skin white as china-clay. Mascara clung in clots to her lashes. Beneath the makeup her cheeks were hollow and her eyes were pouched. Her eyebrows were pencilled into dark circumflexes though her hair was blonde, fading to grey and fastened up with combs that were already working themselves loose. Her dress, made of something black and shimmery, was low-cut and patently unsuitable for a raw spring evening in the country.

'Oh, Lord!' said Lalla, more or less under her breath. 'Mummy, this is Viola Otway. We were at school together.'

'How do you do?' I said, unable to take the slightly trembly hand that was held out to me. 'I daren't let go, I'm afraid. He's getting quite lively.'

'Stick him in this.'

Jeremy had a wicker basket of the sort that fishermen carry – I think it's called a creel – with a lid that fastened with straps. Very carefully I put the rabbit into it and then slammed the lid shut as it began to kick, scratching my hand painfully.

'The darling thing!' Lady Inskip clasped her hands over her thin, veined bosom and tried to see into the basket as I fought with the buckles. 'Is it very badly hurt?'

'I thought its back might be broken but I don't think it could kick like that if it were.' I sucked my bleeding hand. 'We found it in a snare.'

Lady Inskip shuddered. 'What brutes men are! And you rescued it? That was the right thing! I love all furred and feathered creatures. So much better-looking and nicer than people, don't you think?'

'Well, perhaps *some* people,' I agreed, thinking of Sir James.

'What I particularly dislike about men,' she put her hand on my arm and spoke conspiratorially, 'is that they have such scratchy faces.' Then, noticing Giles standing by the fire, steadily eating the biscuits, she extended her hand and advanced on him. 'How wonderful to see you, dear Mr . . .'

'Giles Fordyce.' If Giles was weary of having his part in any conversation limited to the repetition of his name he did not show it as he shook Lady Inskip's hand and smiled. Despite the trials of the journey, the rain, the wind, a little oil on his trouser turn-ups and a hunger-induced pallor, he looked debonair. I was reminded of a picture I had once seen of Beau Brummell on the staircase of the Prince Regent's palace.

'Have you come far? Not too tired, I hope, after your journey? Jeremy, ring for Huddle and ask for more biscuits. Mr Fordyce seems to like them. It's very odd – they always taste stale to me.' Lady Inskip talked on, in a high, strained tone, as though repeating a lesson she had learned. She smiled but her eyes were anxious. 'Very cold for the time of year, isn't it? One feels so sorry for the lambs. Do you like dogs?'

'Well, yes, I . . .'

'Do you ride? I never ride myself, these days. I loved horses as a girl. Those were the happiest times, riding along the beach alone . . .' She lowered her voice. 'They don't like me to go out of doors but I should like to see Rosinante and Major. Horses are gentle and co-operative. They are a woman's best friend. Dogs are like men – greedy and quarrelsome –'

'Mummy!' Lalla's voice was sharp.

Lady Inskip put her hand to her head. 'Sorry. Was I running on, darling? . . . Where is your father? It isn't like him to be late for dinner.'

'I don't know. I expect he's in the cellar with Huddle. You'll be pleased to hear,' Lalla addressed Giles, 'that Daddy's very fussy about claret and port, though one can never get anything decent to eat in this house.'

'Darling!' Lady Inskip laughed and tucked in a comb, making her hair lop-sided as though it were boiling over. 'How you exaggerate! Why, only the other day Mrs Herriot produced a perfectly delicious thing with cherries in . . . What was it called? *Cerises à la neige.*'

'Tinned cherries and bought meringues. Mrs Herriot left six months ago. We've had two cooks since then. And Mrs Clinch, who's the latest, is almost the worst we've had. The liver at lunch was like eating blankets.'

'Don't go on at her, Lal,' said Jeremy, taking hold of his mother's arm. 'Come on, darling. There's the gong. Dinner, everybody. Yum, yum!' He winked at us over his shoulder and walked with Lady Inskip out of the room.

The time had come to take off my coat. I slipped it from my shoulders with reluctance, not only because my dress was stained with blood but because the fire even in its enlivened state had done nothing to take the chill from the atmosphere.

'What shall I do with the rabbit?' I asked Lalla.

'Bring it with you. The dogs will have it if you leave it here.'

Carrying the basket and shivering I followed Lalla and Giles into the dining room.

Predictably it was large and there were great lakes of Stygian darkness around the edges from which emerged, like crouching beasts, the dim outlines of massive side-boards and buffets and wine coolers. We seemed to have been carried by a sort of H. G. Wells machine faster than the speed of light into a different time and a different country. Here the architecture was Scottish baronial with a great deal of varnished wood and animal heads on shields. I was glad to spot several sources of heat. A giant Gothic fireplace harboured a minute, smouldering log, which revealed occasional ruby gleams. I counted twelve candles on the dining table, each flame streaming towards the horizontal. Much the best thing was a food warmer, which stood in the corner like a huge safe on wheels. I passed quite close to it as I came in and felt an immediate desire to jump in and slam the doors.

I sat on Sir James's right, opposite Lalla. I became aware of a strong smell of cows and a disembodied hand with a very dirty thumbnail appeared out of the gloom and placed in front of me something brown on a plate.

'Heavens, not again!' said Lalla. 'It's the third night this week we've had brawn. Watch out, Viola, it's full of the most disgusting bristly hairs.'

Sir James seemed to have the only well-cooked piece of toast for he crunched so loudly that I could scarcely hear what Lady Inskip was saying. My piece of toast was dry and obdurate, like chewing coconut matting.

'What do you think I saw today?' She adopted the bright tone a kindergarten teacher uses to collect infant minds.

'Tell us, Mumsie,' said Jeremy, tackling the brawn. 'God, I must say I agree with Lalla. This really is inedible.'

'I saw . . .' Lady Inskip's eyes gleamed in the candlelight as she rolled them about, building up the suspense '. . . a watch . . .'

'Probably mine,' said Jeremy. 'I left it in the gun room when I was feeding the dogs.'

'Don't confuse me, darling.' Lady Inskip held up her hand. 'I saw a watch . . . of nightingales in the woods down by the lake.'

'Oh, how lovely,' I said. 'I've never seen even one. Are they pretty?'

'Not a bit.' Lady Inskip shook her head, smiling. 'Little brown birds. Quite dull.'

'It's very unusual to see them this far north, isn't it?' asked Giles, who was sitting diagonally opposite me. He was working doggedly through the brawn and the toast.

'I expect they were sparrows.' Lalla put her knife and fork together on her plate with a sigh. 'I'd rather starve to death than eat this.'

'Oh, no, darling. They were nightingales.' Lady Inskip sounded hurt. 'Nightingales do come up here sometimes. I've often heard them singing. I can assure you they were nightingales.'

'Of course, they were.' Jeremy winked at me. 'Hundred of them.'

'I know I make mistakes sometimes, Jeremy, but I don't think you should treat me like a child. They *were* nightingales!'

'It's a charming collective term, isn't it?' Giles said quickly. I wondered if he had noticed that Lady Inskip's eyes were huge with unshed tears. 'A watch of nightingales. I wonder what the derivation is. I suppose it must be something to do with night vigils.'

'I like a murmuration of starlings,' I said. 'And a spring of teal.'

'A sloth of bears,' said Jeremy.

'You must be a bear, then,' said Lalla. 'You're the laziest person on God's earth.'

'Is there such a thing as a spite of cats?' asked Jeremy. 'That would be your category, my darling Lalla.'

'It's a clowder of cats.' As so much of my childhood had been spent keeping quiet and out of the way I had occupied myself by reading whatever miscellaneous material there was to hand. As a result my mind was filled with quantities of trivia. I was glad to find a use for a small particle of it at last. I managed to slip a lettuce leaf from my plate into the hole where the straps went through on the rabbit's basket. I smelt cows again, and the anonymous hand replaced my brawn with a small piece of fish, which was curled up like a baby's fist on a teaspoon of sauce with little green specks in it.

'I think you know my aunt,' I said, as conversation had dried. 'Pussy Otway. She sends her love.'

'You're Pussy Otway's niece?' Lady Inskip seemed pleased. 'How extraordinary! I thought you had come about the money for the house. How is dear Pussy? Always so lovely. Her clothes were the envy of us all. And the Duke – oh, terrifying man – I used to wonder how she could bear to let him . . . I remember, long ago now, we met them at some American woman's house in Paris and the Prince of Wales was there with Mrs Simpson. There was the most awkward scene – Of course, the Americans never understood what the English felt about all that. Do you remember, James?' She looked down the table at her husband who was stabbing at his fish, which was hard to get off the plate, the sauce doubling effectively as glue. He did not look up. 'The Duke – Pussy's duke, I mean, not the ex-King – roared at the top of his voice that Wallis was not fit to be in the room with decent people. Pussy was so clever. She fainted on the spot and had to be taken home. Of course, the Duke went with her. They were still at the stage when he could hardly take his eyes off her, let alone his hands. He was such a passionate man – Oh!' She broke off as Sir James slammed down his fork so hard that it bounced on the plate.

Sir James's lips moved and I heard him say something like 'bloody ass'. I wondered who he meant.

'The Duchess of Windsor must have been mad as fire to be done out of being queen,' said Lalla. 'Think of the ghastly potential of any rows they had. The accusations that might fly! Who had given up what for whom? And did you know she spent the last ten years of her life bedridden with some horrible disease? Apparently she turned black and shrunken like a monkey. Talk about getting one's just deserts!'

As I tried to ignore the horrid smacking sounds from my left as Sir James drained his glass of wine, I could not help marvelling at the power of sexual attraction to make slaves of the cleverest men. If I had spoken in such an extravagant – and probably quite inaccurate – way Giles would have squashed me at once. Although I couldn't see him clearly any more through gusting candle-smoke I heard him laugh.

'When I was a girl in East Africa I had a pet monkey.' Lady Inskip smiled to herself as though the memory was sweet to her. 'It wasn't black but the softest grey with a ringed tail. I called him Arthur after the vice consul, who was in love with me . . .'

'How terrible the world would be if people did get what they deserved,' said Giles, after Lady Inskip, absorbed by reminiscence, drifted into silence. 'One imagines God totting up sins and omissions with a bureaucratic fervour like a bank clerk anxious for a salary increase.'

'You might say that if virtue is its own reward then at least good people always get their just deserts,' I said, as my fish was replaced by a mystery object, grey custard with little lumps in it.

'I call that a clever remark,' said Jeremy. 'Intelligent as well as beautiful. *And* a guardian of our culture.'

'*Your* just deserts would be to end up as slave to a despot.' Lalla seemed rather cross. I wondered if it was because Jeremy was flirting with me. 'You've got a perfectly good brain and enormous charm when you want and you do nothing but start hare-brained schemes that other people have to clear up.'

' "Toiling, rejoicing, sorrowing, so I my life conduct, / Each morning see some job begun, each evening see it chucked," ' recited Jeremy with an air of self-congratulation.

'It was romantic, though,' I continued, with my own thoughts about the Duke and Duchess of Windsor. 'Imagine if a man gave up the throne of England for you. It would do wonderful things for your self-confidence, knowing that you were worth a kingdom to someone.'

'Rivers of ink have flowed on the subject,' said Giles. 'Mostly apocryphal. But his near contemporaries all say that he didn't want to be king. He hated the loneliness and responsibility and always being in the public eye. He wanted affection and domesticity. Also Mrs Simpson didn't want to marry him in the least. She was having a good time being married to a complacent husband who let her do what she liked. The ex-King must have been a burden – spoilt and capricious and really rather stupid as he was.'

'The most interesting thing about the Duchess of Windsor,' said Lalla, 'is that though she was married three times she never had sex with any of her husbands . . . not even poor old Edward VIII. No, honestly it's true! Apparently she was physically incapable. That accounts for her mannish looks.'

'You're making it up!' said Jeremy. 'You don't expect me to believe that after giving everything up for her she wouldn't let him . . . What rubbish!'

'My dear little brother, Edward VIII was as queer as a coot.'

'Might we discuss something else?' Sir James, who had been speechless if not silent, threw himself back in his chair and his voice hooted in the darkness above our heads. 'I hardly think the sexual inclinations of one who was, for a few months anyway, our rightful king are suitable matter for the dinner table.'

'Oh, Daddy, don't be so stuffy!' Lalla seemed delighted to have roused her father to anger. 'You know you don't really give a damn about all that! What was it you said the other day about the Duke of Edinburgh?'

'Arabella!' Sir James's snout-like nose lifted and he bared his long sharp teeth.

And so the conversation went on, with Giles and me throwing in remarks for general discussion, which Lalla and Jeremy swiftly put a stop to by quarrelling. The senior Inskips were ruminative, seemingly in separate worlds of their own. It was a difficult evening and I wondered several times how Aunt Pussy would have handled it.

'What an interesting painting,' I said, into a hiatus. Behind Sir James's head was a portrait of quite the most hideous man I had ever seen. In the dim light his mean little eyes glowed like coals and his broad, flat nose, bald head and fleshy ears made him more porcine than human. Then I saw that he bore a striking likeness to Sir James, and I felt my face grow warm. It seemed positively rude to have drawn attention to it.

'That's Sir Alured Inskip,' said Jeremy. 'He's our most infamous ancestor, not that he was guilty of any misdemeanour. He was repulsively ugly and the local people nicknamed him the Hog of Inskip because he looked so swinish. He married a beautiful young girl, who was literally sold to him by her father. She plotted with her lover and they locked the Hog in the cellar and lived like princes on his money while he starved to death. When they took his body out a few months later he had written on the cellar walls in his own blood, "Vengeance is mine, saith the Lord. I will repay."'

'What a deal of blood that would have taken,' interrupted Lalla. 'He must have hit an artery.'

'Shut up. I'm just telling the story. He needn't necessarily have written it in one go. Where was I? Oh, yes. Within a month the lover had fallen down the kitchen well and drowned and at his funeral the girl's hair caught light on a candle and she was burned to death. So the locals thought there was a curse.' Jeremy lowered his voice and spoke with mock solemnity. 'There are all kinds of stories about the Hog being seen on dark nights when the moon is hidden behind hurrying clouds and the wind is moaning like a soul in torment and the horses are stamping uneasily in their stalls. Then he is sometimes to be seen prowling around the countryside, pressing his face against windows to see whether the locals are behaving decorously. A sort of piggish, priggish Peeping Tom. Woe betide those caught in the act of adultery for retribution is sure to follow. And when any member of the family behaves badly he's supposed to come back and haunt them –'

'I hate that story!' Lady Inskip's face was tense and her hands screwed her napkin convulsively. 'I wish you wouldn't tell it.'

'Well, I hardly ever do. Only Viola asked about him and I thought it would amuse her. There are all sorts of later embellishments. The new wing was built over his grave and he is supposed to –'

'Be quiet, Jeremy.' Sir James put down his knife and fork abruptly. 'Can't you see you're upsetting your mother?'

'Am I, Mumsie? Sorry. It's only a fairy-tale. Of course it's all nonsense.'

'I do think chicken is the dullest thing,' said Lalla, throwing down her own knife and fork.

'This isn't chicken,' said Jeremy. 'It's rabbit. Bowser brought in a couple this morning. I put them in the larder for the dogs. I suppose we should be grateful Mrs Clinch didn't find the lights the butcher left yesterday. Imagine, lung omelettes.'

'That man is a thorough-going murderer.' Lalla looked at her plate with a frown. 'You can hardly move in the garden for mole traps and squirrel snares and rat poison. I believe he'd like to throttle the roses rather than cultivate them.'

'Aren't you being rather a hypocrite? What's the difference between eating rabbits and chickens? Though the poor dead rabbits did look charming, I must admit. Remembering the Beatrix Potter stories and all that, it does seem almost as bad as eating Fluffy's kittens . . .'

'Shut up, you idiot! You're upsetting Mummy again.'

Lady Inskip had put down her fork. '"Once upon a time there were four little rabbits,"' she began in a high childish voice, '"and their names were Flopsy, Mopsy, Cotton-tail and Peter and they lived with their mother in a sand-bank underneath the root of –"'

'Millie!' Sir James raised his head and spoke with a snap.

I found I couldn't eat any more. I thought anxiously about *my* rabbit. The basket wobbled against my leg from time to time. I must be very careful where I let it out as soon as it was better. I did not want it to be lunch for the Inskips. An apple pie with pastry like wet newspaper was followed by a Stilton swimming in pink liquid, which I assumed was port. I gave my rabbit some of both, hoping that its tastes were eclectic. The basket began to shake energetically.

'Have you been following the Test match?'

I was so surprised when Sir James addressed this remark to me that I couldn't immediately think of an answer.

'What do you think of England's chances, sir?' asked Giles. I sent him a look of gratitude, which I don't suppose he saw through the reeling smoke.

Sir James wiped the crumbs of Stilton from his chin and gave it as his considered opinion that the West Indies had now no possibility of winning. He went on to discuss at tremendous length, and with stupefying tedium, the various merits of each side until my eyes watered with swallowing yawns. It was a relief when Lady Inskip stood up.

I had had very little experience of family life and my ideas of it were formed from childhood reading. I had been a fan of E. Nesbit whose intelligent, harassed mothers and fathers were often in precarious financial circumstances but still lived with servants and nurseries in large cosy houses in

Blackheath. On the grounds that absolutely anything fed the young imagination I was allowed to read Enid Blyton, in whose stories Mother wore an apron and kept up a constant supply of hams, sausages and pies and Father was hard at work out of sight in the study. Then there were the William stories with Mr Brown who was wonderfully ironic and Mrs Brown who was continually exasperated but ultimately forgiving. I never read about modern families living in tower blocks with drunk fathers and vandalised lifts and the electricity cut off because no one would have dreamed of giving me such a book. In my imagination, therefore, family life had a retrospective bloom of certainty and safety. I would have given all I possessed to have a brother to cuff me over the ear and tell me not to be such a duffer. The Inskips were utterly unlike any of these delineations. They behaved as though they were in a play by Tennessee Williams, all open strife and latent misery.

I was bending down to retrieve the basket from under the table, thinking lovingly of the fire in the drawing room, when my hostess let out a scream that a banshee would have been proud of. I cracked my head painfully against the table with fright.

'What's up, darling?' Jeremy stood up and put his arm round his mother. Giles half got up and sat down again. The rest of us stared.

'A face! There!' Lady Inskip pointed a trembling finger towards the window where the curtains, carelessly drawn, had left exposed a small triangle of glass. I turned my head to look but saw only darkness. 'There was! A white face with great black eyes and it was staring at me – Horrible!' She shuddered. 'Jeremy, make him go away! Please, darling, make him go away.' She began to weep. 'What shall I do? Oh, God help me, whatever shall I do?'

CHAPTER 8

The conservatory smelt like a garden after rain, ripe to the point of rankness. The panes of glass between florid spears of ironwork, were ink-black except where the brass lanterns made little jumping reflections as they turned in the draught. Giant fronds tickled my neck as Jeremy and I sashayed between the ferns and palms to the tune of 'Love *Is* . . . The Sweetest Thing', which crackled from a portable gramophone. Loose black and red tiles rattled beneath our feet. Giles and Lalla were dancing round the fountain, which was dry and full of rust. Several of the gratings in the floor were broken and we had to be careful to avoid turning our ankles in them.

'Isn't this heaven?' called Lalla. 'I had no idea this evening was going to be such fun!' She put both her arms round Giles's neck. I noticed that some of the liquid in the glass she was holding spilled down the back of his coat. She was fairly drunk. Jeremy had made a cocktail called Angel's Kiss. It was thick and brown and syrupy, like melted chocolate with lashings of gin. I liked it. Giles, refusing it, had finished the remains of a bottle of red wine Jeremy had found in the dining room.

They looked very handsome together, Lalla so fair and Giles dark. She was only an inch or two shorter so their faces were much on the same level. Soon, I noticed, they were dancing cheek to cheek.

'Have some of this, sweetie,' said Jeremy, handing me a clumsily rolled cigarette. 'It's the best dope. I bought it from this bloke I know who got it in Mayfair. Terrific stuff!'

I took it carefully between my fingers and put the end, a filter made of rolled cardboard, into my mouth.

'Not like that, Viola, my darling. Goodness, you are a baby! Look, like this.' He took the cigarette from me, drew on it, inhaled deeply and held his breath. At last he let it slowly out and grinned. 'See? Now you do it.'

I did as I was told. It tasted different from ordinary

tobacco, much sweeter, a bit like hay when you chew it. Jeremy, who was much taller than me, looked down at my face with expectation. 'I don't feel any different, honestly,' I said, wondering what I might be supposed to feel.

'That cut on your lip is incredibly seductive. Hey, you two. Want a drag?' Jeremy called to the others.

'No, thank you.' Giles frowned over Lalla's shoulder.

'I'm as high as a kite anyway,' said Lalla. 'Alcohol's so much sexier, don't you think?' She addressed Giles but I had no chance of hearing his reply as Jeremy took me in his arms and whirled me down to the other end of the conservatory. I was delighted to be nearer the giant pot-bellied stove. I closed my eyes and enjoyed the warmth stealing through my hands and my poor pinched feet.

It had been Lalla's idea to dance. After Lady Inskip's *crise de nerfs* – Aunt Pussy's expression was inadequate but I could think of no other description – Huddle had been sent out to search the grounds for intruders while Lady Inskip's maid came in to take her mistress to bed. We all pretended politely that nothing had happened but it was hard to ignore the sound of weeping that grew fainter as she was led away.

I followed Lalla into the drawing room while Sir James, his face flaming with vexation, remained to drink port with Jeremy and Giles. Lalla said nothing about what had happened so I felt I shouldn't either. I had no idea whether she was upset or mortified or even indifferent to her mother's distress. I asked her if we could do something about the rabbit.

'Come into the kitchen. Bloody Mrs Clinch has forgotten the coffee again. She always makes it as weak as pee anyway.'

Lalla instructed me to put on the kettle and left me alone in the kitchen while she went to look for the old parrot cage, which she said would be perfect for keeping the rabbit in and the dogs out.

The kitchen walls at Inskip Park were built of shiny cream and blue ceramic bricks right to the ceiling, which was very high and divided by a large skylight. Two giant dressers held every shape and size of cooking pot, basin, bowl and jelly mould. A row of bins were labelled 'sugar', 'flour', 'rice' and 'sago', and on the wall above them was a large clock, its hands stopped at half past four. In the middle was a long table, not very clean and covered with plates, serving dishes, knives and forks on which the remains of dinner were congealing. The floor was flagged with stone and there were slatted wooden boards to stand on to escape the cold. An armchair standing by the huge black range looked inviting.

When the house was built the kitchen must have been the last word in modern convenience. I wondered about the cooks and kitchenmaids who had worked in it, proud of the superiority of their situations, homesick for the cottage filled with brothers and sisters, perhaps in love with the newest footman or even the young master. Now they were all dead and forgotten, nothing but human jam. That expression isn't my invention – I wish it were – but Thomas Hardy's, in a brilliantly witty poem called 'The Levelled Churchyard'. It was a great relief to me, after reading his novels about cruelty, misery and injustice, to discover that Hardy could be amusing. Anyone who has read *Tess of the D'Urbervilles* will know what I mean. I gave my copy to the Red Cross but I thought afterwards that this was perhaps a mistake. I hope it didn't go to anyone already wretched and hard-done-by as it would be enough to send them straight down to the river to throw themselves in.

'Here it is.' Lalla came back, carrying a generously sized cage. I decanted the rabbit into it. She – I had decided to think of it as female – sat in the corner refusing to look at us but she had stopped panting. We gave her a bowl of water, some more lettuce, a carrot and a slice of bread. 'The dogs sleep in the boot room so it'll be all right in here for tonight, anyway. It's not looking too cheerful, is it?'

The rabbit stared in a desolate way at the bars in front of it. Just as I had made up my mind that never again would I interfere with the course of Nature, however wrong-headed and objectionable it appeared to be, she – the rabbit, that is – hobbled over to the carrot and began to nibble at it with a concentration that almost amounted to enthusiasm.

'You didn't put the kettle on. Oh, well, don't let's bother. I suppose we'd better go back to the drawing room and wait for the men,' said Lalla. She had been annoyed to find that Jeremy had used her best jersey as bedding in the rabbit's temporary accommodation and that it was not only bloody but sticky with bits of cheese and apple pie the rabbit had spurned. 'I wonder where Mrs Clinch is?' She looked round the kitchen. 'Ugh! Isn't everywhere gloomy. I do so hate being at home!'

'I was just thinking how much I liked it. To me it seems very romantic. I expect the servants had a lovely time among themselves. Dances in the servants' hall. Good food. The servants' ball at Christmas. And it would always be warm in here. I'd much rather have been a servant than the mistress of the house, freezing in lonely grandeur in the drawing room with nothing to do but embroider a set of chair seats.' I shivered at the idea. 'I'm absolutely hopeless at sewing.'

'Are you cold? I know! We'll go into the conservatory. Daddy's a keen pteridologist so it's the one place in this hell-hole that's properly warm.'

'What's a terrydologist?'

'I'm showing off,' Lalla said disarmingly. 'It's the only long word I know. It means someone who studies ferns. Typical of Daddy, really. To be interested in something so unsociable, I mean. I sometimes think my mother would be less dotty if he gave her a particle of the attention he gives his stupid old plants. Let's take the gramophone! All the records are out of the ark but it'll be cheerful.'

'Any effect yet?' asked Jeremy, holding me tighter as I lost my footing for a moment on the damp tiles. 'Steamy in here, isn't it?'

It was so humid that my dress was beginning to stick to my back beneath Jeremy's hands but I had no complaints.

'Did Huddle find anyone outside?' I asked.

'I don't suppose he bothered to look. Mumsie often sees things. Got a terrific imagination as well as a persecution complex, the poor old dear. The worst combination. I *am* enjoying this. What a turn-up for the books. Did anyone ever tell you how beautiful you are?'

'But someone ought to have gone to see, just in case, shouldn't they?'

'If there *was* anyone it was probably Bowser on some nefarious business of his own. Or perhaps one of the charcoal-burners.'

'That does sound romantic. This *is* an interesting place. What do charcoal-burners do exactly?'

'Well, besides making charcoal they trim up the woods – get rid of all the thin stuff that's blocking the light from the other trees. It was my idea to have them in. My father's been hopelessly mismanaging things. We used to have an agent to look after everything but Dad got rid of him a few years ago. Soon we'll be surrounded by impenetrable under-growth like the Sleeping Beauty's castle. We're hopelessly strapped for cash. But you're going to hack your way through with your trusty little SCAB sword and put all that right, aren't you, darling? God, you're a delicious little thing!'

'Well, of course, I don't have any say in it. I'm just what Pierce calls an underling.'

I knew Giles would be furious if I said anything indiscreet about whether or not SCAB would want to donate money. Luckily Jeremy was distracted by the music, which Lalla had changed to a rumba. He placed both hands on my bottom and marched me around very firmly in time to the music. I did begin to have some curious thoughts just then, about the ferns being like tiny supplicating green hands. I wondered if it was a drug-induced hallucination and felt rather thrilled by the idea.

'God, you can really dance!' said Jeremy, as I began to rumba properly, the way I'd been taught all those years ago by Antonio at Monte Carlo.

I knew it was showing off and therefore would not have been approved of by Aunt Pussy, who was very hot on that kind of thing, but it was such fun to do. I admit I enjoyed the others watching me and applauding. I hoped this disgrace-ful exhibitionism was in part due to the drugged cigarette.

'Teach me!' cried Lalla, flushed with drink and excite-ment.

Soon even Giles was trying the steps . . . left, close, forward, pause, right, close, back, pause. Rotate left. Jeremy was beside himself with giggling and got so scarlet with exertion and the heat of the conservatory that eventually he had to stop and drink the remains of the Angel's Kiss.

'Christ! This is beginning to set hard – it's like drinking chocolate blancmange,' he said, wiping his mouth and smearing a brown streak across his face. 'I don't think I got it quite right. I may well have ruined my salivary glands for good. Let's rumba again.'

'Honestly, I can't dance another step,' I insisted, throwing myself into one of the unravelling wicker chairs that were the only furniture.

'I agree!' Lalla gasped, gathering the great mass of her blonde hair into a knot on the top of her head and then letting it fall again. This gesture struck me as extremely provocative but it would never work with my hair which, being wavy, would have bounced heartily instead of slithering sexily. 'I never was so tired! O Bed, where is thy sting!'

Lalla took us up to our rooms while Jeremy stayed downstairs, still practising the rumba. Right cheat forward, left cheat back, underarm walk around. The staircase was very grand, its balusters pierced like Oriental screens, but the landings were dark and the carpets were strangely spongy, like walking on soft earth. Buckets and bowls were strategically placed to catch drips and the whole place smelt like a pond in need of draining.

'You're in here, Giles.' Lalla gave him a wonderful smile and blew him a kiss. 'Sweetest dreams.'

Giles opened the door indicated. 'Good night, Lalla. Thank you for a marvellous evening. It's incredibly kind of you to put us up.' He looked very tired and rather drunk.

'Good night, Giles.' My own attempt at a wonderful smile was wasted on a rapidly closing door.

'This is your room, darling.' Lalla was rather breathless as we had climbed yet more and even steeper spiral stairs. In the event of a fire, I reflected, I should certainly be burned to death as I should never be able to find my way down again. But how deliciously warm those last moments would be. I was very glad that I had retrieved Aunt Pussy's coat from the drawing room on our way to bed. 'Not exactly five stars, I'm afraid. Such fun that you've come. I hope they won't be able to get a new fan-belt for ages and ages. I can't stay awake a minute longer. See you . . .' she yawned noisily '. . . in the morning.'

I looked at my room. I had never slept in anything like it before. It was circular with four arched curtainless windows. I imagined the beams from my tower shooting into the darkness like a lighthouse to guide lost travellers. The walls were papered with tiny pink roses and there was a frieze above the picture-rail of pineapples in relief. The vaulted ceiling rose to a point above the large brass bed so the effect was half exotic temple and half Victorian maid's room. There was a chest of drawers and a wonky three-legged chair made out of antlers. The floorboards were covered in the middle by an ancient holey rug. On the chest of drawers beneath a glass dome was an exquisite bouquet of flowers made out of shells. Two stuffed squirrels were caught for eternity in the act of leaping towards each other in a case on the wall. Opposite them was an oil painting of a burning house. Even to my untutored eye, it was clearly a very bad painting. The flames were crude slicks of red and orange standing up like a shock of hair from the black outline of the house. On the gilt frame was the legend 'Thornfield Hall by Evadne Inskip, May 1948'. I instantly forgave any artistic shortcomings. I may have mentioned before that *Jane Eyre* is one of my favourite books. Altogether it was a most interesting room.

I went in search of the nearest bathroom. This I discovered at the foot of the first flight of stairs. It was exactly what I expected, white tiles, a huge bath encased in mahogany and acres of icy linoleum. By the hot tap of the bath, of which the knobby bit was missing, there was a spanner. There was a towel, a cake of red soap and a tube of toothpaste. As I had no toothbrush I did my best with toothpaste smeared on my finger. I washed my face and hands with the red soap, which lathered like mad into a pink foam like Cherryade. I was mystified to find that the solitary and far from clean towel smelt of onions. Mindful of Aunt Pussy's standards I washed my knickers and stockings with the soap as well. I rinsed them like anything but the knickers remained faintly pink. I hung them to dry on the hot-water pipes then scampered back to my room as quickly as I could for I was now naked beneath my coat and the bathroom had circling draughts like knives on chariot wheels. It was complete bliss to fling off my shoes and get into bed.

I lay and shivered for a while, then got up and spread Aunt Pussy's coat over the slippery green eiderdown and single thin blanket. This was an improvement but cold breezes still whistled about my naked shoulders. In desperation I put on the fur coat, got back into bed and at once I was steeped in heavenly sensations of softness and cosiness. Even the throbbing of my feet was not enough to keep me from drifting slowly away on the tide of sleep.

I found myself downstairs in the drawing room at Inskip Park but in my dream it had become the Victoria and Albert Museum. I was unsurprised to find, exhibited in a glass case all to itself, our broken fan-belt. I asked an attendant where the exit was. The attendant metamorphosed into Pierce. I thought he looked very desirable in his uniform. He took me through the department of eighteenth-century knitted baby clothes – all in shades of 'lemon' – into the garden. A large notice explained that this was an exact re-creation of the gardens at Versailles by Le Nôtre. The famous fountain with plunging horses played impressively in front of us. I began to run down the path between rows of orange trees in tubs. I found I could run very fast and in great bounds so that I was almost flying. I saw that my body was covered with soft grey rabbit fur and I had paws instead of hands and feet. I bounded on like a kangaroo, higher and faster, almost beside myself with excitement. I heard a padding of feet behind me and saw that Pierce had changed into a great golden dog. Suddenly I was terrified for his white teeth were snapping at my tail. 'Pierce!' I called in a strangled squeal. 'It's me, Viola! Oh, stop! Stop!'

'I won't stop! Oh, God! All this nakedness and fur! It's so sexy!' said Jeremy's voice, and I found myself suddenly awake in my turret bedroom at Inskip Park with Jeremy lying on top of me, kissing my neck and face, his hands on my naked breasts.

'Jeremy! What are you *doing*? Get off me at once! You're hopelessly drunk!'

'I know! And you're hopelessly desirable, you little harlot. Now don't resist! Just let Uncle Jeremy in. Ow! You naughty girl!' He giggled wildly while I tried to push him off me – to no avail for he was much stronger. I felt him slide between my knees but just as I resigned myself, with extreme ill grace, to being ravished, he suddenly stopped kissing me and let out a sort of groan. Then his grip on me relaxed and slowly he lowered his head on to the pillow beside me and began to shudder. I thought at first that he was laughing silently. Then I realised that he was crying. He lay beside me, weeping into my hair. 'I can't do it,' he sobbed. 'I'm a failure in everything. I can't even screw a girl. Oh, God! I wish I were dead!'

Quite quickly my anger dissolved and I started to feel sorry for him. 'Come on, Jeremy. Do cheer up. Things can't be as bad as that.'

I know these are the kind of meaningless remarks that, in their lack of any real comfort or empathy, make anyone who is feeling only a little bit miserable want immediately to throw themselves over Niagara Falls but I had just woken up and my reserves of insight and tact were still sleeping. I tried harder. 'All men are impotent when they've drunk a lot. Everyone knows that. I promise I won't tell anyone.'

'You're a darling, Viola.' Jeremy turned over on to his back. In the moonlight his cheeks gleamed wetly. 'I've made an ass of myself. The truth is – God, how pathetic it sounds! I've never been able to seduce a woman. I always go off the boil at the last minute. I really thought this time perhaps – I really fancied you . . . and lying there naked in your fur coat like a wild little animal . . .' He sighed. 'If anything could have done it, you'd think *that* would . . .' He gave a sob. 'I feel awful . . .'

'Poor Jeremy.' I stroked his head and he clung to me like a child. 'It's only the booze. R.D. – the crossest, least sensitive, most bullish man you could hope to meet – used to cry like a baby whenever he got smashed. You'll feel better in the morning, honestly you will.'

'You really are a bloody nice girl. Usually women are furious about it. I'm sorry now I tried to force you – it isn't just the booze – but perhaps I shall feel better in the morning. Mind if I stay here a bit? It's so fucking cold in my room.'

'Well, just for a bit then,' I said, continuing to stroke his head as he seemed to like it. 'But it mustn't be for very long.' He put his arm round me and buried his chin in my coat. It was very cosy and comfortable but I was determined to be firm about him returning soon to his own bed. Having been reared on discretion and decorum with my infant bottle it was not in my nature to disregard the duties of a guest. Which probably included not sleeping with the son of the house on the very first night of one's stay.

The morning sun struck the edge of my pillow with potent brilliance. Jeremy's gentle snores mingled with the cheeps and twitters of the early risers out of doors. A bird looked in through the window and tapped with his beak on the glass. Heavens, I was hot!

I felt the welcome chill of the floorboards on my burning feet as I slid out of bed and went to one of the windows. Far below me waved the tops of naked trees while a herd of brown-and-white cows the size of mice, wandered with bent heads slowly across the park. Big clouds whipped past my tower against a serene blue sky. A sheet of black water lay some way off at the foot of green hills. I could have gazed for hours.

I longed to feel fresh air on my face so I undid the catch on the window and gave it a gentle push. To my dismay the frame toppled out of its hole and the entire window plummeted to earth. The wind hit my cheeks like a smack. There was the faintest crash from below.

I leaned perilously out. There was a wink of sunlight from the depths of the undergrowth. I cursed my luck. The idea of owning up to Sir James was frightening. The best thing would be to retrieve it as soon as possible and ask Jeremy to put it back. Then no one need know.

I consulted my watch, the prettiest thing in diamonds with a tiny lapis-lazuli face, which Aunt Pussy had given to me. It was really a cocktail watch and unsuitable for wearing in the day but my other watch had fallen off into one of Tiffany's chilli soups and had been at the menders' ever since. Eight o'clock. Just time for a quick bath.

'Jeremy! Wake up!'

I leaned across the bed and shook him. He mumbled and groaned and turned over on to his stomach, resuming his snoring almost at once. I ran down to the bathroom and cranked the hot tap like mad with the spanner and managed to produce a moderate trickle. It gave up any pretence of being heated after the first three inches so I splashed and rolled in what there was in an attempt to remove the red soap with which I had carelessly given myself an energetic lathering. It was maddeningly tenacious and the towel was streaked with pink like rhubarb fool when I had dried myself on it. I struggled with a finger and the toothpaste again and combed my hair. After what seemed like enormous effort I was tolerably clean but the bloodstain on my dress undoubtedly detracted from my appearance. I tried to wake Jeremy again and this time succeeded in making him keep his eyes open for at least thirty seconds.

'Do get up before the maids find you wallowing sinfully in my bed. It's so bad for my reputation. It's bound to get back to my aunt. And the window's fallen out. I'm most terribly sorry. Do you think we might be able to put it back?'

'Window? What are you talking about? God! I feel awful! Just five minutes more?'

'I'm going down to find it. Mind you get up now or I shall be angry.'

Jeremy chuckled. 'Reputation's a bubble, dear girl.'

I left him with a last look of strong rebuke.

I let myself out of the front door, pinching my thumb painfully on the latch, and raced round the house to find the missing window. Unfortunately I couldn't identify the exact spot as there were four identical towers, and rampant nettles and brambles, on which I stung and scratched myself, grew like buttresses against the walls. I decided to give up the search temporarily. I paused before going back into the house to admire its extraordinary façade. Beneath the domes, which burned bluish-green in the sunlight, like salt in a flame, ran a stone frieze of marching elephants, trunk to tail. The windows were shuttered with pierced screens. As supports for the portico there were four columns shaped like peacocks with craning necks and spread tails. It was the most original house I had ever seen.

In the dining room Huddle was standing by the side table on which a number of rather tarnished silver dishes exuded little puffs of steam. Alone at the table sat a small boy with very large ears.

'Who are *you*?' he said, a whole sausage held in the air on the end of his fork.

'I'm Viola Otway. Who are you?'

'Nicky. Do you like sausages?'

'Well, yes, quite a bit.'

'You'd better bag one now, then, as there aren't nearly enough to go round. I've just counted them. Mrs Clinch is mad on sausages and eats most of them herself. She gives us all the black pudding. Ugh! I asked Mr Knibbs how it's made and he took me into the back of his shop and showed me a bucket of warm blood, which you stir with your hand and all the veins stick to it –'

'Yes, all right,' I said hastily. 'Good morning, Huddle. I'll have an egg and one piece of bacon, please,' I spoke loudly and clearly.

'Very good, madam. If I may make so bold I wouldn't recommend the black pudding on account of the dogs having got hold of it yesterday. If I was you, madam, I'd plump for the bacon. I did say to Mrs Clinch that it wasn't sanitary – I wouldn't sit there, madam, if I was you.' I sprang up from the seat I had been about to appropriate next to Nicky. Huddle held up a large, unpleasantly bloody bone. 'That Waldemar has got into the habit of hiding his bones from the other dogs in the dining room. Sit here, madam.' He pulled out Lady Inskip's chair. 'Her ladyship never comes down to breakfast. This is a comfortable spot out of draughts. There's a keen wind today. I shan't be able to straighten up until the mild weather comes.'

I sat down in the chair indicated while Huddle delved the dishes with various spoons then placed before me a plate on which were bacon and tomatoes. He had resumed his place at the side-table, his whole body inclined to the left like a melting waxwork. From time to time he shook his head and smacked his ear as though hoping to get something out of it. I picked up my knife and fork and began to eat.

'Would you like to be a butcher?' continued Nicky, displaying a lot of sausage as he talked. 'I think the bacon-slicer might be quite fun but I expect like most things it would be boring after a bit.' The sun shone through the window behind him making his ears glow pink like a pair of seashells from tropical climes. 'I don't think I could bring myself to cut an animal's head in half. Mrs Clinch had half a pig's head in the kitchen last week and I made myself look at it though the eyeball made me feel really sick –'

'For Christ's sake, shut *up*, Nicky!' Lalla had walked in and overheard the last part of this conversation. She was looking remarkably fresh, considering the amount we had all drunk the night before. Her jeans and pale blue jersey looked seductive even though they were old and far from clean. She sat down opposite me. 'You've met my little brother, then. Just keep telling him to shut up. After a while he does. No, thanks.' She waved Huddle away, who was hovering at her elbow. 'I couldn't face anything but toast. Nicky, you're hogging all the toast. Give some to Viola and then shove it over.'

'I'm not hogging it. It just happened to be on the table near me, that's all,' objected Nicky, his lower lip protruding a little in his indignation.

I was surprised to learn that this child was Lalla and Jeremy's sibling. Lalla had never told me that she had a younger brother. Of course, it was perfectly reasonable that he had not come in to dinner. He looked to my inexperienced eye to be about eight years old and no doubt ate his supper in some nursery eyrie.

'I found an adder in the churchyard last year.' Nicky addressed this remark to me. 'Jeremy said it was a grass snake but I looked it up and it definitely had a V-shaped mark on its head. It gave me a very nasty glare.'

'Who could blame it?' said Lalla. 'Even poisonous snakes may have taste.'

'No, you're wrong, Lalla.' Nicky raised his voice with enthusiasm for the subject. 'Things are poisonous if they kill you when you eat them. If they bite *you* and inject poison then they're venomous.' Lalla groaned and helped herself to marmalade. 'I used to want to be a witch doctor,' Nicky went on, speaking a little faster as though at any moment superior forces might stem his eloquence. 'Another word for it is shaman or medicine man. I looked it up. They're the most powerful men in any tribal village and people are always very nice to them for fear of being cursed.'

'But don't they get into trouble if they can't make rain and all the crops dry up?' I said, looking at the eagerness in Nicky's intelligent green eyes, the colour of sea-water, and thinking how very unlike the rest of his family he was. 'I don't think power is a good thing to want. It always makes enemies.'

'I see that.' Nicky was thoughtful. 'Not many really powerful men have gone on enjoying it. Think of Sir Winston Churchill. All those speeches during the war and then they went and elected someone else. And President Kennedy. And Tsar Nicholas. And there was Napoleon. He got to be emperor of almost everywhere but people were terrified of him and he was put in prison and died from arsenic poisoning in the end. It was rotten, really.'

'It *was* bad luck,' said Giles, who had come and sat down next to Lalla. I saw that he looked at her very attentively. From beneath her eyelashes she cast him a glance that was full of enticement. 'Napoleon reformed the French constitution and based his reforms on equality, justice and common sense. And he enfranchised the Jews. So it was, as you say, rotten. Just bacon and tomatoes, please,' he said over his shoulder to Huddle.

'What does enfranchised mean?'

'Oh, don't encourage him, Giles,' interrupted Lalla, as Giles was about to explain. 'The child will dominate every conversation if you let him. Who cares, anyway?'

'It means giving people a vote. Letting them have a say in how they're going to be ruled,' I said, watching Giles's face. He has very straight dark eyebrows and these knitted into a single bar as he stared at the egg that Huddle had put before him.

'I beg your pardon, sir,' replied Huddle when remonstrated with. 'I'm a trifle hard of hearing. It's on account of an accident when an infant, sir. A blow to the head from a parent under the influence of drink.'

'Oh, what rubbish, Huddle!' said Lalla. 'You just want to be interesting. Heaven knows, that takes some doing!'

I wondered why Lalla chose to be deliberately hurtful. R.D. had been breathtakingly brutal on occasion because he could not imagine how it might feel to be the object of wounding remarks. Aunt Pussy had spent a great deal of her time and energy repairing the punctures in the *amours-propres* of his associates. But Lalla meant to annoy.

'It doesn't matter. Don't let's fuss.' Giles began to eat the egg.

'What's everyone planning to do today?' asked Lalla. 'I'm going to drive into the village to pick up some books. Why don't you come with me,' this to Giles, 'and we can call at the garage?'

'Can I come?' asked Nicky. 'Please!'

'No.'

'Oh, please! I want to go to the bookshop. They've got this fantastic book about Tutankhamun with a pop-up reconstruction of the Valley of the Kings at the back. I'm saving for it. I only need another pound and then I've got enough.'

'Don't be a pest, Brat. We don't want you and that's that. Besides, what's the point in coming if you can't afford to buy it yet?'

'I like looking at it, though. Don't be mean, Lalla. Let me come. I'm fed up with being on my own.'

'It's your own fault. You ought to be at school anyway. There's absolutely nothing wrong with you.'

'It's my chest. I can't help having asthma! No one would want it if they could help it. Matron says I'm the worst case she's ever known.'

'I'll agree with her there. Look, don't argue. You're not coming and that's flat.'

Nicky opened his mouth to protest but at that moment Sir James came in and sat down at the head of the table. He shook out his napkin and stared down at the plate of sausage, bacon and eggs that Huddle put before him. He ate with speed and concentration until his plate was empty then he wiped his moustache and looked round at us. His glance fell on Nicky. 'Shouldn't you be back at school?'

'Dr Stoker said I needn't go back until Monday.' Nicky's voice was quenched of enthusiasm. 'He said I was peaky.'

'Peaky?' Sir James pursed his small mouth into an expression of distaste. 'What on earth can he mean by that?'

'He meant I was looking tired, I think.'

'Tired? Good Lord! How can a boy your age be *tired*? I never was.'

Nicky remained silent, hunching up his shoulders and kicking the leg of his chair.

'For heaven's sake, stop that! Have a little respect for the furniture. God knows I can't afford to replace it.'

Sir James's small pink eyes rested accusingly on me. I felt myself blush, as though I were somehow responsible for the family's financial misfortunes. To avoid his glance I looked about the room. In the daylight one could see the collection of weaponry that hung as decoration – claymores, skean dhus and battleaxes, which had the counterfeit look typical of Highland glamour. I knew all about this, having been a great fan of Sir Walter Scott's novels from an early age.

'Do you have any more ideas about what you want to be

when you grow up?' I asked Nicky, who was looking depressed.

'Oh, that's easy! I want to be an archaeologist. I've already started digging things up in the garden and making a museum –'

'I hope you will consult Bowser before you start digging holes everywhere,' Sir James interrupted. 'Why can't you employ your time constructively? Get Bowser to take you fishing. And it's time you learned to shoot.'

'Yes, sir.' Nicky hung his head.

'I can't understand this generation. Last time Jeremy took out a gun he shot a sick pigeon and a beater. Lucky it was only a graze or the fellow would have sued me for money I haven't got. And if you think that's funny,' he eyed Lalla resentfully, 'just you try rearing a pack of idle spendthrifts. Your mother's ruined you all with indulgence. When I was young,' he barked, 'we were taught self-discipline! We had obligations to fulfil. A sense of duty!' He glared at Lalla, who had let out a snort of laughter. 'This family will drive me to ruin!'

'Beg pardon, sir.' Huddle bent respectfully to murmur in his master's ear. 'There's some trouble in the kitchen. About the dispatching of a rabbit. Her ladyship's in hysterics and Mrs Clinch has given notice.'

CHAPTER 9

'It looks quite happy, doesn't it?' asked Nicky.

We were standing in the hen run, looking at the rabbit, which we had released among the chickens. It had been Nicky's idea to put it in there as the only fox-proof place in the whole five hundred acres of Inskip Park. The rabbit crouched where we had put it, blinking and whiffling its nose.

'Perhaps not happy yet but safe anyway. It must feel reassured to be out of doors again.' I stared doubtfully at it.

A fat brown hen walked up to it, clucked softly with its head on one side, examined the rabbit, then ran off purposefully.

'That's St Agatha. Mummy calls them her band of saints. She's very keen on chickens.' Nicky shrugged his shoulders and I recognised the kind of embarrassment I had witnessed at school when girls were afraid that their parents would be laughed at. It had been a small consolation to me then for having parents who never saw me win the egg-and-spoon race or take the deportment prize. I had no need to wince with protective shame on their behalf. 'Mummy likes birds and animals better than people.'

'I suppose animals are less critical. They seem a lot less beastly than humans, actually. But they don't offer quite the same possibilities of interest and happiness and excitement.' Nicky looked unconvinced. 'I can't help wondering,' I went on, 'if I did the right thing by insisting on bringing it. Possibly Giles was right. Perhaps it's gone into shock and will be a nervous wreck for the rest of its life.'

As if to refute this the rabbit suddenly limped at speed to where a cabbage stalk lay in the mud and began to chomp at it. Nicky and I grinned at each other. His teeth looked enormous for the size of his face, which was thin and pointed. His eyes were lovely, though, and any girl would have been thrilled to have his eyelashes.

'Brilliant idea, Nicky. I really am grateful for your help. But I feel awfully guilty about Mrs Clinch and the dreadful fuss this morning. I expect everyone's furious with me.'

'It wasn't *your* fault!' Nicky was indignant. 'It was that beastly woman. I'm *glad* she's given notice. She's the worst cook we've had for ages.'

'Yes, but there's the problem of finding someone to replace her at short notice.'

Mrs Clinch had flounced out of the house half an hour ago, carrying her suitcase, announcing in aggrieved tones to anyone within earshot that she wasn't going to be spoken to like that by anyone, not even her ladyship. It wasn't what she was used to nor what she had a right to expect. Luckily for the rabbit, and unluckily for the domestic peace of the Inskips, Lady Inskip had walked into the kitchen to see my rabbit being pinned down on the chopping block by Mrs Clinch's hefty hand, a knife at its throat.

'How was I to know it was a pet?' Mrs Clinch had demanded, perfectly reasonably, after Lady Inskip had screamed that she was a savage and a brute.

I felt very responsible. Sir James had accepted my apology coldly. Lady Inskip had been collected by her maid, a stout woman with very short black hair who wore a navy trouser suit tightly belted and looked like Mr Plod the policeman, even down to the moustache. Giles had assumed his most severe look, although Lalla had just laughed. I was comforted by Nicky's staunch support.

'I'd better go and get ready. Lalla said to leave by ten.'

'You don't think you could persuade her to take me?' Nicky's eyes were pleading.

'I'll try,' I promised, 'but don't hold out any hopes.'

Nicky hovered near the portico as Lalla brought the battered Baby Austin round to the front steps. I had been engaged in examining the extraordinary fountain that stood in the centre of the circular carriage drive. It was about six feet tall and shaped like a fabulous monster, something like a fire-breathing dragon crossed with my aunt's Pekinese. There were spiral runnels round its stone scales, which must have made a pretty effect, only now there was no water. It had stunning ruby eyes. I was disappointed when Giles told me later they were glass.

'You can drive,' Lalla said to Giles. 'I know how important it is to the masculine ego to be in charge.'

Lalla and I had a short, polite argument about which of us should sit in relative comfort in the front, which I easily won. I got into the back, squeezed sideways to accommodate the legs of the chair that Lalla was taking to be recaned, which took up nearly all the seat.

'Couldn't we fit Nicky in?' I said. 'He could sit on your knee. Or even, just about, on mine.'

Lalla leaned out of the window and beckoned to Nicky. He came running over, stick legs flying, face bright with hope. 'Don't forget to let Nip and Nudge out when we've gone.' She turned to Giles. 'I have to shut them up when I go anywhere or they run after the car. Once they followed me all the way to the village. They're a perfect nuisance.'

Nicky walked away, hands in his pockets, head down.

As we rumbled down the drive I turned to look back at the house. Of all possible styles of architecture it was most like a Mogul palace with a wing thrown out at right angles in the style of Victorian Gothic. The effect was complex and any effort to disentangle the separate elements sent my brain into a spin, like trying to do Mr Phipps's tax returns. I just had time to identify Nicky's small figure sitting on the top step before the front door, his head sunk in his arms, before we whisked round the bend.

Little Whiddon was attractive, consisting of one broad leafy main street, its length punctuated by useful shops. Lalla told Giles to park sideways by the butter cross, in a position which took up three spaces. When Giles pointed this out she lifted her chin and looked at him from beneath half-closed lids. Giles smiled and said no more. I wondered when they would finish dallying and remove the chair, two legs of which had tunnelled deep into my thigh.

I went to the bank while Giles and Lalla went off with the chair. We had arranged to meet in half an hour in Ye Olde Copper Kettle Tea Shoppe. I was sad to make further inroads on Aunt Pussy's emergency fund but I had a few necessary purchases to make. With the ten pounds I drew out, I bought a toothbrush. I also bought some soap in case there was any difficulty with the fan-belt. Carrying this idea further I went to Cox's, the draper's shop, and bought two pairs of knickers. I bought the extra small size but they still looked quite enormous. They were the strangest colour . . . a sort of pale tangerine. Could it be that these thick cotton undergarments, resembling clown's trousers, were supposed to be rendered invisible to the casual glance by this crude approximation of flesh colour? One could only marvel at the innocent optimism of the manufacturers.

As I left Cox's I met Giles coming the other way.

'They can't get the new fan-belt till tomorrow morning.' I noticed he didn't look particularly sorry. 'Lalla says we must stay another night at the Park though I did suggest we went to the Dog and Bone. I'm going to buy a toothbrush. I'll go to the bookshop first and get a better map of the area. See you at the café.'

I also had business at the bookshop but I decided to wait until Giles had come out again as I wanted to make a secret purchase of which I felt sure he would disapprove, so I went back to the chemist and bought a sponge bag and a face flannel. I would have liked to have bought a towel as well as I was fast tiring of the onion smell but I was afraid of running out of money. I went to the post office and sent a telegram to Daniel, saying I would be back the next day. Unfortunately Lalla came in to buy some stamps just as I was dictating it. 'You are a mug, Viola! He's your land-lord, not your father or your husband. Don't you know that you must never pander to tyrants? It only makes them worse. That's just possessiveness – masquerading as kindly meant concern. Any man will smother you with ownership if you let him. And you're not even having an affair with him!'

'But are you saying there *isn't* such a thing as kindly meant concern? How can you tell the difference?' We argued about it all the way down the street. I could see Giles walking ahead of us. 'You go on,' I said. 'I'll just dash into the bookshop. I won't be long.'

'That *is* a coincidence,' said the assistant in the bookshop when I asked him for the book about Tutankhamun with a pop-up Valley of the Kings at the back. 'I've just sold the only copy we had to a gentleman who called in less than a minute ago. And we've had it weeks. I hardly liked to let it go as a young customer of mine has been so keen to have it. I wonder if I should order another?'

The first thing I noticed when I joined Lalla and Giles in Ye Olde Copper Kettle was a large paper bag with Marvell's Book Shop printed on it by Giles's chair. Giles ordered coffee.

'Like a plate of fancies?' asked the waitress, staring at us all with undisguised curiosity. I suppose a party from 'the big house' was always a source of interest in so small a place as Little Whiddon.

'I don't think so . . .' began Giles but seeing my face he added, 'Oh, well, bring us a selection.'

I was hungry, my breakfast rasher having been very small and all the toast having been eaten by Lalla and Giles. I chose a square pink cake with silver balls on top. The icing tasted really synthetic and heavenly.

Giles got out his map. 'I'll speak to Sir James about SCAB today, but that needn't take all afternoon. I'd like to find time to do a little exploring.'

'Oh, do let's.' I sprayed cake crumbs in my enthusiasm.

'I should like to see the church at Clopston. Apparently there are some very fine monuments there. And the alms-houses at Marton Snaithe.'

'We could ride over after lunch,' suggested Lalla. 'Clopston's about four miles. But there are only two nags, these days, fit to ride.' She looked at me. 'Hector can carry Giles's weight easily and then there's Jezebel, my dun mare.'

'Oh, well, I can easily stay behind,' I said at once. 'I shall like looking at the garden.'

'Another cake?' asked Giles, as if he were pacifying a child. I had a huge white meringue filled with mock cream as my reward for not insisting on making an unwelcome third. After I'd finished eating it Giles gave me his hand-kerchief without a word. He went off to get Lalla's car and I went to a small general store I had spotted earlier. Now that I wasn't going to buy the Tutankhamun book as originally planned I had some spare cash. I bought a pair of very cheap white gym shoes. I wore them out of the shop. I expect they looked odd with the mink coat but they felt like velvet cushions strapped to my feet.

I saw Lalla ahead of me, walking with a man with long black hair tied in a pony-tail. They were talking animatedly. I lingered behind politely so as not to interrupt them but at one point the man stopped and seemed to be pleading with Lalla. I paused too and looked in the window of Tooth's Electrical Goods. From time to time I glanced at them. The man had one large earring and lots of rings on his fingers. He wore a pinstriped jacket and a red scarf about his neck. His jeans were tucked into gum boots. He was boldly handsome in an exotic way with a thin black moustache and big dark eyes. He had the panache of a lion-tamer or a buccaneer. Just as I was growing tired of examining the electric drills in the window, Lalla's companion said something exclamatory and walked away from her at great speed. He brushed past me, his face screwed up with anger. When I joined Lalla I saw that she was smiling.

We got back to Inskip Park to find Sir James just getting into his car. The Great Dane, Waldemar, stuck its great grizzled head through the back window and gave a despondent howl that would have made any Baskerville break out in a sweat. 'There's no lunch,' Sir James said very angrily to Lalla. 'A pack of women in the house and no one can cook. I'm going to the Lamb Hotel where I can get a chop in peace. As if it weren't enough to have Mrs Clinch going, Mrs Jukes is threatening to leave on the grounds that there have been what she calls "carryings on". I leave it to you, Arabella, to sort out whatever's upsetting the wretched woman. Your mother is lying down with one of her headaches. This house becomes every day more like a lunatic asylum.' He banged the car door shut and drove off very fast with much spinning of wheels on the gravel.

'Who is Mrs Jukes?' I asked.

'She's one of the daily helps,' replied Lalla. 'She makes the beds and cleans the bathrooms. Actually, it's a lie to say that she cleans. What she does is spray everything, including the dust, with Glosso and rub it into a sort of pudding.'

'Oh dear.'

Jeremy came into the hall at that moment. I gave him my fiercest look. 'Hello, darling.' He took me in his arms and swirled me round. ' "Got a date with an angel," ' he sang. ' "And I'm on my way to heaven." Can you cook? I'm desperate for breakfast. By the time I got down to the dining room Huddle had thrown everything to the hens. Hello, Giles. I know it's no use asking you, Lalla. I remember what happened last time you tried to make your pony a bran mash. We practically had to have a new kitchen built.'

'Even if I could cook I wouldn't make breakfast for you.'

Lalla threw her parcels on to a chair. 'Everyone with any sense of what's good for them has been up for hours. You'll have to wait for lunch now. But what are we to do about it? I wonder what Mrs Clinch intended to cook?'

'Let's go and look in the kitchen,' suggested Jeremy.

On our way we passed a woman carrying a mop and bucket and a giant aerosol can of polish. I assumed it was Mrs Jukes. I gave her a rather soppy, placatory smile and held the door open for her so that she could carry her cleaning equipment into the hall. The minute I let go of the door handle she sprayed it vigorously with Glosso and flapped at it with her duster as though I had something catching.

'What could possibly have happened to upset her?' asked Lalla, surveying the unwashed breakfast dishes on the kitchen table. 'Really, they're all as touchy as a ward of shell-shocked war veterans. What carryings on could Daddy have meant?'

'I fancy she was a trifle startled to find me bollock-naked in Viola's bed.' Jeremy picked at a bacon rind that had escaped the chicken pail. 'Naturally a bloke doesn't go on a seducing expedition wearing his striped Viyella pyjamas. I'd thrown off the covers because sleeping with a girl in a fur coat is sexy but hot. Viola cleared off downstairs, leaving me to face the full blast of Mrs Jukes's shrieks all on my own. It was a ghastly experience, I can tell you.'

Lalla seemed to find this very funny. 'My goodness, Viola, I have to hand it to you, you don't waste time. So Mrs Jukes's sense of propriety is sorely affronted. Stupid creature!'

Giles put his hands in his trouser pockets and leaned against the edge of the table, frowning hard. 'I'm sorry that our advent seems to have thoroughly upset the household.' He gave me a long look in which was blended shock, distaste and reproach. I felt myself blush and was cross.

'Don't be pompous, Giles.' Lalla laughed again. 'What does it matter what Mrs Jukes thinks? Now, let's see.' She opened the door of the refrigerator. 'Oh, Christ! Brawn! Mountains of black pudding. A calf's foot! Something bloody in a bag. Kidneys, I think. Butter. What a relief to find something not drenched in blood! Two wrinkled tomatoes. God! What's this?'

'That's the remains of the lungs for the dogs,' said Jeremy, peering over her shoulder.

'This is horrible! It's like a pathology lab. Oh, for a lettuce leaf or an innocent bit of pasta!'

'There are eggs,' said Nicky, coming in, bearing a basket. 'I've just collected them. I went to see that the rabbit was okay and I noticed that the nesting boxes were full.'

'If you like,' said Giles, 'I could make an omelette.'

'Giles, you're a genius!' Lalla put her lips into a slight pout as though she were going to kiss him but at the last moment turned her head away. I made a note of the manoeuvre as it was definitely beguiling. Giles drew in a deep breath and fiddled with the knot of his tie. I don't know why he was being so prissy and disapproving at the idea of me going to bed with Jeremy. I was prepared to bet every penny I had in the world that if Lalla presented herself at his bedroom door he wouldn't exactly tell her to clear off. Perhaps it was because he thought that I had been unfaithful to Pierce. Men are touchingly loyal to each other in this way, I've noticed. Unless they happen to want the same girl, that is.

In fact Giles made seven omelettes and very good they were too, soft and buttery and brilliantly yellow with chives and parsley in the middle that we found growing outside the back door. We offered an omelette to Huddle but he shuddered dramatically and spoke of his digestive processes with the kind of tender protectiveness one would expect of Achilles, when talking of his heel. Two omelettes were sent up to Lady Inskip and her maid, who was called Miss Tinker. She brought the plates down again and helped Lalla and me wash up in the scullery. At least, we washed and Lalla dried. After a bit Lalla wandered off.

Miss Tinker was very hard to talk to. She had a barking voice and an abrupt manner. It must have been some time since she had last had a bath.

'Lovely view, isn't it?' I gushed. The two great ceramic

sinks stood beneath a window that looked across a small yard over a low stone wall and up to the hills beyond.

Miss Tinker looked and grunted.

'I can see a plume of smoke over there coming up from those trees,' I continued the conversation as I had been taught to do. 'It must be the charcoal-burners.'

'Thieves and layabouts, littering up the countryside,' muttered Miss Tinker. 'No discipline.'

As I knew myself to be deficient in the discipline department I made no comment.

'It must be a delightful life in summer, living in the woods and washing in streams,' I went on, after a pause. 'Perhaps they swim in the lake sometimes.' Then I thought it was probably tactless to refer to bathing and shut up.

'What they need is a spell in the army. That'd get them into shape.'

'Well, perhaps. But it's only one kind of shape, isn't it?' Miss Tinker looked at me as though I were mad. 'What I mean is, it would be a shame if everyone's behaviour was disciplined. We need people to be irrational and unpredictable. We need poets and explorers and inventors and philosophers.'

Miss Tinker grasped the dish mop very firmly and gave the plate she held a violent drubbing. 'When I was in the WRACs during the war we learned the value of unquestioning obedience. It was a hard life but we were fit and could cope with anything. Not like the modern generation. They're not interested in anything but sex and drugs.'

'Well, perhaps a few other things as well . . .'

'We worked hard and played hard.' Miss Tinker gave a bark of pleasure at the memory and her grey pebble eyes gleamed. 'We slept on ground sheets and carried our packs on our backs all day.'

'What a shame! You'd have thought someone could have organised camp beds and proper transport.'

Miss Tinker slammed down the mop. 'I must go and see what Madam is up to. She's apt to go astray.'

I felt very damp and steamy by the time I had wiped the kitchen table and got rid of all the egg shells and given the cat a piece of lung, which was curiously flabby and difficult to cut up. The cat – a long-haired tortoiseshell and rather sweet – gobbled it down and miaowed for more so I gave her some of the kidneys as well. Her gratitude was touching. She trotted after me to the drawing room where the others were drinking coffee. There was the usual hissing and booing that goes on between cats and dogs. When Lalla told them to shut up, Nip and Nudge, the two border collies, flattened themselves into the carpet and inched themselves across the floor like trainee commandos, trying to herd the cat into a corner. She ignored them and began a meticulous wash.

'I told Father I'd go to Bucket's Wood and speak to the charcoal-burners this afternoon,' said Jeremy. 'They've been accused of stealing things from the village. They're all as bad as each other. The people in the village call them gypsies but actually they're nothing to do with the tinkers who come round every year. They all love making trouble, they've got that in common. Anyway the charcoal-burners have got too close to the farm again. Every week they creep forward a little. Burden rang yesterday to complain. I notice Father isn't prepared to throw his lordly weight about. I'm the one that has to do the dirty work. If I'm not back by this evening you can assume I'm tucked up in a clay overcoat, roasting over a camp-fire.'

'Can I come?' asked Nicky. 'I've always wanted to see the charcoal-burners close to.'

'Perhaps they'll kidnap you and put one of their own children in your place,' said Lalla. 'One can only hope.'

'Yes, you can come,' said Jeremy. 'Only don't be a pain and ask questions all the time.'

'Giles and I are riding to Clopston this afternoon. What are you going to do, Viola?'

'Come with me, sweetheart, why don't you?' said Jeremy.

It was a long walk to the charcoal-burners' camp at Bucket's Wood and I loved every minute of it despite a wind that was cold enough to make my ears ache and the shower of rain that made my gym shoes sopping. We set off from the drawing room, stepping out into the garden from one of the french windows. The garden was a sunken terrace about the size of a hockey pitch. The weedy gravel was broken up into sections by a maze of straggly hedges grown to knee-height, which were set out to form small squares and rectangles. In the middle of these divisions were statues of animals and people, all missing noses, arms, paws and, in some cases, heads. Stone baskets of pineapples on pillars punctuated the rows. Thick, grey, dead-looking stems were twisted round a pergola. It had a kind of dreamy, fantastic beauty, like a scene from a fairy-tale.

The park beyond was magnificent with enormous trees, and sheep, cowslips, dandelions and larks. After the shower the sun came out, flinging handfuls of diamonds over the grass, and a rainbow appeared, zinging with colour against the brilliant green of the fields, like that picture by Millais with the two girls and the lamb. I couldn't remember its name.

'The lake's artificial, of course,' said Jeremy, who was wearing a Burberry and plaid wool scarf and looked like a male model, very tall and lean. He was much fussier about his clothes than Lalla. 'It was dug out in the eighteenth century by a classically minded Inskip who constructed a nice symmetrical Palladian villa. He must have somer-saulted in his vault when his grandson pulled the lot down in 1810 and rebuilt it as an Oriental pavilion. That was Walter the Nabob. He was a younger son who went out to India and made a packet of money. He inherited the title unexpectedly, late in life, and came dutifully back to England, but his heart was still in the East. Then in about 1880 a Victorian Inskip added the new wing. We still call it that though it's been in a state of collapse ever since I can remember. Luckily we haven't got any servants any more or they'd be sleeping in boats. The new wing was shockingly badly built and has been leaking for decades.'

'It's unusual,' I said, looking back towards the house, 'but there's something very charming about its eccentricity.'

'I'm fond of it myself. But it's nothing but a liability. I dread inheriting it. Now that is a view, if you like.'

The lake was shaped like a pair of water-wings, two great

lobes with a narrow bit in the middle which was spanned by a lovely covered Palladian bridge, like a little house. I have seen others like it since, at Stowe and Wilton, but at the time I was much struck by its originality.

'I've always wanted to go and live in it,' said Nicky. 'I'd pretend to be on an island and go fishing at night with a lantern. Perhaps I'd have a boat with a sail and it would be like *Swallows and Amazons*.'

'Don't be a fathead,' said Jeremy. 'You can't swim. You'd drown in a couple of seconds.'

Nicky blushed and was silenced.

A burst of sunlight transformed the turbid water into a liquid mirror, which hurt one's eyes. A flight of geese appeared with startling abruptness from the fast-furling clouds and began to circle the lake.

'Oh, they're going to land!' I shouted with pleasure. Nip and Nudge, who had already covered ten times the distance of the walk by running round and round us with tireless industry, spotted the geese and, powered by a stern sense of duty, shot off towards them.

'Don't worry, Viola, I'll stop them frightening the geese away,' said Nicky, setting off in pursuit, his navy school mac flapping above his knees, which were red with cold.

By the time we reached the edge of the water the dogs were barking bossily and Nicky was yelling and gasping in his efforts to keep them quiet. The geese swept up into the sky with a great beating of wings and flew off towards the woods.

'Calm down, you chump! Where's your puffer?' Jeremy was impatient.

'I did want Viola to be able to see them come in,' Nicky panted, taking his inhaler from his pocket. 'She'd have loved it.'

'Perhaps we'll see them on our way back,' I said, putting an arm round his heaving shoulders while he blew out thin cheeks, mottled with exertion. 'It was very kind of you to try.'

After that Nicky was silent all the rest of the way to the charcoal-burners' encampment.

This was a severe disappointment. I suppose I had been expecting something picturesque in the way of jolly painted caravans like Mr Toad's, and tripods bearing cauldrons full of hedgehog stew. I remembered Maggie Tulliver running away to be queen of the gypsies in *The Mill on the Floss* and her terrible disillusionment when she found an unbridgeable gulf of culture and experience between herself and her prospective subjects. At least Maggie found little black tents and a donkey and an outdoor dining room. The campsite at Inskip Park consisted of a row of very large motor caravans sprawling along a gully between two hillocks. There was nothing like a camp-fire anywhere, only mounds of paper rubbish, scrap iron and plastic drums. Yards of dingy garments fluttered on a clothes-line.

A few lean dogs ran out to greet us, curling up their lips at the sight of Nip and Nudge, who retreated to a politic distance.

'Git art of it!' shouted a voice, and from one of the caravans stepped the man I had seen talking to Lalla that morning in the village high street. He assumed none of the coaxing, deferential manner of Maggie's gypsies but stood, hands in pockets, looking us up and down with great deliberation. Then he fixed his bold black eyes on Jeremy's face and very slowly grinned, displaying large numbers of gold teeth. It was not quite an evil smile but it was something near it. He was at least Jeremy's height and much broader, exuding sinewy vigour, just like a character in a novel by D. H. Lawrence, my least favourite writer. He positively dripped male hormones. Jeremy's self-assurance melted instantly.

'Good afternoon. I've come to see Mr Hoggins.'

'That's me uncle.' He continued to smile while his eyes wandered from Jeremy's face to mine. He looked briefly at Nicky and returned his glance to me, where it stayed. 'Hoggins has gone to town. He'll be gone an hour yet.'

'Oh. Well, perhaps you can give him a message from me.'

'Perhaps I could.'

He continued to stare at me. I felt extremely uncomfortable.

'Mm, well. You know you're not supposed to be in this part of the park. You aren't supposed to come beyond that fence.' Jeremy indicated some post-and-rail fencing half-way up the hill behind the caravans.

The charcoal-burner turned round and looked in the direction of Jeremy's pointing finger. 'You don't say.'

'Yes, I do say.' Jeremy attempted to get some authority into his voice. Two little girls with filthy faces and matted hair came round one of the caravans and stared at us, giggling. One of them said something and pointed to Nicky, who took a step closer to me. 'Now, look,' Jeremy went on, 'the people in the village say you've taken some of their things – garden tools and cans of petrol and whatnot. I don't know if there's any truth in it but if there's any pilfering we shall have to end our agreement at once.'

The charcoal-burner smiled pityingly before saying, 'It's a damned lie.'

'Look here, what's your name?' Jeremy obviously felt he was losing ground.

'Zed.'

'Well, er . . . Zed . . . if we find you out of bounds we'll have to make it a police matter. I don't want to do that. We've always allowed you to use the river and collect firewood. We've been pretty liberal, in fact, but we can't have the locals upset. You must see that.'

'I see that my family's been 'ere a lot longer than yourn.' Zed spat to emphasise the point. 'Hundreds of years we've lived in these parts. We moved down 'ere 'cause it's sheltered, see. We ain't taken nothing of nobody's.' Quite suddenly his eyes swivelled back to me. 'That your missus?'

'No . . . I mean – What business is it of yours?'

'Nothing. Only she looks like someone's been knockin' 'er about a bit. I don't like to see that. A bit of a game's one thing. But I wouldn't like 'er to get knocked about any more and the blame laid at our door.'

He showed his teeth suddenly, like a dog, and Nicky pressed against me. Zed's meaning was obvious.

'I hope that isn't a threat!' Jeremy was doing his best but

we now had quite an audience of men, women and children who were gathering to watch the fun. 'As I say, if there's any more trouble I shall call in the police.'

'You do that, sonny,' said one of the women, a brazen girl with permed, bleached hair. 'The narks don't bother us none. Why don't you come with 'em and we'll give you a good time?' She laughed, showing a gap where her front teeth should have been.

'Aye, she'll suck your cock for you,' said an older woman, who might have been her mother. This witticism was the signal for hearty laughter.

'Well, remember what I've said.' Jeremy began to retreat and Nicky and I followed him. 'Any more trouble and I'll –'

'You'll piss in yer pants!' bawled the woman, and they all roared with derision. Zed's bass voice could be heard above them all. The lurchers, probably in response to a signal, came running after us and one took hold of the hem of Jeremy's Burberry in its teeth. Nip and Nudge had disappeared over the hill. We made a fast and undignified scuttle for the gate and I got several splinters in my knee hurling myself over.

'Well,' said Jeremy, breathing hard, as we hastily put another field between us and the campsite. 'I think I made it pretty clear that we don't mean to stand any nonsense.'

CHAPTER 10

'Otway, did Lalla say? Any relation to Pussy Otway?'

Lalla's uncle, Francis Ashton, was a big man, and quite old, at least fifty, but still with an air about him of one who expects to be noticed by women. His eyebrows were very dark in contrast to his hair, which was silvery. He smoked his cigarette through a long ivory holder and showed his teeth a lot when he smiled. Luckily they were good. The expression in his eyes was sardonic. Under his gaze I felt gauche and self-conscious. He wore a slipper on one foot and leaned on a stick.

Lalla had made the introductions very offhandedly while lighting a cigarette. He had kissed my hand with mock-gallantry.

We were standing in the drawing room before dinner. The swirly fabric on the sofas in dismal shades of green, like the liverwort which always makes Dad cross when he finds it growing in his flowerpots, and the smell of damp made me think of romantic woodland glades. Being in the country was all I had hoped it would be and it was colouring all my thoughts.

'Yes, she's my aunt.'

'I suppose we may sit down, Lalla?' Lalla blew out her smoke, managing to put a great deal of disdain into the action, and threw herself down in the chair nearest the fire. Her uncle sank his large frame on to the sofa, wincing slightly. 'Pussy Otway was a beautiful woman. I remember her very well. Before I took orders, of course.' He was wearing a dog collar and a black clerical vest but there was no spirituality in the probing eyes. 'I flatter myself she won't have forgotten me. There was a party at the Dorchester . . . Afterwards we went on to a nightclub, I've forgotten which . . . Well, perhaps these things are best left in the past.' He laughed but his eyes were malicious. 'Susan wouldn't believe me anyway. She thinks her father's a dull old stick.'

We all looked at Susan, who coloured and recrossed her ankles. There was some ambiguous cruelty in the remark. I thought we were supposed to understand that if anything the boot was on the other foot, that it was the daughter who was dull and the father by contrast still engagingly, perhaps even dangerously, urbane.

Susan was somewhere in her thirties, very small and slight, her mousy hair held back by slides. Her face, bare of makeup, was already falling into lines of discontent. There were two frown lines between her brows and wrinkles about her mouth, as though she constantly screwed it up in irritation or self-restraint. Her tiny breasts, like two fairy

136

cakes, were frankly revealed by a pale yellow jersey, too tight, perhaps shrunk in the wash. Her lower half was clad in a frumpish brown skirt, thick stockings and lace-up shoes.

I saw that Lalla's uncle's eyes had dropped from my liberally lipsticked mouth to the bloodstain on the front of my dress. Then they fell to my feet. Damn! I had forgotten to change my shoes. My plimsolls were no longer the crisp white objects I had worn out of the shop but were smeared with mud and grass. He looked away from me to Lalla who was yawning in a rather stagy way. 'Not very flattering to us, my dear Lalla, that our arrival seems to have thrown you into these paroxysms of boredom.'

'We thought of coming to you for dinner, Francis,' said Lalla. 'Our cook's gone off in a huff and Huddle says the agency can't find anyone until next week. But then we remembered that you don't have any staff living in. Well, why should you when it's so convenient just to cross the park each evening? And delightful for us, of course, to have the pleasure of your company so often.'

Lalla leaned her head back and looked at him savagely from below her lashes.

'Clergymen are paupers, as you must know, Lalla.' Francis smiled but his eyes did not. 'I'm afraid the kind of establishment you keep here at the Park would be quite beyond my modest means. And I like to see as much as I can of your dear mother.' He turned to look at me. 'My sister is not strong. You may notice, Miss Otway – in fact, you cannot help noticing – that she takes a somewhat extreme view of the most humdrum events. Her sense of proportion goes a little awry. But, as someone said – I think it was Mark Twain – when we remember we are all mad the mysteries disappear and life stands explained.' He laughed, showing his teeth, and I made a polite noise in my throat, expressive, I hoped, of appreciation of the little joke and, at the same time, dissent from any suggestion that my hostess was insane.

'Very charitable, Francis.' Lalla's look was contemptuous. 'But the end result is that you'll have to make do with scraps tonight. You're lucky to get anything at all. Giles is making omelettes like mad and we've made Jeremy be scullerymaid. Viola did the pudding and I've dressed the salad.'

'Ah, yes. Mr Giles Fordyce. That poor young man so patently captivated by my bad little niece's charms.' Francis took a glass of sherry from Huddle's tray but waved away the biscuits. He shot me a glance of rueful amusement. I understood that he was flattering me by seeking some complicity against Lalla. 'What can we do with her? No young man is safe from her lures.'

It was already apparent to me that Lalla's uncle missed nothing, that his thoughts were preternaturally active and his eyes everywhere. But the most apathetic student of human nature could not have failed to see that by the time they had got back from their ride Giles was completely besotted with Lalla. He seemed unable to take his eyes off her and had wandered about the drawing room in a dazed fashion, responding disconnectedly to anything that was said to him.

'I don't know what you mean.' Lalla shrugged and stared moodily at the tip of her shoe. 'One must be polite to one's guests, I suppose. You're always saying – though what business of yours it is I can't imagine – that I should observe the conventions. Well, I took him for a ride to see the monuments at Clopston. I thought them very boring though Giles seemed to like them.'

'If you confined your attentions to your guests, my dear Lalla, perhaps there would be less cause for complaint. But from what I hear your . . . observation of the conventions has strayed rather far from home. Quite as far as Bucket's Wood, in fact.'

Lalla's cheeks became faintly pink. 'If you believe everything that those gossips say – well!' She attempted to laugh but I saw that she was shaken. 'You really are insufferably officious, Francis. I think it must come from not having enough to do. You and Daddy can wash up after dinner. Neither of you ever does a stroke of work as far as I can see. You two are the drones in the hive.'

Susan, who had been ignoring us all and staring out of the window with a rather fierce expression on her face, shot her father a glance as if to see how he would react to this impudence. I could not help smiling, remembering Lalla's contribution to dinner, which had been to swirl olive oil and lemon juice together in a bowl and tear up a few bits of lettuce according to Giles's directions. She had refused to chop up a clove of garlic on the grounds that her hands would smell.

'I'm relieved to see, Miss Otway, that you do not adopt the mandatory attitude of the liberated woman – one of peevish resentment.' Francis had assumed the air of a man who disdains to be provoked into a display of ill-temper but I suspected that it was costing him something. 'Charming young ladies should remember that, as far as we poor men are concerned, women are never stronger than when they display their weaknesses.'

'Oh, do look out, Viola.' Lalla suddenly threw her cigarette into the fire with an angry movement. 'When my uncle becomes flirtatious, there's hell to pay.'

For a moment Francis looked at Lalla with murder in his eyes but this was swiftly hidden as he closed them to laugh. 'I refuse to be goaded, my dear Lalla. You seem out of sorts. Youth is a time of disappointments. Fortunately it is something we are all bound to outgrow. Ah, Nicky, dear boy, what have you there?'

Nicky, who had been lying on the floor behind the sofa reading his book about Tutankhamun, went up to Francis without any enthusiasm and stood silently as Francis looked at it.

Half an hour earlier I had been coming downstairs, after repairing the ravages to my face and hair caused by the walk to Bucket's Wood, when I heard Giles's voice in the hall below. 'There you are, Nicky.' Giles had sounded almost sheepish. 'I've got something for you. I was in the bookshop, buying a map, and I happened to see it.'

Instinct warned me that Giles would not want a witness, so I had slipped back into the shadows of the landing.

'For me? Really?' Nicky's voice was surprised and hopeful.

There was a rustling of paper. I peered down from my hiding place. If Giles wanted a reward for his kindness he must surely have had it in the expression on Nicky's face. 'It's my book! The one I've been saving for! But – is it mine to keep?'

'Yes. Of course.'

'Oh – but it was dreadfully expensive! Three pounds fifty! Thank you, sir, it's smashing – but won't my father be annoyed? I bet he'll say I oughtn't to accept it.'

'Well, don't tell him, then. If I choose to give you a present it's nothing to do with anyone else. You needn't mention it to anyone. In fact, I'd rather you didn't.'

'All right. It's just what I most wanted. Thank you very, very much.' A pause. 'My father thinks I read too much. He says it's making me weak-chested. You don't think that could be true, do you?'

'Absolutely not. I should say it's quite impossible to read too much. And you needn't call me "sir". Giles will do.'

I had waited until Giles had walked off to the kitchen before coming downstairs.

Now Francis was turning the pages while Nicky looked as if he could hardly bear to let the book out of his grasp. Idly I took a biscuit from the sherry tray and threw it into the snoring heap of dogs on the rug before the fire. At once there was an explosion of barking and snarling as all three dogs laid claim to the biscuit and a lamp – a bronze woman, classically draped and supporting a mushroom-shaped glass shade – was knocked from the table by the fireplace and smashed to fragments on the hearth.

Sir James, coming in at that moment, quelled them with a command, thrown out between his teeth. The dogs crouched down, penitent. One of them, I think it was Nudge, surreptitiously licked his lips.

'I can't think what made them behave like that,' grumbled Sir James, as the bell was rung for Huddle to clear away the shattered remains of the lamp. I felt myself blushing in waves and knew that Francis was looking at me.

'What mad creature was it said, "The more I see of men the better I like dogs"?' said Lalla. 'Nasty smelly brutes.'

'To which genus do you refer?' asked Francis. He was laughing at me now and I was sure that he knew the rumpus had been my fault. 'A very interesting book,' he said to Nicky, when Lalla didn't answer. 'A present from your fond mama?'

'No, sir. May I have it back please? I'd better go upstairs now. Good night, everyone.'

Nicky was half-way across the room when he was stopped by the entrance of his mother. She wore a dress with padded shoulders, long and silvery, which emphasised her drooping thinness. Lips and eyebrows were marked with theatrical emphasis. She wore her hair in a long bob, gathered into a blue net – a snood, I think they're called. A diamond clip glittered in her hair. She reminded me of a child who had been allowed the pick of the dressing-up box.

'Good evening, everyone. Good evening, Nicky. A kiss, darling, before you go to bed?' Nicky reached up and pressed his lips very quickly against her rouged cheek before going out of the room.

'Hello, Francis darling. Dear little Susan, how are you?'

'Very well, thank you, Aunt.' Susan spoke woodenly, with lowered eyes.

'Ah, there you are, Viola! How lucky for us that you and Mr Fordyce are able to stay another day! No, don't move, Lalla, darling. I shall be perfectly comfortable here.'

Lalla, who until this point had paid no attention to her mother, said, 'Nonsense, Mummy. You'll be cold. That's a summer dress you're wearing. Sit here. I'm going to help Jeremy and Giles.' She went out, leaving the remaining four of us drinking our beastly sherrys and trying not to look as though we were shivering.

Giles's omelettes were served with great formality in the dining room and Francis was gracious in their praise. I must say they were a huge improvement on the food of the night before. A dish of boiled potatoes, rather collapsed because I forgot that I was supposed to be watching them, and the aforementioned salad were the only accompaniment.

Sir James ate his potatoes and omelette very fast and refused the salad with a face of disgust. This reminded me of R.D., who thought eating lettuce was morally on a par with buggery. He drank a great deal of red wine that tasted to me of cobwebs and rusty nails. Then he asked Susan, who was sitting opposite me, if she had heard the latest Test match scores. Luckily she had and they had a lively exchange about fast bowlers.

'Excellent claret, James. A Margaux?' Francis was sitting on my right. A second conversation ensued in which I was prohibited from taking part due to ignorance. I heard Giles talking about the monuments at Clopston, though I could barely see him through the eddies of candle-smoke.

'They're the best alabaster sculptures I've ever seen. Of course, gypsum is mined here, isn't it? I remember seeing the quarry marked on the map.' Giles sounded enthusiastic.

'What's gypsum?' Lalla's voice only just managed not to be a yawn.

'Sulphate of lime. It makes plaster of Paris, when combined chemically with water. It was called that because gypsum was first discovered in beds under Montmartre.'

'We once went to a splendid reception for President Truman at the English embassy in Paris,' said Lady Inskip. 'It was just after the war. There was a Russian there who ate all the lobster out of the patties. He seemed to be starving, poor thing. The ambassador's wife was simply furious.'

'Our own natural deposits were discovered in the thirteenth century,' Giles went on, as Lady Inskip lapsed into silence and communed absently with a lettuce leaf on her plate. 'Particularly here in the Trent valley. Alabaster is the massive form of gypsum, a stone so soft it can be cut with a penknife. It takes a high polish, which adds to its beauty. It's the most wonderful sculpting material because you can get a refinement of detail which is almost impossible in harder stones like marble. But you can't use it out of doors – it's vulnerable to wind and rain. It's pure white with varying degrees of streaks of red –'

'Talking of white streaked with red, we ought to have a fanfare for Viola's culinary masterpiece,' Lalla interrupted.

A plate of something faintly steaming was placed in front of me. My pudding. I looked at it with a frisson of pride though it closely resembled the flour-and-water paste with which I had made wobbly bowls in *papier-mâché* with squares of newspaper at school. Milk was abundant at Inskip Park, being brought up daily from the home farm. I had found an old packet of semolina in the larder and there was plenty of caster sugar, which was the only other ingredient needed. I had thoroughly enjoyed stirring it to a thick, granular sludge. This sort of cooking I felt I could master. There had been some tiny brown beetles in the semolina but I thought I had got them all out.

'Oh, Lalla!' I protested modestly. 'Don't build up people's expectations. It's only semolina pudding and jam. I just read the instructions on the side of the packet. But what I want to know, Giles, is how the gypsum got into the ground in the first place?'

'Well, millions of years ago this whole valley was a very salty inland sea. These seas – there were lots of them, of course, all over what's now called England – shrank very fast during the hot desert periods and the hard parts of the creatures that lived in them were deposited in layers and became alabaster or gypsum –'

'Don't take all the jam, Francis,' Lalla interrupted again. 'How typical! Is there any more, Huddle?'

'I'm sorry about the fire, madam, but the logs are chestnut, new cut. I've told Bowser to let us have the seasoned ash but if ever a man was contrary in temperament, it's him.'

'Oh, Lord, never mind. What was the name of the woman you were telling me about this afternoon, Giles? The one who had cosmetic surgery? Giles said my skin was like alabaster and *I* said I'd have to have plastic surgery to keep it as smooth as the woman's on the tomb.'

I could just see Lalla through the branches and knobs of the giant silver epergne in the centre of the table. She seemed to be enjoying herself.

'It was Gladys, Duchess of Marlborough,' said Giles. 'It was a piece of silly gossip, not worth repeating.' He sounded a little annoyed. I suppose a man does not like to have his attempts at seduction broadcast at the dinner table.

'But it's exactly the sort of gossip I love!' Lalla was persistent. '*I* will then, if you're going to be stuffy. She was a beautiful and intelligent American who was determined to marry a duke. Which she finally did, aged forty, after tremendous adventures. She wanted a perfect Grecian profile so she had injections of wax in the bridge of her nose. But the wax slipped gradually downwards and she ended up with a pair of horns on her chin. She had to wear fur collars and things to hide them. In the end she went quite mad.'

Lady Inskip put down her spoon and fork with an abruptness that made her plate ring.

'Now, Millie,' Francis spoke firmly, 'remember the birthday treat I promised you? Well, I've sent for tickets for *Ruddigore*.'

'Oh, Francis, how kind! What a good brother you are!' Lady Inskip smiled with trembling lips.

'What about a duet after dinner?' Francis went on. 'We could have a go at "It's a song of a merryman, moping mum, / Whose soul was sad, and whose glance was glum . . ."'

'"Who sipped no sup, and who craved no crumb, / As he sighed for the love of a ladye,"' carolled Lady Inskip, clapping her hands with excitement.

'If Susan will play for us?' asked Francis, in a tone that made it clear this was a rhetorical question. Susan's glance was glum all right.

'We're going to dance in the conservatory,' announced Lalla. 'If Susan plays for you that'll be perfect. Otherwise we'd have been an odd number, which would have spoiled everything.'

Susan shot Lalla a sideways look of intense dislike.

'Dancing! You are becoming romantic, Lalla,' said her uncle, with a geniality that yet had something hard hidden in it, like a stone in a snowball.

'Oh, no. It's just to save Viola and Giles dying from

144

boredom. And cold. Giles said his bed was so damp that he dreamed all night of drowning.'

'Oh, Lalla, you exaggerate!' I could tell that Giles was embarrassed.

'Don't fib! You know you did!'

They had what sounded to me like a lovers' quarrel, shot through with undercurrents of baffled desire on one side and provocation on the other. But soon I stopped listening. Instead I thought of what Giles had said about alabaster. I imagined tiny transparent shrimp-like creatures scudding through warm salty seas beneath a blistering sun to be transformed millions of years later into a polished white fingertip or an earlobe. Where we were sitting now might once have been beneath an ocean or glacier. It was comforting to be reminded of the absolute triviality of one's own concerns. The best we could hope for was that our flesh and bones would make useful nourishment or building material for whatever life forms might develop in the future. But how could there be all this growing, evolving and transposing without an architect? The more elaborately self-sustaining I discovered Nature to be, the more convinced I was that there had to be a benevolent, busily designing God. Sir James put down his spoon. 'That,' he said, looking at me straight in the eye for the first time since my arrival, 'was what I call a first-class pudding.'

Lady Inskip gathered Susan, Lalla and me with a glance and we went into the drawing room to drink the bitter coffee I had made earlier. I had put in much too much powder. Fifteen minutes later the men joined us. Francis led the way, though I could see from the way he leaned on his stick and the tender manner in which he eased himself into a chair by the grand piano that his foot hurt him. He waved his stick at Susan, and the poor girl went at once to find music and arrange it on the piano. Sir James sat as far from the piano as he could and put up his newspaper as a bastion against the Savoy operas. Waldemar, the Great Dane, rested his enormous chin on his master's knee.

The rest of us legged it as fast as we could to the

conservatory, Nip and Nudge following at our heels. I felt very sorry for Susan but nothing could have persuaded me to stay. I experienced much the same horrible mixture of shame and pity I used to feel at school when some wretched girl was shunned because she was fat or unfashionable. I never had the strength of mind to do what I knew was right and befriend the poor outcast. I was only too thankful to be included in the charmed circle of the *haute monde*.

'Here is my version of the Atom Bomb,' said Jeremy, holding up a jug of something the colour of a London fog, a dirty brown. 'My cocktail book says half brandy, half absinthe but you can't get absinthe any more so I've substituted pernod and Kahlúa – it's a Mexican coffee liqueur. I think it tastes rather good.'

I sipped cautiously at my Atom Bomb. Actually it was delicious. 'I've got something to confess,' I said, as Jeremy took me into his arms and swung me round. 'I felt awful about it all through dinner.'

'"What's the use of worrying? It never was worth-while,"' sang Jeremy. '"So pack up your troubles in your old kit-bag, And smile, smile, smile."'

I told him about the biscuit, the dogs and the lamp. 'I was too frightened of your father to own up at the time. Aunt Pussy would be disgusted with me if she knew. It was very wrong of me and I ought at least to pay for it.'

'I know the lamp you mean. A hideous thing. Now, I forbid you to tell anyone about it. After all, it was the dogs who broke it. Uh-uh!' He held up a finger. 'Not another word. Now tell me about your deliciously named aunt.'

Giles and Lalla were already dancing away to '*I'm no an-gel.*' Holding our glasses, Jeremy and I foxtrotted between the banks of ferns, pursued by Nip and Nudge who were desperate to round us all up. I think the Atom Bomb must have been largely brandy for we were soon giggling help-lessly. Jeremy appeared to find the account of my childhood fascinating and asked me lots of questions I couldn't answer because of my promise to Aunt Pussy so I suggested teaching him to tango. He got the hang of it quite quickly and we had the most marvellous fun travelling the length of the conservatory and incorporating spectacular jumps over the now sleeping bodies of Nip and Nudge.

The other two were dancing slower and slower, Lalla's head, her eyes closed, on Giles's shoulder. I thought it must be wonderful to be in love and felt quite envious until, with a start, I remembered Pierce. I hadn't thought about him once all that day. Surely this was proof that I was not in love with him?

We went up to bed just after midnight. The lights were already turned off in the drawing room. I thought guiltily again of Susan. I brushed my teeth thoroughly and washed my face with my nice new soap, thinking how few luxuries one needed to be really happy. I ran up the freezing winding stairs as fast as I could to find Jeremy already in my bed. 'Just for a snuggle, darling,' he said, opening his arms. 'No hanky-panky, I promise. You don't mind do you, you dear, soft, warm creature?'

'Not if that's really all it's going to be. Oh, my goodness! The window! I forgot all about it! No wonder it's so cold. I'm most terribly sorry.'

'Oh, never mind. What does it matter? Come into my arms and let Uncle Jeremy warm you. We'll pretend we're Saxons lying in our solar under sheepskins, before they discovered glass.'

I lay on my side in Jeremy's arms, gazing out at the stars, which winked back at me in a friendly way.

'England must have looked marvellous in those days,' I mused. 'All untamed forest and just a few mud roads and tiny settlements. It's somehow rather shaming to live in the century that's responsible for despoiling the earth. I was thinking at dinner about the million of years that have gone by without any disturbance of natural processes and then in less than a hundred years we've practically turned everything on its head, burning holes in the atmosphere, poisoning the ground, creating hideous towns and roads, even filling space with rubbish.'

'Not quite filling it, my angel. A small exaggeration there. Yes, but if we can put men on the moon and transplant hearts and communicate instantly with someone on the other side of the world, what's to stop us cleaning all this mess up? Who's to say we won't invent ways of stopping pollution and methods of educating everybody and getting rid of ugly buildings? Perhaps this is one step on the way to perfecting the planet. I like towns. In fact, I'd rather live in London than here. You don't think a nightclub would be an improvement on our conservatory and six gramophone records?'

'I do not! I don't like nightclubs very much. They're all the same when it comes down to it – dark rooms, more or less expensively decorated, with loud music and overpriced things to eat and drink. And then there's the business of trying to keep people's hands off one and their tongues out of one's mouth. Going to a nightclub is tantamount to a girl saying she can be handled like a thing in a shop. Dancing has nothing to do with it any more.'

'I must say you do dance beautifully. It's just one of the many breathtakingly lovely things about you. That adorable face and a body like Aphrodite's. Do you know I really think I'm falling in love with you? We couldn't just try again, could we, darling?'

'I don't think it would be a good idea. Not that I don't like you tremendously – of course I do – but I've got a boyfriend already and you know what they say about being off with the old love before being on with the new?'

'Of course I should have known.' Jeremy groaned. 'Oh, bugger! Who is the lucky bastard? Tell me everything you know about him while I fight to get my jealousy under control.'

So I tried to describe Pierce as accurately as I could. Jeremy questioned me closely and I found myself confiding the details of our love-making.

'No, I *don't* think it's normal to want to inflict grievous bodily harm on one's paramour,' said Jeremy, in answer to my question. 'Obviously I'm not an expert but I've read a lot about sex if I haven't actually done it. I think your Pierce is something of an oddball. Promise me you'll be careful, my sweet one?'

I promised. We talked some more about our sexual expectations in the cosiest way as though we were in the dorm at school until I felt Jeremy's chin, which was resting on my shoulder, begin to grow heavy as he slipped towards sleep. I smiled to myself as I remembered his subtly untruthful account of our meeting with the charcoal-burners at the beginning of dinner. I didn't blame him. Remembering the business with the lamp I was not in a position to wave an admonitory finger at anyone.

'You do seem to have been extraordinarily energetic and firm,' Lalla had said, about the charcoal-burners. 'I'm surprised they didn't set the dogs on you.'

Jeremy had looked a little conscious. 'Much you know about it, Lalla.'

'I wouldn't be in the least surprised to find that Lalla knew a great deal about it.' Francis had raised his black brows slightly as he smiled very unpleasantly.

'What a mean, insinuating –'

'Did you see the wonderful rainbow?' I had said quickly.

'I saw it! From my bedroom window!' Lady Inskip had cried. 'It was just like Millais's painting of *The Blind Girl*. All the colours so bright, the grass so brilliantly green!'

'I didn't notice it.' Lalla had been disdainful. 'We were too busy riding hard. I beat Giles across the ten-acre field, though I gave him a start.'

She had laughed triumphantly. There was something painfully apt about Lalla's answer. She was riding hard towards some goal I could not identify and there was a lot that she wasn't noticing in consequence. Jeremy began to snore gently. I wriggled a little in the blissful comfort of his arms, feeling myself drifting away from dull care. Altogether, I thought, it had been a pretty interesting day.

CHAPTER 11

'I still don't understand it,' said Giles, as he, Jeremy, Lalla and I sat by an enormous fire in the saloon bar of the Dog and Bone at noon on the following day, eating very good pork chops and mashed potatoes. 'Yesterday the garage man swore that he could get a fan-belt without any trouble.'

Giles had telephoned the garage before breakfast to be told that the fan-belt would take three days to arrive.

'I don't know why you keep going on about it,' said Lalla. 'I'm delighted you've got to stay longer and Jeremy looks like a pig in muck.'

'Thank you, dear sister.'

Jeremy, in fact, was looking very attractive, despite some fat from the pork chop shining on his chin, and I was quite sorry that we were not really lovers. But then I remembered Pierce and was glad that my conscience, never quite free from self-reproach, was at least not disturbed on the score of unfaithfulness.

'Well, it's very good of you to have us all this time,' Giles went on, in the grown-up voice of cool level-headedness I had noticed he sometimes assumed, as though everyone else was teetering on the brink of wild and childish irrationality. To be fair, I could see that the combination of the Inskip family and me would unsettle anyone brought up in the temperate ways of The Poplars, Worthing. 'I suppose it gives me another chance to try and talk to your father about the money. When I attempted it before breakfast he looked at me as though I'd accused him of being the Fifth Man and then walked away without a word. Nobody wants pudding, do they?'

Seeing my face, he called the waitress over. I had Brandy Ginger Log – soggy ginger biscuits smothered with cream – and it was delicious despite Giles being very sneering about it. 'You'll end up like the Fat Boy in *Pickwick*, Viola, but yours will be the flesh that's creeping.'

I thought this extremely funny. While I was giggling Giles

allowed himself to smile and silently handed me his handkerchief.

Giles was looking very different from his usual groomed, elegant self. When we had discovered that our stay was to be extended by three more days my first thought had been that I must somehow find a clothes shop and buy myself something to wear. Aunt Pussy's lovely dress was not only dirty, with blood and, unaccountably, jam, but the hem had caught on some brambles during our walk yesterday and was trailing down in a way that made me look slipshod and disreputable. Giles was looking cleaner but he said he absolutely could not wear his shirt another day.

'We'll lend you some clothes,' Lalla had said. 'Why on earth didn't you say before?'

So Giles looked almost Bohemian, and very attractive, in a black Guernsey and jeans belonging to Jeremy. I looked rather ridiculous as Lalla was several inches taller than me besides being larger at bust, waist and hip. Jeremy said I looked like a fetching orphan outcast and he quite understood the desire of King Cophetua to seduce his beggarmaid. Anyway, my wounded vanity was compensated for by the warmth and comfort of the ensemble. I was getting used to looking a figure of fun. When, on rising for breakfast, I had put on my new knickers, bought the day before, Jeremy had been convulsed by laughter.

'Surely,' he said, wiping tears from his eyes and almost sobbing, 'that is not – what the – good women – of Little Whiddon wear? You look like – an Elizabethan courtier. They should be stuffed – and slashed with gold silk.'

He had laughed until he said further sleep was impossible and he had no recourse but to get up in time for breakfast. Then had come the news of the delayed arrival of the fan-belt and fresh plans had to be made over breakfast about the best way to spend the day.

'I'd very much like to drive as far as Haddon Hall,' Giles had said, while doing battle with a piece of bacon, strangely cocoa-coloured and with an obdurate rind. I had cooked it myself. The slices had been stiff as laths and I hadn't been at all sure about them, not knowing how bacon ought to look in its raw state. They were, though, the only thing in the fridge that seemed to speak of breakfast. 'There are some wonderful monuments there. Bakewell, which is the nearby town, is sadly modernised apparently – it grew up round the chalybeate springs in the seventeenth century – but there might be a good pub there where we could get lunch.'

'What's "chalybeate"?' asked Nicky.

'It means waters impregnated with iron. People drank the waters for the sake of their health.'

'Is it really good for you? Can you still drink it? What does it taste like?'

'Do shut up, Nicky. Giles isn't a walking encyclopaedia.' Lalla looked fed up. 'I don't think I want to spend two days in a row looking at churches. Too gloomy.'

She isn't in love with him, I thought in a flash.

'I don't know,' said Jeremy. 'Giles knows more about this area than we do and we've lived here all our lives. It's too shame-making.'

'If you call what you've been doing living. I should rather call it lounging or loitering.'

'Well, I like that coming from you! I'd be very interested to know what you've been doing that's been so extremely productive?'

A row had threatened, which was ended by the appearance of Huddle.

'A gentleman from the Home Office on the telephone for you, sir.' He looked at Jeremy.

'Gosh, that sounds important.' I was impressed.

'It won't be,' said Lalla. 'Huddle makes it all up.'

She was proved right. Jeremy came back and said that the call had been from Farmer Burden, whose land adjoined the Park and who wanted something done about shoring up the bank of the river which acted as part of the boundary. 'He says he's already spoken to my father, who was extremely rude to him. He's threatening to go to law. I said I'd see him about it this afternoon. What a bore!'

So it was decided that after shopping and lunching in Little Whiddon the afternoon was to be spent riding by

Giles and Lalla, pacifying an irate farmer by Jeremy, and picnicking by me.

'You are clever, Viola! This is the most superly brilliant plan.' Nicky looked with appreciation at the tea I had organised. I must say, a little praise never comes amiss. We had apple doughnuts and rum truffles from Ye Olde Copper Kettle, a packet of chocolate digestives, a box of Turkish Delight and some sandwiches – sardine and tomato and cheese – which I had made myself, on the dimly remembered principle that all children's teas should have something savoury for health. 'But you've forgotten something.'

'What?'

'Never mind. I'll bring it. It'll be my share as you've done so much already.' Nicky went away and appeared two minutes later carrying a bag that bulged mysteriously. We let ourselves out through the back door of the new wing, which was a maze of small rooms in a state bordering on dereliction. There were puddles of water on the floor of the corridor and places where the plaster had fallen off exposing brickwork. Nicky set a fast pace, chattering about Thebes and Lord Caernarvon, his face flushing with cold, his large ears purple, the bag swinging against his bare legs. 'Oh, look, Nip and Nudge. You don't mind, do you, if they come?'

'I'd be delighted.'

Nip and Nudge chased round us in large circles with the peculiar intensity of sheep-dogs who know nothing of the pleasures of relaxation. What they wanted was a job to do, and in default of something better they herded us across the lawn and past the walled garden. A few drops of rain began to fall from a shadowed sky.

'We won't have to go back, will we?' Nicky's face was anxious.

'Let's have our picnic on the bridge over the lake. We'll be quite dry inside.'

'Oh, let's! I'm not allowed on the bridge on my own because I can't swim but you'll be able to save me, won't you?' He sounded very confident.

I looked doubtfully at the cold, dark water. 'It would be better if you could manage not to fall in.'

We reached the bridge just as the rain became a torrent. Beneath the arches it was perfectly dry and sheltered from the wind. A wooden bench and a pile of leaves were all it contained.

'This is beautiful!' I exclaimed, looking out at the lake. Now I saw how clever its builder had been. Before us stretched the sheet of sky-reflecting ripples, pocked by raindrops so that the images of clouds shimmered like melting snow and beyond the water two hills rose up, their smooth green folds enclosing a snaking line of tall trees. 'This is just as I imagined Paradise to be.'

'Is it?' Nicky put down his bag and pulled out some round pink-rimmed spectacles from his mac pocket. He put them on and squinted into the distance. 'It's not how *I* imagine it.'

'What's your idea of Paradise, then?' I asked, as I began to unwrap the sandwiches that had got very squashed and pink from the oozing tomatoes.

'Well . . . Nip and Nudge would be there. And Fluffy. There would be lots of things to eat – masses of ice-cream and chocolate. I'd live in a castle and I'd be the baron. But I'd be very fair to everyone who worked for me. No taxation. No raping and pillaging. I'd teach them all how to use the long-bow. And I'd be allowed to wear long trousers.'

'Is history your favourite subject at school?'

'Yes. I like English, too. And maths. I like all the lessons, except physics, really. They're the only decent thing about school. The rest is –' Nicky sucked in his breath and shuddered. 'There won't be any schools in Paradise. And no rugger.'

'Where do you go to school?'

'Bludgeon's Under School. It's my last year there. Next year I go into Middle School.'

'Really? Goodness! How old are you?'

'Nearly eleven.'

I thought I had tactfully disguised my surprise but he added at once, 'I know I look younger. I'm small for my age.

Lots of boys in the form below me are taller than I am. I can't help it. I'd give *anything* to be able to grow.'

'Have another sandwich. You need food to get taller. And lots of exercise to make your bones strong.'

'I know. But I always get out of rugger if I can. I can't see the ball and last term I fumbled a try. They were waiting for me outside the changing room. I got a black eye.'

'Oh, Nicky! What did the masters say?'

'Nothing. I said I'd fallen over. They wouldn't care anyway. Tupman's the only decent beak. He's the English master. He told my father that Bludgeon's wasn't a suitable school for me. My father was absolutely hopping mad and lectured me for hours about what a wonderful school it was and what it's done for him. It wasn't *my* fault. I didn't ask Tupman to speak to him. I'd have known it wouldn't be any good. My father thinks that what was right for him is right for everyone. Of course he was captain of games.' Nicky's voice grew bitter. 'His name's on all the shields. And Jeremy's. He was captain of cricket. Tupman said that Bludgeon's wasn't academic enough for me. I always come top of everything but Tupman says I'm not getting enough competition. My father despises scholars. He would, wouldn't he? After all, he's not a bit clever himself.'

'Another sandwich?' I felt unable to contradict Nicky's assessment of his father.

'No, thanks.' Nicky was eyeing the rum truffles and I gave him one. 'There'll be lots of rum truffles in Paradise.' With the resilience of youth, Nicky had thrown off the cloud that had hung about him as he talked of school. His large white teeth demolished two cakes at speed.

'I know what I forgot!' I said suddenly. 'I didn't bring anything to drink!'

'Aha!' Nicky rummaged in his bag. 'But I did. Look what I brought! Now we can have proper tea.' He drew out a silver kettle and after it a small silver spirit stove. 'It's been in the butler's pantry for ages and no one ever uses it. Look here's the teapot that goes with it and two cups. And I brought a jam jar of milk, some sugar lumps and a bottle of meths which is what you heat the water with.'

'Nicky, you're quite quite brilliant!'

'Well,' Nicky looked modest, 'I only remembered the matches at the last minute, actually. I put them in my pocket to be sure of keeping them dry. Here they are. The sugar lumps have got a bit mucky from the bottom of the bag but we can wash them.'

'You've thought of everything.' I stood the kettle on the spirit lamp and admired it. 'Let's get it going.'

Nicky poured the meths into the container and set light to it. Then we stared at each other.

'That'll pay me out for thinking myself so clever,' said Nicky. 'We haven't got any water.'

We looked over the parapet of the bridge at the lake.

'Do you think it's safe to drink? Won't it be full of liver-fluke? We did that in biology last term. Rather disgusting, actually.'

'If it's boiled it will be all right. Won't it?'

'Yes.' I suspected Nicky was also unsure. 'But how do we get to it? We don't want the muddy stuff from round the edge. And look how far the reeds go out.'

'I know. We'll tie our belts together and lower the kettle from the bridge.'

Which is what we did. Luckily Nicky's mac belt was very long and we fastened it to Lalla's, which I had borrowed to stop my jeans falling down. By leaning over I could just reach the surface of the water, which was much higher this side of the bridge than the other. A few leaves came up with it but we fished them out and put the kettle on to boil. As this was clearly going to take a little while, we decided to play I-Spy. Nicky started first with the letter D.

'Dog,' I said, as Nip came up and laid her head affectionately on my knee.

Her brown eyes were filled with trustful love, which I found very flattering until Nicky said that she wanted a lump of sugar. 'It isn't dog. And they aren't really allowed it.'

'Oh, well,' I said, giving them a lump each. 'It's very dull only doing what you're allowed. Let's form a society for breaking the rules. This is its first meeting. Door.'

'That's cheating,' said Nicky. 'There isn't a door, unless you count the arches.'

'There is, too.' I pointed to a very low door hidden by shadows in the corner.

'I didn't see it! My eyes must be getting worse, I think. I wonder where it goes to.'

The door was locked. Nicky felt along the top of the lintel.

'There you are.' He was triumphant. 'It's silly to lock a door and put the key in the most obvious place.' A flight of steps ran down into semi-darkness. 'Do you think it's a tomb?' he asked. 'Catacombs perhaps, with shelves full of skulls.'

'Let's go and see.'

'Bags go first.'

Nicky led the way. As soon as our eyes became used to the dim light we saw that it was rather unexciting. A room, the same size as the one above and lit by a gap in the stonework at the top, was empty except for a something that looked like a stone altar. A large wheel on a fat screw thread was fixed horizontally in the centre.

'Pooh! Doesn't it stink?' said Nicky with satisfaction.

'It's just damp. This must be right on the waterline. Perhaps it floods sometimes.'

'What do you think this is for? Black magic? Do you think they cut the throats of white cockerels on this stone?'

'I do hope not.' I could see that there were dark patches on the stone, which I trusted were puddles of water.

'Don't you think animal sacrifice is about the unfairest thing in the world? Buying favour at somebody else's expense?' Nicky got hold of the wheel and turned it experimentally. It made a marvellous hollow groaning sound like the Kraken waking after a particularly deep sleep. Nicky was delighted. 'What a row!' He turned the wheel some more.

'Do you think we ought?' I said.

'I don't see it can do any harm. Anyway, what about the Society for Breaking Rules?'

'Perhaps it was for hauling in boats from the lake. Like a capstan. Do let me have a go.'

Nicky and I played at steering aircraft carriers and missing icebergs for some time until the wheel was screeching magnificently and setting our teeth on edge.

'Why are the dogs barking?'

'Perhaps they don't like the noise. We'd better go and see.'

We went up the stairs to find Fluffy crouched on the bench calmly eating the remains of the sardine sandwiches while Nip and Nudge protested vociferously about an inch from her nose. Our kettle was beginning to puff wisps of steam from its spout. The tea when made was oddly delicious though the milk, being very creamy, floated in curds on the top and there was an unidentifiable brown silt at the bottom of our cups when we'd finished.

'Can you eat the last doughnut?'

Nicky blew out his lips. 'Not possibly. That was the best tea I ever had in my life. I'm glad Lalla rang the garage –' He stopped and made a face of alarm. 'Don't tell her I said. I shouldn't have been listening. She'll be furious with me.' I promised I wouldn't. 'Let's go back the long way through Bucket's Wood. Then we could go and look at the rabbit. Perhaps it would like the last bits of cheese sandwich. Nip and Nudge seemed to have got tired of them.'

'What did the D stand for, by the way?' I asked, as we strolled along the muddy track that ran through the trees.

'Doric. There were Doric capitals on each of the columns of the arches.'

'Ooh, you little cheat! That was much too hard.'

'Being difficult and cheating aren't at all the same thing.' Nicky's grin was delighted.

We walked along in companionable silence. Fluffy reappeared from the undergrowth and ran beside us, tail straight up, the orange bits of her coat seeming to catch fire from the fitful bursts of sun. Nip and Nudge chased birds and squirrels furiously as though supercharged by the cheese sandwiches. I loved the smell of wet woods, the dazzling acid green of the young leaves, the sound of rain dripping from the trees. Above all I loved the wildness, the untamedness, the idea of all those creatures going busily about their lives undisturbed . . . nests built, burrows dug, webs spun, eggs laid, babies hatched, food gathered, those hidden worlds unknown to me but, surely, just as important as my own life. Or as unimportant.

Lady Inskip appeared suddenly from among the trees, walking down the path away from us. She wore a mackintosh and gum-boots and her hair hung down in wisps.

'Mummy doesn't like to be interrupted on her walks,' said Nicky, taking hold of my arm to detain me just as I was about to call her. 'We'll let her get ahead.'

We loitered on the path, picking up fragments of bird's eggs and skeleton leaves and pine cones, anything in fact that took our fancy. A few minutes later Miss Tinker came zooming up the path towards us. She was bare-headed and coatless and her shoes were caked in mud. Her little grey eyes, like gravel in a complexion the colour of cement, gave us an unfriendly look as she marched past us, her treetrunk-like legs hammering the ground and her arms swinging as though she was doing Swedish exercises. Nicky and I turned to watch her as she disappeared through the trees.

'Ought we to have told her where Mummy was? It seems like spying, doesn't it? I should hate to have the Stinker hanging round me all the time.'

'It's too late now, anyway. She's gone.' I longed to ask Nicky why Lady Inskip was practically under arrest but of course I didn't.

'I wish we could do this every day,' said Nicky, zigzagging along the track, choosing the deepest puddles for his route. 'Viola, do you believe in God? Jeremy says it's all bunk.'

'Well. Yes I do. Some days more than others. There are times when I can sense something so completely marvellous that I think it *must* be God. It's as though I were standing with my back to a great, wonderful light only I can't turn round. Not just light and warmth, that's just the physical part of it. It's more than that. A feeling of incredible happiness, knowing everything, loving everything . . . passionately with all my heart and soul. Oh dear, it's impossible to talk about these things, isn't it, without sounding perfectly stupid? I imagine that, at the moment of death, I shall turn round and see it.' Nicky walked on his head bowed in thought. 'I should feel very sad indeed not to believe it,' I added, when he did not speak.

'Is Jeremy very sad?'

I remembered Jeremy sobbing in my arms that first night at Inskip Park. And then how cosy and comfortable we had been, lying chastely in each other's arms, on the second.

'No, only sometimes as we all are. Most of the time I think he's fine.'

'Are all grown-ups unhappy sometimes?' Nicky stopped and waited for me to catch up. 'Are you?'

I put my arm round his shoulder and looked down at his pinched face, very white and pink below a fringe of mousy hair, the large intelligent eyes perplexed and anxious.

'Yes. Some things make me very unhappy.'

'I used to pray that God'd make things less . . . awful. But if anything they got worse. I've rather given up bothering. Perhaps it might be worth another go. I could just ask for more days like today. A straightforward request that *anyone* could understand.'

'Yes,' I said. 'If I were you I'd have another go.'

We walked to the hen run – both of us, I imagine, pondering in an indeterminate way the eternal verities. Approaching the hen house from a different angle we had to cross the farmyard. It was churned to a turbulent sea of sucking mud. 'It's always like this after the winter.' Nicky strode into the sticky ooze. 'It's the cows being brought in for milking that does it. Huddle sleeps up there.' He pointed to a loft above the cart shed.

'It doesn't look very comfortable.'

'The roof of the new wing where he used to sleep is full of leaks. My father offered him his own dressing room but Huddle refused. He talked a lot of rot about knowing his place. He likes the inconvenience so that he can complain about it. Once I got completely stuck in the mud and had to leave my boots behind. That's cheating, going round the edge.'

'None the less that's what I'm going to do,' I said firmly. 'I don't want to have to walk back to the house in my bare feet. Poor Huddle, it must be absolutely freezing in cold weather. Oh, look! Doesn't he look happy, stretched out in that patch of sunlight, licking his dear little paws.'

I was referring to the rabbit, of course, not Huddle. We let ourselves into the run and threw down the last remnants of the picnic. The hens ran in circles, conversing hysterically.

'I'll see if there are any eggs.' Such countrified things were still a source of pleasure to me. I bent down and looked into the hen house. Inside, in the shadows, the whites of Lady Inskip's eyes glittered as she sat on the perch up to her knees in straw. Slowly she lifted her finger to her lips.

CHAPTER 12

I was standing in the kitchen at seven o'clock that evening, examining with bemusement the two chicken carcasses we had bought that morning in Little Whiddon, when the telephone rang, making me jump. After a search I found the instrument on the window-sill, hidden behind the curtain. As it continued to ring, I picked up the receiver.

'Mabel Fordyce speaking.' The voice was brisk. 'May I have a word with Giles?'

'I'm afraid he hasn't come back yet. He's out riding. You must be Giles's mother. I'm Viola Otway.'

'Hello, dear. Giles has mentioned you. He telephoned me this morning but I was out shopping. Ask him to let me know what his plans are, will you? I'm trying to arrange a bridge party for the weekend but if Giles comes when my friends are here he moons about looking bored and disapproving and puts everyone off their game. He thinks we're all hopelessly frivolous.'

I was emboldened by this frank confession and by the friendly timbre of her rich, cigarette-smoky voice to ask, 'Would you happen to know how to cook a chicken? I expect it sounds an odd question but you see the cook's left and it's partly my fault and everyone else is out, apart from Lady Inskip and her maid who isn't quite well, Lady Inskip, I mean not the maid. The long and short of it is that there will be eight hungry people sitting down to dinner in an hour and there won't be anything to eat.'

Mrs Fordyce gave a bark of a laugh. 'You're in a spot, my dear, I can see that. Now, have you fat of any kind?'

'Just a minute.' I rummaged in the fridge and found something growing grey silky fur which I threw, pot and all, into the rubbish bin. I ran back to the telephone. 'Hang on, I'm still looking.' I went to search the larder and came back with a bottle of something that called itself corn oil. 'Will that do? It smells positively evil but it's all I can find.'

'Better than nothing. Put the chicken in a roasting pan – check that there are no giblets inside – pour two tablespoons of oil over it, salt and pepper it and put it in a hot oven for an hour and a quarter.'

'Is that all? It sounds easy. Even I can manage that. Wait a minute, though, what are giblets?'

'Goodness, dear, you *are* inexperienced to be left in charge. They're the insides – neck and liver and whatnot – and these days usually wrapped in a plastic bag. Put them in a pan with some wine and water, an onion and a carrot and boil them up and you can make a sauce.'

'Really?' I must have sounded doubtful.

'Gracious, how the other half live! Now don't worry. Any fool can cook. And I'm sure you're far from that,' she added, quickly and kindly. 'I'll give you my number and you can ring me back if you get stuck.'

'Thanks awfully,' I said, with a schoolgirl fervour that was completely genuine.

Three-quarters of an hour and two telephone calls later, the chickens were sizzling in the oven and beginning to brown and there were pans of potatoes and Brussels sprouts bubbling on the top of the stove. I was just looking for sticking plaster, having grazed my thumb painfully trying to grate bread for bread sauce when Susan came in. 'I came to see if I could help. Heavens, what a lot of blood!' Susan found some Elastoplast in a cupboard and ministered to the wound. 'You'd better let me do that.' She took the bread from me and chucked out the crumbs that were stained red. She made a pile of new ones with a practised action.

'You can cook,' I said, with admiration.

'I've had to. My father only has a daily. Everyone – except the Inskips who don't live on the same planet as the rest of us – cooks, these days, don't they?'

'I'm planning to learn,' I said humbly, for there was something challenging in her voice that I didn't feel up to tangling with. 'I'll chop up the onion, shall I?'

'I'd better. You'll only cut yourself.' I knew from experience that the only way to soothe the savage breasts of those who feel disadvantaged is a sort of creeping humility. I held the milk bottle for her and fetched cloves and nutmeg from the larder.

'Those potatoes have been boiled too long,' Susan spoke with satisfaction. 'We'd better mash them. Any butter?'

I ran eagerly about, her willing slave, and by the time she had beaten the potatoes smooth, whatever anger burned within had more or less spent itself.

'We must put dishes to heat in the bottom oven.' Her tone was almost cordial. 'Huddle won't do anything that he considers woman's work. I don't know how my uncle puts up with him. Of course, it's difficult to get people to stay in a place like this and he was in Uncle James's regiment during the war. I've seen photographs of them. You wouldn't believe how young and handsome they both were.'

'Well, I expect Sir James was thinner and less red. And Huddle has a nice face. He makes me think of a friendly polar bear. Not that there is such a thing, I know.'

'You couldn't call Uncle James fat.' The sharpness had returned to Susan's voice.

'Absolutely not. Just – well, of course, compared with Jeremy who's so tall –'

'Oh, yes. But Uncle James was everything that Jeremy isn't. Strong and active and manly. You can tell from the photographs. He was a colonel. Then he went into the Foreign Office. He was quite old when he married Aunt Millie.' Susan's voice conveyed that this had been a mistake.

'I wish I knew what to do about a pudding. I think Sir James is keen on them.'

This little piece of calculation worked like magic, evidence of my double nature. Susan went through the bags of shopping that we had bought that morning and found a bunch of bananas. She sliced them lengthways, sprinkled them with rum, lemon juice and brown sugar and put them in the bottom oven to cook.

'Lalla suggested a tomato salad for the first course,' I ventured.

'Did she indeed!' Susan snorted. 'Naturally Her High and Mightiness wouldn't think of making it herself. It'll always be someone else's job to get their hands dirty.'

'Tell me how and I'll gladly do it. You've already done so much. I couldn't possibly have managed without you.'

'I don't know why you let Lalla get away with it. And yet she always does.' Susan seized the bag of tomatoes, emptied it into a colander and gave the cold tap a fierce wrench, spraying us both with water. ' "To him that hath shall be given . . ." It's perfectly true but it seems very unfair to me.' She looked at me, her skin reddening and her small slate-coloured eyes screwed up with vexation. There was a pause and then she burst out, with a kind of anguish, 'Do you like Lalla?'

I thought for a moment. I remembered how Lalla had taken me up to her room that morning, opened her wardrobe doors and told me to take anything of hers that I liked. Lalla's room had been unexpected – all pink and white with organdie frills and satin bows. 'Gruesome, isn't it?' she had said, seeing my surprise. 'Mummy did it for me when I was a little girl. There's never been the money to change it. I always feel I ought to flounce about sucking my fingers when I'm in it.' She put her finger in her mouth and wriggled her hips in a parody of a winsome little girl. I laughed, wondering that Lady Inskip had once been sufficiently energetic and organised to create such an extravaganza of frilliness.

'That was before she got ill,' said Lalla, as though reading my thoughts. 'She wasn't always the batty old thing she is now. When Nicky was born she had a sort of nervous collapse. Puerperal depression, I think it's called. I was only nine then so I don't remember too well what she was like before. Rather jolly and partyish. And very pretty. Poor old Mummy.'

'She does seem – rather unhappy.' I was feeling my way. 'And she's such a gentle person. I think she needs protecting. It isn't people's fault if they can't stand up to the unpleasantness of life, is it? And she loves you so much.'

'Meaning?' Lalla had stiffened.

'Meaning, I suppose, that when people love you, you have an obligation towards them.'

'I don't recall that I ever asked to be loved.'

'Obligations generally aren't things you ask for. Those are pleasures. Obligations are things required of you whether you like them or not.'

'You think I ought to be nicer to Mummy, is that what you're saying?' When I didn't answer Lalla looked up and caught my eye. 'All right. I know it, anyway. It doesn't make me feel very good about myself, actually, to be mean to her. It's just that she can be so smothering. I mistrust emotion. Particularly my own,' she added, with a kind of caustic irony which made me feel that Lady Inskip was not the only member of the family who needed protection.

'The timing was all wrong. I'd just gone to boarding-school when Mummy had her fit of whatever it was. I needed to know that things were right at home . . . Sorry, I'm sounding self-pitying. But it was worrying like hell. Daddy went to pieces – in a different way – when she did. He just gave up talking. I think he blames Nicky for her decline. Of course, he can be a bloody nuisance but the poor kid didn't ask to be born. Anyway, try on this jersey. It's a bit small for me so it might fit you.'

I undressed. The sight of my knickers had Lalla rolling on her bed in fits. I began to lose sympathy with those stories of the sad clown – the tragic jester whose life is all gallant capering and jolly mummery on stage and bitterness and bale behind the scenes. All any comedian needed was a pair of amusing underpants and their career was effortlessly made.

'That looks terrific,' said Lalla, not looking as I pulled on her jersey and jeans. She lit a cigarette. 'I'm so glad that you and Jeremy get on so well. I worry about him. Promise me you'll try to get him to do some kind of work. He's wasting himself messing about here, doing all the things my father can't be bothered to do.'

'Well, I think you may be overestimating my powers. Really, we're just friends.'

'Rubbish! It's obvious he's nuts about you. You're the first woman I can remember that he's really liked. Promise me you'll use your influence?'

I promised.

'I'm not much good at slopping over people.' Lalla lay on her stomach and unpicked a bit of lace from her counterpane. 'I'm always afraid it might not be true. I hate people professing deep feelings, as though it's a credit to them, proving what kind, sensitive, worthwhile human beings they are. But I love Jeremy more than anyone.'

'Yes,' I said to Susan, as I thought about this conversation. 'I do like Lalla.'

Dinner was hugely successful, as far as the food went. Francis was very greedy and had several helpings. 'We seem to have quite a little cook in our midst.' He spoke unctuously, his lips rimmed with bread sauce.

'Susan helped me. In fact, she was invaluable.'

'Ah. Susan. Yes. She has her talents.' He smiled in a way that drove those talents right to the bottom of any list of desirable accomplishments.

'We galloped for absolutely miles,' said Lalla, in a dreamy voice. 'I'm so tired. I could sleep for ever.'

'I'm glad someone was enjoying themselves,' said Jeremy.

'I had a perfectly bloody time. Old Burden made me examine every single muddy inch of crumbling bank. God, I *hate* living in the country. Why can't we sell up and go and live in Chelsea?'

'Who'd buy this place?' snapped Lalla. 'Perhaps you've seen a gibbering lunatic with a chequebook wandering about?'

I heard a small mewing sound. I thought at first that Fluffy had got into the dining room but then I realised it was Lady Inskip.

'We'll have a go at *The Pirates of Penzance* tonight, I think,' said Francis. I saw him give Lalla a look that would have reduced me to tears.

'I should be grateful if you would remember that this is my house you are discussing as though it were some kind of affliction. I happen to be extremely fond of it.' Sir James glowered over the chicken leg, which he was pulling at vigorously with his teeth, in a way that reminded me of Waldemar. His bloodshot eyes glared round the table. 'Anyone who does not care for it is welcome to leave.'

That put rather a damper on conversation. I saw that something was hiding beneath a sprout on my plate that looked suspiciously like a worm. This was puzzling especially as, on Susan's instructions, I had sieved out the nastier-looking chicken parts from the sauce. It was a relief when a discreet probe with the tines of my fork disclosed a small piece of rubber band. Now I recalled Mrs Fordyce's instructions to remove the band from the legs of the chicken. I distinctly remembered doing this to the first one. Obviously the second bird had gone into the oven with its legs bound and rather horribly stuck into its bottom. But where was the rest of the rubber band? Might people die from eating such a thing? I probed my conscience with the usual shameful result. I kept quiet.

Francis laid down his knife and fork. I suppose clergymen get a lot of practice at breaking uncomfortable silences, their professional lives running the gamut from the sublime to the banal. They have to wrest their congregation from evil, distribute tombola prizes, butter up the bishop and give

167

hope to the dying. I couldn't imagine Francis inspiring anything but the most uncharitable thoughts. Anyone unlucky enough to find him at their bedside as they approached the portals of death would be whizzed off straight away to the stew-pots and gridirons of hell. It's because my mind runs on in this unessential way that introducing new gambits to a dead conversation is almost the least of my talents.

'Dr Johnson,' Francis paused to make sure he had our attention, 'said that a man seldom thinks with more earnestness of anything than he does of his dinner. It is a melancholy thought that we are so little advanced from the primitive clutch of animal appetites.'

'You should know,' flashed Lalla.

Dining with Lalla and Francis was like sitting between two tigers. Watching them snarl and lash their tails was frightening and there was the tiny but abiding fear that one of them might suddenly turn on you with an unsheathed claw. Francis stopped smiling and exercised his lungs with some deep breathing.

'I can't think that's true,' said Giles's disembodied voice through the candle-smoke. 'Great men engaged in great works are well known to be indifferent to basic human requirements. According to Vasari's *Lives of the Artists* Piero di Cosimo ate nothing but hard-boiled eggs. He cooked them a hundred at a time and kept them in a basket by his easel.'

'Think of the havoc wrought on one's digestion!' Jeremy spoke wonderingly.

'And the fiddle of peeling them,' said Lalla. 'Why not apples or tomatoes which don't have to be cooked?'

I marvelled at how much Giles knew and how well-read he was. I wished, not for the first time, that he found me less irritating because being with him was like a complete crash course in the education of the kind I wanted – nothing to do with theorems or copper calorimeters but art, philosophy and history – the things that really interested me.

'But perhaps the great doctor was referring to ordinary folk like ourselves,' Francis made it clear from his tone that his inclusion of himself in this designation was mere modesty, 'engaged in the trivial round, the common task – without genius.'

'How would you define genius?' I asked. I was aware that this question falls into the category of what Daniel would call the jejune but I have always found it gets good results. Most people secretly – and some not so secretly – feel that had circumstances afforded them leisure they would have written the novel or symphony or propounded the economic theory which would have elevated them in a twinkling to that blessed band. This gives them a close personal interest in the definition of it.

Francis screwed up his black brows as he pondered. 'Talent does easily what is difficult for others. Genius does what is impossible.'

'Oh, yes, I like that definition,' said Giles. 'Frédéric Amiel, isn't it?'

There was a tiny pause.

'Aha!' said Francis. 'I wondered if anyone would recognise it.'

After dinner when the men came into the drawing room Francis, Lady Inskip and Susan stationed themselves round the piano.

'Awful, isn't it?' said Lalla to Giles as Susan struck up the tune and Lady Inskip's uncertain soprano was joined by her brother's boisterous baritone. 'It reminds me of those agonising charity concerts we had to go to as children – miners' benefits, the Boys' Brigade and raising money for lavatories for the village hall. Daddy always used to send us to support them because he couldn't bear to go himself. Oh, no!' Lalla put her fingers in her ears as Lady Inskip bravely went full tilt at a top note and only narrowly missed it. 'Now he has it every night in his own house. There's justice for you.'

Giles and Lalla were sitting next to each other on the sofa but I could hear them quite clearly despite the singing. Jeremy was helping himself to coffee. Sir James was stuck behind his newspaper and I was pretending to read *Country*

Life. Lalla giggled and looked so charming that I wasn't a bit surprised to see Giles take her hand and lift it discreetly to his lips.

' "I am the very model of a modern major-general," ' sang Francis, with the violent grimacing necessary for the articulation of Mr Gilbert's patter. I found myself giggling, too.

'Telephone, madam,' said Huddle, looming over Lalla. 'A gentleman from Her Majesty's Constabulary.'

'Goodness. Just like a J. B. Priestley play,' I said. 'What great secrets are about to be revealed?'

Sir James lowered his paper for a second and looked at me as though he doubted my sanity.

Five minutes later I wished I had kept my little quip to myself. Lalla came back in, her mood evidently depressed, and went over to the fire to gaze broodingly at the sulking embers. We all looked at her inquiringly.

'That was Hamish. He's back from Washington. He's coming here tomorrow.'

I saw Jeremy glance quickly at Giles then look studiously at his coffee cup.

'Is that a good or a bad thing?' I asked. 'Who's Hamish?'

'He's something big in international finance. Terribly brainy. And quite rich.' She laughed, but it was not a comfortable sound. 'I'm engaged to marry him.'

CHAPTER 13

I opened my eyes with a start and my dream – something frightening about being wrapped up in bandages like a mummy and rolled into a tomb – slithered away into oblivion. Jeremy's arms held me in a tight embrace. His hand was resting on my mouth. I eased myself carefully out of bed so as not to wake him. He slept deeply, his eyelids twitching, a slight smile on his lips.

I covered my nakedness with Aunt Pussy's coat and went

to the hole where the window ought to have been to look down at the park. Already I had formed an attachment to this particular scene. The miniature trees were sprinkled haphazardly across fluted greensward extending to the horizon. The sun sizzled on the molten surface of the lake, magnifying it to twice its size. Far to the right of it someone was running across the park towards Bucket's Wood. I could just make out a sweep of long fair hair. It was Lalla.

She had asked me to come to her room the night before. 'I know you think badly of me, Viola, and I find, much to my surprise, that I mind.'

'Oh, Lalla, I don't *want* to think badly of you. But poor Giles! He looked so unhappy.'

When Lalla had told us that she was engaged to be married to Hamish I had looked involuntarily at Giles and glimpsed the shock on his face before he leaned forward to take a cigarette from the box on the table. I had never seen him smoke before. His hand was shaky as he lit it but when he looked up again his face was expressionless, apart from his eyes which refused to be governed by his evident desire to conceal his feelings. They were wretched. After that I was careful not to look at him again.

'What'll you do about not having a cook?' I had asked Lalla, to give Giles a chance to recover. 'He won't want to eat semolina pudding.'

'Oh, Hamish won't care about that.' Lalla had spoken offhandedly. I noticed that she didn't look at Giles either. 'He gets the most marvellous food all the time. It'll do him good to slum it.'

As soon as Giles had finished his cigarette he got up and said that he was tired and would have an early night. He said good night to us all in his normal manner but he was very pale.

'I suppose the dancing's off,' Jeremy had said. 'You are a perfect little brute sometimes, Lalla. Let's have a game of gin rummy.'

So we did but, though generally I like this kind of thing, my heart was not in it. I wondered what men do in such circumstances. If Giles had been a girl he would have thrown himself on his bed for a good long cry and then written ten letters of grief, fury and accusation, all of which would, with luck, have gone into the wastepaper basket in the morning. Many sleepless hours would have been spent rehearsing a dignified request for an interview the next day. Lofty phrases would roll round the brain. 'You at least owe me this' and 'I suppose it amused you to trifle with my affections.' Then exhaustion would soften pride. Hope is the great comforter. Engagements can be broken.

I guessed, from the little I knew of men, that a man would be more fatalistic. I could imagine Giles standing at his bedroom window, staring moodily at the moon while reflecting cynically on the fickle nature of women. Probably he would throw himself into a chair, a bottle of whisky at his elbow, emit much bitter laughter, perhaps even dash away a tear or two and get hopelessly drunk. It seemed as good a course of action as any.

'I know I shouldn't have flirted with Giles,' said Lalla, much later, when we were alone in her bedroom. She lay on the bed the wrong way round, stockinged feet on her pillow, smoking and dropping ash on the pink satin eiderdown. I perched on the stool at its foot. 'But I really like him. He's terrifically attractive – much better-looking than Hamish, as it happens. And I like him being so serious. It's very romantic. Hamish is hardly ever serious about anything. I should certainly have let Giles make love to me if he'd asked me. I think he was on the point of it. Damn! It's a perfect nuisance Hamish coming like this.'

'But, Lalla, if that's how you feel – are you going to break off your engagement with Hamish?'

Lalla's skin was the most beautiful creamy colour. Mine is rather inclined to freckle. I could quite understand Giles's infatuation.

'Oh, no! If ever I marry anyone it will be Hamish. I wouldn't dream of marrying Giles. He'd find me out in a minute and then where would we be? No, I just wanted to go to bed with him. It would have been a very brief affair. He's much more intelligent than my usual lovers.'

'What do you mean, find you out?'

'He'd see what a worthless creature I really am and then he'd be disillusioned and reproachful. I couldn't stand that. I'd have gone to bed with him just once or twice and then that would have been it. I'd have got rid of him before he got rid of me.' She laughed with a kind of bleak triumph.

'Lalla! I simply don't understand. Why shouldn't you love Giles and he love you? Leaving Hamish out of the picture, I mean.'

Lalla shrugged. The tip of her ear showed pink through the shiny strands of her hair. 'You're such a little innocent, darling. It couldn't possibly work. I can see already that Giles is suppressing part of himself in order not to disapprove of me. He'd have ended up hating me and who's to say he'd be wrong?'

I was silent for a moment, thinking. 'But, dear Lalla, couldn't you change those things – don't think I'm criticising you, you've been utterly kind to me and I've loved being here – but perhaps things that Giles might not like?'

'No, I couldn't! I hate pretending! I've had to grow up with it and I can't stand it! If I can't be myself then I'd rather be alone. Hamish is the only man I've ever met who's seen me – as I am, without disapproving. Perhaps he doesn't like it, exactly, but he still loves me. But much more important than that, more important than my vanity being flattered, he makes me feel as though I might be – a very little bit – worthwhile. When I'm with him I sometimes feel almost hopeful. I can't explain it.'

I said nothing, thinking how sad Lalla really was beneath the carefree manner.

'So now you know all about it.' Lalla laughed again and reached for an ashtray that stood incongruously on a pale pink tablecloth beside the white, rosebud-trimmed lamp. 'Honestly, darling, do stop looking at me with those huge sorrowful eyes. You *are* the merest child. Why shouldn't I be as bad as men are?'

I refrained from pointing out that I was exactly the same age. I knew she meant in terms of experience. 'All men aren't bad. My father is the most angelic person you could hope to meet. And I don't think Giles deserves to be called bad just because he fell in love with you. He's very disagreeable sometimes . . . because he has high standards, I think. And I expect his mother spoilt him. But he's capable of great kindness too,' I was remembering Nicky's book, 'and he is sensitive to other people's feelings.'

'Unlike me, you mean!'

'No, I wasn't thinking that. Really, I wasn't. Lalla, don't try and make me into an enemy when I'm not! I really do like you very much.'

Lalla looked away from me as she ground out her cigarette. When she looked at me again her eyes were shining. 'I did want to say, Viola, for what it's worth, I'm sorry to have hurt Giles. He's much too good for me.'

I went over and put my arms around her and kissed her.

'What's that for, you little idiot?'

'Just because I'm sorry. Sorry for both of you.'

Lalla got up abruptly and went to look out of the window.

'I'll go to bed, I think,' I said, when she didn't turn round. 'Good night Lalla.'

She didn't answer.

As I gazed down at the prospect of sylvan beauty spread out below, remembering this, I felt a sinking of spirits. If only Hamish needn't come. Perhaps he might be called away on urgent business and Giles would be spared the painful sight of Lalla and Hamish together.

Breakfast was, predictably, tense. Giles seemed to have regained complete self-control. He said good morning with perfect civility to Lalla when she came into the dining room, looking becomingly flushed from her early-morning run. There was a twig caught on the sleeve of her jersey and a grass stalk in her tangled hair. What's more he ate the bacon and scrambled eggs I had cooked without flinching.

Something unexpected had happened to the eggs. One minute they had been golden fluffy cumulus and the next second they had turned to curds of an extraordinarily unappetising grey.

'Lord! This looks like the wadding Mrs Jukes uses to clean the brass.' Lalla prodded the eggs with her fork.

'I'm really enjoying them,' said Nicky stoutly. 'I shall have more.' He went over to the dishes on the buffet and bravely helped himself to the remainder.

Sir James came in with Waldemar and took his chair at the head of the table.

'I'm sorry, sir, there has been a run on the eggs.' Huddle bent solicitously over his master's chair. 'Might I recommend the semolina pudding of which there remains a small helping? Possibly with the addition of a little marmalade, sir, as it's breakfast?'

'Damn it! Is there no consideration in this house?' Sir James threw down his napkin with a grunt of rage, and no doubt Nicky, who shrank lower behind his lead-coloured mound of egg, would have been in trouble but for the arrival of Bowser. 'What now?' snapped Sir James, his eyes like little red pinpoints with anger. 'Can't a man have his breakfast in peace?'

Bowser was a small man with a head that looked as though it had been carved out of a turnip. It had slits for eyes and a mouth and a small flat nose with two round nostrils. His grey bristly hair stood out straight from a low brow, like a sweep's brush. 'Very sorry, sir. It's business as can't wait. Them gypsies have been and tampered with that there sluice hunder t'bridge and the lower lake has flooded.'

'What!' The hyperborean blast of Sir James's cold fury made me knock over my tea-cup and prompted Waldemar to utter his characteristic bark, mournful and reverberating as though we were buried in an underground chamber. This reminded me of the little dark room under the bridge and the large wheel that we had turned with such gay abandon. Nicky and I looked at each other. He was very white and I knew what he was thinking. Quickly he raised a finger to his lip. I had no need of the warning. Absolutely nothing would have induced me to own up.

'Yes, sir.' Bowser was clearly enjoying himself. 'T'ole valley's hunder water and there's sheep stranded and like to drown if we don't get to 'em quick.'

This sounded dreadful. And there were darling lambs too! What if they should drown through our fault? I did not dare to look at Nicky again. I felt that my guilt was emblazoned on my face.

'My God!' Sir James growled. 'Half-wits! Huddle, go at once to Master Jeremy's room and get that lazy good-for-nothing out of bed. Must I think of everything?' Sir James chewed his moustache in temper. 'How many boats have we got, Bowser?'

'Five, sir . . . but only three without holes in.'

Sir James ground his teeth. 'Imbeciles! What is the point of – Oh, never mind! Organise two men to each boat and get those damned sheep in. They belong to that fool Burden and he'll charge me double what they're worth if any of them drown.'

'That'll be me and young Harry in one, sir, and Master Jeremy in another with old Cruikshank – if we can get him into a boat, that is, he's that bad with the rheumatics he can't stand straight. Am I to raise Farmer Burden for the other boat, sir?'

'No, no! Anyone but him. Perhaps Huddle can go.'

'I'm sorry, sir.' Huddle had just come back into the dining room. 'Master Jeremy is not in his bedroom.' For a second his eyes swivelled in my direction so I knew that Mrs Jukes had been talking. 'Most like, sir, tempted by the unseasonable clemency of the weather, he's gone for a walk before breakfast.' It was plain from his tone that Huddle did not believe this nor did he expect anyone else to.

'Don't be ridiculous! You'd better go with Cruikshank –'

'Me, sir? Go in a boat? I'm very sorry to disoblige but my stomach can't take the motion of waves –'

'Goddamn it, man! This is a piddling little lake not the Bay of Biscay!'

Huddle allowed his shoulders and lower lip to droop and hobbled away with a distinct limp.

'Can I help?' Giles stood up.

'Thank you! Good of you!' Sir James bared his teeth as though he would have preferred to bite Giles rather than be grateful to him. 'Do what you can to get the men organised. Pack of idiots! I suppose I'll have to go without breakfast. There's only so much a man can stand!' He fixed Lalla and

Nicky and me with a fiery eye before marching angrily out after Giles.

Nicky and I let out our breaths and Lalla giggled. 'What a storm about nothing!'

'Oh, but think of the lambs! Perhaps we ought to go and see what we can do. I didn't dare suggest it to your father.'

'Goodness, no! Daddy thinks women are only good for two things. One's drawing up guest lists. You can guess what the other is.'

'I can't guess,' said Nicky at once.

'Don't little pitchers have big ears?'

Nicky blushed. 'They call me Dracula at school because my ears and teeth stick out.'

'There isn't anything wrong with them,' I said quickly. 'Your face needs to grow. And it will. You have marvellous eyes.'

'Yes,' agreed Lalla unexpectedly. 'They are the best in the family. Mummy's used to be wonderful before she went dotty. But they're still a lovely colour.'

'Is Mummy quite dotty, then?' asked Nicky. 'How can you tell?'

'Oh, don't keep asking questions, Brat. You know how it gets on my nerves. And I shouldn't have said that about Mummy. She's just a bit – odd. She sees things that aren't there.'

'How do you know they aren't there?'

Lalla stuck her fingers in her ears. 'Don't say another word or I may be tempted to violence. If you want to live to see another dawn, run up to Viola's bedroom and get Jeremy out of bed. Pour cold water down his neck or something. Come on, Viola, let's see what we can do to help.'

'What's he doing in Viola's bedroom? All right, all right, I'm going. Don't get in a wax.'

The grass at the edge of the lake was squelchy beneath our feet. Trees stuck up out of the swirling caramel-coloured water in a surreal manner and the tips of a row of fencing-posts emerged like a string of giant beads. Bowser stood stiffly in the prow, like Nelson boarding the

Victory, as a young man rowed him slowly over the water to where five or six sheep stood on a green mound. Nip and Nudge sat with pricked ears by the shore with the strained expectancy of fishermen's wives during a storm at sea.

'Come on, let's take this boat.' Lalla pulled at a skiff, which lay at an angle near the edge. She continued to give small, graceful tugs while I bent and put my back into pushing it. 'Hang on, you idiot! It's going to float away,' she shouted, as it slithered into the water and began to drift across the lake. I waded in after it and caught hold of the bow rope. Getting into a boat that is not fastened tidily at a landing stage is a very difficult thing. Lalla managed all right by taking a jump from shore while I steadied the boat in the shallows. It rocked madly but just failed to capsize. 'Come on, Viola! Do stop messing about!'

By now I was up to my thighs in the flood. The mud held on to my gym shoes with the suction of an octopus. I struggled to climb aboard. The boat dipped down alarmingly towards me then sprang back, chucking me so hard under the chin that I nearly bit through my tongue.

'For heaven's sake, Viola! You nearly had me in just then.'

'Sorry!' I moved round to the stern and, with a superhuman effort, tumbled in head first, dealing myself a blow in the midriff, which winded me.

'Honestly you are the most complete landlubber! Get up and let's take an oar each.'

As soon as my breath returned I sat down next to Lalla. I was still sucking in air in sobs. My feet were now bare but for mud socks that ended at the knees of my jeans.

'Come on! Row, darling! Look, let me show you how. It's easy to see that you've never been in a boat before.'

I was too puffed to answer but I applied some strength to the oar and at once we went round in circles.

'This is hopeless,' said Lalla. 'You're doing something wrong.'

'Why don't you – turn the end of the oar at right angles – to the water?' I panted. 'We'd have more push.'

Lalla did this and we shot backwards in quite a promising

manner. 'Over there!' I puffed. I gestured with my chin to a small mound where a mother sheep and a baby stood staring at us in consternation.

'All right. Ow! I'm getting blisters. Look!' Lalla showed me a hand that was faintly pink. 'You row and I'll take the tiller.'

I took the oars and after catching a few crabs managed to get into the swing of it. Now and again one or other of the oars would spring out of the rowlocks and I would fall backwards into the bows, causing Lalla great amusement, but soon we were moving more or less evenly along towards our castaways. I felt very wet and cold.

'You get out and hold the boat as you're muddy anyway,' said Lalla, as we reached the island. The mother sheep looked anything but pleased to see us, baaing and trying to throw herself into the water on the other side. The lamb gave itself up without too much of a struggle but the ewe had abandoned the maternal instinct for that of survival and refused to come near the boat. At last I caught her. A fully grown sheep is the heaviest thing imaginable. I thought my heart might burst and my muscles snap as I picked her up round the middle and hurled her into the prow. She managed to plop down into the water between the boat and the island. As she paddled frantically, her eyes glared up at me, mad with reproach.

'Wait a minute, Viola! You'll drown that animal between you!'

Giles rowed expertly alongside. Nicky sat in the stern, holding the tiller. Giles, wearing waders up to his armpits – how had he been so clever as to find them? – leaped into the water and stuck a metal stave into the ground to which he fastened the painter. He seized the sheep and lifted it into our craft. 'I think you girls had better go ashore,' said Giles bossily. 'You'll do more harm than good.'

'You never saw anything so funny as Viola trying to row,' said Lalla, giving Giles a flash from under her lids.

I was too out of breath from the struggle to express my indignation. I rowed Lalla back to land, disappointed at finding myself useless when I was so horribly aware of my own culpability. Getting the mother and baby out of the boat proved almost as difficult as getting them in. Just as I was beginning to lose my temper with her, the ewe decided she'd had enough of being hauled about and made a dramatic bid for shore like Tosca hurling herself from the battlements. I stood in the icy water and pulled the lamb into my arms. As soon as its hoofs touched the grass it galloped away with its mother, bleating indignantly. Nip, or was it Nudge, came streaking round to check any ideas of sheepish independence.

'So much for gratitude,' said Lalla. 'I shall feel much less guilty next time we have lamb chops. Blasted creature's made me wet all over. I shall go and change.'

'I'll stay and see if I can do anything else to help.' It was all right for Lalla. She was not responsible for the débâcle.

I pulled the boat up on to the grass. I was standing by it, trying to get my breath back, when I saw Lady Inskip stepping down into the water by the bridge. I ran over as fast as I could. 'Be careful!' I cried. 'It's terribly deep there!'

She turned her head towards me and, for a second, her face registered terrified guilt. Then she smiled an awful, wobbling smile. There were purple patches of skin beneath her poor bulging eyes. I stretched out my hand towards her.

'Hello, Viola. Dear Viola. See that cloud reflected in the water? I thought it was a lamb. I wanted to save it. "Little lamb, who made thee? I a child and thou a lamb." That's Blake, you know. I learned that poem as a girl. I had to recite to my grandmother every day. Sometimes it was things like "The Lays of Ancient Rome" or "The Fighting Temeraire" – I didn't like those kind of poems, too violent. Blake was my favourite. "Gave thee clothing of delight, softest clothing, woolly, bright." Nanny knitted the clothing. All those little vests and matinée coats. I wasn't well. She sat by my bed and knitted. Click, click, click! Like this.' Lady Inskip made the motion of needles working together with her fingers. 'I used to hear it in my dreams. Click, click, click! Night and day, she knitted on. Sometimes I imagined it was bones rattling. Little sharp babies' bones –' She broke off, her eyes and mouth wide, her lipstick smudged on to her chin. One of her combs had fallen out and a hank of hair hung over her ear.

'Do come out,' I said coaxingly. 'Look!' I pointed to the boats. 'Giles and Bowser are rescuing the sheep. You needn't worry, honestly. Please come out before you catch cold.' She shrank away from me and took a step further into the lake. I became really alarmed that she was going to throw herself in. It was like trying to rescue a butterfly. There was the risk of knocking the precious dust from its wings but if you did nothing it might destroy itself by beating against the pane. 'Lady Inskip! You're frightening me.'

I saw that this had its effect. She took hold of my hand, though with obvious reluctance. Slowly she pulled her feet through the mud until she stood on the grass beside me. I had never seen anyone look so defeated. 'Better come back to the house,' I urged, putting my arm through hers. 'You're shivering.'

Lady Inskip looked down at the weed-bedraggled skirt that clung to her legs. 'How dirty I am. Shall I wash my robe and make it "white in the blood of the Lamb"? Some things can never be washed clean, can they? It isn't enough to break your heart with remorse.'

'There you are, madam!' Miss Tinker stood behind us, breathing quickly, her pasty features shining with the effort of her run. 'You've led me quite a dance. It was cunning to tell me you were going to have a bath. If there's one thing I can't abide it's cunning. We are a sly thing!'

Lady Inskip looked alarmed. 'I saw Viola from my window. I wanted to talk to her. We had a nice little talk about lambs, didn't we?'

'Oh, yes.' I could see that Lady Inskip was afraid of Miss Tinker. 'It was a very interesting conversation.'

Miss Tinker looked disbelieving. 'I think we'll have to brush our hair a hundred times. We're looking quite untidy.'

'Oh, no, please.' Lady Inskip put her hands to her head. 'My poor hair. You know how it comes out on the bristles. My hair was lovely once,' she said to me. 'Now it's wearing a little thin.' She lowered her voice to a whisper. 'Tinker brushes it too hard. It hurts dreadfully.'

'No whispering, please, my lady. Come along.' Miss Tinker held out her stubby hand.

'Goodbye. I have enjoyed our talk. It was so good of you to come.' Lady Inskip inclined her head graciously in my direction before being marched off by Miss Tinker. I remembered how in *Great Expectations* Pip watches Magwitch being led away to the hulks and the torches of the soldiers being thrown hissing into the water as if it was all over with him. I felt very sorry indeed.

I walked round to the upper lake. My heart sank to see a marshland of mud smothered with flattened weeds. This side of the bridge the lake had shrunk to a pond. There were puddles of water here and there in the slime, and I saw something wriggling in the one nearest the bank. It was a stranded fish.

'Hello, Viola.' Nicky was beside me. His expression was chagrined. 'I got chucked out of the boat as soon as Jeremy came. They said I wasn't strong enough. I *could* have lifted a sheep. Of course I can't row because they've never let me learn.'

'Oh, Nicky, never mind! Look at that fish! It's drowning in mud! What shall we do? We'll only sink in if we try to reach it.'

'Wait here,' said Nicky. 'I know exactly what to do.'

He ran off towards the house. I stood looking at the poor fish and, when I couldn't bear to watch its struggles any longer, at the brilliant vapour-streaked sky. Nicky came back with two buckets. 'Fill these with water. I'm going to get a couple of planks.'

By the time I'd filled the buckets from the lower lake and carried them back Nicky was laying a plank over the surface of the mud. Then he picked up the other one and made his way along the first. It sank down a little but held his weight. I handed him a bucket of water. He put down the second plank, stepped on to it and picked up the first plank. He continued in this way until he had reached the puddle with the fish in it. I saw a flash of silver and then the fish was safely in the bucket.

'Brilliant!' I said, as Nicky worked his way slowly back.

Tipping the fish into the lake and watching it swim away, filling its gills with clean water, was extremely satisfying. I filled the bucket again and went back to Nicky. He was making his way to shore. This time he had two large fishes and a tiddler. We worked without stopping for at least an hour until we could find no more puddles with fish in. I think we both felt very much better to have been able to do something useful.

'Ought I to tell my father that it was me, do you think?' asked Nicky, streaking yet another smear of mud across his face with the back of his hand as we stood surveying the soggy desolation we had wrought.

'I'm certain that you *ought* but don't let's. I'm much more to blame than you because I'm older and ought to have known. We'll put a clause in the constitution of the Society for Breaking Rules that we never own up.'

Nicky looked relieved. 'I suppose it does take the daring out of breaking rules if you're going to confess immediately and take the punishment. It's rather feeble.'

'Utterly feeble,' I agreed.

We walked up to the house together. There were voices coming from the drawing room. Lalla was standing by the french windows with a young man. He was of medium height and slight build, with fairish curly hair. He grinned widely as soon as he saw us and held out his arms. 'Nicky! Been taking a mudbath? You're a sight for sore eyes and no mistake.'

Nicky launched himself into his embrace. 'Hamish! I thought you weren't coming until after lunch!'

'I got away early. I've just bought a new car and I couldn't wait to give her her first good run. Got here from London in just under three hours. Flew like the proverbial bird!'

'What sort is it?'

'A Jaguar XJS. Want to try it after lunch? It's automatic so you could easily manage it up and down the drive.'

'You'll let me drive it?' Nicky's face was irradiated by happiness.

'Certainly. Now, listen. I've got a brilliant joke I've been saving to tell you. A smart, snooty woman was walking round an art gallery when she stopped by one particular exhibit. "I suppose this picture of a hideous warty witch is what you call Modern Art," she said pompously. "No, madam," replied the assistant. "It's what we call a mirror." '

I couldn't help laughing myself, not so much at the joke as at Nicky's helpless mirth. As soon as he stopped laughing he broke out again until tears were mingled with the dirt on his cheeks. No teller of jokes could have had a more gratifying audience.

'Hello, I'm Hamish Montgomerie. You must be Viola. How do you do?'

I looked into a pair of amused blue eyes. Hamish was not handsome, not even good-looking. His hair was unfashionably crinkly, his mouth was too large, his nose too short, his skin rather pink. Nevertheless I was at once enchanted by him.

CHAPTER 14

'Sandwiches fit for a king, Viola! I hate meanness with butter.'

Hamish was being kind beyond the call of duty or the bounds of truth. They were very ordinary sandwiches made with the bits of chicken I had scraped off the bones from yesterday's dinner. The butter was cold and stuck to the bread in lumps. Hamish had opened a bottle of champagne – he had brought a case from London – which made them taste much nicer.

'What's this herb? It's got a very odd, bitter taste,' asked Giles, frowning, as he peeled apart his two slices of bread.

'I found it by the back door. I thought it was chives. Isn't it what you put in the omelettes?'

Giles examined a leaf closely. 'It's certainly not chives. It's that stuff bees like – thrift, isn't it called? It grows on chalk cliffs.'

'Chicken and thrift sandwiches! Original!' Hamish continued to eat his, with every indication of enjoyment, though the others picked out the green bits. 'Sounds like a proverb. "It's too late to spare when the bottom is bare." Do they mean the bottom of the money jar or a trouserless bottom, do you think?'

Nicky was rendered incapable of eating by his enjoyment of this remark.

'Clap the boy on the back, my angel,' said Hamish to Lalla. 'I want him sobered up for my next joke. Who shouted, "Knickers," at the big bad wolf?'

'Give up,' Nicky gasped in agony.

'Little Rude Riding Hood. Grab that boy's lemonade, somebody, or he'll have it over.'

'For heaven's sake, Hamish! You seem to have an inexhaustible supply of awful jokes.' Lalla put her elbows on the kitchen table where we were eating our sandwiches. 'Let's go out somewhere. Shall we ride this afternoon, Giles? We could go over to Packer's Mill.'

Giles was leaning against the rail of the range, dropping pieces of thrift into its round hole. 'No. I want to look at the library. It's time I did some actual work. I had a quick look yesterday and noticed some interesting books.'

'You don't really want to look at deadly dull books on an afternoon like this. Stop sulking and come out with me. I must have a good gallop. Hamish won't mind spending the afternoon with Viola. At least she thinks his jokes are funny, which is more than I do.'

'I'm not sulking.' Giles spoke quietly but something in his voice made us all stop and look at him. 'I'd rather spend the afternoon in the library.'

'How very disobliging you are! All right, then, I'll go on my own. I shall go mad sitting about in this dreary place. But it won't be so much fun. I think it's very childish of you not to do what you really want to, just because you're – put out.' Lalla laughed but I saw that she was cross. 'I know a man in a huff when I see one.'

'Well, then, if that's the case, you would be wiser to leave him alone.' Giles smiled but it was obvious that he was angry.

Hamish looked at each of them in turn as they glared at each other. Then he said, 'I'll ride with you, Lalla, if you want. But don't be a pain about it or I might change my mind. Nicky, what happens if you slip on the ice? Give up? Your bottom gets thaw.'

I was surprised to see Lalla handed out the same treatment as she gave others. Except that Hamish softened the reproof with a smile.

Jeremy came in then, having been called away to the telephone. 'You buggers! You've eaten all my sandwiches! Not only do I have to put up with being called a murderer by some bloody woman who says Bowser's poisoned her cat but I don't get anything to eat either.'

'I'll make you some more,' I said, tackling the bones.

'I've got to call on her this afternoon and get her to see reason. She says she'll go to the police. How sick I am of sheep and cats and lakes and the country! I wish I had your job, Hamish, being flown about the place – London, Paris, New York. Plenty of nice dry tarmac and concrete.'

'You'd have to get up a bit earlier if you worked for Steiners Incorporated,' said Hamish mildly. 'And you might not like being sent to places you don't particularly want to go to, to talk to people you don't very much like, and having to read reams of papers that aren't specially interesting. Often I want to chuck it all in. But I don't have any other talents.'

'Giles is the only one of us doing what he really wants,' I said. 'But, then, he's brilliantly clever and amazingly well-read.'

I was embarrassed after I said this. It was the sort of thing Aunt Pussy did, only much more expertly, when she saw someone being left out of things. Once when I was standing by myself, too shy to join the party, she had beckoned me over and said, 'I must tell you that my niece Viola has the most perfect arches.' Everyone had stared down in surprise at my feet while my aunt ran on in her inimitable way, 'Minovska says that she has the conformation to make a classical ballet dancer. But it is an *impossibly* hard life. Margot Fonteyn's feet aren't all they should be, you know.

Too soft. Freddie Ashton used to refer to them as "Margot's pats of butter".' Everyone had laughed and it was enough to give me borrowed glamour and to make me feel included in the group. My praise of Giles was a clumsy attempt at the same thing but it succeeded only in drawing attention to his state of alienation from the rest of us.

'Cultivated he may be but I bet Giles hasn't read *The Insomniac* by Eliza Wake,' said Hamish solemnly.

Nicky burst into an explosion of laughter and we all groaned while Lalla threw the drying-up cloth at Hamish's head and the awkward moment was over.

Libraries are absolutely my favourite rooms. I think there is nothing more completely beautiful and more beautifully complete than walls lined with well-arranged books. Not only do I like the look of them but I love the smell of leather and paper.

'What are you doing?' asked Giles rather irritably, as I stood in the library at Inskip, holding a volume of Clarendon's *History of the Rebellion* up to my face. He hadn't wanted me to help him – I knew that – but one of Mrs Shilling's often-repeated maxims was that 'Two in distress make sorrow less'. On this principle I had decided to risk being in the way to offer a little silent sympathy. I did not hope to be made a confidante. 'Surely you can't be as short-sighted as that.'

'I'm smelling it. It smells of old canvas deck-chairs with a touch of woodsmoke and something growing – heather, perhaps, or hawthorn.'

Giles took the book from me and sniffed it. 'It smells of damp.' He closed the book and examined its binding. 'This is criminal! Look at the title label. It's peeling off. And the stitching's falling apart. This was printed in seventeen three. It's survived all these years only to be left to rot now.' He handed me the book and put his hand into the place from where I had taken it. 'The walls are weeping.' He pulled out another volume and gave it to me to hold. It slipped from my hand and fell with a bang. 'Viola! You idiot!'

'I'm terribly sorry!' I knelt down and picked up the book. The cover dangled by a thread. 'Oh, what a pity! I'll take it home with me and get Daniel to mend it. He does the most beautiful book-binding. I feel terribly guilty.'

'So you should. Who's Daniel?'

'My landlord. I've told you about him. He knows all about antiquarian books.'

'Well . . . if you're sure he'll make a proper job of it.'

'Honestly he will. I have absolute faith in him. He's the most exacting, meticulous person I've ever met. His entire life is spent in pursuit of the refinement of beauty. That's how he described it to me once. I think that's a wonderful thing to aspire to.'

'He sounds interesting.'

I was pleased that Giles had dropped the scolding tone from his voice. 'Isn't this a wonderful room?' I looked at the plasterwork on the ceiling and the elaborate bookcases. The library was part of the Victorian wing. 'Look at those winged angels! They're perfectly lovely.'

'I've seen something like them before. Westminster Hall, I think. And those crocketed pinnacles with quatrefoils between – it's all late Gothic. Wonderful workmanship, though not my taste. But it would be impossible to raise enough money to preserve it. It would need more than SCAB's entire resources. Look at this blown plaster.' He rapped with his knuckles on a pilaster between the bookcases. A chunk fell out leaving a hole. 'Oh dear. We seem to be wreaking havoc between us.' He bent down to pick up the pieces.

'I won't tell if you won't.'

Giles looked at me, frowning, then began to laugh. He has a very good laugh. Deep and slow and rather sexy. Now I had met Hamish I understood why Lalla had become engaged to him. Hamish was a perfect darling. But Giles was undeniably more handsome, with his long, lean face and dark hair and serious, scrutinising grey eyes. No wonder Lalla was reluctant to give him up. I was pretty sure that she would have to, though. Pierce would have delighted in making love to a girl who was engaged to someone else. All the jam without the doughnut, he would have said. But I thought Giles was different.

'What are you staring at?' he asked. 'Have I got ink on my nose?'

'Oh . . . no! I was just thinking . . . What a pity the house is so run down.' I was ashamed of the paltriness of my powers of invention.

'Mm. I see. But *you* have.'

Giles gave me his handkerchief and I stood on tiptoe before the empty grate to see myself in the looking-glass. The end of my nose was smudged in a T-shape like a cat's. It took a lot of spit and rubbing to get it clean. I suspected that the centre of my face was now uniformly grey but the library was so gloomy that it hardly mattered. A bright row of capering motes found its way between curtains of darkest crimson, lending a superficial lustre to the mulberry brocade of the chairs and igniting with fiery colours a tiger-skin stretched before the fireplace. I bent to stroke the noble head. Its poor ears were fraying badly and its glass eyes were crossed in a ferocious squint. I rolled them in their sockets until they were straight, imagining the magnificent creature burning with vigour and simple purpose, that of staying alive, before some fatuous red-faced man smelling of whisky and cigars shot it in the name of fun.

'My God! Look at this!' Giles was standing on a pair of library steps, examining the flyleaf of a book. 'This is the seventeen twenty-eight edition of *The Dunciad*. And it's signed by Pope to John Gay. "Brave fellow member of the Scriblerus Club and *Socius perambulis*". That means partner of my wanderings. "*Forsan et haec olim meminisse juvabit*." A quotation from Virgil. It means, roughly translated, "One day it will be useful to remember all this." This is extraordinary! Pope was an eighteenth-century writer –'

'Oh, I know about Pope. He's Daniel's favourite poet.

> ' "A wit's a feather and a chief's a rod
> An honest man's the noblest work of God." '

It was worth descending to blatant showing off to see the expression of surprise on Giles's face. I suppose he thought my reading was confined to dipping into *Harper's Bazaar*, skipping over the more abstruse articles on the Ten Top Schools to get to the pieces called Silky Summer Legs and the New Hair.

'Well. Mm. Good. Here is *The Essay on Man*.' Giles pulled out another book. He whistled. 'This is marvellous! Signed by Pope to Bolingbroke. He was a philosopher and a great friend of Pope.' Giles took out another volume from the shelf. 'Look at this! Translations from Horace – with Colley Cibber's name in it. You know, this collection's worth a lot of money. Obviously Thomas Victor Inskip, whose bookplate is in every one of these, was a considerable bibliophile. I wonder . . .' He stopped to think for a moment. 'We'd better try to catalogue this. Can you find some paper and something to write with?'

We worked hard for three hours, Giles dictating while I wrote. It was cold in the library but we were carried along by a feeling of excitement as Giles made more and more discoveries.

'Look here, first editions of every novel by George Eliot. *Adam Bede*, signed by the author to Thomas Inskip.'

'Oh, let me see!' I abandoned my role of amanuensis to go over and look. 'It's one of my favourite books! Oh, look! A heavenly drawing of Hetty Sorrel and Arthur Donnithorne in the dairy at Hall Farm. "Will you promise me your hand for two dances, Miss Hetty?" The faithless brute! Poor Hetty. All those dreams she has of wearing pink dresses and riding in a carriage. It's so sad when Arthur won't marry her. He was such a weak and contemptible man. He only thought of how pretty she was.'

'I suppose all men are weak and contemptible when it comes to pretty women.' Giles smiled as he said this but didn't look happy.

'I've loved this afternoon,' I said, turning to pick up my pen again. 'It's been thrilling.'

Giles didn't answer. His thoughts were clearly elsewhere.

*

At half past six I went into the kitchen. Giles said he would come and help me as soon as he had made some telephone calls to people he knew in the antiquarian book world. I took from the fridge a leg of lamb, put it on the table and stared at it, hoping for inspiration. Fluffy jumped on to the table and joined my communing with the Spirit of Domestic Science. It was a pity that when studying this subject at school we only ever made things like miniature *éclairs* and *duchesses pralinées*. I remembered that R.D. had been very fond of boiled mutton and caper sauce. I looked around for a large saucepan. Presumably one boiled it for a while and that was all there was to it. But the caper sauce might be trickier.

'Are you madly busy?' I asked Mrs Fordyce, when she answered the telephone. 'Only I'm terrified of making a muff of it.'

'Not busy at all.' I heard a gulp and then a clink, which sounded like a glass being put down. 'In fact, it's a huge relief to hear a human voice. I can't play tennis at the moment because I've twisted my knee so all my plans for having an event every day are entirely thrown out.'

'Gosh, that sounds very efficient. I never plan anything.'

'Of course not. Nor did I at your age. Things – wonderful things – just materialised. I don't suppose they *were* wonderful – they just seemed that way because everything was new and an adventure. Now things are either familiar or tedious. Generally both. And,' there was the sound of another glug, 'these days I'm lonely. Isn't it pathetic? When I remember the days of my youth, and being married to Giles's father, rushing through the chores to get changed to have lunch in town with a girlfriend, sometimes going to a matinée or shopping at Harrods, back on the four o'clock to pick up Giles from school, doing the flowers, cooking supper and getting the gins and tons ready for Geoffrey. Friends in for drinks, dinner parties, dances at the tennis club. Well, it sounds awfully dull in recital but I was busy then. Never stopped to think. That's the trouble, I suppose. What Giles would call an unfurnished mind. He despises me.'

I heard a note of incipient grief in her voice and I suspected that whatever she was drinking was not the first shot of the evening. 'I don't believe he does for a moment.'

'Oh, yes, he does. And he's quite right. Let me tell you of what my life consists. Monday, meals on wheels.'

'That must save a lot of time and trouble.'

'No, dear, *I* take them round, to the sick and needy in Worthing.'

'Sorry.'

'Tuesday, I visit the hospital, push the library trolley round the wards. Have tea with Geoffrey's uncle who's ninety, deaf as a post and as bad-tempered as a wounded boar.'

'Oh dear.'

'Wednesdays I play bridge all afternoon, a slice of quiche afterwards, dry or rubbery, depending on whose house it is, and brandy and soda, a lot or a little, ditto. Wednesdays are the best day of the week. Thursday, I go to the cinema in Brighton with Pamela Butterworth who was at school with me and mentally has never left. Sorry, that was catty. It's just been a rotten day.'

'Think nothing of it.'

'Fridays, I play tennis. I'm quite good for my age. I've won the tournament twice.'

'I can only serve underarm,' I said humbly.

There was the sound of a match being struck and then some muttered cursing. 'Burned a hole in my bloody cardigan. Sorry, shouldn't swear.'

'I like swearing. It's unfortunate that there are so few swear-words, though. They lose their savour quite quickly.'

Mrs Fordyce laughed. 'You're making me feel better. Now tell me, dear, what was it you rang for?'

'Oh, but you haven't told me about Saturday and Sunday.' I was building up an interesting picture of Mrs Fordyce's life and I wanted to be able to imagine it all.

'Well, if you really want to know – it's sweet of you to be interested – on Saturdays I have my hair done and my nails manicured and I go ballroom dancing. It's the most unglamorous venue, the British Legion Regimental Headquarters, and the others are perms and Crimplene to a man but I love the old steps. When I'm whirling around in the arms of a paunchy retired bank manager I shut my eyes and pretend it's Geoffrey, in uniform. Geoffrey danced like an angel.'

I longed to know more of all this. But before I could formulate a tactful question Mrs Fordyce went on, 'Sundays are spent first of all at Matins and then Beryl and Don come to lunch. Beryl hates the world. She makes me think quite kindly of it. Don is vicar of St Mark's where I worship. He's convinced that all his parishioners are in love with him, despite the fact that he looks exactly like whichever the fat one was in Laurel and Hardy. But I have them because I can't bear to spend Sunday entirely on my own.'

'It all sounds very interesting to me.'

'It's because you're young. If *only* I could recapture the curiosity of my youth. But I'm being silly and self-pitying. It's because I've had too much to drink. Promise me you won't tell Giles?'

'Cross my heart and hope to die.'

'You're a good girl. Now, what was it you wanted to know?'

I explained about the caper sauce.

'Ooh, sounds a bit risky to me. You'd probably have to boil the lamb for at least two hours. What time's dinner?'

'Eight, I suppose, though everyone seems to be out.'

'You'll never have time to do it. Bung it in a hot oven to roast, with mint sauce. Much simpler.'

'How do I make the mint sauce?'

'Heavens, dear, should you have quite so much responsibility? It does seem like throwing you in at the deep end.'

I wrote down everything Mrs Fordyce told me. 'Thank you so much, Mrs Fordyce,' I said when she'd finished. 'You've been more than kind.'

'Call me Mab. Everyone does. I can't bear Mabel – so stodgy. I've enjoyed our chat. I really must get another dog. But somehow since Dodo, our spaniel, died, just after Christmas, I haven't had the heart. She was such a chum. I know I've got to pull myself together. Giles gave me quite a lecture the last time he came to see me. Oh, I've kept myself and the house up to scratch. And the garden. Not a weed to be seen. But what's the point of it all? I ask myself. If only there were grandchildren to come and stay. Tell me, dear,' her voice became louder and breathier as though she was clutching the receiver more tightly to her, 'tell me honestly, do you think Giles is . . . queer?'

'Giles? Good heavens, no!'

'Really not? Only I know it's an odd thing to ask but, you see, he never brings girls home. And he's always been interested in things that other men aren't interested in. Even when he was a little boy he made me make blue silk curtains to hang round his bed and he wouldn't play football with the other boys. He used to shut himself in his room – it was stuffed with bits of china he'd saved up for from local junk shops – and read books and play gramophone records. Nothing but Mozart. Geoffrey used to say it was about as cheerful as living with a consumptive maiden aunt. Geoffrey wanted him to play golf but he wouldn't. I think Geoffrey was secretly ashamed of Giles though he did get that scholarship to Oxford. He thought Giles was what Geoffrey called a pansy. He never said so, of course, but I know that's what he was afraid of.'

'I can assure you that Giles isn't homosexual. He's just got a very well-developed taste and a feeling for beautiful things. Which includes women.'

'That's a great comfort, dear, it really is. Not that I don't like queers – they can't help it, can they, poor things? – but it's the thought of no grandchildren that gets me down.' A pause. 'You sound very certain. I suppose you and Giles aren't . . .'

'Oh, no. We're just friends.' This was an exaggeration but justifiable in the circumstances, I thought. 'I've seen him with other women, though, and one knows these things.'

'Oh. Pity. We could have got along nicely, dear, couldn't we? Never mind. I must stop talking and let you get on. Good luck, dear. Bye-bye.'

I put down the receiver and turned to see Fluffy tunnelling

into the lamb with her sharp teeth. I cut out the nibbled bits and gave them to her. I peeled potatoes and put them into a pan with dripping and salt as Mab had instructed me to do. I burned my wrist quite painfully on the blisteringly hot oven shelf. Above them I put the leg of lamb. This all seemed surprisingly straightforward. I started to peel onions for the onion sauce, which had been Mab's suggestion in place of mint sauce as, after the thrift episode, I had lost confidence in my ability to identify leaves. The kitchen was pleasantly warm and looked romantic with light from the giant central gasolier gleaming dimly in the surfaces of tarnished copper pans. Fluffy curled up to sleep in the armchair. I hummed 'Love Locked Out' to myself, through my tears – at least, the small bit of it I knew.

Half an hour later, when Susan arrived, my mood was less sanguine.

'Gosh, what are those?' she asked, peering into the pan I was stirring. 'Treacle? What a beastly smell.'

'I forgot them. They're onions. I was trying to make a sauce with them.'

Susan took the pan from beneath my poised spoon and took it into the scullery. There was the sound of violent hissing. 'You'd better marry a rich man, Viola.' She came back into the kitchen and tied a drying-up cloth round her waist. 'You've as much chance of becoming a good cook as I have of becoming the face of Estée Lauder.'

I looked at her as she stooped over the kitchen table, in a pea-green jersey pinafore over a grey shirt, her hair pulled tightly back from her forehead, which was corrugated with impatience as she cut the black bits out of the carrots I had already peeled. Frankly I thought she was putting my chances too low. At least, I vowed to myself then and there, I was going to make the attempt to learn.

It was ten to eight when Lalla strolled into the kitchen.

'Hello, you two. We've had the most marvellous time. We rode all the way to Haversage where some friends of Hamish live. The most fabulous house. Queen Anne, quite small and cosy and terribly pretty. They insisted we stayed for tea and then we rode back through the dusk. It was fun!

You're looking awfully cross, Susan. Have you got a headache or something?'

By half past eight Sir James was working his way through lamb and mint sauce, having had two plates of Susan's celery soup and there was still no sign of three of our number. Lady Inskip suggested telephoning the police but Francis was adamant. 'We know Nicky's with Jeremy. Don't fuss, Millie. Of course the boy will be all right. I expect the car's broken down. What do you say to running through the last act of *Iolanthe* after dinner?'

We had begun our rhubarb and custard when Giles, Jeremy and Nicky came into the dining room.

'What a day!' said Jeremy, bending to kiss his mother. 'Sorry we're late, Mumsie. A little contretemps with Dogberry. It took a while for him to unravel the arcane mysteries of everyday life as lived by swells. He couldn't understand why a hopeful scion of broad acres should be trying to knock the teeth out of a feckless *Zigeuner*.'

'What the deuce are you talking about?' As he spoke a little dribble of custard ran down Sir James's chin. 'You keep us all waiting and then you come in gabbling like a –' he caught his wife's anxious eye '– silly boy,' he finished lamely.

'I fancy Jeremy has had a run-in with the police,' said Francis.

'Then why not say so?' Sir James's eyes bulged with temper. 'Who is this Dogberry and what has he to do with it?'

'A comic character in Shakespeare,' explained Francis, in the patronising tone of the civilised man addressing the savage, 'who has become synonymous with the forces of law and order –'

'Shakespeare!' Sir James's teeth snapped shut and he said not another word that evening. Evidently some depth had been plumbed.

'I happened to meet a member of the wandering tribes,' Jeremy was so ebullient that I was certain he had been drinking, 'one Zed by name, in Little Whiddon and I put it to him that in tampering with our sluices he had committed an unneighbourly and illegal act. He punched me in the face. So, not to be outdone I hit him back and Dogberry, in the guise of P. C. Bilker, came up and arrested me on the spot for brawling in a public place. I was allowed one telephone call. Giles answered it. I must say he acted with exemplary speed, hurtled down to the cop shop in the Baby Austin and handed Plod a largish sum of money to let me go. So I am now out on bail. It's rather exciting!' Jeremy felt his face gingerly. 'But I'm afraid my beauty is quite spoiled. The blighter's given me a black eye.'

CHAPTER 15

'Race you to the top of the hill!' shouted Nicky.
'Unfair,' panted Hamish, who was carrying the basket with the wine and the lemonade. But he made a gallant attempt to catch up Nicky, who was encumbered only by tomatoes and watercress. Jeremy refused to run, dawdling behind the rest of us with a bag containing sausages, lamb chops and a small leg of ham. I had one carrier-bag full of fruit and chocolate and another of paper plates and cups. Lalla had the French bread sticks which, she complained, though light were inconveniently shaped for carting about the backwoods of England.

It had been my idea to have a picnic lunch but the smooth execution of the plan was entirely due to Hamish. He had insisted on driving me into Little Whiddon, helping me to choose what we were going to eat and, most importantly, paying for it. He was a very good person to do things with, being admirably decisive about how much we needed and what we could manage to carry, and between us we made the very best of what Little Whiddon had to offer. Lalla had refused to help us because she had wanted to spend the day alone with Hamish and was sulking in consequence.

'It was an inspired suggestion,' said Hamish, as we swooped up and down the hills back to Inskip Park in

Hamish's wonderful car. 'I must admit I felt pretty furious with my prospective father-in-law this morning. He *is* an ass.'

Sir James had evidently risen in a worse humour than usual. He had picked on Nicky the moment the child came into the dining room, asking him why he wasn't in next term's cricket eleven. When Nicky had replied, quite reasonably, that it was because he was hopeless at cricket, a ridiculous row had ensued, which had ended in a frightening asthma attack.

'It was awful not knowing what we ought to be doing to help. His poor little white face and that horrible wheezing! I was terrified he was going to die.'

'He's such a bright, terrific kid. I wish Lalla – Anyway, he cheered up no end at your suggestion of a picnic lunch.'

'Well, it was you deciding to come with us that made him so happy. You're his hero. And it's going to be a much more glamorous affair than the Marmite sandwiches I was thinking of.'

'When Lalla and I are married I want to do something about Nicky. The best thing would be to get him into a decent school but at the moment I can't see how.'

I thought uneasily of Lalla's flight to Bucket's Wood the day before. 'They all need help, really,' I said, and then I felt myself blushing. Often I think things and then find to my horror that I've actually said them. I thought Hamish was going to repeat my hedge trick for he turned to look at me so suddenly when I said that that he almost missed the bend.

'Viola, some time – not now because we're nearly there but some time soon – I want you to tell me just why you said that.' Hamish spoke in a spirit of entreaty, entirely without anger, but my immediate resolve was that I would avoid such a discussion at all costs. I knew my tact wasn't up to it.

'Surely this is far enough,' grumbled Jeremy, when we reached the brow of the hill. 'How the poor pig carted round four of these wretched hams all its life I can't think. Just carrying one has nearly given me a hernia.'

The left side of Jeremy's face was a study in purple. One

eye was nearly closed and there was a cut just below his eyebrow. I had confessed everything to him the night before as we lay in unbuttoned ease in each other's arms.

'You and Nicky opened the sluice? You absolute idiots, you complete lunatics – no word occurs to me that's bad enough. And to think I went up to that great ox and accused him. No wonder he socked me one. Well, I'll be buggered!' And then, much to my relief, he began to laugh and the more I said how sorry I was, the more he laughed. 'It doesn't matter,' he said, when he could speak. 'I've never hit anyone before. It was one of those challenges that I've wondered all my life if I could meet and now I know that I can I feel quite bucked. Like soldiers feel when sent to the front. Will they conduct themselves with superlative courage and save the regiment or will they cry for Nanny and wet themselves? Now I know that when I'm hit, I hit back. It's good to find the reflexes are in tip-top order.'

I thought it was extremely tolerant of Jeremy to take this view. He said he had no intention of telling his father as the less Sir James knew the less likely he was to go about wantonly cutting up other people's peace. We walked past the lake on our way up to the top of the hill. Jeremy had hired a pump which was slowly filling up the top lake and the flood was inching back to reveal drowned, drabbled turf.

Hamish and Nicky collected a pile of large stones, an easy task in this rocky landscape, and laid them in a circle, while Jeremy and I found sticks. This was harder as there were few trees on the promontory. I saw a promising-looking copse just below the brow of the hill on the other side and went to investigate. It was more extensive than I had at first thought. Quite a wood, in fact. I spotted a good stout branch lying beneath the trees and began to drag it out into the open. Looking up I noticed, through a gap in the trees, the outline of a small building. I thought at first it was a large shepherd's hut or a barn but then I saw that it was marvellously pretty with handsome columns all round and a plaster frieze below a conical roof. I dropped my branch and went to have a look.

Double gates in the iron railings which surrounded the building were padlocked. I could have climbed the railings fairly easily but I could see that the doors to the building – a noble pair sheeted with lead – were padlocked too. Inside the railings, standing at angles in the long grass, were lots of gravestones. I read some of the inscriptions. 'BOSUN. Valiant and Faithful Friend. 1856–1870.' 'Miss Mossop. Beloved Feline Companion for Fifteen Years of Hermione Inskip.' 'Fred the Rat. Departed this Life 1905.' There was a large headstone engraved with the words 'Here lies Wellington. A brave hunter who never refused a fence.' Followed by an illegible date. I was tremendously touched by this evidence of sentiment on the part of past Inskips.

I dragged my branch back to the picnic site. Jeremy had already given up wood-gathering and was lying with his head propped on his hand, sipping a glass of Riesling and watching Hamish's attempts to get the fire going. The wind made it difficult. Hamish and I had decided to buy the ham for just this emergency but we both felt that it would be a pity not to have a proper camp-fire. Eventually Nicky crouched down and spread his mac like wings to protect the tiny flame and by dint of feeding it sticks as thin as straws we managed to get it going. After that Hamish piled on the branches and soon the fire was crackling and sending up clouds of smoke. Minutes later sausages and chops were sizzling on the end of sticks and dripping fat into the flames. Of course the outsides were burned black by the time the insides were cooked but we were so hungry by then that we would have eaten anything.

'I do think you might have remembered knives and forks,' grumbled Lalla, bathing her fingers in Riesling.

We had cut up the ham with Nicky's penknife.

'Nonsense. That would have been sissy. Here, have my handkerchief.' Hamish handed her an immaculate silk one.

This made me think of Giles. He had refused to join the picnic on the grounds that he had a great deal to do in the library. I knew that he was excited about the books we had found but I suspected also that he was avoiding being with

Lalla and Hamish. I was pretty certain Hamish had guessed that Giles was in love with Lalla. Hamish was careful now, in public anyway, to treat Lalla in an offhand manner that was strictly brotherly.

'I've got tomato pips all over my shirt,' complained Lalla, 'and chop fat in my hair. I'm going to find a stream to wash in.'

I sensed there was some element of challenge in this but Hamish only smiled and said, 'Don't fall in.'

Lalla set off over the hill in the direction of my newly discovered wood.

'Jeremy, tell me about that building with the animal graveyard.' He was lying on his back shielding his eyes from the sun. He grunted, pretending to be sleepy, so I tickled his ear with a grass stalk. He seized my hand and covered my arm with kisses. I knew this was only the sort of play that we indulged in on our own and that it didn't mean anything but Hamish and Nicky looked slightly uncomfortable.

'That's where Nicky and I are destined to wait for the last trump,' answered Jeremy. 'There's a large pit underneath it filled with the mouldering corpses of our relations.'

'Fancy getting a dead horse up that hill. It doesn't seem the most convenient of burial grounds. Can we get in? It's padlocked.'

'Oh, yes. I've often been inside. I'll show you.'

'Now?'

'No, my darling. Jeremy wants a snooze. Come and lie next to me. I need you, beloved bedmate, companion of my dreams, to soothe me to sleep.'

But I wouldn't. Jeremy wanted the others to think that we were lovers to satisfy some whim of his own but Aunt Pussy's rule was that public displays of affection are always discourteous and excluding. So instead I ate an apple and listened to Nicky and Hamish, who were talking about famous last words. Nicky recited the dying words of Hannibal, which he had learned in Latin last term: 'Let us now relieve the Romans of their fears by the death of a feeble old man.' I was impressed by this serene cynicism. Hamish remembered the last words of Newton, something about being like a boy playing on the seashore, finding a smoother pebble or a prettier shell than ordinary, while the great ocean of truth lay undiscovered before him. I thought it was very clever to think of saying all that, so eloquently, while in the throes of death. I have always liked the words of Lady Mary Wortley Montagu who apparently said, with admirable tranquillity, 'It has all been very interesting.'

While Hamish and Nicky continued to talk I looked down towards the house, which had shrunk to the size of a sardine tin. The wind blew the long grass into waves of running shadows. The sky was a thousand shades of rolling, dissolving blue. All nature was animated by stiff breezes and birds planed above our heads. I had that feeling that comes only occasionally, of intense happiness coupled with the consciousness of being so. I saw a tiny figure walking away from the house towards the lake. It paused for a moment, presumably to examine Nicky's and my depredations, and then resumed a rapid pace towards us. After a minute I recognised Giles.

'My last words will be "Thank God nothing more can be expected from me,"' said Jeremy. 'Is there anything left to drink?'

'Leave something for Giles. He'll be here soon.' I stood up and waved until he saw me and waved back.

'Wonderful!' he said when he reached us, throwing himself down on the grass and accepting a paper cup of wine from Hamish. 'What a view! Anything left to eat?'

'We'd have saved more if we'd known you were coming. There's plenty of ham.' I hunted round and found a tomato and two cold sausages. I was glad to see that Giles looked much more cheerful. 'The bread's in that basket.'

'I decided on the spur of the moment. It seemed too good a day to waste.'

'Can you think of any famous last words?' asked Nicky. 'We've already had Newton, Hannibal and a woman whose name I've forgotten.'

'Lord Palmerston said, "Die, my dear Doctor? That's the last thing I shall do!"'

Nicky thought this extremely funny.

'I wonder what Claud Body's last words were when the tiger ate him,' said Hamish, with deceptive solemnity.

From this it was a short step to silly book titles. Everybody knew *The Cliff-top Tragedy* by Eileen Dover and *A Schoolboy's Troubles* by Ben Dover. Hamish thought of *Jungle Fever* by Amos Quito and I was inspired to produce *The Postscript* by Adeline More, in honour of Aunt Pussy. Giles remembered *The Shattered Windowpane* by Eva Brick. Jeremy's *Springtime* by Teresa Greene got the vote for the best title.

'Let's go and look at the mausoleum,' I said, when we had packed everything back into bags and baskets.

We got over the railings easily enough. Jeremy showed us a small door in the back of the building, hidden in the shadow of a buttress. Inside our eyes slowly grew accustomed to the dimness. There was only one window, which was filled with stained glass so that the light fell in coloured splashes on the central tomb.

'God, what a cheek!' Jeremy laughed, as we saw that someone had spread blankets on the sepulchre. 'Some old tramp's been dossing down in my final resting-place! An empty whisky bottle! And he's left his watch.'

'No, it's mine,' I snatched up Lalla's wrist-watch and fastened it on my arm. 'It must have fallen off just now. I expect it got loose climbing the railings. I've been meaning to do something about the buckle . . .' I was overdoing it and I told myself to shut up. I looked up at the large white tablet on the wall on which were written the ten commandments. 'What do these letters mean? PRSRV Y PRFCT MN VR KP THS PRCPTS TN. Is it Greek?'

'It's English. An instruction to keep the commandments,' said Jeremy. 'Rather late in the day, I should have thought. The key is the letter E.'

'Oh, I see. "Preserve ye perfect men . . ."' The tricky moment was past.

'Under this stone,' Jeremy tapped it with his foot, 'is where the rest of us are put.'

'It's very romantic,' I said, imagining a long procession winding its way up the hill bearing the black-palled coffin, perhaps with a single white rose on it or a regimental sword, 'but rather sad. Let's go. I'm cold.' I had seen a scarf wound up in the tousled blankets, which looked familiar.

'You know,' said Giles, as we stood outside, looking at the animal graves, 'I think this place is the site of a much older building. Look over there where the ground drops away – clearly there's a man-made ditch. See where it does a right-angle? It looks Roman to me . . . something like a signal station perhaps.'

'Could I excavate it?' Nicky was excited.

'Well, I suppose you could. As far as I can remember there's nothing marked on the Ordnance Survey map so it's unscheduled. But you'd have to do it properly so as not to destroy any evidence. You'll have to dig a section through the ditch and make careful drawings of anything you find. It needs patience.'

'I'll be patient. Really I will! Will you show me how?'

We left Giles and Nicky in discussion about sieves, trowels, pegs and string. Hamish said he was going to look for Lalla and plunged off into the trees below the mausoleum. Jeremy and I began to walk back to the house.

'It's lucky Hamish never seems to mind running about after my dear sister,' said Jeremy, as soon as we were out of earshot. 'Ten to one she's taken the other way back to the house and is now speeding into Little Whiddon on some shopping trajectory.'

'I like him so much. Lalla's very lucky. Of course she's lovely and he's lucky too. I'm very fond of her,' I added quickly.

'You're an affectionate thing.' Jeremy put his arm round me. 'Is there anyone you don't like?'

Such a long list at once began to run through my mind that I changed the conversation before I got depressed. 'Hamish is so kind to Nicky, too. It isn't every man who'd bother to be nice to his beloved's little brother.'

'You know, Nicky bothers me,' said Jeremy, with unaccustomed thoughtfulness. 'Do you think he's quite happy? All this asthma . . . I sometimes wonder . . .'

'I think he's extremely *un*happy.'

Jeremy stopped to look at me. His greenish, brown-flecked eyes were, for once, alert and attentive. 'You speak with unusual force, my girl. What's the matter with the kid? He gets plenty to eat and only last week I offered to give him some cricket coaching. Good God, I gave him a new bat last Christmas. He's pretty lucky, *I* think.'

'Nicky isn't like you. He's not athletic. He's a serious, sensitive, intelligent boy. I think he's very clever.'

'Thank you very much.'

'No, really, Jeremy, this is important. I think he's lonely.'

'Lonely? But the house is always awash with people. I can't ever get any peace. Someone's always chivvying me to go and do something.'

'That's not the same thing.'

'Isn't it?' Jeremy walked on head down, brooding. 'I suppose he is a bit of an ugly duckling. Head in a book all the time. Mm.'

'I think somebody ought to take a proper interest in him and arrange something which makes use of his intelligence.'

Jeremy strolled beside me in silence, thinking. 'Aha!' he said, at last. 'I know. I'll organise a treasure hunt. With literary clues. I shall enjoy that.' He seemed thoroughly delighted with the idea.

It wasn't at all what I had meant. But, I reflected, as we strode briskly past the dreadfully noisy pump, Jeremy ablaze with purpose, a treasure hunt would be as good a way as any to spend our last evening at Inskip Park.

'This is the billiard room.' Jeremy waved expansively at a table invisible beneath a holland cover. 'We don't often use it. Francis and I play occasionally.'

'What's that in the corner?'

I pointed to a something shaped like a giant cigar. Jeremy had offered to show me the rest of the house before he went away to write gnomic instructions to assist us in our search for the hidden treasure. We were now in the new wing below the servants' quarters.

'That's a mummy. A three-thousand-year-old corpse lugged all the way back from Egypt by my great-great-uncle. Utterly pointless. You can't see anything but bandages anyway. I'd have been in favour of leaving it where it was. As it is, it makes it damned difficult to get the cues into the rack.'

I touched the case with my finger, imagining it lying with sequestered dignity beneath scorching rocks and sand for century after century until a more barbarous age saw fit to make a trophy of it.

'Come on, Viola. Stop getting sentimental over the decomposing remains of a shrivelled old despot. You can bet he ordered slaves to be buried alive before breakfast every day of the week. I want to show you something that really *is* interesting.'

'A ballroom! Oh, joy!' I looked with anticipation at the sleek wooden floor, shrouded pier glasses and bagged chandeliers. 'We must dance in here!'

'Yes, some time but not now. Anyway, it's perishing. You're the one that's always grumbling about being cold. Now, come and see what's here.'

Jeremy struggled with a pair of large, opulently decorated doors until they yielded to a kick with the sound of splintering wood. 'Bloody things always stick. What do you think?'

'Jeremy! It's wonderful!'

The room was the same size as the ballroom but at one end was a raised platform and a gilded proscenium arch. Crimson curtains edged with gold were drawn across the front of the stage. The profusion of decoration was bewildering. The walls were panelled, painted and gilded in the Pre-Raphaelite style with flowers and birds and four women in flowing dresses, encumbered with various accoutrements of the seasons – baskets of eggs, ears of corn, swirling leaves, fur tippets and so forth. There were two tiny boxes high up on either side of the stage, like large egg-cups, with little spiral staircases to get into them. 'Show me everything,' I said, almost running the length of the auditorium.

There was a short flight of steps to get on to the stage. A door decorated with herons and water-lilies led behind the proscenium arch. It was pitch dark until Jeremy pulled back the curtains. I found myself standing in a wood of flaking, painted trees. On the backcloth was a village straggling up a mountainside with a castle at the top. 'Originally this scenery was for *Comus*. But it does for anything vaguely rural. We did *Jack and the Beanstalk* with it one year. We've also got a seaside set and a village set with lots of flats of houses and windows that open. These are the footlights. You can raise and lower them here like this.' Jeremy pulled a series of levers in the wings and the plank with the lamps on moved up and down. 'So you can have brilliant light or semi-darkness.'

'Can you turn them on? I'd love to see it lit up. It's heavenly!'

'They're gas. I'd have to light each one. Jolly dangerous. That's what all these buckets of sand are for.' He indicated a row of red buckets, hysterically marked 'FIRE!'. 'There's a system for lighting the backs of the flats too so that you can have light shining out of windows – very atmospheric. See those pulleys?'

I peered up into the blackness of the flies. 'Not really.'

'Well, take it from me there are plenty. They're part of a mechanism of tracks and ropes so you can change the scenery very quickly. Must have cost a packet. My great-grandfather married an actress. She was supposed to be a beauty. We had a portrait of her dressed as Cleopatra but my father sold it years ago. She had teeth like a cow-catcher and eyebrows like hairy ginger caterpillars. The theatre was built for her.'

'Do you still put on plays? You really should. It's too good a thing to waste.'

'Haven't done anything for years. No one else is interested. I love doing it but you have to have an audience. There has to be the communication between you and it – a sort of sympathetic energy that makes you take flight. I'm afraid the collective smoulderings of the Stinker, Huddle and Bowser, all sulking like blazes and dying for it to be over, hardly add up to electricity. Besides, there aren't many plays for a cast of one man, one girl and a boy.'

'I hadn't thought of that. What a pity! But couldn't you ask your neighbours to be your audience? You must know lots of people locally.'

'Well, I suppose, yes, but then the play would have to be reasonably good. And we haven't got enough actors.'

'You could have Hamish and Giles and me. I've never done any acting but I'd love to try. And if you didn't need them as audience you could have Huddle and Bowser and Miss Tinker as well. With you and Lalla and Susan that seems almost enough for a crowd scene.'

'I wonder if the locals would come? They're not keen on anything much but keeping down the wildlife population. I'm not sure if a play wouldn't be too cultural.'

'You could choose something light and a bit old-fashioned. What about a revue? Something by Noël Coward.'

'I can barely sing. Can you?'

'I can only manage high notes if I scream.'

'Well,' Jeremy spoke with decision, 'let's not make it a musical.'

'I think most people could understand a play by George Bernard Shaw.'

I was taking R.D. as my yardstick. I remembered that he had laughed a lot through *Mrs Warren's Profession*. The trouble with seeing a comedy with R.D. was that he took a long time to get the jokes and when he did chortle a bit everyone near him felt obliged to laugh like drains, drowning out the next speech. One got a rather patchy notion of the plot.

'Do you know, Viola, my lovely one, I'm beginning to be rather smitten by the idea? You're right. It *is* a waste. You're a tremendously stimulating girl. You wouldn't like to marry me, I don't suppose?'

I laughed and then stopped when I saw that Jeremy wasn't smiling. 'Sorry, I thought you were joking.'

'No. I'm not joking. Though since you came we've done a lot of that, haven't we? I haven't had so much fun for ages.' Jeremy walked up to me and took hold of my hand. His shiny, smooth blond hair flopped a little as he stared at me with unwonted solemnity. I was acutely aware of standing on a stage. I half expected to see rows of upturned faces. 'I haven't ever felt like this about a girl before. You know, I'm dreading you going tomorrow. I don't want to go back to my own bed. I shall be so lonely without you. You don't expect things of me and it's so nice and relaxing. And you're a beautiful girl. Really beautiful. I think if we were married I could – I'm sure I could – consummate the relationship.' He gave a half laugh that touched me infinitely. It sounded so sad. He put his arms round me and looked down into my face. 'Couldn't you learn to love me a little bit, my darling sweet thing?'

'Dear Jeremy. I could love you. Of course I could. I do already. But I'm not sure if it's the right kind of love. For marriage, I mean.'

'What sort of love is that? We'd look after each other and be kind to each other and keep each other warm. It seems to me better than a raging passion that cools to hatred.'

'I expect you're right. I don't know what love I mean. Or how I'll recognise it. How do people know?'

'No idea. It's probably different with each person anyway, isn't it? Are you sure you aren't thinking of something that happens in magazine stories? And if it's romance you want, our relationship *is* romantic. A whirlwind courtship, isn't it called. Love at first sight. Well, I certainly fancied you something rotten the moment I saw you. I expect it's the same thing.'

'I wish I knew! I love you dearly as a friend but I don't know if this is *it*!'

'Let's pretend it is and then perhaps it'll happen.' Jeremy bent his head to kiss me.

I closed my eyes because I didn't want to squint and offered up my lips. The door swung open at the far end and Nicky said, 'I've been looking for you everywhere, Viola. What are you doing? You aren't *kissing*?'

CHAPTER 16

Our departure for London the next day was attended
by expressions of deepest regret on both sides.
Lady Inskip's mild, dreaming eyes were filled with
tears as she clasped me to her bosom. A strand of my hair
became entwined with her diamond brooch.

'We've had such lovely talks, haven't we? And you're
taking Mr Bun with you? I'm so glad. I'm sure he'd be a sad
little man to be left behind.'

For one absurd moment I thought she meant Giles but
realised before making myself look a complete idiot that
she was talking about the rabbit who was stowed in the
fishing-basket at my feet. 'I think his leg's virtually better.
He's really looking quite fat and glossy. Thank you so
much for such a lovely time. You've been angelic to have
us so long.' I kissed Lady Inskip's powdery cheek and she
clung tightly to my hand. I caught Miss Tinker's unfriendly eye as she stared down at me from an upstairs
window. I lifted my hand to wave but she had disappeared.

Lalla embraced me. 'Goodbye, darling Viola. I shall miss
you like anything. It's been heaven to have you.' She turned
to Giles. 'It's been – tremendous fun.' Her expression was
smilingly provocative.

'It certainly has. Thank you,' replied Giles smoothly. She
offered her cheek and he kissed it politely. He smiled back
at her, somewhat wryly, though whether it was himself or
Lalla he was mocking I couldn't guess. He really was good-
looking, I thought then. I wondered what Lalla could be
feeling.

Hamish hugged me warmly. I responded with equal
fervour, then he and Giles shook hands with every appearance of cordiality. Just as I was putting the rabbit into the
back of the Bentley Jeremy came running out of the house.
He was wearing a dressing-gown and from the glimpse I got
as he took me in his arms, nothing else. 'You weren't going
to sneak away without saying goodbye?'

'I didn't want to. But you seemed so fast asleep.' I felt myself begin to blush. 'When I knocked on your door, that is.' Lalla began to laugh. 'I left you a note. With my address.'

' "Don't know why – there's no sun up in the sky – stormy wea-ther," ' sang Jeremy. 'No. I'm too sad to sing. Goodbye, darling, if you must go. But remember what we talked about. You know.' He signalled violently with his eyebrows and I understood him to mean the idea of our marrying. 'As soon as I've found a play you must come back. Remember you promised?'

'I will. Just as soon as I can. Goodbye, Nicky – everyone. It's been wonderful!'

I took a last fond look at the copper domes and marching elephants and the Pekinese-dragon fountain before getting into the car. I was muffled to the neck in mink as Aunt Pussy's dress was a complete rag and not fit to be seen. Lalla had offered to lend me something to go home in but I knew it would be stretching my powers of organisation to intolerable limits to have to wash it, iron it, make a parcel of it and post it back.

Nicky ran down the drive after the car, his arms and legs working frantically, his face reddening with effort. Nip and Nudge streaked around us in circles, inches from the wheels as though the Bentley were an elderly insubordinate ewe. I kneeled up in my seat to wave to Nicky through the back windscreen until, just before the gatehouse, he panted to a standstill and groped in his pocket for his inhaler.

I gave him a last wave before we swung out on to the road. 'Dear, darling Nicky. He's got to go back to that horrible school on Monday. It's very sad.'

Giles grunted.

'I'm glad Sir James didn't come to say goodbye,' I went on. 'Did you have a useful talk this morning?'

'It took me some time to convince him that the books could really be that valuable. Then he couldn't wait to get them out of the house. I've only taken a few for authentication. I couldn't find anything but the car rug to wrap them in. They ought to be properly packed. I've agreed to come back and fetch the rest in a few weeks.'

'We could come back together. I told Jeremy that you'd act in his play. I hope you don't mind.'

'What *are* you talking about?'

'Jeremy's going to put on a play and ask the neighbours round to see it. He's really keen on the idea. We stayed awake for hours talking about it last night.' I blushed again. I should never make a diplomat. 'Anyway, he's rather short of actors so I said we'd both be in it.'

'Well, thank you for offering my services.' Giles frowned as he braked for a flock of sheep who were running up banks, attempting to trample down gates and get under the Bentley, to go in any direction, in fact, but forward. 'You seem to have forgotten that I've got a job to do. Things have moved on a little since *Mansfield Park*, you know. These days, one can't wander about the place indulging whims – a little amateur theatricals here, an assembly ball there, racing a high-perch phaeton down to Brighton for a bet. I have to justify the salary I get from SCAB.'

'What a pity. You'd look so dashing in a curly-brimmed beaver. I bet you're good at acting. Did you do a lot at Oxford? I can imagine you'd be very good. You've got such a lovely deep voice.' We slid slowly forward through the bleating sheep. 'Oh, mind those lambs! Look at their adorable black faces! As though they've dipped their noses in a bucket of ink.'

'I belonged to the Thespian Society.' A smile of reminiscence played about Giles's lips.

I began to think better of my potential in diplomacy. 'I expect you always played the hero. Hamlet . . . so brooding and sexy in black velvet. Or Captain Stanhope in *Journey's End*. Almost my favourite play. Madly brave and repressed. Now I come to think of it you do look very much like Laurence Olivier – languorous eyes, finely chiselled mouth . . .'

I had gone too far.

'You've neglected to mention my determined jaw. Actually, I always preferred to play the villain, seducing silly young women before defrauding them of their money, tying them to railway lines or bricking them up in walls. Gagging the girls first, of course, so as not to be distracted from my fell intent by their unmeaning chatter.'

I took the hint. I sat quietly, thinking about the last few days at Inskip Park. There was plenty of substance for reflection.

First there was Jeremy. Was he really in love with me? Could I possibly be in love with him? I was very fond of him. I fully expected to miss him like anything as soon as I got back to London. I could see that we might be very happy for a while. The four nights that we had spent together we had had to make ourselves stop talking so that we could get to sleep. Jeremy was like the best kind of girlfriend. We could tell each other anything and rely on each other's uncritical loyalty.

One very good thing that had resulted from this was the realisation that my relationship with Pierce was utterly superficial, based on things like vanity and curiosity. Pierce had taught me things that I didn't know – sexual and intellectual in about equal parts. And often he made me laugh. But being with Jeremy had taught me that it was possible to be comfortable and happy in the company of a man. Now when I thought about Pierce I recognised that there had been an element of fear on my part and probably something of contempt on his. I determined to end it at once. I had not the smallest desire ever to go to bed with him again. I shuddered as I imagined it.

But my relationship with Jeremy was based on having fun, being irresponsible, pretending that life was play. Supposing our circumstances changed and reality – in the shape of illness, financial problems or children – intruded? Or, worse, supposing one of us grew up? From the prudential point of view Jeremy was what Aunt Pussy would have called a hopeless prospect. He had no money, no job and a falling-down house. I loved the house but even I, possibly the most impractical person in the world, could see that it was scarcely feasible to think of rebuilding it even if one had trunks of gold. The house was as much a curse as a blessing. And something had occurred the previous day that had made me wonder if the house was not only a curse but cursed. Put that way it seems over-dramatic but I had not been able to put the experience out of my mind.

After Nicky had interrupted Jeremy's proposal of marriage I had left them together on the stage in the theatre, discussing the rules of the treasure hunt, while I went to telephone Mab Fordyce for a consultation on what to cook for dinner. I had walked by myself through the ballroom. The slippery floor beneath my feet was tempting. As I was alone I had allowed myself a small shuffle-spring-tap. It was too good to resist. I began my *Night and Day* routine. It was astonishing how, after four years, most of it came back to me. The choreography was stored in some subconscious part of my brain and I was able to dance nearly the whole of it apart from a couple of hazy patches which I made up. I sank at the end into a sort of curtsy which, in the old days, would have involved leaning backwards over Antonio's arm, my hair touching the floor.

It was then, while I was kneeling to the imaginary applause of an invisible audience, that the groaning began . . . a horrible sound, fearful and agonised like a creature in labour, not loud but deep and insistent. It came from all around, above and below, a desolate moaning, as though, I thought at once, the house itself were grieving over some appalling crime. I fled to the kitchen. Later when my heart had slowed down enough for me to make my telephone call I tried to dismiss it as a rush of blood to the head from over-exertion. Perhaps the wind had been blowing through a grating or down the chimney. There had been a large pile of soot in the fireplace, which had drifted over the floor as I danced. But however much I tried to laugh at my fit of terror I kept remembering that Lady Inskip frequently heard noises that frightened her. I remembered the story of the Hog of Inskip.

I didn't know whether I believed in ghosts. I had never had any experience of them, not so much as a cold stir of air or an unexplained scent of lavender. But if one can believe in the unlikely and quite unsubstantiated idea of God and life after death, as I vaguely did, one ought to be able to believe in anything. One spectral hiccup would be enough. The thought had recurred disturbingly throughout what remained of the day.

The treasure hunt had been a success. It took Jeremy so long to organise that we decided to have it after dinner. Sir James gave his permission for Nicky to stay up. He was quite genial at dinner and asked Nicky what he had been doing with himself all day. I suspected that he felt guilty about the asthma attack. Nicky had explained about the Roman fortification. Sir James's eyelids began to droop quite soon into the explanation but Francis took up the subject and asked Nicky sensible questions. Susan and Sir James discussed the day's play at Edgbaston and Hamish who was on my right talked to me about Mrs Gaskell. It was our best dinner yet, for conversation, if not for food.

Susan and I had made a *ragoût* of beef, at least Susan called it a *ragoût*. I should have been inclined to call it stew, like the stuff we had at school. It seemed quite an easy thing to do once one had chopped everything up. The only difficulty we ran into was that I put it into the hottest oven by mistake and when I took it out after an hour and a half the liquid had magically disappeared. We hastily added water and Marmite and something mysterious from a packet called gravy granules and made a sort of brown syrupy sauce. I thought it was rather disgusting but Sir James gobbled it down.

I had made the first course all by myself and I was quite proud of its appearance. Mab Fordyce had said it was a cinch and she was very nearly right. You hollow out tomatoes and stuff them with prawns, rice, mayonnaise and curry powder. I forgot to ask Mab how to make mayonnaise and as she was busy preparing for a bridge party I did not like to ring again, so I used salad cream from a jar. It tasted a little too much of vinegar, I thought. Perhaps there was too much curry powder as well. The concoction was fiery enough to make one's eyes run. Also it is surprising how frozen prawns ooze water however well you think you have drained them. We didn't have time to make a pudding so we gave them a savoury instead – sardines on toast. Francis and Sir James were complimentary. I had suggested Camembert croquettes, which had been R.D.'s favourite savoury, but Susan had looked at me as though I were perfectly imbecile, casting her eyes upwards and snorting. She did this quite a lot and I made a mental note never to do it myself as it is irritating in the extreme to others. 'Where,' she asked, with an inflection of weary patience, 'do you think we'll find Camembert at half past seven on a Friday night in Nottinghamshire? You really are hopelessly impractical, Viola.'

I longed to tell her not to draw her eyebrows together. She was getting frown lines like ravines. Aunt Pussy always warned me about the dangers of too much animation. 'I know,' I said in a tone that was meant to be humble. It was the attitude I generally adopted to placate Susan. 'I firmly intend to make improvements when I get back to London.'

'Life's just a game to people like you, isn't it? You'll have a brief flirtation with independence and then give it all up for the first good-looking man who can afford to provide you with a house and servants and pay your bills at the couturier's.' This was not how I had visualised my future life but I thought it sounded rather attractive. 'Meanwhile people like me have to put up with being buried in the country where everything's dull and drab, eking out the harvest-festival display with rotten windfalls, putting on an extra cardigan rather than the second bar of the electric fire, making a tin of salmon go a bit further with scrambled egg and frozen peas. I make efforts all the time to suppress selfish thoughts and to put other people first. I always come second. Why shouldn't *I* be first? Why shouldn't *my* needs be considered like everyone else's? Just because I don't make a bloody nuisance of myself!' She stopped in the middle of this outburst and pushed away a strand of mousy hair with the back of her hand, streaking her forehead with a slick of butter. I didn't dare to point it out.

'Would you like to come and stay in London?' I asked, after an awkward little pause during which Susan's eyes were screwed up as though to avoid the spilling of tears.

'You'd have to share my bed but it's an enormous four-poster. I've got such a beautiful room. It would make anybody feel better. It's not a smart part of London but you can get buses anywhere.'

Susan stared at me in amazement. 'You'd let me come and stay in your bed?'

'In winter I have my own fire. It's the most lovely thing to look at just before you fall asleep, so safe and cosy. Of course, now it would be too hot but there's a jasmine which has climbed up to my window and it makes the room smell heavenly.'

Susan stared down at the fragile backbones she had removed from the sardines. 'It's very kind of you,' she said slowly, in a voice that was uncharacteristically soft. 'I couldn't possibly leave my father and – everyone, but I appreciate the invitation.' She looked at me with her pointed nose wrinkled up in what I recognised, seconds later, was an attempt at a smile. 'Don't take any notice of me when I get grumpy. I hate my life but, if I'm truthful, it's my own fault for not having done something about it years ago. I ought to have got away. I had the chance a few times but something – cowardice, probably – held me back. Now I'm thirty-seven and I have to face the fact that this is it. I've made my life by default and I'm going to go on in this dreary way until I die. When I was young I had this idea of what the future would be. Just something conventional. A medium-sized house in a small village. Georgian, perhaps, with a dark blue door and bay trees in tubs either side. A nice husband, not handsome but with a kind face, two children, both girls. I'd make them birthday cakes and party dresses and there'd be a pony in the field. I'd garden and sit on committees and be a churchwarden. It doesn't seem too much to want, does it? But it isn't going to happen now. So I've got into the habit of shutting people out. It's humiliating to let them see how absolutely I've failed.'

I was astonished by this confession. I saw by the unaccustomed brightness of Susan's eyes and the pinkness of her cheeks that it had cost her something to make.

'Do come,' I said, now suddenly really wanting her to.

'We could go to Regent's Park and see *A Midsummer Night's Dream*. There's the V and A and the Soane Museum and the Wallace Collection and we could take a boat down to Greenwich. There are lots and lots of cheap things one can do that are really interesting.'

Susan shook her head. 'Thanks. Not now. It's too late. I'm needed here. And I suppose being needed is, in the end, the most important thing.'

As Giles and I drove south I pondered on this. Was this the key to happiness? Not being loved and loving as I had thought but being necessary to the lives of other people. Were these things in fact inextricable?

'This looks like it.' Giles had stopped the car on the road which ran alongside the wood where we had found the rabbit. 'Here's the gate.'

'I can manage. Don't bother to get out.'

I took the basket from the back seat and carried it into the shade of the trees. The rabbit began to hop about inside. I wondered if it was recognising familiar noises and smells. When I got to the nettle-patch where the snare had been I put down the basket and undid the straps. The rabbit looked up at me with black eyes in which a spark of light trembled. For a while we gazed at each other. I wondered if we had thoughts that even touched at the edges. Did we hear the same sounds, see the same colours, feel things in the same way, warm or cold on our skins? Then the rabbit gave a tremendous leap and bolted off into the undergrowth without a backward glance.

'I hope the rabbit was properly grateful,' said Giles on my return.

'It was so effusive with expressions of gratitude that I was quite embarrassed.'

Giles smiled. 'We can stop for lunch in an hour.'

We rejoined the motorway. My thoughts went back to Inskip Park. We had divided into pairs for the treasure hunt, each couple beginning in a different part of the house so that we would not give the clues away to the others. Nicky was my partner. Lady Inskip was playing with Francis. Hamish had gallantly asked Susan to be his partner and I saw that, despite her offhand acceptance, she was gratified to have her company so unexpectedly sought. So Giles and Lalla had to be partners, which made Lalla smile with mischief. As I opened the first piece of paper I realised that Jeremy's idea of a treasure hunt with literary clues was very different from what I had expected.

> There was a young girl called Jane Eyre
> Who much preferred screwing to prayer.
> She spurned St John Rivers
> He gave her the quivers
> But let Rochester sample her fare.

'Whatever will Mummy think?' Nicky was shocked and delighted. 'Thank goodness my father isn't playing. He'd be livid.'

'I think I know what he means anyway.'

We ran upstairs to my room. Tucked into the frame of the painting of Thornfield Hall was a piece of paper with the next clue, which was in a similar vein. Imagining the entire household thundering in and out of my bedroom I paused to hurl Jeremy's dressing-gown into a drawer in the chest before we rushed away to continue the search.

The next hour was spent in breathless racing around through every room in the house. In addition to the clues, we discovered, in various chairs, cupboards and book-shelves, some long-lost items – several pairs of scissors, chewing-gum, some foul-smelling bones, a diamond ring, a repulsively green, stiff sandwich and Nicky's school pull-over, which he was very pleased about as it would save him a row from Matron. Jeremy's clues lost nothing of their salacious tone – if anything they grew worse. The penulti-mate clue, about the witless Bishop of Balham and some unfortunate birds, does not bear repeating.

'I think it might be the conservatory,' said Nicky, when we'd stopped giggling. 'We had a blue-tits' nest in there last year. You go and look there and I'll try the cases of stuffed birds on the landing outside my father's bedroom. Hurry up, Viola!'

I ran obediently down to the conservatory, passing Lalla and Giles in the hall. They were lagging behind the rest of us, in fits of laughter over the clues, all disagreements seemingly forgotten.

Sir James was standing alone with his back to me before a large fern in a pot. 'Hello, my pretty one.' His voice was unusually gentle. 'You're looking perfectly lovely.'

For a moment I thought Lady Inskip might be crouching out of sight behind the flowerpot. Then I remembered that I had just seen her, looking rejuvenated by excitement, crossing the hall with Francis. I saw Sir James stroke one of the fern's fronds and then lift it to his lips. I could understand this. I had felt very much like kissing the tiny new leaves on my pelargoniums. But I had assumed, I suppose because I was largely ignorant of men, that Sir James possessed the tenderness of a pumice stone. A loose tile rattled beneath my foot and he spun round with an oath. He pierced me with a glance from his ensanguined eye and left the conservatory without a word.

I searched every inch of the room but found nothing. I was just straightening up from my inspection of the grating that ran beneath the benches when I found Francis looming over me. From his alcoholic breath and the way he swayed slightly as he leaned on his stick I got the impression that he had tempered the excitement of the hunt with brandy.

'You look happy, Viola. Have you solved the conundrum?'

'I'm completely baffled. I think I'm looking in the wrong place. I must go and find Nicky and see if he's had better luck. Isn't this fun?'

I knew I was prattling. I was suddenly self-conscious. Francis was standing with his back to the light and his face was in deep shadow but I could trace by intuition the process of his thoughts. He stretched his hand to adjust a curl which had fallen across my forehead. It was somehow a shockingly intimate gesture . . . as though he had ripped open the front of my shirt. The odd thing was, I did not think of rebuffing him. I did not like Francis the smallest bit but I stood as mesmerised as a hapless befurred supper dish before a dancing stoat.

'Don't run away. We never have the chance to talk. In some ways you're like your aunt. Not to look at. Of course, you have your mother's face.'

'You didn't say you knew her.' I could never resist the temptation to hear about my mother, though it always hurt to discover that comparative strangers were more intimate with her ways and doings than I was.

'Didn't I?' Francis was smiling now. I could hear gratification in his voice. 'Oh, yes, I knew her. I remember the evening I first met her. I had taken Pussy to dinner. Luciano's, I think it was. We were just leaving when your mother came in on the arm of a poor stuttering boy, still damp behind the ears. Every other woman in the room was colourless by comparison with her, though she was very young, hardly more than a child. I took Pussy home and then went back to Luciano's. Constantia's face, when she saw me come in, was enchanting. She knew then the power of her beauty. We danced the whole evening together. She was magnificent with elation over her conquest. You have the same amethyst-grey eyes and dark lashes but your expression is softer. That is not without its charm. Pussy was a kitten but your mother was a tiger. Which are you, really?' He moved closer until I could feel his breath on my cheek. 'Now you're shy . . . How enchanting! If only more women realised how attractive that can be. Look at me, Viola!'

To my amazement I obeyed. The light fell suddenly on his face as he took hold of both my wrists. I could see the satisfaction in his eyes. I felt a peculiar sick excitement at his touch. Despite myself I was fleetingly attracted. I knew that he was vain, idle, unprincipled, possibly even dangerous, but this knowledge was part of the physical allure he possessed. I recognised the thrill of corrupt desire, the fascination of cold-hearted profligacy. Dad would have called him one of them Don Junes, as bad as they come. I was my father's daughter. I pulled myself together.

'Goodness, Francis, that's sweet but terribly corny. All

that about tigers and kittens, I mean.' I continued to laugh though he gave my arms a spiteful little squeeze, which hurt. 'These days, women want to be told how intelligent they are and how brainy their conversation is. Oh, Nicky! I was just coming to find you. No luck here, I'm afraid.'

'I've found it. Hello, Uncle Francis. Have you given up looking? I'm sorry, I'm not allowed to tell you where it was.' Nicky became helpless with giggling. 'I don't completely understand this one but I'm sure it's very rude. I wrote it down. You mustn't let Uncle Francis see it.'

I read the squiggles on the scrap of paper.

> I, Caesar, when I learned of the fame
> Of Cleopatra, I straightway laid claim.
> Ahead of my legions
> I invaded her regions
> Vidi, Vici, Veni.

Nicky exploded into giggles. Francis had let me go. He was livid with temper.

'I don't get it, either,' I said. '*Vidi, vici, veni*. What does it mean?'

'I saw, I conquered, I came,' said Francis, meanly depriving Nicky of his chance to show off.

'Something to do with Cleopatra,' suggested Nicky. 'That painting we used to have.'

We were off – on a false scent, as it turned out – leaving Francis, leaning on his stick, the very picture of a dejected, ageing roué.

Nicky opened the mummy-case in the billiard room. I hardly dared to look. The thing inside bore little resemblance to humankind. It might have been a log of wood wrapped in filthy bandages but for the extra width of the shoulders and the prominence of nose and feet.

'It's here! We've found it!' said Nicky excitedly, removing a parcel fastened by a safety-pin to the loins of the corpse. 'Chocolates! Cadbury's Milk Tray! My favourite! Oh! Jeremy's signet ring, look, pinned to the arm. I hardly call that treasure except I suppose it's gold.'

I took the ring and put it on the third finger of my right hand. I guessed that Jeremy had selected the clues so that Nicky and I would have the best chance of winning and that I was to have the ring. I said Nicky could have all the chocolates. No one could have accused me of being fastidious but somehow they didn't appeal.

I looked at the ring now as we flew down the fast lane of the motorway. I must be careful not to lose it. I was always losing things, especially jewellery –

'What the hell! Why did you scream like that?' said Giles angrily. 'I nearly drove into that van.'

'Sorry. I just realised that I've left my watch at Inskip Park. It's Aunt Pussy's. Diamonds. Awfully valuable.'

'You'll have to telephone them when we stop for lunch. I expect someone will put it in the post. What are you flapping at? It's extremely distracting.'

'Sorry. A bee. The poor thing's desperate to get out. Where's the map?'

'Can't you leave it until we stop for lunch? It won't sting you if you leave it alone.'

'I read somewhere that they can only find their way home within a certain distance. It must have got in when we stopped to let the rabbit out. Every second we're carrying it further from its nest.'

'What *are* you doing?'

'I'm getting it to climb on to the map. Okay – got it. I'll just put it out of the window. Oh – oh dear! I *am* sorry!'

Giles was very restrained, confining himself to a short angry expletive, as his map bowled away behind us down the motorway. 'I think I'll turn off here. There's bound to be a pub in the village.'

There was – a very pretty one, called the Hanged Man, thatched and painted white, overlooking a crossroads. Nearby a gibbet cast its ominous shadow, a tattered rope swinging in the wind.

'How horrible!' I was indignant. 'Imagine being *able* to do that to someone! It's murder, whatever they've done. Think what you'd feel all the time in prison, knowing you were doomed to die. And people used to come and watch! I despair sometimes of the human race – what are you laughing at?'

'I can see from here that it's three pieces of plywood rather clumsily nailed together and heavily varnished, *circa* nineteen sixty. I expect the owners of the pub put it up to attract tourists.'

I didn't mind being laughed at. I was too relieved. I had been taken to the Chamber of Horrors as a child and had been led out in tears. The friend and her mother who had taken me were furious. They were very cold and snappy as I sniffed and gulped through a delicious tea at the Savoy afterwards. I had had nightmares for ages. I suppose it is a contemptible weakness not to be able to view things dispassionately.

Lunch was really good. We had steak and chips and mushrooms. Even Giles seemed to enjoy it. 'The steak's overdone and the chips are greasy but anything would taste all right after what we've been eating for the last five days.' He shuddered eloquently and then saw my face. 'I forgot how much hard work you put in. Really, I am sorry. I ought to have helped you more. But those books had to be catalogued. And the night before I had to spring Jeremy from gaol.'

'I know I can't cook. But I'm going to learn.'

Giles's smile was kind if disbelieving. 'You had the most difficult conditions to work in. And very bad ingredients. Raw curry powder! The dead hand of Middle England. Just the sort of thing my dear mother produces.' He shuddered again. 'But it's thanks to you there was anything to eat at all.'

'Susan helped a lot.'

'She seems to be in a permanent temper. She was very snappy last night, flouncing off without saying goodbye.'

'She's rather strait-laced, I think. I don't imagine Jeremy's clues struck her as being amusing.'

Giles began to laugh. 'I like Jeremy. No one could help liking him and, despite the Bertie Wooster impression, he's very bright. But he *is* odd. It's none of my business, I know, but you ought to be careful.'

'What of?'

'He seems rather unstable, that's all. And you're too young to know what you're doing.'

'Well, I like that! I'm only six months younger than Lalla!'

I left the rest – about how Giles had been ready to seduce Lalla at the drop of a hat – unsaid.

'You seem much younger – oh, now, don't get cross. All right, I apologise. Most women want to seem younger than they are, don't they?'

Giles was willing to make amends so I accepted his offer to ring Inskip Park to tell them about the watch to save me the ordeal of telephonic communication with Huddle.

The waitress brought coffee while he was gone. I drank it pensively, my thoughts still at Inskip Park. I was very fond of Huddle, who had wished me goodbye with a fatherly tenderness and begged me to take care of my health. But it was impossible to tell whether Lalla was right about his infirmities being invention. The family themselves were sufficiently odd to make it unsurprising that everyone who worked for them seemed slightly unhinged. Though whether Lady Inskip was quite as unbalanced as they all thought her I was beginning to doubt. After all, I too had heard that phantasmal din in the ballroom.

At the conclusion of the treasure hunt I had gone back into the conservatory to look for Jeremy to thank him for the ring when I had seen a face pressed against the glass. It was contorted and demonic, with a hideously flattened nose and goggling eyes. I had screamed and the face had disappeared. A ring of mist marked the spot where its open mouth had been. Encouraged by the conviction that any creature with warm breath could not be supernatural I had thrown open the door of the conservatory and gone in pursuit. I saw a small figure ahead of me running through the gloaming in the direction of the charcoal-burners' camp. The night was chilly and I had come without a coat but I was determined to catch up with him. We were almost level with the lake before his legs, shorter than mine, began to tire. I put on a spurt and grabbed hold of his shirt collar. He swore and tried to kick my shins.

'Which Hoggins are you?' I demanded, as soon as I had recovered my breath. 'If you kick me again I'll complain to your father.'

'Barry,' retorted the child, who could not have been more than six or seven. 'An' I'll tell my dad of *you*. You've torn me shirt.'

'What were you doing peering into the conservatory? You frightened me.'

'I wanted to see t' mad lady. Shane says she has fits and foams at t' mouth. I weren't doing no harm.'

'Have you done this before? Stared in at the window, I mean.'

'Wot if I have?' The boy was sulky and had stopped struggling. 'There ent nuffink else to do. Only t' telly. It's borin'. Me and Shane likes to see t' mad lady.'

'Is Shane your brother?'

'Yeah. Shane's ten.' He offered this piece of information defiantly, as though hoping to impress.

'Then he ought to know better. You shouldn't look into other people's houses. It isn't polite.'

'Sucks, then. *I* don't care.'

'Do it again and I'll tell.'

'So what? Dad can't do no worse than hit me. I don't mind bein' hit. So there.'

He stuck his tongue out at me. We had reached an impasse. I let him go. I was just wandering back to the house when a shadow springing out of a neighbouring bush made me yell with fright. I thought at first it was Francis and prepared to fight for my virtue. It was almost a relief, after that, to make out the vegetable features of Bowser. 'It isn't safe to be out after dark, miss. There's gyppos and all sorts in these here parts, up to no good. And worse than gyppos.'

'I only came out because I saw one of the Hoggins boys staring in through a window. They've been frightening Lady Inskip.'

'There's more than boys in them there woods.' Bowser

spoke menacingly. 'I seen things that would have frighted a lesser man into his grave. Things what you wouldn't believe if I told you. You'd best be getting indoors, miss.'

I was beginning to weary of the sinister-henchman routine. It was obvious that if anyone was up to no good it was Bowser.

'What's that you're holding?' I put out my hand in the dark and touched warm, furry bodies.

'Just seeing to it as no harm comes to Sir James's chickens and pheasants. 'Tis my bounden duty to watch all hours, day and night. There's minks and there's stoats and there's foxes, all wanting to eat what don't belong to 'em.'

'Isn't that an owl?' My eyes were beginning to adapt to the darkness. 'Don't tell me an owl takes chickens.'

'This be a particular bad 'un. Take a pup if it could. I been after this owl an age, I have.'

By now Bowser had walked me round to the front door. The light fell full on him and I saw that he had a string of birds, little ones like starlings and thrushes, all hanging dead from his arm.

'Oh, how horrible! You shouldn't kill those poor little things!'

'You'd best be getting inside, miss.' Bowser was deaf to argument.

'I shall speak to Mr Inskip about it. You ought to be ashamed of yourself.'

'Tha's right. Speak to Mr Inskip.' I saw something like a smirk on the disagreeable turnip countenance.

I had gone in and slammed the door.

'There seems to be uproar at the Park.' Giles sat down and looked disapprovingly at his coffee, which was thin and grey and had little black bits in it. 'Apparently someone left the conservatory door open last night. There was a frost and all Sir James's rare ferns are dead. Nicky says the house is in deep mourning and no one dares to speak in his father's presence. Do you want me to slap you on the back? Naturally, if you try to inhale coffee you're bound to get into difficulties.'

CHAPTER 17

I did not confess to Giles then my responsibility for the
swift and comprehensive dispatch of Sir James's ferns.
Instead I made good use of his handkerchief, which he
said I might as well keep as I seemed to have more need of it
than he. Snuffing hot coffee up one's nose is unpleasant and
humiliating and even when my sinuses were restored to
something like normal I was in no mood for confession. The
waitress brought me a large portion of trifle, which Giles
said he had ordered.

'I'm not a baby, you know,' I said, perhaps ungraciously.
'I can choose my own puddings.'

'All right.' Giles called the waitress back.

'There's fruit salad, cheese or trifle, miss.'

'Oh. Trifle, then.' The waitress looked at Giles, widened
her eyes slightly, and went away again.

'That looks pretty horrible.' Giles drank his coffee, his
lips pursed with distaste. 'Like the packet jelly we used to
have as children. Shouldn't trifle have custard in it? Will this
country ever acquire civilised habits of eating and drinking?'

I know a rhetorical question when I hear it so I continued
to eat and enjoy the bilious green jelly with curious white
foamy stuff on top, which was gay with hundreds and
thousands.

'More coffee?' asked Giles. 'If one can call it that. Mine
tastes oddly of sardines. You look hot. Why not take off
your coat?'

'I'm boiling.' Sweat was beginning to prickle on my
forehead. 'But I look an absolute mess. I'll have to find a
really good dry-cleaner's who can do invisible mending as
well.'

I mentally added another five pounds to the wretched
total of indebtedness. There was the fiver I owed Giles for
the hedge and the ten pounds – at least – I ought to send Sir
James for the ferns, with a note of profound apology. I
played with the wording of this letter as I ate the last

spoonful of hard, yellow sponge. Or I could send it anonymously. That might, after all, be simpler. Perhaps I ought to pay for the hire of the pump that had drained the lower lake. 'It's surprising how expensive staying in someone else's house can be.'

'You can say that again.' Giles looked at me thoughtfully. 'You've dropped jelly on your coat. It cost thirty pounds to get Jeremy out of prison.'

'Oh, no!' I mopped energetically with the handkerchief. 'Do you mean no one's paid you back?'

'They probably forgot about it. And they were very hospitable. It really doesn't matter.'

'What an extraordinary few days it's been. It feels like very much longer.'

'I was thinking that myself. It's another world, isn't it? Different things seem important there, and one feels different oneself.'

I looked at Giles in surprise. 'Did you feel that too? How interesting! I've just been wondering why that is. One thing, though, I've come to the conclusion that there's nothing quite so sad as effete aristocrats. And also – of course I'm not an aristocrat myself – I don't want to fall into the same Slough of Despond. It's only too easy, I can see, to muck about not doing anything very much and then suddenly find all your chances to really do something with your life have gone because you're too old, too tired or too depressed.'

'Aren't you an aristocrat? I thought you were.'

'Not a bit of it.' I smiled to myself as I thought of my darling old dad. 'But it doesn't matter who you are. The same thing applies. It's more poignant with people like the Inskips who seem to have so much to begin with, that's all. But when I get back to London I'm going to begin.'

'Begin what?'

I thought I could detect something between cynicism and amusement in Giles's eyes but I didn't mind much. 'I'm going to live my life properly. I'm not just going to fit in with whatever seems to be going on. I'm going to chart my own course. I'm going to do all the things I've wanted to do

229

and find out about all the things that interest me. First of all I'm going to get a proper education.'

'Well, certainly nobody could disapprove of that.' I could tell Giles was humouring me, not unkindly but as though I were a child. 'How are you going to go about it?'

'I shall go to evening classes.'

Giles looked surprised. 'If you do, and if you stick at it, I shall take my hat off to you.'

'I know you think I'm a frivolous birdbrain with no ambition but to polish my fingernails and catch a rich husband but you'll see!'

'I honestly never thought that of you, Viola.'

Now he was laughing at me. 'What's funny?'

'I'm sorry. You look so hot and indignant. Take that wretched coat off, for goodness sake.' I gladly complied since I was feeling like a kettle about to whistle. 'Now, look, I'm on your side. It's a long, slow process to acquire even the beginnings of an education but there isn't anything more worth having. Not fame, not money, not power, nothing! Let's drink to your success!' He drained the wine in his glass. 'Eugh! When will pubs start to stock decent wine?'

'Thank you. I can see you don't think I really mean it. But I'll show you.'

'All right. I'm truly not as sceptical as you think. We'll make a pact, if you like. You'll be educated and I . . .'

'What?'

'I'm going to learn to take things less seriously. That's what *I*'ve learned about myself in the last few days. I'm inclined to be too intense, too exacting, too . . . earnest. *I*'m going to study frivolity.'

'How interesting that we should have discovered such important things about ourselves and that they're quite opposite.'

'While you were out picnicking yesterday morning I was reading Pope. *Windsor Forest*. Do you know it?' I shook my head. 'It's a political polemic but also it's a celebration of pastoral, of the countryside. "In the clear azure gleam the flocks are seen, And floating forests paint the waves with green." Beautiful! I happened to look out of the window and was struck by the greenness of the grass and the depth of blue of the sky and I wondered what on earth I was doing moping about indoors, sulking.'

'Were you really? That's rather unkind to yourself, I think. You had every reason to feel wounded.'

Giles shook his head. 'I was flattered by Lalla's interest in me. I was conceited enough to think she meant it. It went to my head. I wanted very much to go to bed with her, that's all.'

'You weren't in love with her?'

'No. I pretended to myself I was because I like to wrap simple lust in poetical garments to make it more justifiable and more interesting. But I discovered – very quickly, luckily – that I was cross, not broken-hearted. Once I decided to chuck the hurt pride I felt fine. I think it's a kind of vanity to require love as well as desire. Other men don't, after all.'

'I'm so glad. I mean, that you aren't broken-hearted. And I don't think you and Lalla were at all well suited. You're so different.'

'As darkness to day,' said Giles, with perfect good-humour. 'Do you want any more trifle?'

I thought about this conversation as we drove into the northern suburbs of London. It was the first time that Giles had spoken to me as though I were capable of anything more than the most primitive reasoning. I felt that we were on a much better footing now than when we had begun our journey to Nottinghamshire. I was quite sorry to say goodbye at Hyde Park Corner. Giles had offered to take me all the way to Spitalfields but it really was just as quick to get on a bus. Several people looked at me curiously, swathed as I was to the eyebrows in mink on what had turned out to be quite a hot afternoon.

Tolgate Square, bathed in sunshine, was its usual elegant, tranquil self. The door of number 46 was open and on the threshold was Josephine, who began to screech and jump up and down as soon as she saw me.

'You're back.' Daniel spoke in tones of disgust. He was coming up from the kitchen as I came in with Josephine in my arms and before I could say more than 'Hello Daniel, I –' he had walked into his sitting room and slammed the door.

'It's just how my Tibby behaves if I goes away,' said Mrs Shilling, who was putting on her felt beret to go home. She always wore it with the rim turned out and rammed far down over her ears, making her hair stick out in woolly grey triangles. 'Fogg's very like a cat, now I think about it. The way he creeps about the place on velvet paws.' (Mrs Shilling pronounced it 'welwet'.) 'Affection's got to be on his terms. If you can call it affection. Still, the dog don't know what the donkey has to bear and he's got a deal to put up with. It's good to see you back, Miss Viola. He's been that hoity-toity. And Miss Tiffany moping like a hen on addled eggs. Miss Barlam's as thin as a blade of grass with pining. It'll be nice to have some cheerfulness about the place again.'

'It's lovely to be home, Mrs Shilling. It seems an absolute age, though it's been less than a week. I brought you something – just a tiny present.'

I had made Giles stop in Little Whiddon so that I could buy some presents for the household with the remains of the ten pounds. For Mrs Shilling I had chosen a box of violet creams, which I happened to know she liked. There were eight of them in a pretty oval box tied with mauve ribbon.

'Ooh, Miss Viola! You shouldn't have! I *shall* enjoy them, though! Bless your heart! I can manage these without me teeth in.' Mrs Shilling was a walking advertisement for regular visits to the dentist as her false teeth were constantly giving her 'gyp' due to ulcerated gums. 'It's a lovely box!' She stroked the cardboard quilting with a rough, red finger. 'I shall keep me earrings in it when I've eat the sweets.'

'This is for Tibby.' I gave her a tin clockwork mouse from the enterprising little toy shop in Little Whiddon.

When Mrs Shilling had closed the front door behind her, bearing away the little things I had given her with an expression of gratification out of all proportion to their worth, I paused for a moment to breathe in the distinctive smell of the hall while Josephine tried to separate my ear from my head. It was one of the ways she sought attention and it was effective. I went upstairs and knocked on Tiffany's door.

'Viola!' cried Tiffany flinging wide the door when she saw me. 'Am I pleased to see you!'

Against a background of winking brilliance, Tiffany looked magnificent. The colours of her home-made patchwork curtains and bedcover glowed like boiled sweets and sparkled with beads and sequins. Her red hair was loose and fell like flames down to her elbows. Her long, slim feet were bare. She might have been a pagan goddess of fertility and fruitfulness. When I told her so, the corners of her mouth trembled and then she burst into tears. Josephine leaped from my shoulder to the window-sill with her paws over her face. I put the present I had bought Tiffany from the junk shop in Little Whiddon – a pair of Victorian ivory glove stretchers (Tiffany loved wearing gloves because she was self-conscious about her large freckled hands) – on her bedside table and took her into my arms, stroking the yellow chenille shawl that clothed her shaking shoulders. Eventually the sobbing grew less. I lent her Giles's handkerchief, which was now far from clean. 'Have a good blow,' I advised. 'I've got to wash it anyway. Do tell me what's the matter. Is it something to do with Montague?'

'You bet it is! I'm going to have his baby!'

'Oh, Tiffany!' For a moment all comforting words deserted me. 'Are you sure?'

'Practically certain. I've been worried at the back of my mind about not having had the curse for ages but I couldn't remember when it was due so I wouldn't allow myself to face up to it. And my breasts are tingly and much bigger. But yesterday morning I was sick as a dog and again this morning. And I've got this tremendous longing to eat pickled walnuts. I'm on my third jar in two days!'

I stared at her dumbly for a moment, trying to imagine what I would feel in the circumstances. Why had God made conception such a haphazard business? Physical desire and having babies have absolutely nothing to do with each other. It must be some grim, divinely prescribed test of self-control but how brutally unfair that the punishment for failure falls exclusively on women. Supposing I had become pregnant by Pierce? We never did anything to prevent it. Whenever I had tried to talk to him about it he always said I was fussing about nothing and putting him off. I felt cold when I thought of the risks we had run. All of which was very selfish of me. It was Tiffany who was in trouble and this was no time to consider myself. 'You must see a doctor and make sure. Then we must think what's the best thing to do.'

'There are only two options that I know of. Both unthinkable. I shall kill myself, that's the solution.' Tiffany looked round her room as though seeking an instrument of execution. She was always dramatic but this time there was an air of desperation about her that was quite real.

'Please, dear, dear Tiffany, don't talk like that. You're in a state of shock. We must try to be calm and think what's best – for you and the baby. Oh, Tiff! Imagine! A darling baby, belonging just to you, like the most miraculous present!'

I tried to imagine what it would feel like to hold one's own baby. Perhaps like Josephine – less hairy, of course, but warm and nestling, something you couldn't help kissing.

'But I don't want a baby on my own. Babies need families, don't they? I don't want to be an unmarried mother, struggling on the dole, trying not to resent the poor little thing. Above all, I don't want Monty's baby. I should be worried all the time that it was going to grow up a philanderer.'

'It might be a girl. With your beautiful hair.'

'Women can be philanderers, too. Except that they aren't usually interested enough. Oh, God, how I hate men! Cold-hearted, selfish, sex-obsessed bastards!'

This was no time to argue in defence of men. What Tiffany needed – and it happened to be the only thing I could give her – was sympathy. We spent the next half an hour denouncing the male sex in the most extravagant terms. It seemed to do good for Tiffany stopped crying and we finished off the sherry.

'The fact that this is such a horribly commonplace

disaster makes it worse. I feel humiliated. I'm nearly twenty-nine and I should have known better. I've prided myself on my independence and town bronze and then I go and trip up like a lovelorn schoolgirl.'

'Think of all those poor little servants who were seduced by the young master and thrown out into the snow. Have you ever read *Esther Waters*? Honestly, it's the saddest book. And then there's Hetty Sorrel. Giles and I were talking about her only two days ago.'

'That's just what I mean. It's a positively banal situation.'

'Yes, but you won't be thrown into the streets. All your friends will help. It isn't considered a disgrace any more.'

'I'm pretty certain that down in Yeovil things haven't changed that much. A basket in the family is still seen as a scandalous event.'

Tiffany's parents, Lieutenant-Colonel and Mrs Wattles, lived near Yeovil.

'Well, I don't suppose they'll like it at first but they'll get used to the idea and when they take a gurgling, smiling grandchild in their arms their hearts will melt and everything will be all right.'

'How lucky you are to have this rosy view of life.' Tiffany sighed. 'My mother has the melting capacity of ingot iron. She already thinks I've let the family down because I haven't married the heir to a baronetcy.'

I thought immediately of Jeremy but dismissed the idea almost as quickly. 'Well, I'll take your word for it. I know as much about mothers as I do about men. That is, almost nothing.'

'Poor Viola!' Tiffany put a hot, damp, sympathetic hand on mine. 'Were you very young when she died?'

'Actually she isn't dead. People always assume that she is and I let them because it's easier. A child didn't happen to suit her scheme of things. But I've never worried about it, honestly, as Aunt Pussy was the best mother-substitute anyone could want. Will you tell Monty?'

'I don't know. I don't see there'd be much point. He'll be full of his nuptials with Bebe Ballantine. I suppose I could ask him to pay for the abortion.'

'Oh dear. That does sound horrible. Is that really the best thing to do?'

'I wish I knew. Is it better to be born, whatever the circumstances of your birth? If no one genuinely wants you it's a hell of a start. Of course, you may turn out to be Mozart or Newton or Dickens. The other thing that bothers me is, is it too late? I just can't remember when I last had the curse.'

We pooled our knowledge on abortions. Needless to say, mine was virtually non-existent. Then we discussed its moral implications, without coming to anything like a conclusion, until the clock on the church at the end of the square struck five o'clock. I jumped up. 'I'll go and buy something to drink. And I must make a couple of telephone calls. But I'll be back in half an hour.'

'You're a darling thing.' Tiffany got up and kissed me. 'Talking about it has made all the difference. I did mention it to Mrs Shilling and she was full of comfort but it was clear that to her an abortion is unthinkable. Her recommendation was to marry Monty and make myself respectable. The Baa-lamb's such a deep-dyed Catholic she'd be shocked to the soles of her shoes. I daren't tell her. And Daniel will absolutely hate it. You know how he loathes the idea of human beings reproducing. It offends his idea of beauty. I was so desperate to have someone to talk to that yesterday I spilt the beans to one of the girls at the theatre but she immediately burst into floods and said that Monty was the only man she had ever loved and she was never going to get over him.'

As I walked to the telephone kiosk I asked myself several pertinent questions. How was Tiffany to support herself and a child? And what would Daniel and Veronica think about a baby in the house? Ought I to be encouraging Tiffany to keep the baby? None of these could I begin to answer.

I stepped into the kiosk. I had not yet changed my clothes and the kiosk was hot from the sun beating on the glass sides. It was used regularly as a *pissoir* by roving youths and as regularly disinfected by a hygiene-conscious neighbour. I was nearly asphyxiated by sweltering antiseptic vapours. First I telephoned Aunt Pussy to tell her I was safely back. 'Darling, how was it? How is poor Millicent Inskip? Was it too dreadfully uncomfortable? I suppose James is just as disagreeable. He had a way of looking as though he wished you would drop down dead on the spot. Not *quite* what one wants in a diplomat. No wonder they were continually posted to places like Outer Mutoboboland. It was a good thing when old Sir George Inskip died and they could come home.'

'He still does that. He is rather horrible. But Lady Inskip is sweet, though rather . . . peculiar.'

'She always was, a little. People don't change, you know, as they get older. They just get *more* so. I was thinking that this morning. I've been indolent all my life. I've made the most awful sacrifices just to keep the peace. Now I'm positively *su*-pine. Soon I shan't get up at all. And your mother – well, let's just say that she always was rather flighty.'

'Have you heard from her?'

'She rang me at six o'clock this morning – *six o'clock* . . . I suppose, to be charitable, the time is different in New York – to tell me that she was leaving Mackenzie Jackson as he was a drunken swine. It was quite apparent to me at the wedding reception that that was exactly what he was but, of course, she wouldn't listen to me.'

'Jackson Mackenzie.'

'Well, it's all the same. Anyway, she says the scales have fallen from her eyes and she has run away with a man she calls the Flying Dutchman. Apparently he has an enormous yacht. From what I remember of the opera she's in for an extremely bad time.'

I promised Aunt Pussy that I would visit her the next day and rang off. I searched through the yellow pages until I found the number of the family-planning clinic. I made an appointment to go and see them on Tuesday. My last call was to the Courtauld Institute. Giles had suggested that this might be my best bet for evening classes. I don't think he had any expectation of my actually ringing them up. I spoke to a charming woman who told me that most of the evening courses began in September and were two-thirds of the way through. However, there was a new one beginning, which was due to run throughout the summer, called From Giotto to Cézanne, and would that interest me? I said it certainly would, and could I start at once? She told me to fill in a form, which she would send me, and bring it to the class next Thursday at seven o'clock. I gave my address breathlessly, partly from excitement and partly from suffocation as the temperature in the telephone box was nearing flashpoint. Jotto to Sayzan, I wrote on a piece of paper. I had heard of both of them, which was a comfort.

I emerged with relief from the kiosk and walked to the little shop on the corner two streets away where nice Mr Dring, the owner, always gave me credit. I bought a bottle of wine, which he said was the best in the shop. Luckily it was very cheap. I also bought two jars of pickled walnuts, some eggs, a loaf of bread, a large bar of chocolate and an envelope. Sitting on a bench in the middle of Tolgate Square, amid the sparrows and squirrels and drifting litter I addressed it to Bludgeon's School and enclosed the chocolate and a note to Nicky. I posted it at once in the pillar-box on the corner, hoping the chocolate's arrival would coincide with his arrival and cheer him up.

'Here's to the future.' I lifted my glass to Tiffany, who was enthroned in the most comfortable chair in the kitchen with all the cushions behind her, a pickled walnut speared on her fork. 'Whatever it may hold.'

'I expect if we knew that we'd both drink ourselves into a stupor of grief. As Mrs Shilling always says, it's not work that kills but worry. If only we were like animals without the ability to anticipate.'

'I'm sure it's the worst thing possible, to worry when you're having a baby.'

'Who's having a baby?' Daniel had materialised suddenly and soundlessly in his usual fashion and stood scowling at the end of the table.

'I am,' said Tiffany. 'But don't scold because I'm only just able to talk about it without screaming.'

Daniel folded his arms and looked at Tiffany over the top of his reading spectacles. 'It does not seem to me a circumstance in which scolding can do much good. I've been expecting it. Modern young women slide into any man's bed with the impartiality of a hot-water bottle.'

'Well, goodness, how unfair! I'm twenty-eight and I've only had three lovers . . .'

'Spare me the sorry details of your sexual intrigues.' Daniel held up his hand. He had the most beautiful hands, though spectrally thin. 'I suppose you have considered what this will mean. Crying at all hours of day and night, nappies drying in the bathroom. Oh, God! A pram in the hall!' Daniel screwed up his face in agony at the thought. 'All women want babies. Why, I can't imagine. You really are a bloody fool, Tiffany. Now, for heaven's sake, girl, don't mope.' Tiffany's eyes had begun to fill with tears. 'Stop it, stop it, stop it! I really won't bear crying. What's this you're drinking?' He sniffed at my glass.

'It's Mr Dring's best,' I said.

'Then heaven defend us from his worst. It's not even fit for cooking. I'm going down to my cellar and, mind, one more tear and you won't get any.'

Daniel's cellar was filled with precious bottles and he only fetched them up for drinking with us on very special occasions, like birthdays and the day I got my job at SCAB.

'He's a dear behind all that *Sturm und Drang*,' said Tiffany, winking away her tears. 'I know I'm going to be a frightful nuisance to everyone.'

'This is Dom Pérignon and you won't drink a better glass anywhere.' Daniel had returned with a bottle of champagne. 'Viola, see if you can get any ice out of that damned machine.' I tackled the ice-box, which was very old and unpredictable and consisted of one box inside another, the space between which was packed with charcoal. It had to be topped up with ice from the fishmonger every other day. We were in luck. It was so frosty that I could hardly unstick the lid and there were lumps of ice positively smoking with cold.

'While we're waiting we must think of a toast appropriate to little Algernon. Or shall it be Sapphira?'

'I like short names,' said Tiffany.

'I know a man called Zed,' I said.

'Zed? Oh, that's romantic! It makes me think of flashing white teeth and olive skin and castanets.'

'If I were you I should try to curb these sensual fantasies for a while. You're in quite enough trouble as it is.' Daniel looked sourly at Tiffany, then threw back his head with a great laugh.

He has the most marvellous eyes, very deep in their sockets with amazing browbones and eyelids. Although he did not pretend that Tiffany's pregnancy was anything other than a catastrophe he said enough to make her feel that it was a ruin of peace and order in which he would bear his share and this must have been, for Tiffany, the most consoling thing yet.

Later, when Tiffany had gone, very drunk, to bed, I gave him my present, which Giles had helped me choose – a second-hand volume of Richard Crashaw's poems, bound in navy blue cloth with edge-gilding. 'Hm, not a bad little book. They knew a thing or two, those seventeenth-century men,' was all he said.

As I lay in my own bed in my beloved room that night, communing with the familiar shadows and smelling the jasmine, which poured its sweetness in through the open window, I thought how happy I was and how I would love Tiffany's baby.

On Monday I went with Tiffany to the local surgery. She came out half an hour later, looking white. 'It's true. I really am going to have a baby. He says I'm too far gone for a termination, probably fifteen weeks. Oh, bugger!'

I treated her to lunch at Wheeler's on the grounds that fish is good for you and would counteract the amount of wine we drank. Aunt Pussy's fund was almost emptied by this extravagance.

On Tuesday I went to the family-planning clinic and came away with a prescription and my first packet of pills.

On Thursday evening I went to the Courtauld Institute. I

was nervous. Everyone seemed to look frighteningly intelligent and to know what they were doing and where they were going. Eventually I found the room in which the lectures were to take place. A group of people of assorted ages were gathered there already. Some of them smiled at me, a few talked together in low voices, most seemed to be reading from books they had brought with them. I sat down at a desk near the projector and turned back the cover of my new block of A4 file paper. I took my newly sharpened pencil and a rubber out of my bag.

'Evening, everybody.' A young man came in and pushed the door shut, dropping several books as he did so. A woman rushed forward to pick them up for him. He had long mousy hair parted in the centre and pushed back behind his ears. A pair of silver-rimmed spectacles drooped on his large nose. He came up to the table on which the projector stood, threw down his books and began to peel off his denim jacket. Then he saw me. 'Hello. Who are you?'

'Viola Otway.'

'I'm Julian. You've missed the first talk on the background to the Early Renaissance in Italy. You'd better stay behind afterwards and I'll give you a reading list. Okay, everyone. Now we're going to look at the work of Giotto di Bondone *circa* twelve sixty-seven to thirteen thirty-seven.'

'Jotto de Bondonay 1267–1337,' I wrote and suddenly my eyes were filled with tears, my heart beat until it hurt and I could barely hold my pencil for joy for I felt as though a door had opened before me into some vast new world and I was invited to dwell with the blessed of this earth.

CHAPTER 18

The summer of 1976 was the hottest for years. It began in May, when temperatures soared from a cool spring to scorching summer in a few days. For months not a drop of rain reached a steaming, sweltering

London. Windows were grimy, pavements were caked with dirt, tarmac melted, the plane trees hung their scorched leaves, the grass in the parks grew corn-coloured and the flowerbeds turned to sand. Grit was in our eyes, our nostrils and our hair. I remember those sultry days as a time of fierce self-absorption.

'Must you encourage every pigeon in London to defecate on *our* balcony?' Pierce, who was lying horizontal in a deck-chair, sighed as he ran his hand through his impeccably cut locks, which were already becoming attractively streaked by the sun. It must have been about four weeks after my return from Inskip Park. 'One day the whole building will topple to the ground under the weight of birds. We could go into guano production.'

I was topping up their drinking bowl and bird-bath as he spoke. 'Sorry. But birds have to bathe to keep their feathers weatherproof. And they're as thirsty as you are.'

My pelargonium cuttings were standing in a row outside, putting forth emerald leaflets with a vigour that seemed to me miraculous. At one end of the balcony I had rigged up a canvas awning beneath which we retreated when we were in danger of sunstroke. In its shade was a table and an ice bucket, replenished by me at intervals, for the pints of water, lemonade and alcohol consumed. Below us the traffic droned through a fog of dirt and heat but we in our lofty eminence were breathing a purer air and could look down on the gilded city with a happy sense of remoteness from the dusty clamour.

Pierce was wearing shorts and a T-shirt. Formal dress had been abandoned by everyone in London except undertakers and guardsmen. Even Giles had taken to coming to the office tieless and with his shirtsleeves rolled up to just below the elbow. I had to go out and spend the last of Aunt Pussy's money on cotton dresses and a pair of sandals.

Pierce was sipping Campari and soda through a straw. He finished it with a noisy sucking. 'Make me another, honeychile.' He held out the glass towards me.

'Should you? That'll be your third. You've got that meeting at five. You seem a bit drunk already.'

'What a puritanical little thing you are now you're so wise. All work and no play makes Jill a very dull girl indeed.'

I couldn't see his eyes since they were hidden behind sunglasses with mirror lenses but his mouth looked sulky. He never lost an opportunity to let me know how much he resented my efforts to improve my mind. 'I'll make you one more and then you really must sober up. But there aren't any more oranges. Do you want a slice of lemon instead?'

'Certainly not. Campari *must* have a slice of orange. Nip down to the deli and get some more, there's a good girl. And see if he's got any of those delicious little black olives in garlic and olive oil.'

'I thought you wanted me to type out the guest list for next week's drinks party. It'll take me at least three-quarters of an hour. And I'm going home at five on the dot. You said I could.' I had an essay to finish before my class that evening, on Botticelli's Vision. I had written my first essay on Giotto the Revolutionary in a state of passion mingled with terror. After a few sentences in which I tried to capture the tone of the lecture my pen broke away from all restraints and I wrote whatever came into my head. When my essay was returned to me at the beginning of the next session there was a cryptic 'See me afterwards' scrawled at the bottom of it.

At the end of the lecture, after an hour of Masaccio, Fra Angelico and Fra Filippo Lippi my head was a briar-patch of information, which I needed to go away and disentangle. Julian had a crowd of eager disciples around him so while I waited I scribbled notes about anything I could remember, mostly consisting of things like – what mean F. Angelico's conservatism? Who Donatello? Ask Giles. What poliptick?

'It's a panel with more than three folds, usually an altarpiece,' said Julian's voice above my head. 'But it's spelt p-o-l-y-p-t-y-c-h.' We were alone. Julian smelt faintly of sausages or bacon – something fried, anyway – which made me feel terrifically hungry. 'Your essay.'

'Yes?' I was immediately in a state of the most horrible suspense.

'At first I wondered what language it was written in. It didn't seem to resemble any of the Western European languages I'm familiar with.' Julian looked at me with large, vague, burnt-sienna-coloured eyes over the top of his spectacles. Burnt sienna, I had just learned, is a rich, reddish-brown made from iron-bound earth. Julian had been telling us about egg tempera and how colour was obtained during the medieval period. I could hardly believe that he was serious when he said that egg yolk made a perfect natural emulsion to mix with pigments and purified water. To me it was extraordinary that the homely egg was the foundation of those ancient and beautiful works of art.

When he made that remark about the incomprehensibility of my essay I felt a sharp pain of disappointment exactly where my supper ought to have been. 'I know I can't write.' To my shame I felt tears welling up. I had worked so long over that essay and been so thrilled when writing it. Suddenly I was in despair, all my hopes crushed.

'Oh, now, look – come on. It was meant to be a joke! It's not as bad as that.'

Tears were plipping off the end of my nose. 'Oh, no, I know – it's just – I tried so hard and I was so loving it – Don't take any notice. I cry at anything when I'm hungry.'

'Let's go and find something to eat, then.' Julian offered me a handkerchief of such violent hues, all Prussian blue and crimson lake, like bruised flesh, that I dabbed only the smallest part of it on my cheek, reluctant to acquire a freakish striped appearance. 'Sorry, it isn't very clean. I wait till I run out of socks before I go to the launderette and as I've got six pairs and only two hankies there's always a period of drought where handkerchiefs are concerned. I know a good caff round the corner where you can get pie, chips and mushy peas for seventy-five p. The waitress is a friend of mine.' We picked up our books and went out together into the street. 'This way. It's not the most salubrious of joints but they make the tea good and strong.'

Actually, I hate strong tea and prefer to drink it the colour of honey without milk and sugar but Julian was so patently trying to cheer me up that I tried to look pleased. We turned into a café called the Kozy Kavern. It was bright with red plastic banquette seating, and the walls were painted with crimson gloss. A girl with dyed black hair in a pony-tail and lots of dark eye makeup flapped a hand briefly at us as she operated a coffee-machine. 'Usual?' she shouted across the clamour of the customers, who were all young and quite rowdy.

'Twice.' Julian held up two fingers. 'Now, the end of hunger is in sight so let's talk. You know, when I started to read your essay I was taken aback by your swashbuckling style. But then I found your idiom, as it were. The way you try to pin down a painter's technique by very exact definitions of what you see in the picture. I got very interested then.'

'Really?' I started to feel better.

'Yes. All my other students reiterate what I've told them or they get it from books. They haven't the confidence to tackle the work afresh for themselves. You know, despite its lack of structure, I came to the conclusion that I liked your essay the best.'

'Gosh!' I felt a tingling sensation that was pure pleasure run up and down my body.

'You'll have to do something about your spelling and learn about phrasing. More full stops and not so many ands just for starters. But your excitement is contagious.'

The pie and vegetables came – so hot that Julian's spectacles misted up in the steam. When he took them off to polish them his face was shining and bluish-white like nacre and there were two red marks where the nose-grips rested. The pie had something like minced kidneys in it – horribly strong and with a sweaty layer of sodden dough where it joined the crust. The mushy peas had an odd taste but were quite good.

'I'll eat that if you don't want it.' Julian speared the remainder of my pie with his fork and chewed it up quickly. While he ate he told me about his job at the Institute and how he painted terrible daubs to sell on the railings of Green Park to supplement his income. 'I do Swiss mountain scenes, waves rolling on to moonlit beaches, kittens sharing baskets with spaniels – I know no shame. I like to eat.'

'Which sells best?'

'Possibly the kittens. I've discovered that you can sell anything if you paint it very smoothly, with a sort of licked-all-over look. People respond to the sensuousness, perhaps.'

'Do you get time to paint what you really want to?'

'Yes, occasionally. And then I become enraged with the difficulty of it. I sometimes wonder if it's worth it.'

Julian talked a great deal. He was a wild enthusiast about painting and its history and I was thrilled to pick up whatever crumbs he let fall. The waitress brought us our tea and said, 'On the house, Ju,' with a wink. By the time I'd got down the tea – it tasted as though it had been used to embalm Lenin – Julian and I were on the way to becoming friends.

'I suppose you've got a bloody evening class again.' Pierce lit a Passing Cloud and flicked the match over the balustrade of the balcony. 'Shall I pick you up afterwards and take you out to dinner?'

'Well . . . if it is just dinner.'

When I had returned to London from Inskip Park, I knew that I must end my affair with Pierce at once. I did not envisage any difficulties. Our relationship had been confined to drinks parties and dinners and bed. No words of love had passed his lips, nor had he required any from me. Probably he would not have cared much if Jeremy and I had been lovers, as long as it did not interfere with my availability. I was amazed now that, inexperienced as I was, I had been contented with such a sham for my first affair.

Pierce had seemed surprisingly pleased to see me when I arrived at the office the morning after my return. I felt guilty at once because of Jeremy, and this was not lessened by Giles's studied indifference to Pierce's sweeping me into his arms and pretending to derobe me on the spot. 'How I've missed you, my darling! Dins tonight? At the Caprice?'

'Thank you.' I was uncomfortably aware that Giles, who

was opening the letters that had arrived during his absence, was affecting not to listen, his brows creased in a frown. I had actually done nothing of which I need be ashamed but I still felt like a Jezebel. 'That would be lovely. We must talk.'

'Talk? I should think so! It's not my idea of fun to spend the evening staring in moody silence at each other across the grub.'

While changing for dinner that evening, I heard Veronica's shoes go tapping past my door. I put out my head.

'Hello, Viola.' Veronica appeared pleased to see me.

'Do come and talk to me while I get ready.' Veronica sat in the wing chair, politely averting her eyes from my semi-nakedness. 'I had a fascinating time, thanks,' I said, in answer to her enquiry. 'And I brought you this tiny present.'

I gave her another treasure from the junk shop in Little Whiddon, a mother-of-pearl shell, the two halves of which were held together by a band of green velvet ribbon, the whole thing being filled with sand. 'It's a pin-cushion,' I explained. 'The sand keeps the pins sharp.'

'It's perfectly lovely.' Veronica caressed the smooth shininess with her fingers. 'I shall always treasure it! How sweet of you to think of me.'

'Are you all right?' I stopped combing my hair to look at her more closely. Her thinness was more noticeable because I had not seen her for a few days. Her eyelids were puffy, her general appearance depressed.

'Oh, yes, really – I'm just the silliest creature imaginable, that's all. I despise myself. Now, let's talk about something more worthwhile. What's Nottinghamshire like?'

I told her about the countryside I had seen and about the Inskips and the house. I saw that she was doing her best to seem interested but that her mind was really on something else. 'I hope you won't think me very interfering,' I said at last, 'but you do seem just a little sad. Is everything all right at work?'

Veronica sighed. 'Yes, really. Mrs Potter's retiring and they aren't replacing her, which is rather discouraging. Circulation's down again this month. But I've known for years that we're dwindling into extinction. I've applied for another job but I haven't heard anything yet. Designing greetings cards.' She pulled a face. 'It doesn't sound my sort of thing. However.' She appeared to give herself some sort of mental shake. 'I feel I've made some fundamental mistakes in my life and now it's too late to put them right.'

'But you aren't even middle-aged yet! Of course you can change things!'

'The trouble is that I'm not the sort of person who can change very easily. I wish I could. When I'm fond of someone I can't stop loving them even though I know it won't be any good.'

The door to Veronica's inner world had opened the smallest chink and I was ready.

'Is it . . .' I paused, fearful of wounding this most private of human beings '. . . is it something to do with Daniel?'

Veronica's large, beautiful eyes closed as she drew in a great breath and burst into tears. For the second time in two days I held a weeping girl in my arms but, unlike Tiffany, Veronica cried with restraint, just a few small sobs before her body became stiff and she held her breath to stop herself crying.

'It's very good for you to cry,' I reassured her. 'It does something to your brain – I can't remember what – and restores your chemical balance. I cry a great deal, I expect that's why I'm generally very happy. Oh dear, that sounds like complete nonsense, doesn't it?'

Veronica mopped her face with a tiny lace-edged hand-kerchief and tried to smile. 'I'm sure you're right. Granny thought it was self-indulgent to cry so I always feel guilty when I do which stops it being much of a release.'

'Has Daniel said something to upset you?'

Veronica shook her head. 'Not intentionally, no. But I did something awfully stupid. I can't imagine what came over me. Last Friday I saw some bunches of cherry-blossom in the market. They were beautiful, purest white, so – innocent, really, if flowers can be such a thing. I had to buy some. On the spur of the moment I took some branches to Daniel's room. I knew he'd love them. I hoped he'd think

Mrs Shilling had put them there. I was arranging them on his desk when he came in. He started to frown terribly. I realised at once that I'd given myself away. I couldn't control my face, you see. I felt myself blushing, my eyes filling with tears – I suppose of shame. I wanted to make some explanation about having bought too many, about how I knew we both liked wild flowers but I was tongue-tied with embarrassment. He said "What have I done to deserve this?" Just that. But in the angriest way possible. That's how I knew that he knew.' I looked questioningly at her. 'Well, I'd better be truthful. I'm obviously no good at subterfuge. He knows I love him. Probably the whole world knows.'

'By no means. Mrs Shilling and Tiffany have guessed, I expect, but that's all.'

'Well, that virtually is the world – my world. I'm not ashamed of loving him. Don't think that. He seems to me eminently worthy of love. But I wish my love wasn't so conspicuous. I try to make myself eat, try to behave sensibly, to treat him like a good friend and nothing more. I tell myself that it's a disgrace to pine for the love of humans and that God's love is what's worth having. But inside there's this desperate impulse . . .' Veronica forced her lips into a smile. 'Let's not dwell on the indignity of unrequited love. I want to give him everything and, ironically, I know really that the only thing I can do for him is to keep out of his way.'

'There must always be hope,' I said. 'I'm sure that he likes you. And there can't be anything more winning than someone loving you as much as all that.'

Veronica looked at me with infinite sadness. 'There is no hope. I am quite sure of that. But please don't ask me how I know.'

Under the circumstances, I felt myself bound not to say anything more. While I finished my hair and face we talked about the awfulness of modern Christmas cards.

As I walked downstairs to wait for Pierce, Daniel was coming in through the front door, Josephine on his shoulder. She made a jump for my arms.

'I have sold my walnut secretaire for a good profit.' Daniel looked unusually good-humoured.

'What a pity, in a way. I've always thought it was lovely.'

'Lovely! It was more than that, much more. It was exquisite. But I shall buy another thing. One cannot expect that money comes floating down from the sky.'

'Once a pound note blew on to our balcony at SCAB. But I agree it would be unreasonable to expect a regular income from such a source.'

I liked to hear Daniel laugh. It didn't happen that often. It made his eyes soft and you could see that he had been very . . . well, beautiful, if you can say that about a man. I told him about my evening classes.

'I hope you keep at it. It will not be easy. If you do, I can lend you some books.'

It was annoying to find that the common reaction to my efforts to acquire knowledge was one of disbelief in my ability to stay the course. Tiffany had said, 'But you'll be so tired doing a job as well.' And Mrs Shilling had tutted with disapproval. 'A man doesn't want a wife to know more than what he does. On the shelf with poor eyesight'll be the end of it. Still, you'll find it dull enough, I dare say.'

'I'm quite determined to stick it,' I told Daniel. 'I want to know everything. Who Petrarch was and why Socrates drank hemlock. What was the South Sea Bubble. I'm going to read Gibbon's *Decline and Fall* and *Finnegans Wake* –'

Daniel held up his hands in mock astonishment. 'My God! You really *are* going to go at it. What has brought all this about? I don't believe that boyfriend of yours has complained of your lack of erudition.' His mouth took on a twist of sarcasm.

'Pierce, you mean?'

'He is the only boyfriend of whom I know. Unless you have acquired another in the last five days.'

'Well . . . ah, Pierce prefers women to be stupider than him, I think.'

'Of course he does. You are an embellishment. Someone to look at, someone to show off to his friends, someone to – let us put it politely – to be subject to his love-making.'

I was annoyed by the accuracy of this description. 'You've never even spoken to him. I don't know why you should be so hostile.'

Daniel looked steadily at me, his dark eyes full of derision. 'Let us just say I know a conceited donkey when he brays under my nose.' The tooting of a car horn from the street, to the rhythm of 'Colonel Bogey', prevented my reply. I opened the front door. Pierce sat in his open two-seater, fiddling with the radio. A blast of rock and roll, followed by the top notes of a coloratura soprano made Josephine flee for the stairs and several windows round the square were thrown up.

'Get a move on, doxy. I booked the table for seven thirty. We're going to a party afterwards.' Pierce turned his mirror-lensed eyes towards me. 'Are you going to stand there all night? The champers is getting warm.'

I looked back to say goodbye to Daniel but the hall was deserted.

Over dinner Pierce was especially nice to me, paying me compliments on my dress (blue silk with a *pointe de Venise* collar – a birthday present from Aunt Pussy) my hair (newly washed) and my earrings (pearl drops bought from the pawnbroker's next to Mr Dring's). 'Eat up, my lovely little tit-bit. I shall enjoy showing you off at the party. You're looking perfectly edible. Come on, you don't want a pudding. You'll get fat.'

I looked longingly at something smothered in chocolate and raspberries at the next table. 'Whose party is it?'

'Julia's. Or, rather, her mother's giving it but Julia particularly asked me to go.'

'Julia Sempill-Smith? Oh, I don't think I want to. She doesn't like me at all.'

'Rubbish! She's crazy about you. Well, she's crazy about me anyway and I'm not going without you. I've just got to nip back to the flat and change into black tie. I had to come straight to you from a meeting. Bloody nuisance you living at the back of beyond. Perhaps you ought to move in with me.'

'I don't think that would be a good idea. Besides, I like living where I do . . .'

Pierce had turned away and was asking the waiter for the bill. I hadn't been able to talk about Jeremy at all. Every time I tried Pierce brought the subject back to the merits of Inskip Park as a project for SCAB, or whether or not he should change his MGB for an E-type. We drove fast over to Rutland Gate. I went in with Pierce to comb my hair while he changed. I was standing in the bathroom washing the traffic smuts off my nose when my eye was caught in the mirror by a very pretty nightdress hanging on the back of the bathroom door. I had a good look at it. Pink and silky, the same make as Aunt Pussy's underwear, exorbitantly expensive. It was drenched in a strong scent of lilies of the valley. Out of curiosity I opened the bathroom cupboard. A pink toothbrush, certainly not mine, stood in the glass next to Pierce's blue one. I wandered into the sitting room. A copy of *Vogue* lay on the stool in front of the fireplace. A girl of frightening thinness peeped coyly out between two headlines 'The Ten Most Eligible Royals' and 'Serious Secretarial Schools for Sloanes'.

'Is this your latest attempt at mind expansion?' I asked Pierce as he came into the sitting room and stood before the looking-glass over the chimney-piece, fastening his bow-tie.

'What?' He turned briefly to look. 'Oh, that. Probably Mrs Sansome left it behind.'

I had met Mrs Sansome, Pierce's daily help, which I think he must have forgotten. She was a large woman in a shrimp-coloured cardigan, sensible shoes and a hair-net. She had complained a great deal about her prolapsed womb. 'I do think my going to Julia's house is a bad idea.'

'Nonsense! She'll be ecstatic to see you.'

Ecstatic would not have been the word I would have chosen for the look on Julia's face when we clawed our way through the throng on the ground floor of Julia's mother's smart Belgravia house. She was one of those girls whose faces are all points . . . terrific cheekbones, a high, sculpted brow, sharp retroussé nose and a neat, triangular chin. Her short, straight hair was dyed an eye-crossing chestnut red. The expression in her eyes was stormy. She allowed Pierce to kiss her polished cheek, said, 'Hello,' to me with a droop of glittery green eyelids, and then said, 'You really are a fucking bastard, Pierce,' before blowing cigarette smoke over both of us and walking off.

'Julia's a malapert hussy,' said Pierce loudly, with some admiration. 'I must say, I find it not unattractive. Look, there's the Bravington girl. What's her name?'

'Angelica.' I ought to know as she rang the office to speak to Pierce at least once a week. I was interested to see her in the flesh. Very short blonde tufty coiffure, like a long-haired guinea pig, false eyelashes and a deep tan. She was wearing a white dress so tight you could see the outline of her bra and knickers.

'Doesn't go for the subtle approach, does she?' Pierce laughed. 'Got "screw me" written all over her.'

'Pierce! Darling!' Angelica had seen him and was undulating through the crowd holding her champagne glass high above her head. Pierce went to meet her. I stood amid a sea of backs, bare and freckled, one with a Laura Ashley label sticking up, one in which the zip was held by a thread, several broader and in dinner jackets, and wondered which to engage in conversation. To my surprise I saw Giles over by the window. As far as I knew he and Julia had only the most slender acquaintance. He looked very serious, listening and nodding while a man with long grey hair and a pink face talked energetically. Julia walked over to them, put her arm through Giles's and, with a smile at Pink Face, bore Giles swiftly away. Pink Face was disconcerted for a moment but a rapid reconnoitre brought him to my side.

'Hello. Don't you know anyone here either? My name's Teddy Titt-Praed. We two lonely souls must look after each other. Have you known the Sempill-Smiths long?'

'No, I –'

'Nor me. I met Robert Sempill-Smith for the first time at a school governors' meeting last week and he absolutely insisted that I come but now I discover that he never attends his wife's parties. Very odd behaviour, I call it.' For a moment Teddy looked petulant then he brightened. 'But I must do my best to cheer you up, you poor little lost girl. You remind me of Mary Rose in the Barrie play. You remember, the one that was stolen away by fairies. You've got that wistful, hexed look. What happened to the little girl, can you remember?'

'She came back and –'

'Yes, yes, so she did. Now, how can I bring a smile to that sad little face? Let's really get to know each other.' Teddy's eyes beamed above his fat cheeks at his own suggestion. 'I'm the luckiest man alive in that I absolutely relish my work. Most poor devils have to nerve themselves to go into the office day after day but I skip to work.' Teddy made a vague bouncing movement with the upper half of his body to suggest the motion of skipping.

'What do you –?'

'I'm a musicologist. There! That's alarmed you, now, hasn't it?' I politely did my best to look startled. 'But you needn't worry. I'm not going to bore you with talk of concertos and symphonies. I study music that is so fascinatingly universal that a baby couldn't help kicking up its toes to it. I explore the music of trance and possession. Particularly of West Africa – the Putoo cult of Narasunga. Every spirit has its own tune. The spirit of Motherhood and Fertility has a song that goes something like this.' Teddy threw back his head and let forth a strange high-pitched howl. Several people standing near us turned to look. 'And then there's the Spirit of the Hearth and Cooking-pot. That's more of a low warble with emphasis on a rising a-ah! at the end, which is the demon of maize blight being overcome.' Teddy flexed his shoulders, lowered his chin and gave a slow moan, which ended in a shriek that made me jump and spill my champagne. 'Fascinating, isn't it? And this is the Healing song.' Teddy opened his tonsils to the ceiling and began to whoop. By now we had collected a crowd.

'Take several deep breaths with your arms raised and I'll bang you on the back, old chap,' said an elderly man with a monocle. 'Swallowed an olive stone the wrong way, I think,' he explained to the woman at his side.

'Try the Heimlich manoeuvre,' suggested someone else.

'No, no.' Teddy had grown pinker with the effort of

ululation. 'I'm explaining to this young lady all about the songs of the spirits. There's a really unusual rhythm for the spirit of the lano-lano tree. Quite hallucinogenic.' Teddy rolled his eyes upwards and blew out his cheeks as he trumpeted on one note.

'It's a fit, I think,' said a woman standing nearby.

The party began to dwindle just after midnight.

'Let's go to Sibylla's and dance.' Pierce, whom I hadn't seen all evening, stood beside me. I could always tell when Pierce was drunk because he appeared so much more sober than usual. He was unsmiling and held himself very upright, which told me he was as tight as a tick. I had spent much of the evening locked in Mrs Sempill-Smith's bathroom, which was a haven of strawberry-pink with a large comfortable armchair by a table on which stood a glorious arrangement of peonies and lilies and a pile of the latest magazines. Several times the door handle had rattled urgently but I was resistant to entreaty and had worked my way through *House and Garden* and *Tatler* from end to end until I judged it likely that Teddy had given up waiting for me at the foot of the stairs as he had promised to do.

'I think I'll go home,' I said. 'I'm very tired. You'd better not drive. You're much too drunk.'

'All right, Miss Goody-Goody. As it happens, Giles is driving. So come and say goodbye nicely to your hostess and we'll be off.'

'I really think I'll take a cab and go home,' I said to Giles as he, Pierce, Julia and I stood in the hall.

Julia pushed a cigarette into her holder. I caught a gust of lilies of the valley. 'Light, sweetie,' she said, to anyone in general. Giles went away to look for matches. 'Do come, darling,' she said to me. 'Giles and I want to dance. He's the most tremendous poppet. I adore clever men. It'll be such fun.' I wasn't particularly convinced by the cooing tone of her voice. I thought there was something of menace in it.

Pierce grabbed my arm and pulled me to one side. 'Can't you see that those two are desperate to get off with each other?' He pointed to Giles who was lighting Julia's cigarette.

'Well, I'm certainly not stopping them,' I said rather snappily, nursing my arm which Pierce had hurt. 'What do they need us for?'

'Don't you see how much jollier it will be for them if we go too? Besides,' Pierce whispered in my ear, 'Julia wants to make me jealous. It wouldn't be very sporting if we went away and spoiled all her fun, now would it?' Pierce looked at me solemnly, his eyes gleaming wickedly in the light from the overhead lantern.

Weakly I resigned myself to being carried, full of resentment, to our next rendezvous with fun and frolic. As it happened, the moment fresh air hit Pierce he collapsed like a felled oak on to the pavement and the three of us had to haul his unconscious body into the back of the Bentley and drive him to Rutland Gate. Giles gave him a fireman's lift up to his flat and we left him snoring on the sofa in the sitting room. Luckily a taxi was driving past as we came out into the road and I hailed it and got in.

I lectured myself sternly all the way home. What had I said to myself on the way back to London from Inskip Park about not falling feebly in with the plans of others? I had resolved to steer my own course and do only what was useful or enjoyable or strictly required by duty. My entire evening had been wasted because of a foolish inability to make a fuss. I had an overweening spirit of co-operation, which must be mastered and crushed out of existence.

I let myself quietly into the blackness of the hall of number 46. The house was solidly reassuring, smelling of Daniel's supper – something with herbs and oranges – and the bowl of dried rose-heads on the table. The tranquil ticking of the long-case clock and the faint gleam from its dial, like a single considering eye, seemed like a commentary on the folly of my efforts to take my life in hand. I felt for the candlestick that always stood beside the rose-heads. In the candle's glow I saw that there was a letter addressed to me. The light was too poor to read the postmark. I opened it.

Dear, dear Viola, Since you left I have been like a poor animal with a spear stuck in its side. I can do nothing to escape the pain of missing you. I did not realise until after you had gone how much I love you. Several times a day I run up to your/our room and shout your name across the valley like a muezzin calling the faithful to prayer. I sleep there at night breathing your scent from the pillow. I have not let Mrs Jukes change the sheets. There are nearly enough hairs from your coat to plait for a mourning ring. Come back and marry me at once, Your lonely, heartsick, Jeremy.

CHAPTER 19

'How does *anyone* know when they're in love?' replied Tiffany, when I asked her if she thought that I ought to marry Jeremy.

Tiffany lay in Pierce's deck-chair on the balcony at SCAB. A voluminous scarlet sarong was hitched up above her knees, exposing snow-white legs faintly downy with chestnut hair like a Chinese gooseberry. She was stitching blue-and-white glass beads to a lampshade. Beside her was a catering-size jar of pickled walnuts.

The only drawback to living at Tolgate Square was that not much sun came into the house and there was no garden, only a tiny cobbled courtyard like a pit, lined with ivy. Mrs Shilling, who was a fount of advice and told us in great detail about her pregnancies (which alternately encouraged and terrified us), was adamant that sunshine was good for pregnant mothers. Tiffany had had to give up her wait-ressing job at the vegan restaurant because the merest whiff of soya made her vomit instantly. So I had asked Pierce and Giles if they would object to her coming to the balcony.

'Not as long as she doesn't stop you working, my demon of efficiency,' Pierce had said, with the sarcasm that he tended to use in addressing me these days.

'I suppose she can't do anything useful like type or add up?' Giles had asked, with despair in his tone.

'It's a question that's been puzzling me since I was fifteen,' I said, while attempting to add up the latest donations received after Pierce's mother's last 'big push' in fund-raising. 'Damn these figures. I do believe they're changing of their own accord. I've added this column six times and never once got the same result. The answer, to whether one is in love or not, might be that there is no such thing. Simply varying degrees of sexual desire. I really think it might be better to like someone very much.'

'One might marry in order to belong to someone. Or to be the same as everyone else. Or so as not to feel a failure and unattractive to the opposite sex.'

'I bet loneliness has a lot to do with it,' I said, stopping to sharpen my pencil, fruitlessly blunted in an effort to carry beneath the line. 'I think Jeremy's lonely, really. That doesn't necessarily mean that he doesn't love me as well but I fear it may warp his judgement. That's not to say we couldn't be happy together, though. I'm pretty sure we could be.'

'What about you? What do you *really* feel about him?'

'I enjoy being with him. We have masses to say to each other and we make each other laugh. It's comfortable and cosy and I don't have to make efforts not to say something stupid. Usually talking to men is like trying to find a door in a rock. Occasionally you think you see a gleam of light but seconds later the surface is impenetrable again. He's very honest and good fun and I'm very, very fond of him but I don't know if that's a proper basis for marriage.'

'You haven't mentioned sex with regard to Jeremy.' Tiffany rolled her eyes as she popped another pickled walnut into her mouth. 'Yum! These are especially good ones. As soft as cream cheese. God! Suddenly I long for some.'

'Sex or cream cheese?'

'The latter.' Tiffany shuddered. 'I couldn't feel less sexy. Broodiness and sexiness are opposites. I want to fluff out my

258

feathers and go into a dark dream. Though I thought Giles was rather delicious. He reminded me of Gregory Peck. I like men who look complicated.'

Giles had appeared briefly in the office that morning to collect some papers before rushing away to an important lunch given by SLOPS – Scottish Land Owners Preservation Society. Though I had sometimes talked about Giles, it was the first time she had seen him.

'Complicated? Mm, actually that's a pretty accurate description. But he's well and truly bagged, I'm afraid. Julia Sempill-Smith hardly ever lets him off the leash. I see her waiting in her Daimler Dart outside the office every night like a fox after chickens. I thought at first she just wanted to pay Pierce out for taking me to her mother's party but now I think it may be more serious. Mrs Sempill-Smith keeps ringing Giles up, too, and talks to him for hours. He told me yesterday always to say he was out.'

'Shame.' Tiffany bit off a thread. 'Still, as I say, I'm not in the mood for passion with anyone, however desirable. But you didn't tell about sex with Jeremy. Am I being too nosy?'

'Of course not. But, really, there isn't anything *to* tell. Though we spent five nights in the same bed we didn't actually make love, though there was plenty of hugging and quite a bit of kissing.'

'How odd. Rather nice, though. If only men would realise that a girl likes to be spoken to in bed. Was he too gentlemanly to insist after such a brief acquaintance? I warm to him by the minute. Perhaps this is the genuine thing.'

'I think it's something more obscure – but I don't really know.' I didn't want to tell Tiffany that Jeremy had a sexual problem. It's hardly the kind of thing it's fair to broadcast . . . especially not if you're going to marry the man in question.

'And what about Pierce? Is that completely over?'

'Well, yes, on my part it is. You know that awful row we had?'

Tiffany had been sympathetic when I had arrived back at number 46 unexpectedly early the second evening after my return from Inskip Park. Despite the rather disastrous experience of the Sempill-Smiths' party, I had accepted Pierce's invitation to have dinner with him the next day so that I could tell him about Jeremy. He had picked me up from home and driven straight to his flat and said he wanted to make love before eating.

'Get those things off,' Pierce had said, as we walked through the door of his flat. 'I'm going to fasten you to the bed by your hands and feet. Corny but fun.'

'Perhaps Julia likes that kind of thing but it sounds ridiculous to me. I shouldn't be able to stop laughing. Anyway I've got something to tell you. I'm thinking of marrying Jeremy Inskip.' I suppose this was rather bluntly put but he was already beginning to feel for the buttons on the back of my dress and there wasn't time to think of a more delicate way to break it to him.

'Ha! Viola has gone stark, staring mad! Never mind, a little lunacy adds piquancy – as Lord Arthur said to Lucia di Lammermoor.'

'Honestly, I mean it. Do leave my dress alone, Pierce. I'm practically engaged to Jeremy.'

'You're sacking me!' Pierce's blue eyes were wide with indignation and disbelief. 'You little – stop talking like a madwoman or I'll put you over my knee and spank you.'

It had taken me ages to convince Pierce that I was serious. He said it was perfectly ridiculous to think of marrying someone after having known them for a few days. I had tried to explain about those five days being a peculiarly intense period of time that had changed me a lot in important ways. I pointed out as well that if you added up the time Pierce and I had spent actually talking to each other it probably didn't amount to anything like as long as five days.

'Well, *I* haven't asked you to marry me,' Pierce had pointed out. 'Not yet anyway,' he added, his eyes full of reproach. He had then sulked tremendously and refused to take me to dinner. I had got a taxi home, only just able to bear making him so unhappy by reminding myself of the nightdress and toothbrush. Tiffany had reassured me that I had done just the right thing and shared with me her bean and pickled walnut casserole.

'Pierce has virtually ignored me since then.' I looked hopelessly at the columns of figures as Tiffany put down the lampshade to spear yet another walnut. 'He's been incredibly grumpy, with Giles as well as me, and made me do all sorts of unnecessary tidying jobs which he knows I'm no good at. I've Ajaxed the kitchen until I haven't got any fingernails left. And he has long lascivious telephone conversations with other women in front of me. I'm afraid I haven't minded in the least. I could tell he wanted me to listen so I did and I must say it was rather amusing trying to guess what the person on the other end might be saying. But yesterday he dragged me into the conservatory, kissed me violently, and said he wanted to marry me.'

'Two proposals of marriage in hardly more than a month!' Tiffany paused, her fork half-way to her lips, and stared at me in awe. 'I'm eight years older than you and I've never had one! I'm *madly* jealous.'

'I don't believe for a minute Pierce would go through with it if I accepted him. He doesn't really want to marry me. It's just that no one has ever denied him what he wanted before. His mother spoils him completely and girls are always dotty about him – because he's so brutally unkind to them, probably. Other men are a little afraid of him because he's so ruthless. I honestly think my sacking him has acted as a sort of aphrodisiac.'

'I must say he does sound rather exciting. But no – what am I thinking of? I'm soon to be a mother and, according to Dr Spock, my thrills will come from an extra ounce on the baby scales and a well-formed stool.' Tiffany had begun to read all sorts of manuals on childbirth and child-rearing. The diagrams of episiotomies made us both scream. Giles came out on to the balcony at that moment and Tiffany turned the colour of her sarong in fear that he had heard her last remark.

'This place looks like the Bower of Bliss – thoroughly decadent and degenerate. But a wonderful haven from heat and noise. I wish I could stay.' Giles was looking cool in a blue open-necked shirt, which set off the slight tan he was acquiring – no doubt from being driven about in the Daimler Dart. He looked at Tiffany's flaming face. 'You've caught the sun quite badly, you know. You ought to be careful.' He turned to me. 'I'll be in tomorrow at about eleven. Any luck with those totals?' He leaned down to look over my shoulder. I was drowned in a drift of lilies of the valley. 'I don't think a fraction can be right, Viola.'

'That's my method of carrying figures beneath the line. I'm trying to take this lot away from that lot to see if the answer is anything like the same . . .'

Giles laughed. Two weeks ago he would probably have been annoyed by my incompetence. His resolution to be less serious was clearly bearing fruit. About a minute after he went away I thought I could detect the roar of a sports car revving up to join the traffic.

'Actually, Viola, if one were going to be in love with anybody I would have thought the obvious candidate has just driven off with La Sempill-Smith.'

'Oh, no! Giles is terribly clever and knows virtually everything. He wouldn't be interested in a butterfly brain like me.'

'And Julia has PhDs in Oriental Semantics and the Last Seljuk Dynasty?'

'Well, no. Of course she isn't at all suitable. But, you see, Giles wants to learn to be less serious.'

I explained about the effect Inskip Park had had on Giles and about his resolve to be more frivolous. Tiffany was gripped by the tale. 'Well, well. It ill behoves me to be critical of others when I'm an object lesson to the improvident. But poor Giles. Lalla does sound just a hint self-centred.'

'I really think he's absolutely over it.'

'I don't know Julia but from the glimpses I've had of her she certainly looks pretty *and* pretty silly. Perhaps that was mean. Pregnancy isn't doing my morale any good. I'm getting crabbed and envious. Here's to cultivation and frivolity, without either of which life would be unendurable.' Tiffany drained her glass of Mr Dring's bargain white wine, which came from a barrel at the back of his shop. 'It feels delightfully sinful to be drinking at four in the afternoon.' She squinted against the sun to thread her needle. 'Though this wine is an acquired taste. An unusual flavour of ink mingled with gents' lavs.'

'It isn't that bad. You've probably ruined your palate eating those walnuts. Don't you think you'd better put more cream on? Your legs are looking pink.'

'This is heaven up here.' Tiffany rubbed in more Ambre Solaire. 'One feels tucked away from the big, bad world. It's like being a god on Mount Olympus. We could lean over and watch the struggles of the teeming hordes below and make capricious decisions about their destinies. What do you think?'

Tiffany held out the lampshade, which was shaped like a witch's hat. She had done something very brave with what, in the old days, I would have called purple and orange but, having just finished reading a book about pigments in oil paints, I would now describe as Cobalt Violet and Naples Yellow. I admired the originality of the design with perfect truth. I had never seen anything remotely like it. 'This is my first commission actually. I'm rather excited about it. This bloke I used to know has opened an art gallery somewhere in Chiswick. He admired my skirt – you know, the one I made with the stripes of sequins – and asked me to do something for his exhibition of contemporary domestic furnishings.'

I looked with fondness at the pleased smile on her broad face, which was charmingly dappled with freckles. Everything about Tiffany was generous, including her capacity for enthusiasm. 'I'd love to come to the private view, if you can get me an invitation,' I said. 'Perhaps I'll ask Pierce to take me. He begged me to say I'd have dinner with him. In the end I promised to think about it. Only, would it be unfair to encourage him? I wonder if Jeremy would mind.'

'I must say, Viola,' said Tiffany, with a dreamy look on her face, 'you do have an extraordinarily good time.'

*

'Here you are,' said Giles, with an air of triumph the next morning, putting down a rectangular object in front of me.

'What is it?'

'It's a calculator. It's the latest thing. Look, it will add up for you.' He pressed various buttons with dizzying speed and numbers appeared in a little box.

'Heavens, how clever!'

We spent some time playing with it before Pierce came in with a face like a Scottish Presbyterian minister finding his congregation frolicking with goats, Pan pipes and bunches of grapes on the Sabbath. 'I'm going to do some work,' he said pointedly, slamming down his briefcase on the table.

Giles raised his eyebrows at me, and I tried to signal sorrow and helplessness with my eyes. We worked in a tense silence for an hour until Pierce got up, gathered his papers together and said, 'I don't think I can remain in this atmosphere of funereal gloom any longer. I shall go and have lunch with people who are capable of being amusing company.' He banged the door on his way out.

Giles sighed. 'How are you getting on?'

'I don't think I've quite got the hang of this.' I frowned at the calculator. 'It can't possibly be such a huge sum.'

'You're supposed to press the plus sign between each addition.' Giles showed me again with what was, for him, exemplary patience. 'How's the essay on Botticelli going, by the way?'

'Oh, well – slowly, thank you. I'm a bit stuck on something to say about the *Man with the Medal*. I don't like it very much.'

'Probably you need to see it. It's a pity it's in the Uffizi. But you could go and look at the *Portrait of a Young Man*, which is just up the road in the National Gallery, and talk about Botticelli's portraits generally. You can say something about the Renaissance bringing about a revival of interest in the individual man. And have a look at the exquisite *Venus and Mars* while you're there. What are you doing about lunch?'

'I shall have to get a sandwich somewhere.'

'Would you like to have lunch with me? I'll see what I can dredge up about Botticelli from my student days.'

'Would I!' I ran my hands through my hair, passed a licked finger over my eyebrows, grabbed my bag and was ready.

We walked together across Trafalgar Square and into the Strand. Heat radiated from the surrounding buildings. Sweating knots of tourists dutifully craned their necks to see Nelson's statue and queued at the stall selling pigeon food. The restaurant, called La Petite Sonnerie, was dark and cool and smelt wonderful, of lemons, bread and coffee. A young French waitress greeted Giles with shy deference and showed us to a table by the window. She brought us, unasked, a carafe of house wine and a basket of bread, which we ate off the paper tablecloth – a thing I had never done before.

'How odd not to have a menu,' I said, as the waitress brought us our first course. It was a little dish of pink radishes, still with their green stalks on and of pearly whiteness inside when you bit them. With them came a few pats of palest yellow unsalted butter. 'It's much more exciting – not knowing. And it cuts out the agony of wondering whether you made the right choice.'

'I expect they would cook you pretty well what you wanted, within reason, but I like to have what the family themselves eat. The grandmother is the cook, the daughter does the managing and the granddaughters wait and wash up. I come here whenever I'm not lunching on business.'

'It's perfect.' I looked around the room. It held eight tables, all spread with white cloths with wide blue borders beneath the paper covers. It was already nearly full and we seemed to be the only English there. The walls were painted dark green and hung with a collection of paintings of gardens and dogs. Squeezed in between them were plates painted with flowers. 'I've never actually been to France. Only Monte Carlo. It wasn't anything like this. Not nearly as nice.'

This seemed to amuse Giles and he asked me to tell him about Monaco. While we talked the young girl brought us our next course, pale-pink succulent flakes of fish, which Giles said was salmon trout, accompanied by new potatoes and a sauce like sea foam. Giles said it was a *beurre blanc*.

'This is absolutely delicious. What a lot I've got to learn about everything. It's amazing to me that you can know so much – I mean, how can you possibly recognise salmon trout from ordinary salmon or trout and know which sauce it is?'

'It's written on the blackboard behind your head.'

'Oh. Well, anyway, you do know a lot about food. I'd like to learn how to make this. It was one of the vows I made at Inskip Park – to learn how to cook, I mean. I'd forgotten about it in the excitement of starting my history of art course.'

Giles seemed pleased by my enthusiasm. I suppose it is always gratifying to have one's favourite things admired. Madame herself came out from the kitchen as we were finishing the fish and made a beeline for Giles to ask him how he liked it. She was a magnificent woman, tiny and wrinkled like a dried fig but with the most terrific presence. Giles spoke in what sounded to me like perfect French but I must admit I'm no judge as mine is of the schoolgirl variety and when Giles pointed to me and said something about my liking the food I could only stammer 'tray, tray bonne, Madame. Ex-keys!' while feeling myself turn the colour of a bishop's vest. She cackled at me, said something very fast to Giles and went away. 'What did she say? Oh, heavens! Look at this!' The waitress had brought us a dish of broad beans like pellets of jade and little stripy purple and green artichoke hearts. 'Now I've started really looking at things, I wonder how I could possibly have been so unnoticing before. The colours alone are a banquet for one's eyes.'

'She said you had beautiful eyes, actually.'

'Really? It took her a long time to say just that.' I did not receive so many compliments that I could afford to be careless about them.

'Something about your witty and intelligent face. I'm not sure if she meant that you looked amusing or had your wits about you. Probably the former.'

266

'Thank you.'

'Now, don't sulk but have some cheese.'

After we had eaten some salty, crumbly Roquefort Giles began to talk to me about Botticelli and everything he said struck me as so brilliant and pertinent to my essay that I wrote it down in the notebook I took everywhere now. 'I suppose you want a pudding,' he said, catching the waitress's eye.

'I don't think I could. I've had so much and it was honestly the most delicious lunch I've ever eaten in my life.'

'You'll have to have it now or Madame's feelings will be hurt,' he said, as the old lady herself came out from the kitchen and with great ceremony put before me a small dish of something golden like distilled sunlight.

It was an orange soufflé, light in texture and intense in flavour. After we had drunk our coffee Giles and I had an argument over who should pay the bill. 'I really hate ruining a good lunch squabbling about money,' said Giles, very firmly. 'I earn ten times as much as you do. I can assure you that by buying you lunch I won't feel that I have purchased a right to sexual favours of any kind.' He looked at me severely when he said that and I knew he was thinking of Pierce and Jeremy.

'You seem to have your hands pretty full as it is,' I returned sweetly, and Giles laughed.

'Here's to Inskip Park,' he said, lifting his glass. 'And to our good intentions. May you grow as wise as serpents and as harmless as doves.'

I lifted my glass in reply. 'May you never grow sober. I take it the serpents and doves are a quotation?' I wrote it down. 'I hope you're enjoying your reformed self as much as I am. Honestly I thought I was going to cry when Julian showed us the slide of the Rose-garden Madonna. It was so absolutely beautiful.'

' "Pleasures newly found are sweet." That's Wordsworth. No, W-O-R-D. Really, Viola! How could it possibly be W-H-I-R-D.'

I smiled as I corrected my spelling, pleased to find that being told off by Giles no longer troubled me at all.

CHAPTER 20

O n the way home that evening I stopped at a second-hand bookshop and bought *French Country Cooking*. I chose it because it had a recipe for *beurre blanc*. All the way on the bus back to Tolgate Square I dipped into the pages and found them quite as interesting as a good novel. The writer suggested the sauce as an accompaniment for pike but, remembering my experience with the sturgeon, I thought not.

'What are you making?' Daniel peered over my shoulder as later that evening I stirred the contents of a pan, my face hot from the fire. I was attempting to see by wavering candlelight whether the concoction of finely chopped shallots, white wine and butter was going to boil, in which case, warned the author of the cookery book without mincing her words, 'disaster will ensue'.

'*Beurre blanc*. I hope you don't mind me using two of your shallots. But I haven't got three tablespoons of something called *court bouillon*. I wanted to practise the sauce before I spent fifty p on a Dover sole. What do you think it is? I hope not something disgusting like brains because if so I'll never be able to make it properly.'

'It means water, acidulated with vinegar or wine and simmered for perhaps an hour with vegetables and herbs. I think it unlikely that even the largest fish possesses three tablespoons of brains.' Daniel picked up the book and flicked through the pages. 'Hm. This is an excellent cookery book. I can borrow it sometimes?'

'Whenever you want.' I was flattered that Daniel, always so severely critical, should approve my purchase.

'So. You begin your cooking at the wrong end but perhaps that is to the good. Mastery of sauces – yes, as important an accomplishment as any. But careful! It is a little too hot.' Daniel seized a cloth and snatched the pan from the trivet, which was suspended over the flames. He poured the shallot mixture into a pudding basin. 'That will cool it at once. Now wash out the pan and fill it with hot water from the kettle. Then we sit the bowl in the pan and there you have a *bain-marie*. You see, it says here that it is a wise thing to do.' He pointed to the page.

'I hadn't got as far as that.'

'But, Viola, you must read the whole recipe before you begin. Ach! What a little idea you have of doing things. You can add warm water and white wine to replace the *court bouillon*. It will not be as good but it must do. Now you need to whisk in more butter piece by piece. Like this. A loose motion in the wrist. Patience. Air is the secret of this sauce. Light, light, light! Now a little cream, so! A few grains of salt. Taste.'

I did and was thrilled to recognise the sauce of lunch. I told Daniel about La Petite Sonnerie.

'And who led you to this epiphany? Not the young man so amusing with his car horn, I think?'

'No, it was Giles.'

'The man who took you to Nottingham. The one who thinks you are a fool. But why does he then take you to lunch?'

I had described my relationship with Giles to Daniel in the early days of my joining SCAB. 'He's not nearly as disagreeable as I thought. He wanted to help me with my Botticelli essay.'

Daniel looked at me with some scepticism before returning to the book. 'Now we shall try sauce Espagnole. As this excellent writer observes, it is the basis for several important classic sauces. Fortunately there is a good beef stock in the larder. Fetch me the flour.'

'You seem to get a lot of letters these days,' Tiffany said to me, the morning after my discovery of French sauces as Mrs Shilling brought down the post. It was Saturday and we were drinking tea in the kitchen. The door to the well-shaft, which pretended to be a garden, was wide open to counteract the heat from the range. This was one of the inconveniences of living in the past. It was romantic but hot in summer. Mrs Shilling had accepted our offer to help her with cleaning the silver, though she insisted on inspecting our work before the knives and forks and salts and coffee-pots could be put back, for Mrs Shilling was a stickler for perfection.

'Here you are, duck.' Mrs Shilling gave me an envelope. I recognised Jeremy's writing. It was the sixth I had received from him since my return to London.

Darling girl,

Two court appearances next week. One for disturbing the peace – when I so famously reduced *lo zingaro* to a bloody pulp – and the second because that bloody old bitch did press charges over Bowser's slaughter of her cat. If it weren't for having to be here to answer these grave imputations I'd throw everything up and climb the ivy to your window, drop over the sill and make slow, sumptuous, heart-breaking love to you. I know now I could. I'm filled with the most hideously ungovernable lust and have to take cold baths to stop myself combusting. I will do something soon about your watch – or get Lalla to, don't worry. I think I may have A PLAY! Your own BURN-ING Jeremy.

I was pleased that the tone of his letter was more cheerful. I opened the second.

Dear Viola,

The Mars bars were great. Thanks. I didn't eat any of them because Bugger Boreham took them but in return he wouldn't let the others flush my head down the bogs. Bugger is captain of cricket this term and his voice has already broken. I was glad because the water goes back up your nose when they hold you down for a long time. This has been a good week. The cook is ill so we didn't have porridge. I know you are right about the swimming and I mean to try but I've been off games all this week because of my verruca. No more news, love Nicky.

'I'll answer that,' said Mrs Shilling, as the front door bell leaped on its spring. 'Give me tea a chance to cool.' Mrs Shilling lived in terror that anything hot would melt her false teeth so she always let her tea get cold and scummy before she drank it.

I read aloud Nicky's letter to Tiffany. 'Poor little boy!' Tiffany was horrified. 'What beasts boys are!'

'I'd better send him some more chocolate at once. What makes people want to torture their fellow men?'

'Telegram for you, dear.' Mrs Shilling held it out towards me at arm's length as though it might go off. 'I hate the things. You better sit down before you open it.'

'It's probably another proposal of marriage. I shall spit if it is,' said Tiffany. 'I'm the one that needs to get married.'

'"Hardly dare to think you may not be already engaged,"' I read aloud, '"but would you have dinner with me tonight? Love Hamish."' A telephone number was appended. We were all impressed by what Mrs Shilling called the 'pound-foolishness' of this message.

'He's going to pop the question. I know it,' moaned Tiffany. 'Is he heart-stoppingly handsome like the rest of your friends?'

'Not really. He's tremendously nice and kind besides being clever and rich. But he's engaged to Lalla.'

'With the swathes you're cutting through the male population at the moment I can't see that that will make any difference. Anyway, it wasn't bad news. You can relax, Mrs Shilling.'

Mrs Shilling had braced herself, hand on heart and scarcely breathing, while I opened the telegram. 'You're too young to remember the war, that's what it is. We used to feel our hearts go pit-a-pat when we saw the telegraph boy. It was a terrible thing. Women made widders and kiddies orphans at a stroke. Not to mention all the poor gels that lost their sweethearts. How's that boyfriend of yours?' Mrs Shilling thoroughly enjoyed the vicarious excitements from our romances.

'Oh, pretty cross still. He pretends I've broken his heart. But all the time I was in Nottinghamshire Julia Sempill-Smith was staying at his flat. He admits it but says it didn't mean anything. He says I'm a "necessary love" and Julia is a "contingent love", according to the philosophy of Simone de Beauvoir and Jean-Paul Sartre. It sounds to me like a feeble excuse for promiscuity.'

'The tea-leaves said he'd be unfaithful. They never lie.' Mrs Shilling bit into a jam ring with satisfaction. 'He's not a good bet for marrying.'

'I'm sure of it. I said I would always want him as a good friend but that made him more furious.'

'That was naïve of you, Viola, if I may say so,' said Tiffany. 'Men consider themselves insulted by the offer of a relationship which excludes torrid sex on demand. Disinterested friendship holds no attractions. Perhaps they feel the same about blokes. No immediate and obvious gain. I think cases of Damon and Pythias are in reality few and far between and that's why such relationships are famous.'

Tiffany was rather more acerbic these days, I had noticed.

'They don't know what's good for them, that's the trouble,' sighed Mrs Shilling. 'Poor mad dears.'

'Mad, certainly,' said Tiffany.

I met Hamish in the Rivoli Bar at the Ritz. He embraced me warmly and I recalled Tiffany's parting injunction to bear it constantly in mind that he was already spoken for. He was a delightful companion, ready to be amused and amusing. He was looking important and glamorous in a pinstripe suit and a beautiful tie. We drank North Pole cocktails. They were three parts French vermouth and one part pineapple juice and the edge of the glass was dipped in sugar, to look like ice. I wrote the ingredients down to tell Jeremy when next I wrote.

Hamish had spent the last two days in Rome, which he said was beautiful and inspiring but so hot that London felt almost chilly by comparison. I was wearing a pale-green, sleeveless linen dress, cheap but fetching and Hamish said I looked as enticing as pistachio ice-cream. He had been to see the house near the Spanish Steps where Keats died and we talked a lot about his poetry and which were our favourite bits. Hamish admired the lines from 'Sleep and Poetry'. ' "Stop and consider! Life is but a day: a fragile dew-drop on its perilous way from a tree's summit." I have always loved "When I behold upon the night's starr'd face, Huge cloudy symbols of a high romance."' It was a very satisfactory conversation.

Over dinner Hamish told me about his parents' house in Scotland and the cottage on the estate which was his. 'It overlooks the seashore. Often the sheep wander down there. They look delightfully incongruous on a beach, ambling among the seaweed. And there are seals who put up their heads from the waves and call out to each other like this.'

Hamish imitated the mournful honking of a seal and the people on the next table turned their heads discreetly to look at us. This reminded me of Teddy Titt-Praed. Hamish laughed until he cried real tears at my description of Teddy, and our dining neighbours swivelled in their chairs to find out what was so funny.

We began with asparagus and the head waiter came over in person to describe how the sauce Maltaise, which came with it, was made. I wrote it down carefully in my notebook.

'Are you going to be a cook?' asked Hamish.

'I don't know. It isn't very likely. But I really have no idea. That's what's so marvellous about being twenty. I might be anything.' I tapped my notebook. 'In here are just the seeds of possibilities. Anyone of them might be an enormous tree with hard work.'

'I wish Lalla saw things like that.'

We hadn't talked about Lalla or Inskip Park until that moment. I knew that we would but I had decided to wait until Hamish introduced them as subjects of conversation.

'What do you mean exactly?' I lowered my head to sniff my lobster *à l'enfant prodigue*. Delicious little flakes of truffle gave off a tantalising scent. Being interested in cooking added another important dimension to the business of eating.

'She seems to want to run from everything. From having a job, from travelling, from friends, from being happy like any other girl with looks and brains ... from me.' Hamish looked at me intently just as I had speared a delicious-looking hunk of red-and-cream marbled flesh dripping with champagne sauce. It seemed insensitive to be chomping at this moment of revelation so I put down my fork. 'I don't know why she won't marry me and let me take her away from Inskip Park. I think – I practically *know* – I could make her happy, yet she shrinks away when I suggest it and changes the subject. She tells me she loves me, that she doesn't want to marry anyone else but I feel that she wants to get away from me. It's like having a terrified animal on a string. They pretend to walk quietly beside you but you have the feeling that if you let them off the lead they'd be away like a shot and over the next hill. What's eating her, do you know?'

My eyes involuntarily swooped down to my lobster at the mention of eating but I forced them back to Hamish's worried face. 'Well . . .' I could not betray a confidence but I wanted to encourage Hamish. 'I think it has something to do with not feeling worthy of you. Lalla thinks of herself as being . . . not bad exactly . . . perhaps – I don't know . . . culpable in some way.'

'Is that it? But how absurd! . . . Though, yes, I see that you could be right. Ridiculous as it seems . . . the notion that she's somehow *persona non grata* . . . Now I think about it, that fits with some of the things she's told me.' Hamish looked more cheerful. 'I hope that's what it is. I can soon get rid of such a silly idea. My great terror, if I'm going to be honest, was that she might find me, well . . . boring. We always get on so well when we're alone together but as soon as we're with other people she seems to turn away as though almost anyone else's company is better than mine.'

'Nobody could find you dull – ever,' I said truthfully. 'And I'm absolutely positive that Lalla doesn't. It's to do with her not you. Honestly, I know I'm right.'

'I feel so much better for talking to you. I'll never love anyone else, you know. I hadn't been with her five minutes before I knew she was the girl for me. And she can run away from time to time if only I can be sure that she'll come back.' Hamish's face, when he said that, looked so wistful and

274

hungry that I was tremendously touched and at the same time I felt a twinge of shameful jealousy. Would anyone ever love me like that? Because I wasn't the sort of person to run away probably they wouldn't. Hamish cleared his throat and smiled. 'But I've been thoroughly egotistical, bothering you with my problems. It's because I could see how much Lalla likes you – how relaxed she is with you. Usually she doesn't like women much. And they seem to find her intimidating.' I remembered Lalla at school. It was true, I thought, that the other girls had been a little afraid of her because she had done so completely exactly what she wanted. It made her seem at the time much more grown-up than the rest of us. Now, oddly, it struck me as being rather childish. Perhaps I was beginning to grow up. The idea was exciting. 'You aren't eating that,' said Hamish. 'Would you like to order something else?'

When Hamish kindly took me in his taxi all the way back to number 46, I had to struggle to bend my protesting stomach to get out. I had eaten strawberries Romanoff for pudding and had just had room for several petits fours with my coffee. Hamish had said he was bored to death by girls sucking on celery stalks and that it was a great treat to take a woman out to dinner who was beautiful and also a hearty trencherman.

'I hope you don't think I'm greedy.' I looked up at him as we stood together on the doorstep. He had insisted on seeing me actually to the door though the taxi was ticking away pound notes in the street. Hamish was going straight from Tolgate Square to Heathrow to fly overnight to Japan. His kind, intelligent face was illuminated by the light from the street-lamps.

'I don't think that for a moment. I can see that you're hungry for life. I think it's charming.' He stroked my cheek and then kissed it in a sweet brotherly manner. Lucky Lalla, I thought. 'Promise me something, Viola.'

I prepared myself mentally. These days I always seemed to be making solemn promises to people and it behoved me not to forget what it was I was swearing to do. 'Lalla's unhappy. She needs you. If she sometimes seems to behave badly, try not to be angry. I know it's a lot to ask. But will you always stand her friend, for my sake as well as hers?' Just then I would have sworn to cultivate Jack the Ripper, if he had asked me.

I let myself into the hall and knelt on the window-seat with my head out of the window to watch the tail lights of Hamish's taxi as it turned at the end of the square and disappeared into the traffic. I could with very little effort have imagined myself in love with him or, really, with almost anyone. I gave myself a stern lecture. It must be the champagne and the dreamy summer night working in tandem to encourage me to make an absolute fool of myself. I shut my eyes. The lush scent of jasmine climbing past the window befuddled my senses.

'Viola,' said Daniel's voice behind me, making me knock my head sharply on the open sash.

'Ow! Can't you whistle or something when approaching a girl from behind?'

'I'm worried about Miss Barlam. I know that you and she are friends. Has she said anything to you?'

I gathered my thoughts. 'What's the matter with Veronica?'

'She has left this note on my desk. I don't know what I ought to think about it.' In the gloom of the hall I could barely see Daniel's face. He held out a piece of paper. 'I found it when I came home at about six o'clock. I thought I had better – goodness knows what maggots you women have in your heads. I waited to speak to her when she came home. But she has not come back.'

'Just a minute. Can you light a candle?'

As the flame grew Daniel's anxious face appeared from the shadows. I read the note.

Dear Daniel,

I am so sorry to be such a trouble to you. I realise after our encounter this morning that that is what I am and your annoyance is quite justified. It has all gone on long enough. I have made a perfect fool of myself and it is time to make an end of it. I want to set your mind at rest. I cannot bear to think that I am adding to your burdens when my one desire is to ease them. I shall act at once. Believe me, your sincere friend, Veronica Barlam.

'What happened this morning?'

'Well,' Daniel looked at me angrily and then turned his head away to stare at the lights of the square. 'I was making my breakfast. You know how I like to be alone. The society of my fellow men is insupportable to me for the first hours of waking. I make no excuses.' He resumed his fierce look but didn't meet my eye. 'Miss Barlam came in as I was preparing my bread and butter. She apologised for intruding over and over again until my head was ringing and made a ridiculous tiptoe to the cupboard and opened it so –' Daniel hunched his shoulders up and made the gesture of opening a door with finger and thumb in an exaggeratedly careful manner. 'I was irritated. I said something like "Please, Miss Barlam, that mincing is, if anything, more exacerbating to the nerves than a slamming of the door."'

'Oh, Daniel! That was rather unkind to someone as sensitive as Veronica.'

Daniel threw out his chin and glared at me. 'I dare say. I am, after all, a brute. I acknowledge it.'

'Was that all you said?'

Daniel looked down. 'I may have said – let me be truthful – I *did* say something about society being a curse. I merely quote Ovid, amongst others. Ha! Who would think someone would be silly enough to take this to their hearts. You, for example, would have told me I was a curmudgeon who deserved to be chained and beaten –'

'I doubt it. I think it *was* rather hurtful. Particularly first thing. You're not the only person who feels fragile when they wake up.'

'You think I am a selfish monster, inconsiderate, unmannerly . . .' Daniel paused to fold his lips back over his teeth like a dog. Then he expelled his breath violently and clutched my arm. 'Well, it is true. And now I am desperate. Viola, I admit I am everything that is bad but tell me that Miss Barlam has not killed herself!'

277

We stared at each other. Daniel's face was wreathed in dread as his eyes urged me to reassure him.

'I don't know! You say she hasn't come back?' This was extremely worrying since Veronica always returned from work without fail at half past six and had never, in the time I had lived at number 46, left the house again until morning. 'Where might she have gone?' I thought of the river and of the tube station and of the nearest tall buildings. 'We must telephone the police and report a missing person.'

'She has been missing all of three hours. The police will tell us she is visiting friends, out to dinner, at a concert.'

Daniel was right. They would not take us seriously.

'What can we do? Shall I go down to the Embankment?' I picked up my evening bag from the window-seat and opened the front door.

'Well, you can walk up and down but most likely you will be picked up and murdered by some passing maniac and that is all the good you will do. No, if anyone is to go to the river it must be me.'

'All right. You go to the river and I'll go to the Underground. What else can we do?'

'I am the most wretched creature alive! How could I lose my temper with that poor, lonely woman. Oh, Viola!' He groaned and took my hands in his. 'I would give the rest of my life to have the chance to unsay those ridiculous – those cruel words of temper!'

'Hello, Viola. Hello, Daniel.' Veronica stood in the doorway. Her eyes moved from our faces to our clasped hands. 'It's a lovely evening isn't it?' she said, as we gaped at her. 'I haven't been out after dark for such a long time. I've been for a long walk by the river. At night the city has quite a different kind of beauty.'

'Oh, Veronica!' I exclaimed, letting go of Daniel's hands. 'We were so worried about you!'

'You needn't have been.' Veronica smiled with an obvious effort. 'I went for an interview. I didn't get the job. They want someone younger. It's a pity since they were offering a flat over the premises.' She looked at Daniel. 'I think, though I've loved living here, the time has come for a change. I'm sure you agree.'

Daniel brushed past her and walked out into the night, slamming the front door behind him.

Veronica's face fell. 'I'm always annoying him. I can't seem to say the right thing.'

'It isn't that.' I held out her note, which I still had crumpled in my hand. 'He thought you'd gone away to kill yourself.'

'What?' Veronica glanced at the note. 'Oh dear, yes, I see that someone who didn't know me very well might have thought that. How sorry I am to be the cause of yet more trouble to him! But, of course, the Church's teaching forbids the taking of one's own life. It's a mortal sin. I should never even contemplate such a thing. Surely *you* didn't think – oh, Viola, I *am* sorry.'

I thought, but did not say, that not everyone was as dutiful and law-abiding as Veronica and that there might be circumstances in which some people would decide to disobey the tenets of their religion.

'I think I've made a fool of myself again.' Veronica's head drooped with weariness. 'I know at the time when I do and say things that I'm annoying him but I just can't stop – being – me!'

'Thank goodness for that. I don't want you to change the smallest bit.'

Veronica smiled sadly. 'Thank you for that. But I must change at least my outward circumstances. It's killing me. I'm growing mean-spirited, jealous. Sometimes I'm even jealous of Josephine. I want to get away, if only for a while. Anywhere. Perhaps, after all, I'll apply for that job as receptionist at the Great Westminster Hotel.'

'I've got a better idea,' I said. 'Don't do anything yet but let me make a few telephone calls. I really think I may have the answer.'

'Oh, Viola!' Veronica clasped her hands together as though in prayer. 'I'm desperate. If you really think –'

'Is this a private talk or can anyone join in?' Tiffany stood on the staircase, her face lit by the candle she was holding. 'Sorry to butt in but I'm feeling quite –' She stopped speaking and began to sway. Veronica and I stared up as though mesmerised by the weaving flame. 'Christ – sorry, Veronica, but I feel so rotten, there's so much blood – I think I'm having –' She sagged at the knees and her head fell back. Then the candle dropped from her hand and bounced down the steps, followed in slow motion by Tiffany.

I ran as fast as I could to the telephone box. I kicked off my silly strappy shoes somewhere on the way so as to run faster. I panted out a request for an ambulance and ran back to find Veronica kneeling by Tiffany's side chafing her hands. Tiffany was just beginning to come round. 'Darling Tiff,' I sobbed, partly from emotion and partly from breathlessness, 'don't worry about a thing! They'll be here any minute.'

Tiffany's eyes rolled alarmingly. 'Horrible mess. Daniel's blessed Aubusson.'

By which she meant the hall carpet, which was particularly pretty and the apple of Daniel's eye. I suddenly saw on its pale cream and pink beauty a pool of dark red. I knelt down and put my arm round her.

'I'll scrub it. Don't worry! There they are!' I added as the doorbell pealed.

I held Tiffany's head as Veronica went to open it.

'Hello. Does Viola Otway live here?' said a voice I recognised immediately.

'Lalla!' I stared at her by the light of the hall candle, the flame of which was streaming in the draught.

'Sorry to barge in on you like this, darling,' she said, walking in, 'but I'm in rather a jam.' She looked from me to Veronica and down at Tiffany who lay with eyes closed, her head lolling on my knee. 'Well the party must have been good.' No one spoke for several seconds. I think Veronica and I were too frightened and confused to be able to think of anything sensible to say. 'All right,' continued Lalla, tossing her head and looking rather discomfited, 'don't stare me out of countenance. I've very stupidly got myself in pod and I shall have to get rid of it at once. Isn't it *drôle*? I must say, though, I'm not exactly killing myself with laughter. Has there been a power cut?'

CHAPTER 21

'Are you sure it's the right thing to do?' I asked Lalla, as we lay side by side in my bed. I had blown out the candle seconds before and the sharp smell of wax and smoke drifted across our faces. It was too hot to close the shutters. Gradually it became possible to identify objects in the room in the light from the street-lamps in the square.

Veronica had returned from the hospital an hour before with the news that Tiffany was comfortable and in no danger. Veronica had been allowed to walk beside Tiffany's stretcher to a cubicle in Casualty and was then told to go home. They would let only one of us go with Tiffany in the ambulance and it had seemed sensible for Veronica to accompany her so that I could look after Lalla.

'The ward sister was very brusque, I must say.' Veronica looked exhausted on her return. 'When she said, several times, about Tiffany being in the best hands I did wonder. The ward was filthy and there was no washing of the much vaunted hands or the thermometer. I suppose they're short-staffed. Perhaps I ought to train to be a nurse. Only my head did swim rather at the sight of quite so much blood. The ward sister was quite cross with poor Tiffany for getting it on the sheets. I'm going straight to bed. Try not to worry, Viola. She really was looking better when I left.'

Of course I did worry, but Lalla's presence was a distraction and a concern of a different kind. 'Are you sure having an abortion's the right thing to do?' I repeated my question as Lalla did not seem to have heard me.

'I thought I could rely on you not to ask that kind of thing.' Lalla's voice was cold. She lay very rigidly on her side of the bed. The charms of Tolgate Square were quite lost on her. 'If I'd known you were living between the pages of a Dickens novel I'd have risked being talked into a persistent vegetative state by Fiona Parks-Bentley,' was what she had said when I had shown her the bathroom in the basement. 'I should have thought the whole point of being in London was to avoid the beastly discomfort of the country.'

'I don't mean to bully you, Lalla.' I turned on my side in bed and tried to make out her profile against the dark opacity of the bed curtains. 'I just wanted to be sure that you've really thought about it.'

'Christ! I've thought about virtually nothing else for the last two weeks! It's been an absolute nightmare.'

'How can you be certain that you're pregnant? Have you been to see a doctor?'

'You think I'd go to that stupid Dr Curran in Inskip Magna? He'd be on the telephone to my father in two seconds flat! Of course I haven't! But I'm as regular as clockwork. To the hour practically. I'm sure, all right. My breasts have started to hurt.'

'Poor Lalla.' I felt for her hand under the sheets but the bed seemed to have doubled in size. 'It must be miserable. I'm so sorry.' Then, greatly daring, 'You haven't thought about keeping the baby? After all, you and Hamish could get married at once and no one would even know that you'd got pregnant beforehand. Not that it would matter anyway. It isn't anyone else's business. I suppose your parents would mind but –'

'Oh, don't be such a simpleton, Viola! The baby isn't Hamish's. And even I shrink from the paltriness of pretending that it is. Besides, he'd know the minute it was born it wasn't his. Imagine! A little swarthy thing with black hair and an earring in its ear.' Lalla laughed but I couldn't. 'It's Zed's baby.'

'Are you . . .' I decided to risk Lalla's scorn further '. . . quite positive?'

'He's the only man who's made love to me in the last twelve months. I wouldn't let Hamish.'

'But – I expect I'm being stupid – it does sound rather

odd. To be engaged to one man and be sleeping with another.'

'It must have happened countless times before. You're rather a baby, Viola. You think people do things according to the rules. Well, children do, mostly, because they have to, but the idea that grown-ups behave themselves is just a myth. Everyone just does what they want and be damned to everyone else.'

'I expect that's often the case.' I spoke slowly because I was thinking. 'But I do know people who at least attempt to live by a code of behaviour. And I'd say Hamish was one of them. My father has very strict ideas of duty, as does my aunt . . . though they're rather unorthodox. Then there's Daniel, my landlord and Giles and Tiffany and Veronica –'

'Oh, all right.' Lalla sounded impatient. 'So I've behaved badly. So what? It doesn't change the situation. I'm carrying a child I don't want by a man I don't want to marry. So I've got to get rid of it. End of story.'

'But it isn't, is it? The end of the story, I mean. It doesn't take account of the fact that you've been sleeping with Zed and not with Hamish. *That*'s the story.'

Lalla was silent for so long that I wondered if she had fallen asleep. When she spoke much of the anger had gone from her voice. 'I suppose I'm afraid that if I let Hamish make love to me then he'd really be convinced I was his. And I would be. He's the only man who's ever made me feel that I might belong to the conventional world of happy, good people living an ordinary, constructive existence. Sometimes, especially when I'm with him, I want that more than anything in the world. But at other times I feel it wouldn't be being true to myself. I want to live dangerously. It's exciting to feel that you may be about to destroy yourself. Giving myself to Hamish would be like letting him put a collar on me . . . agreeing to walk to heel for the rest of my life.'

'Dear Lalla, you're wrong! You're absolutely wrong. Hamish would never try to change you. He understands you better than that.'

'Have you talked about me with him? You seem to know a lot about it.'

'I had dinner with him tonight, actually. He left only minutes before you arrived –'

Lalla sat up in bed with a swiftness that rent the sheet where I had painstakingly repaired it the day before. 'Hamish is in Japan. What the hell are you talking about?'

'He's at the airport now. He just stopped in London for a few hours.'

Lalla's face was turned towards me but it was too dark to see her expression. 'Why did he ask you to have dinner with him? Is there something between you? God, that would be funny, wouldn't it, after all I've been saying? You and Hamish . . . Well, anyway, what does it matter? When Hamish knows about Zed and the baby he'll ditch me. And who could blame him? I've cast my lot with the sinners of this world.' Her laughter had a wretched sound. 'Still, perhaps Hamish isn't quite the saint he seems. *Is* there something between you two? You've got to tell me, Viola.'

'No, there isn't anything – nothing at all. I like him enormously but that's absolutely all. No other woman's got a chance. He's utterly besotted with you.'

'You're telling the truth? I know he's fond of you. And I couldn't really blame him . . .' She stopped and I heard her swallow. 'It would be a kind of justice to lose him to someone else after having treated him so badly.'

'Yes, I really think it would,' I said, considering. 'If deserving's got anything to do with it then I suppose you ought to lose him. But as worthiness has absolutely nothing to do with affection I don't think he'd stop loving you whatever you did.'

'That's plain speaking anyway.' Lalla's voice cut through the darkness with something of bitterness about it.

'Well, not sleeping with him is one thing. But making love with someone else is quite another.'

'You're perfectly right,' said Lalla, after a pause. 'I'm guilty on all charges. And now I'm going to have to take the consequences. I think, if you don't mind, I'll get some sleep.

My appointment at the clinic's at nine o'clock. It's going to be a hideous day.'

She turned over on her side with her back to me and pulled the sheet around her ears.

'Lalla? Don't let's quarrel. I shouldn't have said that. I wasn't really thinking. Lalla?' There was no reply.

Sleeping in the same bed with someone with whom you are not on the best terms is a wretched experience. All night my dreams were uneasy. Whether I dreamed about being in Baden-Baden with Aunt Pussy and R.D. or about trying to ride a monocycle down Pall Mall while playing a piano accordion, Lalla appeared sooner or later in my anxious visions and each time her plaintive presence filled me with self-reproach.

When I awoke I thought at once of Tiffany. The ward sister had said to telephone for news at half past eight. I looked at Lalla's sleeping face. She had turned towards me. Her hair was looped on the pillow in shiny strands and she looked so much younger and softer that I was moved by remorse to stroke her head. Her eyes flew open at once and she stared at me fiercely.

'I'm so sorry I was unkind last night,' I said, feeling tears rising. 'Please forgive me.'

'What *are* you talking about? Oh, God! The clinic. What time is it?'

'Half past seven. I shouldn't have said that you didn't deserve to be loved by Hamish. It was mean of me. I think I'm a little jealous.'

'Oh, that! Goodness, don't give it another thought! I shan't. You were quite right anyway. Don't make a drama out of nothing.' She must have seen from my face that I was still worried for she patted my hand. 'Come on, let's get up and bag the bathroom. I suppose I should be grateful we haven't got to wash under a pump.'

The kitchen, where we ate our breakfast, made Lalla clutch her head and groan. 'An open range and one tap. My God, Viola! Why don't you wear a wimple and be done with it? What is this longing for scourging the flesh?'

'I think it's romantic,' I said, placing before her a warm

285

brioche which I had bought the day before from a French bakery Giles had told me about. I opened a jar of loganberry jam.

'I must say this is delicious,' Lalla admitted, as she broke off a piece of the soft sweet bread. 'Oah!' she screamed suddenly. 'What the hell is that?'

Josephine had come into the kitchen and run up the chair into my arms. She clung tightly to me and peeped at Lalla from behind a fold in my dressing-gown, which she pulled over herself as a shield. 'This is Josephine, Daniel's monkey. She's adorable. Really, she won't hurt you.'

I stroked Josephine's beautiful, delicate ear and kissed the top of her warm hairy head. Lalla stared at Josephine then rolled her eyes. 'A mad house. That's what it is. Perhaps it's all part of the nightmare.'

Veronica and Daniel had already breakfasted and gone out and Mrs Shilling didn't come in until nine so we had the house to ourselves. The kitchen, with its crackling fire, singing kettle, beautiful old china and delicious smells all seemed to me to offer sanctuary but I could understand that Lalla was beyond such trivial comfort. I offered to go with her to the clinic but she was adamant that she didn't need me. 'It will be grim, I expect, but the doctor I spoke to on the telephone said that they could do it at once if I was less than thirteen weeks gone. I shall have to wait until the anaesthetic's worn off. So I'll be back this evening if that's all right.'

'Do let me come. I'm sure I can get a day off work. I hate the thought of you being alone among strangers. You'll feel so sad afterwards.'

'I shall be in seventh heaven. No more horrid little Zedlet growing inside me. You can't think what a foul feeling it is. Like a parasite.'

'I don't see why dependency should necessarily be bad. Think of mistletoe and orchids.'

'Well, I don't like the idea. I don't ever want to have children. Ruining one's figure and one's sleep. Plus the hideous expense. Think of having to endure speech days again. Thank God, these are my last few hours of motherhood. Now, for goodness sake, stop worrying. I'm not. The days of dirty knitting-needles wielded by wicked old women with hairy chins are over.'

Lalla set off to walk to the end of the square. I watched her until she turned the corner and was out of sight. As soon as it was half past eight I telephoned the hospital. Tiffany was comfortable. Yes, I could visit her between two and three o'clock. No, they could not undertake to give her my love. They were too busy to run back and forth with personal messages for all the patients. After this snubbing I went humbly to work.

I spent the morning, for once, quite productively. Pierce had given me the job of designing an invitation for the next drinks party for SCAB's chief supporters. I had the idea of copying an eighteenth-century drawing of one of the houses we had contributed funds to and writing the details of the invitation in one single line following the complicated roof of towers and cupolas in my best handwriting and black ink. I thought it looked quite effective. I was just holding it out at arm's length, admiring it, when the telephone rang.

'Hello, dear, is that you?'

'Hello, Mab. How are you? Giles hasn't come in yet. He's gone to see the bank manager.'

'Oh, good. How's everything? How's Tiffany?'

Mab rang every few days to be filled in on the events in my life and what little I knew about Giles's. I knew that she was lonely and bored but also I felt that a real friendship had sprung up between us in the course of our telephonic communications. I told her about Tiffany being rushed to hospital and Mab was properly sympathetic. 'I suppose she's lost the baby.'

'I've no idea. Is that what a lot of blood inevitably means?'

''Fraid so. Or will it be a good thing? You did say she didn't want the baby.'

'Well, no. But recently I thought I detected some tenderness creeping in. She'd stopped calling it Monty's by-blow. And she's started to look quite wonderful. Her hair's become very silky – it's the most heavenly Titian – and her complexion looks like something from *Vogue*. Apparently it's hormones.'

'I remember when I was expecting Giles I felt marvellous. I suppose, until the bump grew, I was at my prettiest. I've never been what you might call a beauty. Too mannish, I dare say.' She gave a husky laugh. 'I'm five feet nine and I've got broad shoulders and narrow hips.'

I was glad to have this useful addition to my picture of Mab. I knew already that her hair was what she described as pepper-and-salt and cut short and that her taste was for flat shoes and tweed 'costumes' and that she had a wardrobe full of evening dresses dating back twenty years which she no longer had the chance to wear.

'Geoffrey was such a handsome man. I expect everyone wondered how I'd managed to catch him. Tall and dark. Just like Gregory Peck. Giles takes after him. Geoffrey was quite different from Giles in personality, though. He liked golf and fishing. Conan Doyle was the most intellectual he got. He and Giles didn't really hit it off. I don't remember that they ever had what you might call a proper conversation. It was Geoffrey's terror that Giles might be queer that made them awkward with each other. I remember when Giles showed us what he'd bought with his birthday money – his sixteenth birthday, I think – it was a woman's hairslide. Geoffrey really went off the deep end.'

'Gosh, that *does* sound rather unusual. Was Giles actually wearing it?'

'No, dear. It was Roman, something BC. He got it from an antique dealer. I thought that made it all right. I mean, I could see that he'd wanted it because it was a piece of history but Geoffrey accused me of mollycoddling the boy and making him a sissy. It was one of our worst rows.'

'Well, he's certainly proving your husband wrong now. Julia never lets him out of her sight if she can help it. I don't imagine she wants intelligent conversation. Pierce says she's a nymphomaniac.'

This was unkind of me but I knew this was the sort of thing Mab liked to hear. She laughed long and loudly before saying, 'That's what I could never be. Geoffrey liked sex much more than I did. But I've sometimes wondered if he was any good at it. As he was the only man I've ever been to bed with I can't tell but it wasn't anything like the kind of thing you read of in books. I never felt even a fleeting desire to breathe faster let alone moan.' Her voice became confidential. 'Talking of men and sex, there's been quite an interesting little development in my life.'

'Oh, Mab, that sounds exciting.'

'That's putting it a bit strongly. But the house round the corner's been let again, to a man of about sixty, very dapper and straight-backed, really quite nice-looking. He came round the other day to ask me if I'd seen his cat. Apparently she's upset by the move and keeps wandering off. Well, anyway, I said I hadn't and asked him to describe her and then we got talking and it turns out that he was in the Navy during the war with Geoffrey. They vaguely knew each other. Wasn't that a coincidence? He asked me to have a drink with him that same evening and when I went I found a very cosy little bachelor's nest, tidy and well organised and a bottle of champagne – no less – cooling in a bucket. We got on like a house on fire. His wife's been dead two years, cancer, no children. He's asked me to go to Covent Garden with him. *Turandot*. I must say I'm rather looking forward to it.'

'How marvellous, Mab! You'll be able to dress up.'

'I know. I was wondering whether my black silk . . .'

'Hello, Giles,' I said, as Giles came in just then.

'Oh, he's there, is he?' said Mab. 'I'll ring off, then. Tell you all about it later. Bye-bye, dear.'

Mab never bothered these days to pretend that she wanted to speak to anyone but me. Without actually saying so, we had agreed to keep our friendship a secret from Giles. I suppose we both thought that it might annoy him without, for my part anyway, knowing why.

'Did you do this?' Giles had picked up my design for the invitation.

'Do you think it will do?' I asked with, I hoped, becoming modesty, though I was secretly convinced that it was inspired.

'It's pretty good. Yes. It'll do.'

He looked at me hard, with a critical expression. I imagined he was seeing new artistic depths to my character and gave him my brainiest appraisal in return. I was disappointed, therefore, when he said, 'Did you mean to make yourself look like a proboscis monkey?'

I ran to the mirror. Somehow I had transferred black ink palm-prints to my forehead when leaning it on my hand during my conversation with Mab and I had managed to smudge a long black stripe the entire length of my nose.

'I was going to ask you if you wanted to come to the lunchtime concert in Smith Square with me as you're now so culturally inclined. But you must do something about the war-paint. It might frighten the musicians.' He offered me an immaculate handkerchief which I accepted – the only alternative being the cloth I used to clean the kitchen sink with. I scrubbed like mad at my face until my nose felt as though it had been broken and reset and was fiery red with shadowy grey blotches where the ink refused to come off. The manufacturers had not lied when they described it as permanent. 'It'll wear off over a few days,' was the only comfort Giles offered.

The concert was wonderful. The Heidelberg Ensemble played Schubert's Quintet in C. The *adagio* is the nearest thing to the musical expression of a slow ascent to heaven that I could possibly imagine. While I was listening to it I forgot my preoccupations, even what dreadful things might be happening to Tiffany and Lalla, and floated in a paradisal ether on a cloud of lilies of the valley, which drifted around my head in wreaths every time Giles moved.

'Thank you so much for taking me,' I said, as we were walking back through St James's Park afterwards. 'I've never heard chamber music live before. It's like an incredibly intimate conversation about tremendously important and worthwhile things on which you're permitted to eavesdrop. My musical education has been utterly neglected but now my eyes are opened.'

Giles laughed. 'I hope you won't have brain fever with all this intellectual cultivation. You don't want to overdo it.'

'I seem to think that more people, on the whole, have come unstuck with too much frivolity.'

'*Touché*. I must say, it's enjoyable to take out someone who's enthusiastic. It's a pity your appearance always lays me open to suspicions of violence. I'm sure the programme-seller thought I'd been beating you up. She gave me a very cold look.'

'Oh, Lord! I'd forgotten about my face. Do I look very inky in daylight?'

Giles turned to consider me. 'An Ancient Briton covered in woad might feel outclassed. Oh, no, come on, I was teasing you. You just look as though you haven't washed for a week. It's no good licking and rubbing. You're making your nose red. But you seem less knocked about these days. When you first came to SCAB I wondered if you had one of those bizarre illnesses, like Lesch-Nyhan syndrome.'

'What on earth's that? It sounds very glamorous.'

'It's a personality disorder. The people who have it injure themselves deliberately. With an emphasis on biting. Would you call that glamorous? You always used to look bruised and cut about.'

'That was Pierce. He's a very violent lover. But now I'm practically engaged to Jeremy naturally that's all over.'

Giles stopped in his tracks. 'Engaged to Jeremy? I had no idea. Why didn't you say?'

'I didn't think you'd be interested, I suppose.'

'Well.' Giles walked on, looking down, the forefinger of one hand in the loop of his jacket, which was slung over his shoulder, the other hand in his pocket, 'of course it isn't any of my business . . . but are you certain you're doing the right thing? You're very young.'

'I have no idea. How does one know if something's the right thing or not? Supposing there isn't any right thing? I mean, the future isn't written. It must be just what you make it.'

'Oh, yes, but you can give yourself a sporting chance of being happy or you can court disaster. That's just common sense.'

'Jeremy's very good-natured. We get on like anything.'

'Good-natured. Yes. He's genial enough. But he's also irresponsible and penniless. I don't think feckless would be too harsh a word.'

'This is my future husband we're discussing,' I said, with a degree of hauteur.

'Oh, don't get sulky, Viola. You must know that I'm only thinking of your own good.'

'Yes, I know,' I said, coming off my high horse immediately. 'And he is, as you say, feckless. But I think that's what I like about him, in a way. I haven't got much feck myself. He's like a good chum.'

'You seem singularly in need of advice and protection. What does your aunt say?'

'I'm nearly twenty-one. I don't know why everyone insists on treating me like a baby.'

'Perhaps it's because you behave like one.'

We stopped walking and glared at each other. The sun made Giles's hair glossy like a blackbird's plumage and a few drops of perspiration stood on his upper lip.

'Don't let's quarrel,' I said at last. 'It's much too hot and it's a shame when we were getting on so well. And you've just given me such a treat. I'll say I'm sorry.'

Giles smiled. 'It *is* hot. And I shouldn't lecture you.'

'*Pax*?'

'*Pax*.'

'Do look at those people sunbathing.' I pointed to where office workers lay in rows, their sleeves and trouser legs and skirts rolled up, desperate for all the sun they could absorb. 'They look exactly like grilling sausages, grey and pink with burned stripes.'

Giles made a frame with his thumbs and forefingers and held it before his face. 'I prefer to look at the trees. And those spires in the distance. Look at the blue of those shadows. And the brilliant yellow of the treetops.'

I imitated Giles with my hands. 'I see. It sort of concentrates the picture. You can pick out details better. Prussian blue and gamboge.'

'In the eighteenth century people took something called a Claude Lorraine glass with them to view the countryside.

They were dark convex mirrors, which shrank the scene into miniature landscapes.'

'What a charming idea. Have you got one?'

'No. I've never been lucky enough to find one.'

I made a mental note to ask Daniel to look out for one on his antique-buying trips. Giles had insisted on paying for my concert ticket as he said he knew I was paid practically nothing working for SCAB. I expect he thought I had to live entirely on what I earned. I decided that, rather than tell him about Aunt Pussy's allowance, I would find something really exciting to give him for his birthday, which was some time in September, Mab had said.

As we left the Park for Birdcage Walk a flock of pigeons, their wings blindingly white in the sunlight, swept in a parabola above our heads, so close that I could feel a stirring of the torpid air. 'They must be heading for our balcony.' Giles shielded his eyes to watch them beat upwards over the rooftops. 'Someone ought to tell the poor things about the countryside.'

'Don't you like towns?'

'Not very much. Not on days like today.' We passed an old man with a nose like a plum who was huddled in a blanket tied round his waist with string. He was singing 'My Old Dutch' over and over again at the top of his voice between taking swigs from a bottle. 'It's somehow much sadder to see people like that in a town than in the country. They seem to be more brutally outcast. Thinking about aberrations, were you serious about Pierce giving you all those cuts and bruises?'

'He likes sex to be a conflict. He's much keener on me now that I won't allow him to make love to me.'

'And you let him hurt you like that?' Giles shook his head in disbelief. 'Are you a masochist?'

'I hardly know but I think not. Pierce was my first lover. I had very little idea of what to expect.'

'I suppose you've noticed that the rest of the population is not walking about looking as though they've done fifteen rounds with Sonny Liston.'

'It was precisely that which tipped me off that there was

something unusual going on,' I said, attempting irony. 'But you needn't look so disapproving. I didn't enjoy it much. In fact, hardly at all. I was flattered by Pierce choosing me as his girlfriend when he could have had practically anyone. That's human, I suppose.'

'It isn't *you* I disapprove of. But no one should allow themselves to be tyrannised. That can't ever be right.'

'Oh, look! It's Julia.' I had spotted a blazing chestnut head like a bonfire walking down the street towards us. 'Doesn't she look cross? I expect she's wondering where you've got to.' I smiled very sweetly and innocently at Giles as I said this.

'Rubbish, Viola! You don't suppose she wanders all over London on the off-chance of running into me?'

'I left a note for Pierce saying where we were going.'

'There you are!' It was indeed Julia. She looked chic but hot in a skin-tight black-and-white spotted dress and high-heeled peep-toe shoes. Her lipstick was running into lines around her mouth and darker strands of hair were stuck to her forehead. 'I've had to walk miles in this heat and I'm famished. I got away from the dressmaker's much earlier than I expected. I want to go to the Mirabelle for lunch.'

She ignored me. I walked on by myself, much amused by Giles's expression of annoyance. Then I remembered Lalla and Tiffany and my mind lurched back into a state of anxious speculation.

CHAPTER 22

'Viola!'

I would not have recognised Tiffany if she had not called my name as I walked past her. She was lying in one of a row of beds. Her hair was taped up into a bun on the top of her head. She looked diminished, fragile and colourless. Her bedclothes were thrown back and she was engulfed by an ill-fitting white hospital gown.

'I'm so hot.' She lifted her eyes to my face as though with an effort. 'Could you open the window a bit more?'

It was close to the head of her bed. I fought with it for a while to no purpose. After she had watched me struggling for at least a minute the woman in the next bed said, 'They don't open no more 'n that. It's to stop folk throwing themselves out.'

I caught Tiffany's eye and saw the faintest smile cross her face. 'How are you?' I said, sitting down on the end of the bed.

'They don't like you to sit on the beds,' said the woman in the next bed. 'You have to get one of them.' She indicated with a sideways movement of her head a stack of plastic chairs. I fetched one.

'I've brought you some fruit. And some sherry.' I put them on Tiffany's locker.

'They won't like her having drink,' said Tiffany's neighbour.

I began to feel that the woman was rather intrusive. She leaned on one elbow, looking at us in an unblinking way. Her hair hung in clumps like my old dolls' hair. Her eyes were pale brown, the colour of sultanas, and protuberant. But I reminded myself that she probably had something ghastly wrong with her and it was sad that she didn't have a visitor.

'How are you feeling now?' I repeated my question.

'If I had the energy to get up I might well think of chucking myself out of the window.'

'As bad as that?' I stroked Tiffany's arm sympathetically. It was like caressing a radiator. 'You *are* hot. Have you got a temperature?'

'The ward sister says it's just the weather. She says they're all hot. She made me feel very self-centred.'

I could see drops of perspiration on Tiffany's forehead and nose. 'Have you had any treatment? Have you . . . I lowered my voice ' . . . stopped bleeding?'

'They had to change her bed twice,' chipped in Next Door.

'They gave me something called a D and C this morning.

It's a womb scrape.' I let out a little scream. 'Don't worry, I had an anaesthetic. It was painless. I've stopped bleeding and I'll be able to go home the day after tomorrow. I just feel a bit weak but otherwise fine.'

'I'm so glad. I'll come in a taxi, shall I, to take you home?'

'That would be lovely.' There was a pause. 'I've lost the baby, of course.'

'Oh, Tiff!'

'Well, we both know that it's probably a good thing. It's only that –' tears began to slip down her face '– it's only that I'd almost managed to persuade myself to love it and want it. I can't help feeling, poor little blighter, it didn't have a chance. It's the silliest thing but I feel it was a real person already. A red-headed boy, not like Monty but thoughtful and gentle. I can see him – as though he really existed. Isn't it quite stupid?'

'It's her hormones,' said Next Door. 'Doctor said she'd be bound to feel depressed.' She unwrapped a toffee from a paper bag and jammed it into her cheek, still staring at Tiffany's face.

I moved my chair to screen Tiffany from scrutiny.

'One thing I do know,' muttered Tiffany, wiping her cheek on the sleeve of her hospital gown, 'I've done with men.'

A nurse strode purposefully up to me at that moment. 'You can wait in the corridor. Dr Singh wants to have a look at Miss Wattles.'

'I'll be back in half an hour,' I told Tiffany. 'I'm just going to nip over to John Lewis.' Tiffany nodded and sighed.

When I returned twenty minutes later, Next Door's eyes met mine as I pushed open one half of the double doors. 'They've taken away the sherry,' she said, as soon as I was in earshot.

Tiffany was lying on her side, one knee drawn up, her mass of hair escaping from the bun and falling over her ear. Next Door began on a crackling packet of chocolate digestives. I plugged in the electric fan I had bought in the department store and trained it to blow cool air from Tiffany's head to her feet.

'This is – bliss!' murmured Tiffany. 'I shall be grateful for this for the rest of my life. Thank you, dearest girl.'

'She's not the only one who's hot, you know,' grumbled Next Door. 'Some people expect luxury, I must say.' She rolled on to her back, turned her mouth down in a sulk and closed her eyes.

I promised to come the next afternoon and left Tiffany to sleep.

It was nearly ten o'clock that night before Lalla came back to Tolgate Square. I was sitting by myself in the kitchen, too worried to write or read or do anything but nurse Josephine and scratch behind her ears, which she loved. I heard the peal of the front-door bell and ran upstairs. When I saw Lalla in the hall I thought at once of the Jackdaw of Reims who was so comprehensively cursed by bell, book and candle for stealing the Cardinal's ring. Lalla looked depleted of strength. Her eyes were sunken and ringed with shadows, her hair was lank, her shoulders drooped. She seemed scarcely able to drag herself across the hall. If she had possessed a claw it would have been crumpled.

'Lalla! I'm so glad to see you! You're so late! Are you all right?'

'Of course I'm all right. Don't fuss.' The words, though defiant, lacked Lalla's customary starch. I took her bag and led her upstairs to my room. She didn't protest when I pushed her gently towards the bed but fell back against the pillows with her eyes closed. I stood beside her, wondering whether to take her hand or fetch her a glass of water or swing her legs up on to the bed. In the event I did none of these things for she opened her eyes and said, 'Darling, I think the only thing which *might* make me feel human again is a drink.'

I ran downstairs and poured her a glass of Mr Dring's best and then, on second thoughts, grabbed the bottle as well.

'Better,' sighed Lalla, leaning forward as I put a pillow behind her and holding out the glass towards me to be refilled.

'Do you think it's all right? Haven't I read somewhere that alcohol encourages bleeding?'

'I couldn't care less. I just don't want to think too much about anything. It's been a hell of a day.'

'Does it hurt?'

'Not really. Perhaps a bit. It was okay, really. It's over anyway. I'm just tired, that's all, and rather . . . fed up.'

'Want anything to eat?'

'No, thanks. A ghastly nurse stood over me and made me eat a repulsive ham roll. She said I was too thin and needed fattening up. She was built like a traction engine herself.'

'Perhaps she meant it kindly.'

'She didn't *look* kind.'

I dared to take Lalla's hand and was surprised to find that my grasp was returned.

'Were they nice to you, otherwise?'

'The bloody doctor fondled my breasts. He knew I was desperate and wouldn't kick up a stink. The whole thing – handing over the money in notes, undressing in a dirty little room with sealing tape over the cracks in the linoleum somewhere in Bushey, having him dribbling over me – was unbearably sordid.'

I shivered in sympathy. 'Can't you get a termination on the NHS these days?'

'Yes, but it goes on your medical notes. Dr Curran worships the turn-ups on my father's trousers. There'd have been a hideous fuss. It was much easier to have the thing done privately.'

'But where did you get the money?'

'You might well ask. I had fifty pounds of my own. I borrowed twenty-five pounds from Jeremy and another thirty from Mrs Bradwell, who runs the Dog and Bone. I made up some ridiculous story about needing it to repair a damaged wing on my car which I was afraid to tell my father about. Then, by a miracle, I found twenty pounds in an envelope in my father's desk drawer. I don't expect he'll notice it's gone.'

I knew that it was no miracle as I had sent Sir James

twenty pounds anonymously a few days ago in payment for the various catastrophes I had unwittingly brought about.

'Anyway, you needn't worry any more. It's all over.'

'Yes, it's all over,' Lalla agreed, without enthusiasm.

Half an hour later, as we were lying in bed in the darkness, Lalla said, 'Are you too tired to talk?'

'No, not a bit.'

'Do you think it possible that Hamish will ever forgive me?'

'Possible? Yes. But have you got to tell him? I know it would be dishonest not to but it will hurt him so much –'

'I've already written to him. I've asked him if he'll send me the money. He's my only hope. I've got to pay Mrs Bradwell back. Besides, there's the twenty pounds from the desk.'

Poor Hamish, I thought. I could only admire Lalla's courage. 'I expect he will forgive you. He does love you so much.'

'I suppose I want to be forgiven.' Then, before I had the chance to say anything, she went on, speaking hurriedly as though out of breath, 'Actually, I do. If I'm honest, I know I do. I've done something that feels as though I've put myself on one side of a great divide. And there isn't any going back. What's happened can't be laughed off or be made to seem amusing and daring. I don't seem to be able to see it like that, anyway. From one point of view it was the sensible thing to do. Thousands of babies are got rid of every day. Half the girls I know have had abortions. But when I woke up this afternoon . . . there was a light right above my head and it was hideously bright and made my eyes water. I couldn't focus properly and I felt sick . . . I was in despair. There was a smell of hot rubber and disinfectant and school mince. I could hear two nurses gossiping outside the door of my room, about going to the cinema. One of them came in and said, "You're awake now, that's good," and went out again without once looking me in the eye. It was so dreary and sad. And I thought about the life I'd just paid to have ended . . .'

Lalla paused, took several quick deep breaths and then

went on. 'That little collection of cells, growing so fast and comfortably inside me until it was rudely yanked out and chucked away, was my first child . . . the person who should have been more important to me than anyone in the world, who deserved, at the very least, my protection. Instead I . . . Well, finally I've proved to myself at last that I *am* bad. But there isn't any triumph in it. It isn't the freedom I thought. Instead, stupidly, I found I wanted my mother.' Lalla's voice sank lower as she talked. 'As she used to be when I was a child. She always seemed so permanent and imperishable. It was such a shock when she changed. Everything seemed different after that. It was the end of something precious. I couldn't really be happy any more.' I heard a sharply indrawn breath. 'She really was lovely and she was such fun, not like other mothers, cold and expensive-looking. Sometimes she'd wake me early in the morning so that we could go and see badger cubs playing in the woods. We made a bee garden together, planted with things like catmint and borage that bees love, with a bee skep in the middle. It's completely overgrown now. Bowser makes compost there. Poor Mummy! I've been hateful to her. I couldn't bear her to be weak and frightened. I wanted her to be as she used to be. But there never *is* any going back, is there? No wiping the slate clean. Just the piling up of worse and worse thoughts, and the accumulation of stupid, destructive deeds. Now I wish so much that I'd lived my life better.' There was a distinct break in her voice on the word 'much'.

'You're hopelessly tired and under the weather,' I said, putting my arm round her. 'Of course it was a horrible thing to have to go through and I wish you hadn't had to, but you aren't in the least bit wicked or bad. I think you're very brave and honest. I particularly admire that because I'm such an awful coward. What is it that's given you this ridiculous idea that you're so sinful?'

'I've felt like it for a long time, ever since . . . Well, I suppose it won't matter if I tell you. What does matter after all? Nothing very much.' She sniffed hard.

'What? Tell me, Lalla. I'm sure it's something you've exaggerated.'

'When I was fifteen I had an affair with Francis. Now you know and you can despise me, if you want.'

'Oh dear. Yes. Now I see. That's why there always seemed to be sparks between the two of you. It was pretty obvious that there was some unfinished business, as they say. I never imagined . . . but that was hardly your fault, was it? It was very wrong of Francis –'

'Oh, no. It was nothing as corny as a wicked uncle seducing an innocent niece. I seduced *him*. He was the only grown-up I'd ever liked, though he could be mean, sometimes. He was awful to Susan. But he was fascinating. I really thought I was in love with him. That it was a great passion worth risking everything for. I'd got to the age when all my childish preoccupations had palled and everything seemed dreary. Except for Francis. He was so attractive. I suppose he still is.'

'Yes. I know what you mean. The nastiness is part of it.'

'Can you see that?' Lalla rolled over on to one elbow to look at me. 'I didn't think I'd be able to make you understand. Well, anyway, one evening we were walking together back to the Rectory after dinner. I'd made the excuse of needing to exercise the dogs. Susan had gone back earlier with one of her headaches. It was one of those stuffy, warm nights that you get after rain. I was flirting with him. He suddenly grabbed hold of me and kissed me on the mouth. I responded as well as I knew how. I'd never kissed a man before. Then he pulled me into the cover of the trees and we made love. The ground was damp and we got very muddy. The fact that he was my uncle, that I'd known him since I was born, that he was miles older than me, added to the thrill and the shame of it. I was exultant and horrified at the same time. I didn't have an orgasm, it was much too quick. But I was fearfully excited in a mad, sick kind of way. I ran home and lay in my bath until after midnight, my heart beating so hard that I could hardly breathe. I felt like a new, quite different person. The next morning he came up to the house early. We walked together round the lake and he begged me to forgive him. He'd always been so authoritative. I was very moved to see him agitated and uncertain. I didn't know then about the law and being underage and all that. I thought his concern was all for me. I told him that I was in love with him and that I didn't regret it and I swore that it would always be our secret. I felt so . . . powerful. He'd been so frantic when we were making love, so passionate . . . Of course, I didn't realise how little it means to men. After that we met whenever we could – at the Rectory when Susan was out, in empty bedrooms at home, once on the bridge over the lake. I didn't particularly like the sex but I loved the feeling of giving somebody something so wonderful. He used to call me his gateway to paradise. Disgustingly trite, wasn't it?' Lalla made a hard, angry sound, between a laugh and a groan. 'I went back to school for the autumn term. I didn't do a stroke of work. I thought all the time about him. He'd said we mustn't write. That if people found out, he'd have to give up being in the Church and go away and we wouldn't be able to see each other any more. The risk he was running made it seem so – important. When I went home for the Christmas holidays he came up for dinner as usual. He looked wonderful, so confident . . . He shows all his teeth when he laughs. I've always liked people who seem open. He didn't look at me once. I waited and waited for him to come up the next day. In desperation I went down to the Rectory. He was out and there was no message. Day after day it was the same. I thought I'd go mad with doubt and hope and longing.'

'I can imagine what it felt like. Poor Lalla!' I could, too. I remembered Jack and the exhausting, turbulent flights of fantasy about him in which I had indulged, to no end but the increasing of unsatisfied hunger.

'I realised eventually that Francis was arranging things so that we were never alone together. Then I heard the gossip about Mrs Thrall, a middle-aged divorcee with a double chin. I expect she had a nice comfortable double bed and a few love-making skills. I was standing in Bracey's, the newsagent's, and I heard two women talking about it, how Francis knew no shame and someone ought to speak to the bishop. I went home and was physically sick. I spent the rest of the holiday in my room pretending I had a bad cold. My first weekend back at school I broke bounds and went to a party in London with Fiona Parks-Bentley. I made love with a guards officer on a pile of coats in one of the bedrooms. He was the most stupid man you've ever met. He called me his princess but the minute it was over he buttoned up and flew away downstairs with scarcely a goodbye. I did it partly to hurt Francis, though he neither knew nor would have cared. And partly to hurt myself because I wanted to stop myself thinking about Francis. That was just the beginning.'

Lalla gave a great trembling sigh. I lay staring into the downy grey of darkness and tried to think of something comforting to say. But before I could formulate a thought Lalla said, with a vehemence that made me jump, 'Do you know something? I absolutely hate him! He isn't worth it, I know, but I do. I hate him so much that I can't think of anything that would be too awful to happen to him!' Putting her face on the pillow, with her hands clasped round her head, Lalla started to cry with croaking sobs wrenched out of her with the utmost pain as though she were being tortured. I took her in my arms, my own eyes hot with sympathetic tears. After a bit she leaned her head on my shoulder and I felt her slowly relax until she was weeping more quietly and with less effort. I didn't try to stop her.

'Oh, Viola,' she said, when the crying seemed at last to have worn itself out, 'what have I done? What *have* I done?'

CHAPTER 23

'I wish you'd stay a few days.'

I sat on the bed, watching Lalla eat the breakfast I had brought up on a tray – toast and an egg, coddled in a special lidded china pot painted with strawberry leaves.

Daniel had recently shown me how to cook eggs – boiled (coddled, *mollet* and hard-boiled), baked (with tarragon, cream and mustard), poached (with watercress and a delicate onion sauce) and scrambled (with scorzonera), and I was quite proud of the result.

I had picked the only rose that had so far managed to bloom in the garden of number 46 and put it in a glass on the tray. I don't know if Lalla noticed but, anyway, it made me feel better to try to do something for her. It seemed to me now, in the light of last night's conversation, that hardly anyone had done anything for Lalla since she was a child. She had been left to struggle alone. I had no difficulty in keeping my promise to Hamish. Affection, rather than obligation, bound me to her. I hoped that Hamish would be understanding and forgiving. My experience of men so far had not led me to think them inclined to consider other people's needs before their own dignity. My father, of course, had forgiven my mother innumerable crimes but he was an extraordinary exception to the general run.

'Thanks, but London's only good for shopping and going to the theatre and things and I haven't got any money. And I'm too depressed to be good company.'

'I wouldn't mind that. You could come and sit on our balcony – it's the most heavenly place – and read books and drink and sleep. You look so tired.'

'You're a Norland nanny *manqué* really, Viola.' I was glad to hear a return of Lalla's customary sharpness. 'You ought to have an enormous brood of children to fuss over, making sure they're wearing their stomachers and have taken their senna pods. I haven't read a book in years and, anyway, I don't think Giles would be particularly pleased to see me. I hurt him quite a lot. I'm afraid I didn't behave very well. As usual.'

'Oh, Giles wouldn't mind at all.' Tact, as I may have said before, is not my strong suit, particularly first thing. 'He's involved in a steamy relationship with a girl called Julia Sempill-Smith. It's all to do with his new resolve not to be serious. She's a very pretty noodle, only interested in one thing. You never saw a man so sated with sex and frivolity.'

'Really?' Lalla looked as though she did not entirely like the idea. 'I should have thought Giles would have had better taste.'

'That's the whole point. He was fed up with being an aesthete. Luckily she never comes upstairs to SCAB. I think it annoys her to see me ensconced. She's got this ridiculous idea that I pinched Pierce from her, which is completely untrue. A lot of the time I'm on my own up there. Tiffany comes quite a bit . . .' I paused. Lalla had listened politely to my bulletin of Tiffany's health but it was clear to me that she was not in the mood to sympathise with the sufferings of a complete stranger, particularly one who had had an unpleasant decision taken out of her hands by Nature.

'God! It would be like a convalescent home for fallen women. No, thanks! Though it's nice of you to offer. I'll go home and lick my wounds and wait to hear from Hamish. He'll get my letter any day now. I really am so bloody exhausted. I'm worn out with crying.'

'I bet it did you good, too.'

'Could be.' Lalla's tone was noncommittal. But when, an hour later, she stood at the front door about to get into the waiting taxi, she put her arms right round me and hugged me so tightly that I could scarcely breathe. Her eyes, green and speckled as moss agate, were bright. 'Goodbye, Viola, I shan't forget how marvellous you've been to me. Come and stay soon. Promise!'

'I will. Give your mother my love.'

'Poor Mummy. I really will make an effort to be a better daughter. I shan't bother to give your love to Jeremy.'

Lalla had recognised Jeremy's handwriting on a letter waiting for me on the hall table. She had been astonished to learn that we corresponded. 'That must be the most trouble he's taken about anything since he left school. I got the impression he was pretty dippy about you but I hadn't realised he was quite so saturated in love. Well, well, how little we know about those we're closest to.'

Lalla got into the taxi. I saw her go with a real sense of loss. I went to the office and typed up some lists for Giles, which took me ages as I lost my place constantly, thinking about Lalla and Tiffany. I had a sandwich for lunch then went to the hospital.

I was surprised to see the curtains drawn around Tiffany's bed. I was just wondering how to make my presence known – you cannot knock at a curtain – when the ward sister called to me from her desk and said that Tiffany had a fever and was not allowed visitors. She told me to telephone the hospital for news the following morning. I half made up my mind to defy her and make a rush for the cubicle but early habits of obedience won and I slunk away. I noticed that a fan identical to the one I had bought the day before was standing on the ward sister's desk, sending a cooling breeze across her paperwork.

I decided not to go back to the office as I had signed myself out for the afternoon and instead went home to do what I now thought of as my real work. Giles had lent me his copy of Vasari's *Lives of the Artists*, which he said, though frequently inaccurate, was an important book for anyone interested in the history of art. I was astonished to find that Vasari had lived in the sixteenth century and had been a contemporary of Michelangelo. As soon as I began to read the mettlesome prose, full of enthusiasm and insights and gossip, I was transported back to Florence and the Cinquecento.

'How astonishing!' I said to Daniel, who happened to come into the kitchen at six o'clock that same evening as I was reading the life of Giotto and making mayonnaise for a *sauce rémoulade* at the same time. 'Fancy Cimabue coming along just at the moment when Giotto was scratching a picture of a sheep on to a rock with a flint. And imagine it being good enough for him to offer him an apprenticeship! Isn't it romantic? I can practically hear the sheep baaing and smell the rosemary on the hot hillside.'

'Very romantic and, without doubt, apocryphal.' Daniel laughed. 'Vasari isn't to be trusted. But it is good that you read him. Very good. Giotto's master is pronounced "Chimah-booay". Not *Sim*-aboo. But you are putting the oil in too fast. Remember, you must drip it in like rain. Now it has separated.'

'Oh, damn! There's so much to learn! I never seem able to do more than pick at things. Now I realise that I could spend my whole life learning about the Italian Renaissance and still only know a fraction of it. Doing it in a few weeks is ridiculous. What can I do about the sauce?'

'But you must start somewhere. It will give you a valuable idea of chronology. Begin again with a fresh yolk. And put down the book or you will get the food on it. This is a good edition, excellently bound.'

Daniel turned to the fly-leaf and saw 'Giles Fordyce' written in an elegant sloping hand. The smile disappeared from his face. 'He must think a lot of you to lend this book. It is of some value. Thank God he does not see you with a cruse of oil suspended above the page.' Daniel looked at me very coldly. His black eyes narrowed accusingly. 'He is the man who took you to lunch, no? It is not he who writes you the letters that I see constantly upon the hall table?'

'What? No! I can assure you Giles isn't in the least interested in me. He sees it as his duty to encourage me to throw off the yoke of my ignorance, that's all. It's just kindness. He's very much someone else's property.'

'Ah. Kindness. I see. And the other lover? The young man with an assurance to match the vacuity of his spirit?'

'Pierce? Gosh, I do think you're unkind about him. Anyway, he isn't my boyfriend any more.'

'Then why does he come here last night, very drunk? Not, I suppose, to admire my collection of *blanc-de-Chine*?'

'I didn't know he was here. Why didn't you tell me?'

'It was late. You and your friend were already in bed. I also but I heard the bell. I explained that we do not receive visitors after ten o'clock. He was inclined to be argumentative but I was intransigent. He told me that you are the only girl for him and that he is thinking of killing himself. I was sympathetic but remained firm.'

'I'm sorry. How annoying for you.'

'No matter. We elderly people are inclined to be disagreeable about disturbances.'

'Oh, really, Daniel! You needn't talk as though you were a hundred and fifty. It's just an absurd affectation to pretend to be in your dotage. I never think of you as being any older than I am.'

'No?' Daniel raised his eyebrows and smiled a cold, thin smile. 'I am complimented. Now, you need to add mustard and herbs. Tst! You cannot put in the capers whole! You must chop them finely. Never did I meet a woman with less culinary intuition.'

He went away while I attempted to atomise the remaining ingredients to meet Daniel's exacting standards. I was half-way through reducing a knobbly celeriac root to julienne strips when he returned. 'I intend to outdo Mr Giles Fordyce in kindness,' he said, in a sarcastic tone, as he placed a pile of books on the kitchen table, well out of reach of the sauce. 'If you truly wish to be educated you must go back to the beginning. Here are the eight books of the Ancient World which are considered to have shaped the early political history of mankind. You may begin with the *Laws of Hammurabi*, written in Babylon eighteen centuries before Christ. Then the *Book of the Dead*, which explains the preoccupation with another world, which was responsible for the static character of the Egyptian civilisation. Third the Torah. It is the Book of Moses, the Jewish law. Fourth the Epics of Homer that made a single Greek culture possible. Fifth, the *Institutes of Manu*, which characterised Hindu India. Sixth, Confucius, who formed the minds of the literati who ruled China for centuries. Seventh, we have Plato's *Republic* and eighth Aristotle's *Politics*. That brings us to 330 BC. Then, if you have stomach for more education, we go on with another seventeen works ending with *Das Kapital* of Karl Marx. I am kind, am I not?'

'Very,' I said, looking at the pile, not without something of an inward sigh. I picked up the copy of the Torah which was the only book that was well worn. On the fly-leaf was written 'Daniel Ezra Ebelmelech 1946'.

'That is my own copy of the Torah. You see, I refuse to be outdone in kindness.' He bowed stiffly from the waist, almost glaring.

'You mean – is that really your name?'

'It is. When I came to England I decided that I would

cease altogether to be a Jew. So I took the name of Fogg simply because the day I arrived in London you could not see your hand in front of your nose for dirty yellow smoke.'

'How interesting! I had no idea you were Jewish.'

'Ach! A man with my physiognomy called Daniel, and you have no idea that I am of the Chosen People.' Daniel's laugh, which had a dry, angry sound, became a cough.

'I'm very sorry.' I spoke humbly because I had the sinking sensation of being on sticky ground. 'It was stupid of me. I'm afraid I haven't known many Jewish people. If any.'

I tried to remember if I ever had. R.D. had sometimes spoken about men as 'Jew-boys'. It was obviously a term of derision, though what it implied was unclear to me. I did not think any of the girls at school had been Jews. What little knowledge I had of the Jewish race came from things I had read. I recalled, with an increasing feeling of apprehension, Riah the Jew in *Our Mutual Friend*, whom Dickens made so superior in character to his Christian master but who is downtrodden and abused by nearly everyone. George Eliot made some apology for the characterisation of Shylock and the Jew of Malta when she wrote *Daniel Deronda* but there was an uneasy suggestion of vindication in her portrayal of 'good' Jews as excepted from the most part of the Hebrew people. Fragments of a speech from *The Merchant of Venice* floated in my brain: 'Hath not a Jew eyes? If you prick us do we not bleed? If you poison us do we not die?'

'I imagine that among the English upper classes Jews are as welcome as pathogens.' Daniel looked at me with an expression I could only describe as intense dislike. I made an apologetic murmur but Daniel closed his eyes and held up a stiff, protesting hand. 'You need not look embarrassed. In my own country, after all, there was an actual attempt to eradicate the troublesome bacteria.'

Then something of the horrifying nature of the Nazis' treatment of Jews during the Second World War, which I had occasionally read articles about in newspapers and magazines, began to trickle into my mind in still pictures of wasted bodies and piles of spectacles and artificial limbs. I remembered a photograph of a line of naked adults and children beside a pit, kneeling before uniformed men with guns. The candle flame on the table beside me wavered as I breathed slowly out. A piece of coal shifted in the range and a trickle of condensation ran down the distempered wall. The shameful truth was that, though I was nearly twenty-one, the concept of Jewishness had made almost no impact on my understanding.

'Wasn't it a pity to give up being Jewish?' I tried not to look nervous but the way Daniel was staring, with a look both impregnable and angry, was intimidating. 'I think you should be proud of it. Aren't Jews terribly intelligent and artistic?'

Daniel snorted and bared his teeth. '*Ach was!* You think in truistic platitudes. There are many Jews not clever, not gifted, just as many as illiterate Gentile boors. Such remarks, made to appease, are banal.'

'It was a stupid thing to say. I see that now.'

Daniel seemed a little softened by my submissive penitence. 'What can you know? You are so young, so silly. But it is not your fault.' Daniel was about the only person in the world I would have allowed to call me silly without protest. 'Yes, I *am* proud. At least . . . I am not one whit ashamed. But what good is pride? It does not cure hunger, it does not shelter from cold, it is no armour against kicks and blows, against the villainy of one's fellow men. Pride is worthless unless you have nothing left, when you are reduced to scrabbling on the ground for a shred of human dignity. It is a last recourse.'

'I suppose so,' I said weakly.

'When I found that I could not give up being a Jew, that other people would not let me forget it – that *I* could not forget it – then I tried to become more Jewish even than Baal Shem Tov. I studied the Torah, the *Talmud*, I worshipped at the synagogue, I learned Hebrew, acquired phylacteries and ate kosher food. I refused to carry anything on the Sabbath. I wore a *yarmulke* and the *tallith*. I held myself aloof from Gentiles. But I became impatient with these restrictions. I chafed within the limitations of other men's ideas of virtue.

I could not conform. I found no comfort in ritual, no joy in festival. So I reverted to what I had ever been, a Jew by blood but not by religion. I am first and last a humanist and I must carry my burdens until my dying hour without expiation – with little help from man and none at all from God.'

'I'm so sorry,' I said, without thinking.

'Sorry? What are you sorry about?' Daniel's expression was hostile. But a fit of coughing made him press his handkerchief to his face and by the time he had taken it away he looked less angry.

'Oh, just that you sound so sad.'

Daniel smiled then but I saw it was an effort. 'I am nearly fifty years old. One gets sadder. There is a loss of belief in the sense of things, that is all. *Schluß damit!* Enough of this introspection. It is an indulgence of the moment for which a price must be paid.'

'Do you mean that talking about your feelings is something to be punished for? I can't believe that.'

'With regard to myself . . .' Daniel spoke slowly as though he were pondering the truth of it '. . . there is an accompaniment to any exploration of the emotions that is painful almost beyond bearing.'

'Oh! In that case,' I felt, not unnaturally, alarmed, 'don't let's even think of continuing. Thank you very much for the books, and won't you try the sauce?'

Daniel dipped his little finger in the bowl I held out towards him. 'Not bad. A little fiery – too much pepper. Like me. Too much pepper in my nature.' He brushed round the curve of my cheek with his hand. I was startled by this uncharacteristic demonstration of affection. 'You are so like her. So like my sister. You will not take offence at me?'

I saw a look of grievous sorrow spring into Daniel's eyes. He turned and went away at once, not giving me time to answer and ignoring Josephine, who flung up her arms with a wild, angry chattering.

'Did you know Daniel was Jewish?' I asked Tiffany, a week later, as she sat on the end of my bed, drinking lettuce milk, which she had read in one of her vegan journals was good for recovering invalids. The lettuces had been stubbornly reluctant to yield up their juices and had required much perseverance with mincer and sieve.

'Oh, yes. It's obvious, really – I mean, he could hardly be anything else. You don't mean to say you didn't?'

'I cannot tell a lie,' I said humbly. 'At least, I can and frequently do, but in this case I won't. I had no idea. He got very prickly as soon as we began to talk about it. I don't know why but I felt guilty, as though something was my fault.' I took a reflective sip of my Horlicks and huge lumps of undissolved, incredibly sweet powder bobbed against my lower lip. Luckily I liked it like that.

'Well, I suppose we all ought to feel guilty, in a way,' said Tiffany. 'Of course, you and I weren't born then but really we should all bear responsibility for the crimes of humanity. And the awful thing is that it goes on happening all over the world still. Think of the gulags and what the Khmer Rouge did in Kampuchea. No one's learned anything from what happened in the Second World War, have they?'

I looked at her over the rim of my cup, hoping not to have to reveal the extent of my ignorance. I rarely read newspapers and current affairs at school had been limited to things like the Queen's visits to Fiji and other far-flung remnants of the British Commonwealth, as though what happened off British territory was irrelevant and even rather distasteful.

'Gosh, this stuff is pretty unexciting, nutritious or not.' Tiffany swilled round the contents of her glass gloomily. 'Mrs Shilling told me that Daniel talked to her once about being in Auschwitz. Apparently he survived because he was a musician.'

'Oh.' I was silent for a moment, thinking of Daniel among those imprisoned, emaciated bodies. The idea was intensely hurtful. 'I wondered why as soon as he began to talk about being Jewish it made him cough.'

'Some psychological reflex, I imagine. You can't go through something like that and not be impaired for life. Also, of course, you will have insights and a sort of wisdom that no one else can have. On the whole, though, it seems to be very much more minus than plus. Survivors of the camps have an appalling weight of guilt. An awful lot of them have found it impossible to live with and have killed themselves, sometimes years afterwards. What must it feel like being haunted by your dead companions?'

'I don't know. I don't think I can bear to contemplate it just at the moment.'

'All right, neither can I, actually. Let's talk about something else. Isn't it quiet without the Baa-lamb? Not that she ever made any noise but somehow one knew when she was there, a steady force for good emanating from above. I took her for granted but now I miss her.'

'So do I. Though it's only been three days.'

I had helped Veronica to carry down her suitcases and had seen her into a taxi. Daniel had come down the steps at the last minute – he must have been watching from his room – and put into her hand a little red book. He told me afterwards it was a volume of verse by Coleridge. We waved her off.

'It was awfully clever of you to find her a job. What about the rest of her things?'

'Daniel says they can stay in her room until she's sure she doesn't want to come back. It's very nice of him since he'll have to do without the rent. On the other hand, I suspect he's dreading finding the next lodger has fallen in love with him. Are you sure you shouldn't be in bed?' Tiffany had been out of hospital for two days now but her complexion was still pale green and she complained of legs like stewed rhubarb. We had donated the fan to the hospital as Sister had seemed so attached to it and it would be useless at number 46.

'I suppose I should. But I'm really much better. And much less depressed. I'll come to the balcony tomorrow, if it's okay with you, and soak up a few rays of ultra-violet. I'll get on with that cushion for the exhibition. There's nothing like creative effort for restoring the tone of one's mind.'

I lay in the darkness after Tiffany had gone to bed, thinking about our conversation. The war had ended thirty-one years ago. Daniel must have been seventeen or eighteen. Handsome and clever and gifted. And alive. But carrying a weight of death. Other people's deaths. What must it have felt like to find oneself helpless in the power of the brutal and the ignorant? How could you reconcile yourself to the human race after witnessing such displays of sickening cruelty and injustice – almost worse, a lack of awareness of what cruelty and injustice were?

'I've been much too sheltered,' I said suddenly into the ether, looking up from my list of foreign subscribers.

Giles glanced up from the books and pamphlets he was sorting through, preparatory to chucking them all away. 'What's brought this on suddenly?'

I hadn't intended to speak my thoughts aloud but now that I had a tolerably sympathetic audience nothing could have stopped me from continuing. 'I never realised before what dreadfully sad lives other people have. At least, in theory I knew it and I've cried like mad through *Random Harvest* and *Madam Butterfly* and *Diana of the Crossways* but I've never really felt before how terrible real people's lives are. My aunt has always been able to make troublesome things seem nothing but tiresome hiccups in the broad flow of *douceur de vivre*.'

'For instance?'

'Well.' It would have been disloyal to talk about Lalla and Tiffany. But there could be no harm in discussing Daniel. So I told Giles about Daniel having been in Auschwitz. 'I feel I've been amazingly stupid and ignorant not to have known. I saw the number on his arm weeks ago when he rolled up his shirtsleeves to cook. Quite honestly, I thought it was his National Health number or something he was afraid of forgetting.'

'It was ironic that the Nazis tried to make those work camps models of efficiency – they could never be that because the workers kept dying off from starvation and disease. Those who went to the death camps, like Treblinka, Chelmno and Birkenau, weren't granted the luxury of a tattooed number. They were effectively already dead.'

314

'Why did the Germans hate the Jews so much?'

'You have to see it in a much wider context.' Giles put down his pen and adopted the measured tones of his lecturing voice. I never minded being lectured because he was so good at explaining things. 'Throughout the Middle Ages, Jews were held responsible for the murder of Christ. Wherever there's been an outburst of religious fervour the Jews have been persecuted. In fact, England expelled all Jews in the thirteenth century. Whenever there was a disaster – plague, fire, famine – the Jews were scapegoats. It's how people reinforce a national identity in times of crisis – by excluding others. In fairness it ought to be remembered that in the nineteenth century Jews were assimilated better in Germany than anywhere else in Europe. But with the advent of Hitler Germany lost all sense of proportion. It was a kind of hysteria produced by many things, not least, of course, the humiliations of the First World War. It's important to remember that, from nineteen forty-one onwards, the English had detailed reports of the death camps but our Foreign Office – well known to be anti-Semitic – preferred to call them atrocity stories. Ten thousand Jews were dying every day but still the Allies hesitated about bombing the gas chambers at the death camps on the grounds that it would endanger the lives of too many aircrew. It's easy to look back from this distance and express horror at what was done but I'm afraid the blood is on all our hands.'

'I feel ashamed that I've never thought about it properly before. Daniel's so intelligent and scrupulous. He's devoted to whatever is beautiful and fine. He's an ascetic . . . He looks for purity and truth in everything. The idea of him being subjected to such hatefulness . . . I just can't imagine such horror.'

'But now you *have* begun to think about it you can begin to understand so much more. Art, great art, isn't just about technique. Or visual appeal. It's about ideas. You have to encompass a vast range of human experience before you can grasp those ideas. If you have no proper knowledge of suffering you can't fully understand those paintings you write essays about, for example.'

I was struck by the evident truth of this. While I was gazing at Giles and digesting the implications of what he had said, the telephone bell broke the silence. Giles picked it up. 'Hello? Hello, Julia.' Silence. 'Mm. Of course, I see your point. But I wonder whether it really would be better to –' A longer silence, though I could hear energetic talking from the other end. 'Well, if you're sure it would help. But won't it just prolong the agony?' Julia's voice became louder, though I still couldn't hear what she was saying. I pretended to study my list, wondering if I should get up and go into the kitchen. 'Naturally I'm sorry, very sorry. It was never my intention to –' Just as I had made up my mind that I absolutely must leave them to it, Giles said, 'Really, Julia, you're getting hysterical. I made it clear from the beginning –' He stopped and looked at the receiver with annoyance. 'She's rung off. Oh dear. She's quite right. It's entirely my fault. I should never have let things go on so long. It seems I'm condemned to be serious after all.'

'You've broken it off with Julia?'

Giles nodded. 'I began to worry that she was getting too – No, damn it, that sounds disgustingly conceited. Let's just say that I realised that we had quite different objects in view. I'm so sorry to have hurt her.'

He stood with hands in pockets and head bowed for a while. 'From the momentous to the ridiculous. I think we both need cheering up. What about lunch at La Petite Sonnerie?'

CHAPTER 24

A week later Aunt Pussy and I went down to Kent for my cousin Miranda's wedding. Bert was brought out of retirement and my aunt's Rolls Royce, unused since a visit to Cap Ferrat five years ago, was serviced and buffed to a blinding sheen for the occasion. Bert was nearly eighty and had had a stroke the year before but he was indignant at the suggestion that he might not be up to it. He sat with extreme uprightness behind the wheel, hands at ten to two, looking neither to right nor left and giving no quarter. This provoked much tooting in heavy traffic and several cyclists nearly came to grief. Luckily he drove so slowly that no one was actually hurt. In fact, we could have had brimming glasses of champagne in the back without spilling a single drop. It was disconcerting though when other cars, and even lorries, paused alongside as they overtook and stared in at us, wondering if we were important state functionaries or part of a funeral procession.

Even more embarrassing, once we reached the country-side he tapped the horn at frequent and regular intervals until Aunt Pussy was moved to protest. Bert's explanation was that he was anxious not to run over the flocks of birds in our path. We stared out of the window at the empty sky and birdless road and then looked at each other. My aunt raised her eyebrows eloquently.

As we drove through the village of Westray and I saw again the familiar landscape of my childhood I felt a rush of excitement. We drew up outside the church as Miranda was about to enter the porch. She was wearing a yellow dress, a deeper shade of her hair, and a chaplet which I saw, when I got close enough, was made of tiny yellow roses. She held the arm of a much older man with a splendid head of white hair, who was dashingly attired in a dark green suit with a waistcoat of coral.

'Heavens!' breathed my aunt. 'Who on earth is that?'

'He's rather stunning,' I said, lowering the window. 'Miranda!' I called. 'Sorry we're late. Hang on a minute!'

There was a crunch as the back of the Rolls Royce met the stone of the churchyard wall.

'All right, Bertram, never mind!' My aunt sounded unusually flustered. 'Let's just get out and worry about the car later.'

We had to scurry out on the other side as the door was jammed tight against the lychgate. I had never in my life seen my aunt run but this was the nearest thing to it, an elegant loping movement down the path and into the church where we stood blinking in the dim light, panting like hares. An usher directed us to the front pew and told us to squeeze in as tight as we could. I found myself almost sitting on the knee of Miranda's sister, whom I scarcely knew at all. 'Hello, Beatrice,' I whispered. 'It's Viola. Sorry to have to crush you to death.'

'Viola! It never is!' Beatrice's round face was suffused with pleasure. 'Fancy you being grown-up! How are you, darling? Isn't this lovely? Have you seen Miranda's gorgeous husband?'

I leaned forward to look as a man with dark curly hair stepped into the aisle from the opposite pew. The organ, which had been making the sort of rumty-tum twiddles organists do when their eyes are fixed expectantly on their mirrors, broke into ear-splitting chords. I felt a sympathetic twinge of nerves for the bridegroom, who was very pale and seemed to be gnawing his lip. Then, as we all shifted sideways in our pews to sneak a glimpse of Miranda coming up the aisle, he turned right round and smiled at her. I was won completely by that look. Weddings have a most undoing effect on me and my eyes misted over so much that I could barely see Miranda's face as she came towards us but by the time the Vicar, a man owlishly bespectacled and transparently meek and mild, began to speak, I had control of myself more or less.

The elderly man with the coral waistcoat gave Miranda in marriage then squeezed into our pew. His girth was broad and Aunt Pussy and I had to think thin like mad to make room. Beatrice's bottom was amply fleshed and on her other side was a man with a black beard who had the burly physique of someone who shoes several horses before breakfast.

'Dearly beloved, we are gathered . . . this man and this woman . . . for the begetting of children and the avoidance of fornication . . .' I heard snippets of the service as I looked at the church, which was more like a jewelled casket than a place for Christian worship. Almost everything was gilded or painted and the ceiling was blue with tiny gold stars flung in handfuls across it. I had been to services there before but I suppose I was too much of a child then to appreciate its opulent beauty.

The bride and bridegroom gave the responses without stumbling. I couldn't see Miranda's face as I was on her side but I caught a glimpse of his – I knew his name was Rory McCleod, from the wedding invitation – whenever he looked down at her. The thought flashed into my mind that I would want my husband to look at me like that while we were being married and the second after I knew that it would be a mistake to marry Jeremy.

I had never seen two people in love before. If Aunt Pussy had once been in love with R.D. she had fallen out of it before I was old enough to take notice. There was no doubt that the love between my mother and father was fearfully one-sided. All Aunt Pussy's friends were too worldly for love other than the temporary, concupiscent kind and all the young people I knew were too brittle and energetically self-seeking to feel the passionate adoration I saw on Rory's face. The babble of love was constantly on people's lips, in poetry, novels, plays and films, but I had not until now seen a single real example of it.

After the exchange of vows the Vicar began his address. He set off very promisingly with a poem by Elizabeth Barrett Browning which began 'How do I love thee? Let me count the ways' and had wonderful lines in like 'I love thee with the passion put to use / In my old griefs, and with my childhood's faith.' I wrote them in my notebook and made a mental note to look the poem up when I got home. I waited eagerly for more cultural droplets to fall into the vast ocean of my ignorance. But somehow we had wandered into the text 'All flesh is grass'. By the time I had worked out that it was intended to be a reminder of the fleeting nature of physical love the Vicar had strolled down a byway into types of grasses. I had thought there were perhaps three sorts, short and green (lawn), long and yellow (hay) and brown (dead). Instead I learned that there are hundreds of different kinds all with impossible double- and triple-barrelled names. I tried to concentrate on the botanical erudition that flowed in a cataract from the Vicar's lips but, as usual, my mind wandered and I imagined myself saying, 'Allow me to introduce Sir Peregrine Festuca-Ovina. This is Mrs Dactylis Glomerata-Variegata.'

The congregation was growing restless by now and the crushed buttocks of those on the front pew were, if mine were anything to go by, causing acute pain. I decided to let the grasses go by the board and to concentrate instead on the charming arrangements of wild flowers with which the church was filled. But instead I found myself reflecting on the fact that, given the brevity not only of our loves but of our lives, everything was really rather a mess and the best one could hope to do was to pin down and identify those matters nearest to one and leave the rest in unfathomed chaos. A hymn book was snapped violently shut behind me and we would have jumped out of our skins if we had not been wedged fast into them. The Vicar faltered, glanced in the direction of the noise, and announced the next hymn without coming to any sort of conclusion. I discovered afterwards that the woman sitting behind me was his wife.

'I can't see Fabia anywhere,' I said to Beatrice. We were standing outside the church after the service. Fabia was Beatrice and Miranda's mother. I had met her only three times in my life but those few occasions had reduced me to inarticulate dismay.

'She couldn't come. Her boyfriend is a ballet dancer and he's opening tonight in Vienna as the male bit of the Bluebirds. Apparently he said he couldn't go on if Fabia wasn't standing in the wings holding his wrap. I think the truth is that he's terrified that we'll try to persuade her to change her will so he pretends to be completely artistically dependent. She's leaving Sergei half her worldly goods.'

'Sergei? A Russian? How glamorous.'

'Not if you met him. He's less than half Fabia's age, has long greasy hair in a pony-tail and thigh muscles like hot-water cylinders. Anyway, Fabia's rather miffed about Miranda marrying Rory. To her, doctors are lowly artisans.

You know her passion for creative geniuses. Hello, James, darling.'

My cousin James, with whom I had so often played bandits, knights and pirates, stood before me, now a dazzling young man. He had Jack's white skin and flame-red hair. It wasn't the first time that day that I had thought of Jack. But I saw at once that James was in possession of an interior world and, unlike his father, would not need to torment others to satisfy his craving for reassurance. You may think that this was a great deal to assess in ten seconds but one glance at his face assured me that this was the case.

'Hello, Viola,' was all he said but I felt that we were friends again.

'You've got a lot older,' said Henry, James's younger brother, who came up to us then.

'Only by the same amount you have.'

'Ah, but you're grown-up now,' said Henry, with all the gravity of fourteen years. '*I'm* still a schoolboy. 'That's a *very* pretty dress,' he added, and for a moment, despite the freckles and the grin and the grey-flannel school suit, Jack was there.

'Viola! You are a darling to come!' Miranda threw her arms around me.

'He's delectable! Clever, clever girl,' I whispered into her ear, because Rory was standing quite near by.

'I'm so wickedly happy you can't imagine,' she whispered back. 'This is Maurice Tremlow – a dear family friend,' she said aloud, introducing the man in the coral waistcoat who had given her away.

'Hello.' I shook his hand. He was like Father Christmas in civilian dress. You felt that he was the bringer of good things. He looked wise and jolly and sympathetic all at once.

'Maurice is the most marvellous painter. I must somehow manage to show you some of his work before you go. Aunt Pussy! I'm thrilled to see you. It must be three or four years. Too long, anyway. This is Maurice Tremlow. This is Adeline Otway but we all call her Pussy.'

'Hello, Michael,' said Aunt Pussy at once. 'What a very long time since we last met.'

'Maurice,' I muttered *sotto voce*.

'I beg your pardon.' Aunt Pussy looked confused. 'Maurice, of course.'

By this time we were being organised into groups to go up to the house so the *petit moment d'embarras* passed more or less unnoticed. Bert had managed to unhook the car from the wall and drove us, plus Beatrice and her husband – the black-bearded man who turned out to be a potter not a blacksmith, rather to my disappointment – up to the house. I defy anyone to catch their first glimpse of Westray Manor through the woods without losing their heart completely. It is the most marvellous tangle of styles and periods and every part of it leads harmoniously into the next with a dramatic blend of grandeur and friendliness. I thought suddenly of Giles and wished that he could see it.

My reunion with the house was marred by Bert backing the car at speed and almost knocking down the medieval gatehouse. We all screamed simultaneously and it was enough to make him jam on the brakes in time.

'What will Bert do during the reception?' I asked my aunt, as he finally drove the car away to the coach-house. 'Poor thing. He looks quite shaken.'

'I don't think his eyesight is quite what it was,' replied Aunt Pussy, with masterly understatement. 'Don't worry, darling. He'll have a good time in the kitchen with the other drivers.'

I looked about. It was unlike the kind of wedding that my aunt was accustomed to attend. For a start there was not a single male guest wearing a morning coat. Little children and dogs ran about unchecked and there were very few important hats. In fact, as it turned out, it was the nicest wedding I'd ever been to because, unlike all the others, it largely ignored ritual. There weren't any speeches, there was no cake and no going away. Miranda said they were going to France in a few weeks' time with Henry and Elizabeth. Food was delicious and plentiful, the house was crammed with flowers, everybody relaxed and wandered

322

about and got more and more cheerful. All Rory's relations were Scots and they got plastered within seconds of the corks being popped. I need not have worried about Bert. He was included in the party as a guest and seemed to have a very good time.

'Hello, Elizabeth,' I said to Miranda's daughter, whom I found lying on the grass in the quincunx garden with a can of beer in her hand. She seemed rather drunk. 'I love your tattoo.' She had a bee on her cheekbone. It was very well drawn when you looked close to. From any distance, I'm afraid, it looked like a repulsively hairy mole. 'How brave! Didn't it hurt like mad?'

'Acksherly,' Elizabeth's speech was slurred, 'I drew it on myself with ink. But you mustn't tell anyone. I want people to think it's permanent.' Elizabeth hadn't changed. She was four years younger than me but I had always admired her and recognised a superior strength. She had been rebelling since she was old enough to hurl her rattle from her pram. 'What have you been doing, Viola, all these yearsh?'

'Well, nothing very much, I must confess. But I've got a job now, working for a charity which looks after old houses.' Elizabeth yawned, not bothering to conceal it behind her hand and took a swig from the can. 'I'm so sorry about your father,' I said in softer tones. 'I wanted to come to the funeral but I was ill.'

Elizabeth looked at me. 'I'm glad someone here's thought about Dad. I hate the feeling that we've just pushed him away.'

'I bet there isn't anyone here today who hasn't thought about him. People may not like to mention him just now but no one's forgotten. I remember him very clearly. So attractive and well . . . powerful perhaps isn't the right word.'

'Thanksh,' said Elizabeth. 'I only wanted to hear someone say something nishe about him. Of course I know what a bastard he was to Mum. But still.' She sighed. 'I do think parents are toxic.'

'Miranda seems to me to be just what I would have chosen, if I could.'

'Really? What's your mother like?' Elizabeth's attention was arrested.

'I hardly know. I've only met her about six times in my life.' I told Elizabeth about Constantia. She seemed much struck by the contrast between my upbringing and her own. Then we discussed Fabia, about whom Elizabeth said some extremely rude things, which made me laugh.

'I suppose it's rather feeble to blame your problems on your parentsh,' said Elizabeth in conclusion.

'It's certainly a complete waste of time,' I agreed.

When we were in the hall getting ready to leave I gave Miranda a tremendous hug. 'It's been the loveliest wedding,' I said. 'You've got a smudge of ink on your cheek.'

'That must be Elizabeth's bee coming off.' Her eyes were soft. 'She came up to me a little while ago and kissed me and said I was the best mother anyone could have. It was the happiest moment of the entire day.'

All the way back to London Aunt Pussy and I gossiped shamelessly. We agreed that it had been much more enjoyable than weddings usually are, that Elizabeth had fulfilled her early promise of beauty, that Henry was a character and James an absolute dear. We thought Beatrice was a saint to put up with Roger and that the Vicar was a duck. I was voluble with praise about Maurice and his paintings but Aunt Pussy was unusually reticent about him though they had spent a long time walking round the garden together after lunch. We had no doubts whatsoever that Rory was intelligent, agreeable and breathtakingly sexy and that he was just the person to make Miranda happy.

The countryside we drove through was staggeringly pretty, with tile-hung cottages and high hedges, pink and white with dog-roses. I made Bert stop so that I could gather a few for Daniel as he had once said that he liked wild roses best of all flowers. The scent was sweet, the birds sang and the sky was enticingly blue. This made me think again, for at least the hundredth time that day, about getting married as it has always seemed to me that living in the country on one's own could be rather lonely.

'Do you know Jeremy Inskip?' I asked, in what I hoped was a casual way.

'Millicent's elder boy? Isn't he rather a problem? Like all the male Inskips. No push. I seem to remember hearing something . . . Why?' Aunt Pussy's mind suddenly focused. 'Darling, you haven't – you aren't thinking of – Oh, no, darling, let me beg you to put it out of your mind at once! No Inskip ever made a woman happy. Bad blood.'

'It's all right. I know now it wouldn't work. But Jeremy isn't like his father at all. He's much more like his mother. I do like him very, very much but I realise I'm not in love with him.'

'Let me see . . . I can't remember who Millicent's family were.'

'Her brother is Francis Ashton.'

Aunt Pussy let out a scream. 'Worse and worse! Francis Ashton! The wickedest roué in London. I remember your mother – good heavens! Darling, I really think perhaps it would be wise not to go to Inskip Park again.'

'I don't know why everyone thinks I can't take care of myself,' I complained to Daniel later that evening as he showed me how to make a *bourride*, which is a kind of fish soup. Actually all I had wanted to do when I got home was to go to bed and digest everything I had eaten and drunk but Daniel never believed in this sort of self-indulgence and he was severe when I hinted my intentions. I was busy pounding cloves of garlic for the *aïoli*, which is stirred into the soup at the end of cooking when Daniel remarked that I was dangerously inclined to accept people at their own estimation. I had been telling him about the wedding and how much I had enjoyed talking to everyone. 'It's not as though I like everyone I meet. I'm quite critical, really, I think. After all, that sort of occasion isn't meant to be a symposium on moral values and their relevance to modern society. One's simply obliged to get on with people as best one can for the sake of one's hostess who has slaved for days. Not being a nuisance to put it at its lowest.'

'Aha! Exactly. But the vast majority will do precisely that.

They will travel along with whatever the loudest voice says and they will never question it. But you – you are too intelligent for that. And therefore you have a duty to ask the questions, to check with rigour the credentials of the behaviours you meet with.'

'Well, thank you for saying I'm intelligent. You said the other day I was silly. I suppose I can't be both.'

'Of course you can be. We are all sometimes silly and sometimes inspired. You have the background that makes you conform to absurd ideas of caste and money. But you have also the curiosity which will save you.'

'Hang on.' I stopped pounding the garlic and looked angrily at Daniel. 'I feel rather insulted. I don't think I'm a snob or a materialist.'

'Oh, Viola! How you deceive yourself! Does not your aunt give you money? You play at independence. You have whatever you want as soon as you want it. You like to play at being poor in this house with us because it seems to you romantic. But the minute that it seems so no longer you will go away to something more luxurious. No doubt to the arms of a man who can give you all the things you want. And we shall be your so amusing acquaintance of whom you like to tell occasionally, our eccentricities, our ridiculous ways and so forth. It is all a delightful little game. Who are your friends? They have grand houses, servants, cars, they belong to the upper classes. It is just chance? You are not a snob?'

'That's the meanest thing you could have said!' I was furious now, my heart pounding and my throat tight. 'I told you about Miranda's house because I thought you'd like to hear about how beautiful it is, not because I wanted to impress you. Actually, she hasn't had any money for ages and she's just married a man who's a doctor and quite poor. She's had to take in lodgers to make ends meet. Neither of us would dream of marrying anyone for their money and you're just – you're just bitter because – I don't know why!' Then, probably because I was tired, I burst into tears.

'*Mein Liebling*, don't cry!' Daniel took me in his arms although I was still holding the mortar of crushed garlic.

'You are right. I wanted to hurt you because I am jealous. It was very cruel and stupid. You are a lovely, intelligent girl and I *am* a bitter old man who is disappointed in life and cannot live with himself. Forgive me, fool that I am.'

'It's all right.' I sniffed, anxious that my nose should not run into the garlic. 'Only you *were* mean. But I'm often mean myself. And you've been so good to me and taught me so much – of course I can forgive you much worse things than calling me a greedy snob.'

'I lied. You are none of these things. I can find no fault with you, other than those of youth and ignorance which will cure themselves.' I couldn't help smiling at this. It was a typical Daniel compliment. Daniel let go of me. 'You feel better now?' He looked at me anxiously.

'Oh, yes. Don't take any notice. I cry very easily. Really, I've absolutely recovered.' I gave a silly grin to reassure him as he continued to look troubled.

'Ah, that is a horrible grimace!' He shuddered. 'Never willingly spoil your beauty. It is precious. Preserve it as long as time will allow.'

'I refuse to walk about with a face like a log of wood for fear of being ugly. Anyway, I don't think I'm beautiful at all. I look very ordinary to myself.'

'Well, I could tell you what I think of your beauty – but I shall not because conceit is ugliness also.'

'Besides, think how embarrassing!'

We both laughed.

'That is good. We are quite friends. I am very sorry. I must be more careful.' Daniel held his arms away from his sides and let them fall again in a gesture of exasperation. 'I seem so bad with women – always sending them into tears.'

'You're thinking of Veronica? Yes, but there can't be many women in the world who haven't cried over a man.'

'Is that so? Can they be worth it?'

'Not usually. Probably never. But at the time you convince yourself that you can't live without that particular one. Don't men cry about women?'

'I have never done so. I have not cried since – since –' Daniel stopped talking and began to cough.

327

'Oh dear. Don't say if you'd rather not. It's something to do with the camp, isn't it?'

Daniel sighed and made a gesture of impatience. 'Yes. I cannot go back – in my mind – because of it. Neither can I go forward in my life. Everywhere it hems me round. It has crippled me.' He hunched up his shoulders and folded his arms across his chest.

'You don't think that talking about it might make it easier to live with? Isn't it supposed to be terribly bad to suppress things?'

'I tell you the truth. I am afraid.'

'What are you afraid of?'

'I don't know . . . madness, perhaps. A few years after I came here I tried to talk about it. I was recommended to an expert in shell-shock. You know what that is? When soldiers have seen too much horror. This man also had helped camp victims.'

'Yes?' I said encouragingly as Daniel paused.

'I went to this man. I start to tell him. He is very kind, very wise. He listened, he nods, he is all sympathy. But suddenly as I begin on the worst part, he moves. Through the window the sun falls on him. I am dazzled by the buttons on his coat. He is in uniform. All at once I begin to sweat, I wish to vomit, I tremble with – oh, the most degrading terror. I run from the room, I do not go back.'

'Oh, Daniel! What a pity! If only you could find someone you trusted enough. Men ought to cry. I saw my father cry once. He said he felt much better afterwards.'

Daniel began to walk about the room, still clasping his arms, his face white.

'Well, then, if you will listen, since you urge it I shall try. When I have found sympathy I have been tempted. But, of course, people are made bashful. Some things are difficult to hear as well as to say.' He began to give little coughs, like a motorbike starting. I felt apprehensive. 'But I don't know if you can understand. It was another world. We were not civilised beings. I do not speak only of my captors. You know what was perhaps the worst thing about the camp? That one could trust no other human being. The first blow I received was from another prisoner – a Pole, a Jew like myself. He knocked out a tooth from my head because I questioned why he was beating an old man. But the pain of that blow was disillusion. The Nazis were clever. They used the temptation of privileges to divide us – extra food, shoes, clothing. We wanted to live, but the price was self-respect.'

'I see – how awful! That's not how I imagined it. I thought the prisoners would be united in their suffering, supporting each other.'

'They – the prisoners in charge of our barracks – were called *Kapos*. Generally they were political prisoners, the élite. They were as pitiless as the Nazis. Everywhere there were spies who would betray their fellow prisoners for a piece of bread. We were brought so low, starving, thirsty, cold, fatigued, diseased, that we lost even the crudest sense of honour. The *Sonderkommando* were also prisoners, mostly Jews. It was their job to make the victims strip, to push them into the gas chambers. They pulled out the corpses, cut off the women's hair, extracted the gold teeth, sorted the clothes and shoes. Then they transported the bodies to the crematoria, piled them in to be burned and raked out the ashes afterwards to be spread on the fields. Their own people. Even though life was a purgatory, still they were willing to do this filthy work in order to live. And the irony was that the Nazis slaughtered them all to get rid of witnesses.'

He paused to cough. I could think of nothing to say that would not have sounded trivial and impertinent. But he stopped pacing and fastened his eyes on my face as though requiring some response.

'No one could blame you for hating them,' was all I could think of to say.

'I have often wished that I could burn myself up with hatred. Then I should be fired by a belief in my own rectitude. But men are universally violent. One sees and reads of terrible things every day. Malice, cowardice, brutality, they are not the peculiarity of one nation only. You know what saved me each time they selected for the gas chambers? I played the viola. Our commandant was a sensitive, cultured man.' Daniel's face became strained with sarcasm. 'He liked to hear the classics and to have them very well played. Was he not a god among beasts? When we were liberated I decided that I would not play it again. Some sacrifice seemed obligatory. I had literally nothing else to give.'

'But surely playing music to stay alive was quite different from punishing and executing other prisoners.'

Daniel shrugged. 'At the time I thought so, yes. It seemed to do no harm. Despite weakness from hunger – we had only soup, dirty water with turnips, and a morsel of bread to eat – and sick with my lungs from the hard labour and intense cold, I played always my best because I was enamoured of this painful, filthy, lice-ridden thing called life.'

Daniel paused with a bout of coughing, so racking that I was frightened. I ought not to have persuaded him to tell me. I was much too inexperienced to help him. I longed to ask him to stop. He rested his hands on the back of a chair, fixed his eyes on the fire in the range and began to speak very quickly. 'There was a day in April when the cold had receded and I saw that a *feigwurz* – a little yellow flower – was blooming among the concrete slabs on which the barracks stood. We were lining up to march to work. I bent to pick it but my hand was stayed by the thought that I would be its executioner. I was moved almost to tears by this living thing of beauty. As I looked up moments later I saw my sister Mirah among a transport of new arrivals and I conceived that the flower was a symbol. I would be a preserver – a liberator. I would put all my effort to save something better than the thing I had become. I watched Mirah take her place in the line for the stripping, shaving and delousing. She had lustrous dark hair like yours.'

Daniel stared at my hair as though trying to commit it to memory.

'She was fifteen years old. I thought how sweet hunger would become if I could smuggle her some of my bread ration – if I could devote myself to sustaining life in this innocent girl, pure, lovely, unconversant with corruption. I did not call out because it was forbidden to talk when going to work. I knew the dangers. We had seen people shot for less. But I had to pass very near. I turned my face away so that she could not see me. But at the last moment I turned to look back – for one second I looked – and she saw me. Her face at first was surprised – then there was horror and pity in her eyes. She called my name. I shook my head. She left her place in the line and began to run towards me. I heard the guard shout – saw him lift his rifle. I stopped – and covered my face – I felt the crack of a rifle butt on my head, to make me keep walking. I walked on. I knew she was dying – but I – walked on.'

I put my hand over Daniel's where it rested on the chair. His face was convulsed with anguish, screwed up as though to weep but no sound came. His mouth trembled, the corners of his dark eyes drooped, his shoulders were stooped with grief.

'Poor, poor Mirah!' I saw a young, dark-haired girl, shocked, frightened, running to her brother for protection. 'Oh, poor girl!' I flinched from imagining the impact of the bullet.

'I might have died with her.' Daniel's voice was constrained, so quiet that I could hardly hear what he was saying. 'I might have held her, kissed her – what was my life worth that I left her to die alone?'

'I suppose something stronger than your will didn't allow you a choice. When you touch something hot your hand flies away before you register the pain. The instinct to survive is the same thing. A reflex.'

Daniel looked exhausted and a bad colour, a sort of olive-grey. He pressed his handkerchief to his lips, coughing. 'I abominate talk of these things. It induces a violent physical nausea. I should not have attempted the explanation.'

'But I think you ought. How can you live properly if you can't examine your past? You only looked back,' I trembled at my own temerity, 'you didn't kill her. You loved her. That wasn't wrong. It wasn't your fault.' Daniel looked at me then, and I knew he longed to believe me. 'What happened was terrible but it can't be changed,' I went on. 'You ought to embrace life because you've got it and the others haven't.' I took his cold thin hand in mine. 'Play the viola. Make it an act of defiance. I know it's easy to say and that I've never had to stand up to anything remotely as bad and I wouldn't be able to do it myself. I expect I'd want to kill myself with sorrow. But because it didn't happen to me I can see what you ought to do.'

'Ah,' Daniel paused and took a deep breath. I heard his chest rattle. 'You are perfectly right. I take the coward's way. Either way I cannot tolerate to contemplate myself.'

I was silenced by the sadness of his face. I felt my own inadequacy to offer comfort. Daniel turned away and walked up the stairs. I heard the sound of his sitting-room door close.

I waited for a while wondering if he might come back but he didn't. My heart was no longer in the sauce so I washed up and went upstairs to my room. I paused for a moment by his door but I didn't dare go in.

I sat down at my table and made myself begin to read and take notes for my essay. From time to time I went over my conversation with Daniel. I was terrified that I might have done something wickedly destructive. How could I have been arrogant enough to think that I might help? I wished now I could undo it all. I felt exhausted. The image of Mirah running came into my mind over and over again. I put my head on the table and wept for pity.

The time dragged by. I felt worse. I contemplated going to bed but it was only nine o'clock. Work was the only possible comfort. 'Jan Van Eyck – Father of the Northern European Renaissance?'. Julian liked to put question marks at the end of his essay titles to kindle debate. When, as so often happened, I wandered from whatever argument I was positing and lapsed weakly into eulogy, Julian always wrote 'slush' in the margin, which was both humiliating and salutary. I hoped I was beginning to grasp the technique of organising an essay.

Poor Daniel. I tried to imagine what it would be like to have to live with so terrible a memory. I longed to go down and try to comfort him but I was afraid he would be angry with me.

I managed to lose myself for a while in Vasari's description of Van Eyck's discovery of oil paints. I was engrossed by his magical depiction of the fur in the photograph I had of *The Marriage of Giovanni Arnolfini and Giovanna Cenami* – which is one of the paintings everyone knows, of a Dutch interior with the betrothed couple and a convex mirror in the background reflecting the artist, when I heard the clock in the hall strike. It was ten o'clock.

Tiffany had said that many camp survivors killed themselves because they could not endure their feelings of guilt. I had persuaded Daniel to relive his sister's death. What if he found that the pain was too much to bear? Josephine was sleeping on my lap. I took her in my arms and went downstairs. The hall was quiet but for the clock and the faint sounds of traffic. I lifted my hand to knock at the door of his sitting room but an unfamiliar sound from within made me hesitate. It was, I recognised seconds later, the sound of a stringed instrument being tuned. Standing in the dark hall, a smell of verbena and dust in my nostrils, I listened as Daniel began to play.

The piece was slow and elegiac, a rising sweep of notes. I imagined ghosts of the prison-house passing through Daniel's room, tormented souls, which in their turn tormented him. Josephine bared her teeth and made a clicking noise with her tongue, which meant that she was upset. I stroked her head. After a minute the music stopped. There was silence and then a strange grating sound, like a saw running with regular strokes against the grain of a plank. I realised that it was the sound of breathing, from a chest painfully constricted. I sat on the stairs, clutching Josephine for comfort. Daniel was crying.

CHAPTER 25

'**W**ell, Viola, you've certainly grown. You need to put on some weight. I suppose *some* men find the *gamin* look attractive, but generally I think a few curves are appreciated.'

My mother blew cigarette smoke emphatically from her nostrils and gave me an appraising look from beneath eyebrows plucked into thin curves. Even from the distance of several feet – from the doorway of my father's cottage to his favourite chair in which she reclined – I could see that they owed a great deal to the pencil. She was beautiful still but there was a suggestion of reconstruction about her appearance. Her hair was very well cut, dark with a blonde streak at the front, and her tobacco-brown linen dress and crocodile shoes yelled money. Her eyes were still large and lovely and her scarlet lips exquisitely shaped but her jaw-line was blurred and her throat had swollen into a second chin. Even though she was sitting down it was apparent that she had gained a stone or two since the last time I had seen her.

'Now, Connie, is that the way to greet your own child?' My father spoke softly as he stood with his arm about my shoulder. He smelt deliciously of outdoors. A sprig of herb, I think it was rosemary, was poked into the buttonhole of his shirt.

'I wish you wouldn't call me that. You know I hate it.' My mother's tone was petulant. 'Come and kiss me,' she said to me.

Her cheek was soft and smelt of something exotic, a mixture of mimosa and pencil-boxes. Close to, I saw that there were lines and patches of darker skin beneath her eyes. I thought she did not look happy. For the first time in my life I felt a stirring of something like sympathy for her. Before, she had always seemed so bright and distant and fast-moving that it would have been like feeling sorry for a shooting star.

'I suppose Pussy spoils you as much as ever? You look well enough. How old are you?'

'Twenty.' I knew that my mother knew this – she could hardly fail to – but she always asked me on the few occasions we met. It was a way of distancing herself from the unpleasant fact that she had once given birth to me, I suppose.

'God! Twenty! What an age to be. Marvellous! You can make mistakes and get away with them. Well,' she laughed, 'usually anyway. I'm nearly forty-two. And not a thing to show for it. Jenks, get me a drink, will you, darling? I'm parched. Whisky. With ice.'

'I've nothing but my own parsnip wine, Connie. You should've told me you was coming.'

'Parsnip wine! How revoltingly bucolic! We'll be skipping in circles and singing hey nonny no next. Oh, well, it'll be better than nothing.' My father poured us both a small glass of liquid the colour of Turkey umber. It tasted very interesting, sweet and flowery. 'The truth is I didn't know I was coming. We went ashore at Cannes to do some shopping and have lunch. I can tell you there is *nothing* more stupefyingly dull than a yacht. I never want to see another wave. On the spur of the moment I grabbed a taxi to the airport and managed to get on a flight to England. They'll be wondering what's happened to me!' She laughed. 'Pieter – that's the Flying Dutchman – was being tiresome. He adores a row so he can come crawling all over me to make up. I came straight here, Jenks darling. I hope you're pleased.' She gave him an arch look and drew on her cigarette without puckering her lips, presumably to avoid getting 'dog's bottom' lines. 'We were supposed to have lunch with these ghastly friends of Pieter's – terribly pretentious and *so* dull. Seven courses with ancient retired ambassadors and obscure *principi* trying to rub their trembling shrunken shanks against one's legs.' She giggled. 'Pieter'll be mad as fire.'

'You'd better telephone him from the house, Connie,' said my father. 'Doesn't do to make folks anxious. 'Tisn't the right way to carry on.'

'Oh, don't be so stuffy!' My mother looked defiant. 'What do *you* care about Pieter?'

335

'Not much. But I care about you, lass, and I don't like to see you behave shabby to anyone and let yourself down. You always was headstrong and I respected that – loved you for it, even. You was bold and brave and full o' spunk. But you was never small. I don't hold with spite. Making folks unhappy, that's something else.'

To my surprise, my mother burst into tears. 'Oh, Jenks! You're the only person in the world who loves me enough to care what I'm like. The others are such bloodsuckers. They only think what they can get out of me. It's just endless, endless sex. No one thinks I'm good for anything else.' She cried without screwing up her eyes or making a face, just allowing the tears to slide down her cheeks, looking up at my father and holding out her hands to him as though she were a child.

'Now, Connie, don't upset yourself,' he said, taking a large, earthy handkerchief from his pocket and sitting on the arm of her chair to dry her tears. She rested her head against his arm and gave him the faintest, most fetching little smile with swimming eyes.

I left the cottage and walked up through the orchard to visit Aunt Pussy. My mother would require all my father's attention. He was a lamb to the slaughter as far as she was concerned. I paused for a moment by the fountain in the formal garden to look at the splashes of sun sliding like butter melting on the dimpled surface of the water. I could do nothing to help him. He knew my mother through and through and he still loved her.

I had badly wanted to talk to my father and had come to Richmond to ask his advice. But Aunt Pussy would have to do instead. As it was only half past eleven she was in bed, lying back on the pillows, looking like one of those allegorical portraits of the seasons by Arcimboldi, which are composed entirely of fruit and vegetables. She had what appeared to be strawberries pasted over her forehead, nose and chin and pieces of pineapple balanced on her cheeks. She lifted a slice of cucumber from one eye when I came in. Pooh Bah lifted his chin from his dish of biscuits and wagged his tail.

'Thank goodness it's you, darling. I feared it might be Marcel. He's taken to coming every day. I can tell it means a proposal and, you know, it's so silly at my age but I still rather shrink from the *coup mortel*. One so dislikes wounding. If only men would believe me when I say that absolutely *nothing* would persuade me to get into bed with anyone.' Aunt Pussy shuddered and a piece of pineapple slid down her cheek. 'Oh, damn! How messy fruit is! Mamie Stewart-Buchanan swears that she owes her new complexion to spending an hour every day looking like a market stall. You should see her – cheeks stretched tight like two tennis balls and not a wrinkle in sight! I'm not sure I altogether believe her. Americans are so *brave* about plastic surgery. And she *was* away for rather a long time, visiting her daughter in Boston. The strawberries counter the oiliness of the centre panel, do you see, and the pineapples have enzymes which tone sluggish circulation. Cucumber is good for bags under the eyes.'

'Did you know Constantia's here?'

'No! Is she?' Aunt Pussy half sat up. 'I suppose she's tormenting Jenkins. He's so loyal, poor sweet. Of course she'll never stay with him. Hasn't an ounce of taste in men. And I suppose it wouldn't be quite – Well, darling, I hope she won't upset you, that's all.'

'Quite honestly she's always so indifferent to me that I might as well be upset by a passing cloud or a shower of rain.'

'Darling, that does sound sad, whatever you say. Now bring up that chair and let's have a nice cosy chat.' She held out her hand to me.

I did as bidden and placed a kiss on her hairline where there were no strawberries. 'What would I have done without you, Aunt Pussy? You really are my guardian angel.'

'Stop! Stop! You know how easily I cry. My cucumber will go limp. Is this a flying visit or did you want something, dearest?'

'Actually, I'd like some advice.'

'It's a man, of course. Oh, horrors! The Inskip boy! I implore you, on my knees – well, imagine me on them, darling, because I can't disturb the fruit.'

'No, it isn't Jeremy. Don't worry. That's all over.'

And it was. The day after my return from Miranda's wedding I had spent at least three hours struggling over a letter explaining that I couldn't marry him because we weren't really in love with each other and though he would always be my most undying bosom friend – you can imagine the sort of thing. Anyway I sweated blood over it and shed quite a few tears at the idea of hurting him so badly. When I had finished it I went down to make myself a reviving cup of coffee and found a letter from Jeremy on the hall table. It was the first I had had from him for over a week. It turned out that he had come to exactly the same conclusion and though he considered me a terrific pal, he didn't think we should consider tying the knot at such a young age, et cetera, et cetera. It was only half the length of mine and had a breezy tone which mine, I hope, lacked but I forgave him because, after all, he was a man. Of course I tore mine up and spent half an hour on a much easier letter, agreeing to all he said, pledging eternal friendship and so forth. I felt so much better after that that I realised how much the whole thing had been worrying me.

'Jeremy and I are just chums.'

'I'm glad to hear it. It isn't Pierce Topham? I heard something about him the other day from Margot Sempill-Smith that I didn't quite like. I believe you know her daughter.'

'Vaguely.'

'Well, Margot told me that he favours tying girls to dining-tables and smearing them with chutney. Or was it jam? In itself not dangerous, I agree, but what is wrong with a comfortable bed and clean sheets? What I wondered was – how could she know? It's hardly something a daughter would tell her mother. Margot's always liked younger men, of course. I can't think why. So little conversation and so much sex – one quails at the thought. I suppose I've answered my own question, really. Too sordid. What were we talking about, darling?'

'Do you think it matters if a man is a bit older?'

'Well . . . no . . . I don't think it does. Poor Roddy was fourteen years older and I found it generally a good thing. A man is always so much keener on the bed side of things. Though Margot, if one can believe a word she says, is still ex*traord*inarily enthusiastic – but I'm straying from the point. A man tends to slow down when he gets to sixty whereas most women seem to cool off at about forty. I'm generalising, of course, darling – if Harriet Winstanton's account is anything to go by Count Fuseli was ninety and still able to make love to three women at once though either my notion of anatomy is adrift or – However, that's neither here nor there. So the age gap fits in rather well. Roddy fretted about being impotent later on but quite honestly it was a relief.'

'Supposing it's quite a lot more than fourteen years?'

Aunt Pussy lifted a slice of cucumber to look at me. 'How much more?'

'Um – twenty-eight actually.'

'Sweetest girl! What can you be thinking of? That's more than twice your own age! He'll be in a bath-chair, mumbling biscuits soaked in tea, before you're even middle-aged. What could have put the idea in your head? I *can't* believe you'd sacrifice yourself for money or a title.'

'No. He hasn't got either. He's quite poor. But he's a very fine man. And he's had such an awful life. I'm practically certain he's in love with me, if that doesn't sound very conceited.'

'Darling, *that* doesn't surprise me. With that face – your mother had half London at her feet and her nose was always the teensiest bit too short. I'm glad to say that yours is perfect.'

'I don't think he's the sort of man who falls in love with the length of a nose. He's terribly clever and knows so much and so badly needs someone to . . . humanise him. He's the most fascinating person I've ever met. His life has been almost destroyed by things he couldn't help. He's suffered

339

unimaginably. It would be marvellous to give a man something really worthwhile – supposing one could – rather than just the usual thing of spending his money and seeing that his newspaper's on the breakfast table.' My grasp of domestic duties was vague. I thought for a moment. 'I suppose I feel like Dorothea Brooke did at the beginning of *Middlemarch*.'

'Is that Quentin Brooke's eldest girl – the one with a face like a chest of drawers? It would be a mistake to compare yourself with her, though she has fifty thousand a year of her own. Why has this man suffered so frightfully? I don't understand.'

'Well . . . he's a Jew and he was sent to Auschwitz.'

'Oh dear! Not that I've anything against Jews though Roddy couldn't bear them. I've always found the Rothschilds utterly charming. And they're all so clever and artistic. Minnie Golding's a Jew and she's an absolute poppet. But, you know, Jews or not, when people have suffered dreadfully at the hands of others they are inclined to make everyone else go on paying. Poor dears, they can't *help* it, I don't suppose, but I shouldn't like to see you trying to make up single-handedly for two thousand years of persecution or whatever it's been.'

'I don't think Daniel would do that. He's not like other men.'

Aunt Pussy took away both slices of cucumber for emphasis. 'Darling, if I had a gold coin for every time I've heard a woman say that and another when the same woman's admitted after two years or so that he's practically identical to all the others, I should be as rich as Crocus or whoever it was.'

All the way home on the bus I turned over Aunt Pussy's words.

'Heavens, Viola!' said Tiffany, when I took her into my confidence that afternoon on the balcony at SCAB. 'No, naturally I won't breathe a word to anyone. Daniel! But, my lamb, he's so much older than you! Of course he's wonderful, I do agree. I've always thought that. Even his moods and tempers are exciting. He's an exotic creature – like an emir or a margrave or the Dalai Lama. I suppose his remoteness is what makes him romantic and mysterious. But can you imagine what everyday life would be like? I think one ought to be able to discuss everything with the person one lives with. I can't see you chatting about something amusing that you saw on a bus. Or telling him you've got a curse pain. I blush even to think of it. And what do you mean you'll have to do the asking yourself?'

'I don't think he could ever tell me what he feels. It's so hard for him to talk about anything that really matters to him. After he told me about his sister – the one who was shot – he was in bed for three days afterwards. He said it was a putrid throat, do you remember? but I'm certain it was what my aunt calls a *crise de nerfs*.'

'I see. It's a mission. You want to restore him to life like Dr Manette in *The Tale of Two Cities*.'

'Well, yes, though that does sound rather calculating. But I'll admit I've always had a longing to be actually useful to someone. I've been an encumbrance all my life, though Aunt Pussy has done everything to make me feel that's not the case. But I know how difficult things were for her sometimes because of me. This is my chance to do something worthwhile. Like Dorothea Brooke, you know.'

Tiffany was much better read than my aunt.

'Hm. Do remember how that ended up. Though of course Daniel's nothing like Casaubon. But I'm riveted. Why do you think he's in love with you? Now I come to think about it he's always been incredibly possessive about you, hasn't he? When you were in Nottinghamshire he was like a stung bear, charging around trying to bite one's nose off. And I've noticed him watching you when we're all in the kitchen together. He has a sort of hungry look which I assumed at the time was wanting supper.'

'Mrs Shilling told me that he keeps a copy of Richard Crashaw's poems under his pillow. It's the book I gave him when I came back from Inskip. And inside are some pressed dog-roses that I brought back from Kent. I suppose it isn't evidence by itself. But you're right, he does watch me. When I leave the house to catch the bus I've got into the habit of looking back – just because I love the look of the façade with the sun on it. I always see Daniel watching from his window. And in the evening when I come home he's there again. Probably he doesn't realise that I can see him since he stands in the shadows. He's waiting in the hall when I come in, pretending to read his letters. I know this doesn't add up to anything much.

'But two nights ago I woke up and found Daniel in my room. He was standing by the window leaning against the shutters. The light from the street-lamp was full on his face. He looked so brooding and sad. Luckily my face was in the shadows because of the canopy. I closed my eyes at once and pretended to be still asleep. I heard him walking around – you know how quiet he is, he pads like a cat – and I squinted through my lashes. He was right by the bed, looking down at me. I felt him touch my hair, very lightly. Then he went away.'

'I wonder you weren't frightened. I think I might have been. Aren't people usually murdered by people they know and trust?'

'Daniel is the last man on earth who would inflict physical violence on anyone. I felt completely safe.'

'And do you love him?'

'I . . . reverence him, if there is such a verb. I want desperately to make him happy. Isn't that love? To feel that you'd make any possible sacrifice for someone?'

Tiffany lifted her tawny eyebrows. Her needle was poised over the piece of velvet she was stitching. 'I'm no authority on love. And I don't know anyone who is. I believe we're all fumbling in utter obscurity whatever we may say. But the word "sacrifice" in the context of love strikes a warning note in my mind.'

'Perhaps I didn't quite mean that. I spoke without thinking.'

'Perhaps so. Which makes it all the more revealing.'

Just after Tiffany left to keep an appointment with her art-gallery friend, the telephone rang.

'Mab! How lovely! I've got something I want to ask you. But first I must know. How was *La Bohème*?'

'Glorious.' Mab's voice was huskier than ever. I suspected that excitement had upped the cigarette intake. 'Superb production and faultless singing. Afterwards we went to a little Italian restaurant David knows. It was small and cosy, red lampshades, you know the sort of thing. I wore my navy in the end. I had my hair and nails done specially. I looked as good as I can look these days. Which is to say, ladylike and tidy if not actually seething with promise.'

'Did David make a pass?' You will judge from this how intimate Mab and I had become.

'Not quite. I thought he was going to when we got to my front door. I was suddenly horrified by the idea. I went to jelly, just like a schoolgirl again. But he only kissed my hand and said he hoped we'd be able to do it again soon. Then I was disappointed. I couldn't get to sleep for hours wondering what it might have been like to kiss a man other than Giles's father. Honestly, I'm behaving like an adolescent.'

'I don't think so. Pressing your lips to someone else's is not a thing that should be lightly done. Just being that close to another human being makes one feel vulnerable, I think.'

'How refreshing to hear this from one of your generation, dear. I thought you all believed in making love with any and everybody all the time.'

'That was the sixties. We're a bit more circumspect, generally.'

'What of Giles and his floozy? Though it's rather mean of me to call her that. Maternal jealousy, I expect. It's rather hot at the moment for untamed lust, I should have thought.'

'As it happens he's broken it off. I can't help feeling sorry for her. She still lurks about the place but in dark glasses and a veiled sun-hat. I'm afraid she's got it bad, poor thing. She keeps ringing here and when I answer she hangs up. I can always tell it's Julia. She's a very loud breather.'

'Well, I'm both glad and sorry. I was pleased that he was behaving like a red-blooded male. Of course he's had girlfriends before but they've never lasted. He's so pernickety. But Julia didn't sound like someone who would have had much time for mothers.'

'I think he's just looking for something above the commonplace,' I said, thinking of what I knew about Giles.

'I hope you're right, dear. Now what was it you wanted to talk to me about?'

I told her, briefly, about Daniel.

'Goodness, Viola! What a girl you are for challenges! How much older did you say? And a Jew. Well, your family won't like it, I don't suppose. I've nothing against them myself, of course, but Geoffrey was very anti them being admitted to the golf club. They were always blackballed.'

'But why?' I felt angry.

'Now, don't get cross with me, dear. I'm only saying. Goodness knows why! Because men are like nasty little children, I suppose, when all's said and done. They like ganging up. Geoffrey was a freemason. It's all much the same thing. Stupid, I call it. All this mystery and pomp when it's nothing more than who'll play with whom in the playground. Just like war. Senseless, isn't it, really, but they love the self-importance. More to the point, what's this man got that makes you want to give up the world for him?'

'I don't think I'd be doing that. He'd be giving everything to me. He knows so much more than I do.'

'I should hope so. He's more than twice your age. Make no mistake, dear, you'll find that you've given up a great deal. As a couple you won't fit into ordinary society. I'm not saying that that's the be-all and end-all but you must think how awkward it'd be to have your relationship constantly under puzzled scrutiny. Being married to a very much older man will immediately become the most interesting thing about you – like having a wooden leg or being a dwarf. Those are misfortunes that have to be lived with but I don't see why you want to put yourself on the fringe. I've grown very fond of you, dear, so you must allow me to speak my mind. No doubt you'll say I'm a conventional old woman who doesn't understand anything but one thing I do know – life is never easy and there's no need to go making it harder for yourself. He'd be a rare man indeed to be worth the sacrifice of your youth and all the habits of simple enjoyment. He sounds rather on the gloomy side, to say the least.'

'I don't think for a moment you're either old or conventional and I'm very, *very* fond of you, too. I promise I'll think about what you've said and I know that in many ways you're only telling me what everyone else – Hello, Giles. You're back early.'

'I'll ring off, dear. Now, you just be careful. Bye-bye.'

'Giles,' I said, after we had worked for an hour in companionable silence. 'Can I consult you?'

Giles looked up and smiled. 'I wish you would. I'm trying to decide whether we ought to take away the most hideous Victorian porch you ever saw from the front of a perfect Georgian house.'

'That doesn't sound a very difficult decision.'

'Ah, but if we do that we can't afford to save the two Chippendale pier tables that are more worm-hole than wood in the drawing room. There simply isn't enough money.'

'Oh dear, and we've had so many fund-raising events recently. People ought to be given a rest from our importunate demands for a bit, shouldn't they?'

'Exactly. So it has to be the pier tables. The porch can wait. What painter are you researching this week?'

'Leonardo da Vinci. Vasari calls him marvellous and celestial. I think that's possibly an understatement. I went to see *The Virgin of the Rocks* yesterday. That little piece of boundless sky among the dark primeval stones! But though I long to know what you think of it, it wasn't that I wanted your opinion about. Julian wants me to do a proper degree course.' I couldn't help a slight blush of pride as I said this.

When I had found 'See me afterwards' written on the bottom of my Van Eyck essay, I had experienced the customary foreboding. But over pie and chips at the Kozy Kavern Julian had put me out of my misery. He said that he usually discovered one or two people each year from his part-time students who would benefit from more serious study. Although I still couldn't spell and my grammar was freakish, the construction of my essays was improving by leaps and bounds and, more importantly, I had intelligent things to say and an ability to absorb painterly concepts. 'He thinks I ought to spend next year doing A levels and then apply to read history of art at university.'

Giles looked at me for a moment with an expression of one taken wholly by surprise before saying, 'I think that's the most satisfactory thing I've heard for a very long time. In fact I'm absolutely delighted. Of *course* you must do it. There can't be any question about it. This deserves a celebration! Let's go and share a bottle of Madame's best champagne.'

'It's four o'clock in the afternoon.'

'The French are more civilised about these things than we are. Come on, I'm hot and thirsty and tired of the Victorians.'

'Isn't that Julia over there?' I said, as we entered the burning air of the street. Despite the hat, which hid the trademark red hair, I recognised the sinuous walk, the forward thrust of the hips.

'Let's go the back way. She hasn't seen us.' Giles grabbed my arm and pulled me back into the building. We went out into the yard by the dustbins and by a circuitous route to La Petite Sonnerie. 'I really have a great deal to answer for. I should never have believed her when she said she was only interested in a good time. Poor Julia is so busy reacting to her grisly mother that she has no idea what she really does want.'

'It may only be a desire for high drama, you know. In which case she's getting it.'

'Do you think so?' Giles stopped to look at me. 'I'd like to believe that.'

In the cool gloaming of La Petite Sonnerie Giles lifted his glass in my direction. 'Here's to the future occupant of the Ruskin Chair.'

'What sort of chair is that?' I asked, imagining something Chinese Chippendale in style.

'A chair is what a professor gets elected to. John Ruskin was a famous Victorian writer, painter and social reformer. Very keen on the Pre-Raphaelites. He was Slade professor of art at Oxford at one time.'

I was busy writing this down in my notebook which was filled to nearly the last page.

'How do you spell Pre-Raffle-ites? One F or two?'

I put Giles's immoderate laughter down to the fact that he had drunk a whole glass of champagne very quickly. Naturally enough, given the weather, we were insanely thirsty and it wasn't long before we had finished the bottle. Giles ordered another, this time of Chablis. I felt rather drunk.

'There is something else I'd like to ask you about,' I said, borne on an alcoholic wave into the confessional. I started to tell him about Daniel.

'Just a minute.' Giles put down his glass. 'You're thinking of some sort of passage of love with your landlord? Is this to take place before, after, or to run concurrently with your betrothal to Jeremy Inskip?'

'Oh, didn't I say? Really, Jeremy and I were never properly engaged and by mutual consent we've decided that we never will be. Neither of us is the least bit hurt and we're still the best of friends.'

'I see. That's a very good thing. So, start again from the beginning.'

As I talked Giles stopped smiling and listened intently, leaning back in his chair with his arms folded in a relaxed way across his chest.

'So you see, I know he would never consider it right to tell me what he felt,' I concluded. 'He always talks about himself as though he's antique. He's inured to renunciation. If you only knew how good he is. And how unhappy.'

Giles was silent for a while, thinking. 'I suppose everyone's told you that it won't work?'

I nodded.

'And this hasn't deflected you in the least?'

'Well, I know it's silly to ask advice and then not take any notice of it. But I'm surprised how conventional other people are when it comes to it.'

'Is it convention or is it common sense?' Giles narrowed his eyes and looked at me in a considering way. 'Tell me everything you know about this man,' he said, when I was unable to answer.

So I described Daniel in the greatest detail possible. I could see that Giles was genuinely interested.

'If he really is all that you say, I think you'll find the answer to your dilemma very quickly. I don't imagine there's too much to fear from making your proposal, if I may call it that. I suppose you're hesitant because you're afraid of finding that your own feelings are not strong enough to withstand a torrent of emotion, once unleashed. Is that it?'

I sat with my mouth unattractively open until I realised that that was what I was doing and shut it fast. 'Is it?' I asked in my turn.

'In my experience people rush into doing something they want to do and ask advice only when they've got into a mess. You're doing this not out of desire but out of compassion.'

'I think he's amazingly attractive. It's not because I feel sorry for him.'

'Objects of compassion can be attractive. Animals, children, whatever makes us want to make the world a less hurtful place.' Giles smiled. 'Go ahead. I'm pretty certain that you'll find the answer to your quandary.'

This response was so different from others on the subject that I was puzzled. Giles was the only man I had asked – perhaps that had something to do with it. Anyway, I decided on the bus going home that I must stop talking about it. Four confidants was excessive, almost disgraceful. Had I so little faith in my own ability to make sense of things? The answer to that was a resounding yes.

In the kitchen at number 46, Tiffany was stirring a pan of walnut and butter-bean soup, the steam frizzing her hair into a halo of marigold rings round a face that was reminiscent of Cranach's *Venus*.

'I've got a letter from Veronica,' I said, tearing open the envelope, 'I'm terrified. Suppose it's all a disaster? I shall feel utterly responsible, if so. Shall I read it to you?'

'Yes, do. I'm hopping with curiosity.' Tiffany stopped stirring to listen.

'Dear Viola,

'This is the first opportunity I've had to write to you. Ever since I arrived here I've been frantically busy, writing invitations, organising lunches and dinners, answering letters and sorting out the Duchess's engagements. The Duchess – she has asked me to call her Marie-Louise – is kindness itself. I'm always afraid of making a mistake but she has a talent for making one feel worthwhile and valuable and I'm beginning to get a little more confident. Only think, yesterday I sat down to dinner with a cabinet minister, a belted earl and a bishop! And their wives, of course. The Duchess – Marie-Louise, I must get into the habit, she is really insistent – likes me to attend all her little parties and says how useful I am when the conversation is slow. Granny used to make me discuss an article from *The Times* every day at dinner so I dare say it has helped.

'I imagined before I met the Duchess that she would be like my grandmother but even more imperious and demanding. Instead she is surprisingly shy with people, considering the sort of life she has led, and we have found a great deal in common already. She has been good enough to confide in me about her marriage and I feel for her, very much. For your aunt, I must quickly add, she has nothing but the greatest affection. I had better say no more.

'The best thing that has happened is that when she discovered that I was an artist with the *Lady's Companion* – isn't it extraordinary that I should have become one in fact? – she has asked me to give her drawing lessons. She showed me some of her sketches and they are very promising. When I showed her the pair I brought with me of mine she was good enough to praise them quite above their deserts and had them hung in the drawing room immediately. She has drawn attention to them each time anyone has called. So the result is that on Saturday I am to instruct a small circle of the Duchess's – Marie-Louise's – friends. I am both excited and nervous at the prospect.

'I can't tell you how grateful I am, my dear, dear Viola, for your goodness in finding me this situation. I have great hopes that I may be able to be of service to the Duchess and do something to earn the more than generous allowance she has made me. I thank God each night on my knees. Already the unhappy past seems like a bad dream, though, of course, I shall always continue to pray for one who is above other men. Marie-Louise had never heard of Samuel Taylor Coleridge and we have fallen into the way of reading a few verses to each other over our bed-time cocoa. I really do think we shall get on. I must close now. Marie-Louise and I are going to walk in the Park with the Dandie Dinmonts. She particularly asked me to send you her love and to tell you – but I cannot repeat her praise of me. She is too good. I shall write again soon. I trust you are well, and still enjoying your studies. I can never express my gratitude sufficiently.

'With fondest love, Veronica.

'PS I have borne in mind what you said about Lord Percival and have kept him very much at a distance though there is no danger that he would take any notice of a dull, almost middle-aged woman like me.'

'Well!' said Tiffany waving her spoon in the air and accidentally flicking soup on to the wall. 'I call that a resounding success! Imagine the dear Baa-Lamb cultivating the Duchess's mind and presiding over her table. I'm so glad! You can congratulate yourself, Viola.'

'I really think I can. Isn't it marvellous? I couldn't be more happy. Is that burning I smell?'

'Oh, blast! I forgot to stir it.'

Tiffany scraped at the pot but it was too blackened to save. In the end she threw the soup away and I gave her some of my broad bean, cucumber and orange salad, dressed with a *sauce vinaigrette aux oeufs*. The eggs were a difficulty but she decided her first loyalty must be to the theatre and ate two platefuls before rushing away.

I went up to my room and read about Leonardo's astonishing diversity of talents, brilliance of intellect and restless inability to stick to things, thus confounding the definition of genius as 90 per cent perspiration, which is pretty sad for most of us. I was particularly pleased to discover that Leonardo bought caged birds whenever he saw them in order to set them free, thus proving himself a man after my own heart. The clock in the hall below struck eleven and I was beginning to pack up my books when I heard Daniel coming upstairs. He trod quietly as usual but I had left the door of my room ajar. His footsteps stopped outside.

'Hello,' I said opening my door wide.

For a fraction of a second Daniel's self-possession deserted him and he appeared disconcerted. 'I was going to look at something beautiful. Do you want to come with me and see it?'

There could be only one answer to this. I followed him up to the second floor and passed the door to Veronica's room. What looked like a cupboard revealed a ladder. I climbed it after Daniel.

'You are not afraid of heights?' We were outside on the roof of the house. A parapet three feet high protected the gully in which we stood, looking out over London, our backs to the steeply sloping roof. 'Look up. What I miss most living here is not being able to see the stars. The sky is too light and there are hazes from traffic and so on. But tonight – a new moon – is one of the times when you can just make them out. See them glitter.'

I looked up into the great dark vault of the sky, the colour of Mars Violet, and watched the stars shimmering – sending out messages of hope or nullity, according to one's beliefs. 'They are beautiful. I wish I knew more about them.'

'You will be familiar with the seven stars straight above you, the most significant constellation in the northern hemisphere, the Great Bear. You see they look a little like a pan with a crooked handle. Running in a line from the two stars at the round end of the pan – they are called the "pointers" – you will see the brightest star, which is the Pole Star. At about the same distance from the Pole Star as the Great Bear but on the opposite side are five bright stars in the shape of a W. That is Cassiopeia. These constellations are circumpolar. They remain visible above the horizon at all times. Going outwards you will find constellations that rise and set daily. To the left of the Great Bear is a semi-circle of stars known as the Crown. Sweep your eye from there towards the southern horizon and you have Arcturus, a star of the first magnitude.'

I listened as Daniel talked, straining my eyes until they watered to follow his explanations. Gradually I began to see more and more pricks of light as my eyes grew accustomed to the darkness.

'Now I have lectured you enough,' said Daniel, after a while. 'You will not remember it all. We can do this again if you like. In winter we shall see Orion, with the magnificent ruddy star, Betelgeuse, and Sirius, the most brilliant of the stars, immensely brighter and bigger than our sun. Strange, is it not, to realise that our sun, accompanied by its planets including earth, is rushing through space towards the constellation of Lyra at a speed of perhaps something like twenty thousand miles in an hour. It will take more than a million years to cross the great abyss.'

'I find it completely impossible to imagine.' I rubbed my neck, which was stiff from bending my head back. 'Doesn't so much beauty make you believe in the existence of God?'

'I looked up at these same stars from Auschwitz. No. There is nothing orchestrating our fate. We are solely in charge. But it makes me feel, as people have felt no doubt since they crawled from the bottom of the lake, that our worst troubles and difficulties cannot be of moment in this vastness. That is comforting. And, after all, belief in God is about comfort. We wail to God for assurance that we do not shiver naked and alone in this harsh world, that there really is no such thing as death without end.'

'But we aren't alone. What about the comfort human beings can give each other?'

'Ah, yes. We poor creatures may comfort one another. But it requires not only generosity but an enthusiasm for life and its potential good that I have no faith in. You, however, yes, I see that you have the power to console . . . with your youth and beauty and your relish for living.'

'I wish . . .' I stopped and because I could not find the

words I wanted, I took his hand and lifted it to my lips. My heart beat very fast.

'What is it you wish, *meine Liebste*?' Daniel looked down at me. His face was in shadow, with stars radiating outwards round his head. When I didn't answer he bent and kissed me on the forehead. The next moment I was in his arms, his mouth on mine. The constellations circled above our heads, for the moment forgotten.

CHAPTER 26

The train left St Pancras and dawdled through the dreary north London suburbs. Between the tracks the purple flowers of self-sown buddleias were host to countless white butterflies. I looked into back gardens filled with home-made sheds, coal bunkers, prams and cabbage patches and wondered about the lives of the people who lived there. In one garden naked children played with a garden hose, screaming and happy. In the next a woman struggled with pegs, sheets and shirts. They made squares and rectangles of blinding light beneath the sun, which burned a silver hole in the opaline sky. I thought of the famous picture called *The Snail* by Matisse, which is made of shapes of gouache-painted paper assembled into a montage of intense colours, at first sight like something a child might do. Julian had warned me against becoming a *seicento* junkie.

'There are other kinds of beauty. Matisse wanted to show colour as light – energy flowing through space. He opened up form. His desire for expression transforms a piece of painted paper into an object with its own density.'

There was much more besides, which I only partly understood and had now forgotten. There was so much to learn and I was so lamentably ignorant. Two women sitting opposite me in the carriage were having an impassioned conversation about whether Princess Margaret should have been allowed to marry Peter Townsend or not. They got very heated about it, even though they seemed to be in perfect agreement that it had all been a crying shame.

I opened my book, entitled *The School of Fontainebleau*, and read about foaming silvery-green foliage in a sinuous expanse of landscape twisting and winding to the crystalline pale mountains, which made me look longingly out of the window again. My mind reverted to the subject it had scarcely been able to leave alone for the past four days. Daniel.

When, on the roof under the stars, he had stopped kissing me he held me for a very long time against his chest. I could hear the wheezing of his breath like a cat miaowing far off. Then he said, in a calm voice, 'Go to bed. Don't argue. Go.'

I had gone, without the vaguest idea of what to expect. Lying in bed watching the headlights from a car which was trawling the square glide across my ceiling I wondered whether Daniel was going to come rushing in, in his dressing-gown or perhaps even naked, and whether I would be pleased if he did. I was almost completely certain that I would be. The thought made my heart beat very fast indeed. I loved him. I was also just a little afraid of him in a way that I had never been of Pierce, despite his roughness. I knew that Daniel would have cut off his arm rather than allow himself to harm the smallest creature. So what was I afraid of? I had found no answer as some time later I drifted into sleep, alone.

In the morning I awoke abruptly and remembered at once the events of the preceding night. Daniel had not come. I looked at the clock on my bedside table. Nearly eight. Should I go to his sitting room, where he always break-fasted, and ask him why? I lay and dithered. Tiffany's words about being confident and unreserved with one's lover came into my mind. I felt as nervous and uncertain about Daniel as though he had been a Mogul emperor and I had just accidentally shaved off his moustaches. But, then, he was not yet my lover. A scratching at my door, which I recognised as Josephine, got me out of bed. I saw that she was trying to pull out something square and white which lay on my bedroom floor. I let Josephine in and picked it up. It was a letter.

My dearest girl,

You have penetrated my secret. How absurd of me to think that I could conceal it. Lord, what fools these mortals be! I have wanted for a long time, perhaps – yes, to say the truth – from the very beginning, to make you my own. When you so sweetly and generously kissed me last night I allowed myself for a moment to pretend that your desire was the same. But I am not able to deceive myself. Whatever destruction was wrought by those experiences in my youth they have at least the merit of making me fearful of anything dishonest.

You do not love me as I love you, nor is it fitting that you should. I am old enough to be your father and, perhaps more important, I am aged – worn-out would be a truer word – beyond my years. Certain attitudes of the mind I never can recapture – faith, sanguinity, merriment – these and their attendant feelings I have lost. My moods are frequently black and it would be a crime to draw a beautiful young soul into proximity with these regions of darkness. You will say – see how well I know you – that love is sharing these despairs and that I mistake the strength of your feeling. [He was right. It was exactly what I thought as I read those words.]

What you feel for me is a kind of love admixed with pity, which from you I shall not scorn, and a wish to serve and to protect. All these things are, of course, good. But they are not the essential part of what should be between a man and a woman if they are to live together as man and wife. And I have too old-fashioned, too serious a nature to live with a woman on other terms. There should be, must be if there will be lasting happiness, also a recognition of one's own self in the other person. This is the basis of friendship, so strong is human self-interest. It is an unconscious process this seeking of the self in others, it will not be gainsaid. I see in you my unfettered youth, my appetite for knowledge.

But you, what could you see in me? What can there be in me that you recognise? I should say, nothing. Race and age need not be a barrier but combined with the vastly different experiences of our lives they would become so. We have tastes in common and there is much that we could teach each other. But your heart would not leap up at the sight of me. You would feel anxious, tender, dutiful and perhaps, I dare to suggest, a little of that admiration which one so young might feel for one so old who has not entirely driven himself to rack and ruin by profligate ways. Of course many marriages have been based quite on these grounds and no doubt some have proceeded without great hurt to the participants.

But for you I want much better than this. I want you to be able to give your heart and mind in unconstrained rejoicing to a fit companion for, if you are lucky, the rest of your long life. You must not waste the sweet years of your youth on a husk. You will know him when he comes and then you will be thankful for what I say now.

Of our sexual union I have not spoken specifically. I am quite as other men – selfish, weak, desirous. To me you are very beautiful. But the difficulty I have to write about it to you confirms my strong sense that it would be a deep disgrace to take advantage of your innocence. Enough. I am going away the moment I have delivered this letter.

As soon as I read this I ran downstairs with the letter in my hand. Daniel's rooms were empty. There were signs of a hasty departure, drawers half open with articles of clothing hanging out, papers screwed up and lying on the floor near the wastepaper basket. I sat on his unmade bed and finished the letter.

I am afraid that a very little persuasion from you – and I know you would feel in honour bound to try – would undo these resolves which I know to be right. Dear heart, believe me when I say that it is a measure of my love for you that I do this. [I felt a hard lump form in my throat when I read this. I did believe him.] Send a line to the above address when you can write to assure me that you concur with my convictions on this matter. Only then shall I return. I give you up because the sacrifice of your happiness is too great a price, even if it were possible that the old wrongs could be repaired. I shall always love you for attempting to make it. Daniel.

I folded up the letter with shaking hands. Outside a blackbird flew into the garden well and began to sing lustily, as though pleased with the echo. Mrs Shilling's voice calling Josephine trumpeted up from the basement. I would write to Daniel at once, telling him to come back. Here was yet another case of someone treating me like a child when I was quite able to look after myself. Taking advantage of my innocence! The notion was Victorian, ridiculous. I would acknowledge the strength of his argument but explain that . . . what?

The clothes that hung in his open wardrobe blurred and a constriction in my chest and a pricking in my nose ignored all my reasoning. I wept for Daniel's blighted life, I wept selfishly for the loss of an opportunity to make something better than it had been. I lay on Daniel's bed and cried into his pillow. It smelt deliciously of verbena. I tried to imagine his thoughts as he had lain there only a few hours before. I did love him tenderly, fiercely. I was quite certain of that.

Then I cried some more because I recognised, though I did not want to, that he might possibly be right. There had been something that frightened me when I imagined living with Daniel as his lover. I had been afraid of the intensity of his feelings – about the past, about the experience of being alive, about me. I was violently attracted to the beauty of his person and of the things by which he had surrounded himself, even the beauty of his suffering and expiation, but it was a dark, melancholy beauty. I had felt myself akin to Proserpina, descending to the infernal regions to be the wife of Pluto.

When, later, I went down to the kitchen, Mrs Shilling was cutting up pieces of fruit for Josephine and Tiffany was stirring something beige and granular in a saucepan. They were both too tactful to remark on my red eyes.

'Here's a turn-up for the books,' said Mrs Shilling. 'Gone away and never said when he'll be back. I've never known anythink like it, not in twenty years. Just a note on the

357

kitchen table to say will I see to Josephine. Which I will, won't I, my precious?' she added, offering the monkey a grape, which she took in her elegant hands, piercing the skin with her sharp teeth and sucking it noisily. Mrs Shilling glanced at me. 'I hope he hasn't had a quarrel with anyone. He does go off the deep end something shocking.'

I couldn't think of anything to say that might explain his absence so I kept quiet. Tiffany poured her breakfast into a dish. It had turned a nasty shade of khaki and resembled wet cement.

'That's a peculiar sort of mush, if I might say so,' said Mrs Shilling. 'Them lumps look as unappetising as anything I've seen since Ernie's ma used to make suet dumplings. Ernie and me lived with his ma when we was first married. She was the worst cook it's been my misfortune to meet and a temper like a prowoked wasp. Ernie and his ma never got on. She were too busy running her sweetshop to have time for him so his auntie Glo, what was head cook where I was kitchenmaid, more or less brought him up. Sherbet lemons and acid drops was right for Ernie's ma. She made you shudder like a cart over cobbles with her sour cooking and sharp tongue and she was that offish you'd have thought she was a duchess. Ooh! She were hopping mad when Ernie told her I was in the family way.'

This was just the sort of conversation to distract me from my current state of misery. It being Saturday I was at liberty to stay in the kitchen and question Mrs Shilling about her early life which we both enjoyed.

'What was it like being a kitchenmaid? Did you have to scour pots with sand?'

'Bless you, duck, I'm not as old as that. We had wire wool and soap in the thirties. And a nice gas cooker. Auntie Glo wouldn't put up with nothink but the best. Put on Black Sal,' this was what Mrs Shilling called the kettle, 'and I'll tell you about the time Ernie and his ma had such a row that he chucked a tray of coconut ice at her, walked out and got a job as a hot potato. That's a waiter to you. Chuck them slops down the sink, pet,' this to Tiffany, 'and have some of my Wictoria sponge made this morning afore I come.'

'It's bran,' said Tiffany, prodding a lump with her spoon. 'Ever since the miscarriage I've resembled nothing so much as an exhausted halibut.' It was true that the abrupt change in hormones had not only made her very weepy but also her lovely hair was falling out in handfuls and her complexion was grey. 'So that I don't get constipated. Apparently a good bowel habit, at least twice a day, is essential for a clear skin.' Tiffany did not believe in prudishness about bodily functions.

'Thank you, Miss Tiffany, but I were enjoying my piece of cake.' Mrs Shilling, on the other hand, was shy of discussing anything digestive though she was quite open about sex. 'Come on, you have a bit and stop worritting your insides. A little of what you fancy does you good.' She gave a cackle at the innuendo.

'A little bit of what I fancied – and it was a *very* little bit – did me no good at all. Which reminds me, guess who came oiling into my dressing room last night, oozing seduction? Monty. He'd heard a rumour that the reason I'd been away for a week was because I was having an abortion. I said certainly not. Well, it wasn't a lie, anyway. He actually looked quite disappointed. He walked up and down for a bit in a stormy sort of way and I just let him. I'd got to a difficult bit in the quilt I was making so I concentrated on that. After a bit he said that he didn't wonder I was bitter, he'd behaved very badly and he wanted to make it up to me. What do you think? He asked me to marry him!'

Tiffany took a huge bite out of her slice of Mrs Shilling's excellent sponge cake and watched our faces, enjoying the sensation she had caused.

'The devil a bit!' This was Mrs Shilling's favourite expression when she was really surprised.

'But what about Bebe Ballantine?' I asked. 'I thought the wedding was to be next month.'

'It seems Bebe's left him for a pop star called Simon Spangles. Shoulder-length hair and a heroin habit. But the owner of a pink Rolls Royce and similar tasteful accoutrements. Monty was extremely resentful. I made sympathetic noises, not very sincerely I'm afraid. Then he took my hand

and got sentimental and talked about how much he had always loved me and how Bebe was a harlot and very stupid to boot.'

'So what did you say?'

'I said that I had no intention of marrying someone who was on the clearest possible evidence disloyal, faithless and conceited. I said I knew quite well that I would be chucking my happiness away with both hands if I married him and that I wanted to be independent and free of men altogether. You know, it wasn't until I found myself saying it to Monty that I realised that that was what I *did* want. Autonomy. Self-sufficiency. Freedom from emotional trammels.'

'Bravo! Tiffany, you're wonderful!' I got up and kissed her cheek. 'I'm incredibly impressed. Of course, you're quite right. He's a dead loss. But I shouldn't have been as strong in your place, I'm afraid.'

'That's because you're still optimistic about men. I've had more affairs than you and I can tell you there have been more debits than credits. Perhaps it's my fault. Perhaps I'm too unattractive, too boring, too romantic, too broke – I don't know. But I'm fed up with crying over some rat who can't be bothered to behave decently. Of course, the minute I didn't want him Monty grew as keen as a dog after aniseed. To think that once my entire happiness depended on a few hasty moments spent with Monty with his trousers down. I was a fool.'

Mrs Shilling was of the opinion that, at Tiffany's age, a husband with an income was not to be sneezed at. 'You won't find one that doesn't want to wander. Once you've got him, though, you can knock some sense into him. Men want telling. They don't know what's best for 'em until you hammer it into their silly heads.'

But Tiffany was adamant that she had done with men and sex for good. I could not put Daniel entirely out of my mind during this conversation but I was delighted to be distracted, however temporarily.

I had gone upstairs an hour later and found on the hall table three letters postmarked Little Whiddon, Notts. I read Jeremy's first.

Darling Viola,

Sorry about not writing. Have been incredibly busy of late. HAVE FOUND THE PLAY!!! It's called *The Lighthouse Keeper's Daughter* by Jacintha Plumbe – a little known but startlingly talented Victorian playwright. It's perfect for our sea scenery and we can use nearly all our sound effects as it has a storm in the third act which is when Bess, the lighthouse keeper's daughter saves the crew from drowning by her gallantry, wins her father's consent at last to her marriage with the son of his most hated enemy, only to see him perish beneath the waves at the last. Terribly affecting! Should have the audience crying like waterspouts. Lalla is to play Bess. She grumbles about it all the time but she looks good in the part if only she wouldn't drawl out the lines like an exhausted debutante after too many cocktail parties. You'll never guess who is to play Cedric, Lord Cobblestone's son and the hero of our tale. None other than Zed, the bestower of black eyes! I happened to meet him ten days ago in the Dog and Bone. He raised his fist when he saw me but just before he laid me out again I confessed that I'd accused him falsely over the business of the flooding of the park and offered a pint of beer as an apology. We got talking – and both got very drunk in fact. He's the strangest bloke I ever met, hardly any schooling, as one might expect, but by no means unintelligent. In fact in some ways he's a lot sharper than I am. He wants to get on in the world and give up being a charcoal-burner but he's got bigger ideas than settling for one of those permanent campsites the council build, which he calls monkey cages. He thinks he's the by-blow of some Hungarian prince though looking at his mother – nose like a freshly dug truffle and a ginger beard which would make a coconut envious – I somehow doubt it. Anyway he makes up all these stories about what he's going to do out in the world, wowing Larry Olivier with his acting ability and rising to the House of Lords on the strength of revolutionising the entertainment industry single-handed and much more besides. The long and short of it is that he wants to act so I asked him to come and read some lines for me. Do you know, the man's got magnetism? You can't take your eyes off him when he's on the stage. And he can mimic too. He spoke

Cedric's words as though he'd been to Eton. When I asked him how he could do that he said he just copied me. So I engaged him for Cedric on the spot. Lalla kicked up a bit of a stink. I hadn't realised what a snob she is. But I've insisted. She hardly speaks to him but luckily Zed seems to think it's funny. Now the trouble is I'm desperately short of stagehands and I need someone to play Cedric's fiancée. She dies in the first act so you needn't be afraid of too many lines to learn. Then you could help me a lot with the storm scene. You'd like that. Do say you'll come at once, my angel. I'm counting on you. Remember you PROMISED. Wire me which train to meet. Your devoted Jeremy.

Nicky's letter was much shorter.

Dear Viola

Thanks very much for the chocolate. Now it's the holidays I am eating it myself instead of having to give it to Bugger Boreham. Does your shop have any nut chocolate as this is my favourite? I hope this doesn't sound greedy but my father doesn't give me any pocket money and I'm saving the 50ps Uncle Francis gives me for a book about archaeology. But even with the pound Hamish gave me before he went to Japan I've only got half. My dig is going brilliantly. I've found a bit of leather I'm practically certain is a Roman sandal. And a Roman cloak pin. I think, anyway. No one here is the least bit interested. Jeremy only thinks about his play and Lalla lies on sofas looking miserable. Mummy isn't very well. I wish you'd come and stay. It was very much better when you and Giles were here. Love Nicky. PS When I read this letter again the bit about the nut chocolate did sound greedy so better forget it.

I opened Lalla's letter.

Dearest Viola

Life here is too grim to be endured. *Still* no word from Hamish. There must be a black cloud over Japan. I suppose it's to be expected. It's entirely my own fault. I did think at least he'd write if only to tell me to push off. Perhaps he's too angry and upset to put pen to paper. Or doesn't care any more. Anyway, I know that I've been an ass and that I shan't look upon his like again. Oh, shit! Anyway.

Mummy is really in a worrying state, all jitters. I think she'd be better off in hospital or something. I'm sure it's this house that gets her down. I *am* trying to be a better daughter but old habits die hard, as they say. But the other day we went for a walk together and she told me all about migrating swifts and I managed to be quite interested. Then she insisted on holding my hand. Remembering what you'd said I didn't pull away. I see what you mean about longing for love. If any good can be said of Francis it's that he does genuinely care about Mummy. Apparently some men do like their sisters better than other women. The Prince Regent for example. Hamish must have told me that in the good old days before I spoiled everything. I'm amazed to remember how happy I was when I was with him. If only I could have it all to do again. I've been a bloody fool. However.

I suppose you've heard from Jeremy about this tiresome play? I have to learn endless lines and make a complete ass of myself . . . [The sentence was unfinished. Scrawled after this in different-coloured ink and much less tidy writing were these words] Sorry, forgot to finish this yesterday. Have just had a telegram from Hamish. My letter was redirected to Rome. The idiots! Anyway it must have hung about there for ages before being returned to Japan. He's coming to Inskip! His plane lands on Monday and I'm to meet the four o'clock train from London! Nothing about the abortion but I suppose a telegram is hardly the place. I'm terrified. Viola, if you ever cared twopence about me come at once. I can't face him on my own. Say you will. I think I'm going mad. Love Lalla.

As I seemed to be so flatteringly in universal demand it did not take me long to decide to go.

CHAPTER 27

Jeremy was waiting for me on the platform at Nottingham station. His face was brown and his hair was bleached to ivory by the sun. He held wide his arms and had I not been burdened by a suitcase, magazine and a carrier-bag I would have flung myself into them. As it was we could manage nothing more dramatic than a one-sided embrace and a hearty kiss.

'Darling, how I've missed you! I'd quite forgotten what a delicious girl you are and how madly I love you.'

I, too, had experienced a leap of the heart at the sight of him – not the kind of somersault that has to do with passion but more the pleasure of seeing someone of whom I was very fond. Jeremy took my luggage and led me to the car park. Nip and Nudge, who were leaning out of the Land Rover window, began to howl as soon as they saw me. I submitted to being licked and panted over. Jeremy drove at high speed, ignoring things like pedestrian crossings and traffic lights and in no time we were in the country, rushing through lanes and woods on the way to Inskip.

'I can't wait to show you the theatre. We've got nearly all the seascape scenery up. It looks amazingly convincing from the back of the auditorium.'

'I'm dying to see it. Who's we?'

'Zed and his brother Wat. Wat's playing the part of the bo'sun of HMS *Unity*. He's not handsome like Zed or very bright but he's good with his hands. He's making some extra flats and a backdrop for the first scene – the one you're in – where Cedric proposes to you and there's a touching bit when Lord Cobblestone gives you his blessing as his future daughter-in-law. Cedric then confesses in a soliloquy to the audience that he is really in love with Bess, the lighthouse keeper's daughter, whom he saw through the window of an inn, dancing to the tune of a fiddle – Nicky's going to play his Grade Three piece in the wings for atmosphere while he's talking, rather a subtle touch, I thought – but has discovered that she has been betrothed from the cradle to Jonathan Stubbs. He's the son of a smuggler. So Cedric decides he'd better please his father if he can't please himself and marry you – your name's Clorinda, by the way and you're the most frightful wet week, always in a swoon about everything.'

'Who's going to be lucky enough to view this affecting spectacle?'

'There's a slight problem there.' Jeremy's exuberance was temporarily depressed. 'I've sent out invitations to everybody I know in the area, more than a hundred in fact, and so far I've had ten replies, all from people who are my father's tenants and obviously don't want to risk offending him. You'd think that people would be desperate to slake their thirst in this cultural desert, wouldn't you?'

'I'd expect them to be curious anyway. Perhaps you ought to offer them an added inducement. A glass of wine in the interval or something like that. With fund-raising for SCAB I've found that people are terribly lazy about anything the least bit intellectual but they'll travel half-way round the world for a free peanut.'

'People's minds ought to be loftier.' Jeremy's tone was offended. 'But I dare say you're right.'

'Even better, why don't you give a party afterwards? Everyone would want to come to that. We could buy the wine out of the ticket money and I could help with the food. I've been doing quite a bit of cooking since I was last here. It would be a challenge.'

'Ye-es.' Jeremy was thoughtful. Our progress down a narrow lane was impeded by an old man who was hobbling along crouched over two sticks. Jeremy gave a cheery blip on the horn and the old man achieved for a moment the upright posture of his youth as he skipped high into the air with fright. 'Hello, Mr Tringle. How's the rheumatism? Mrs T pretty chipper? Coming to our play, I hope,' shouted Jeremy through the open window. Mr Tringle's oaths were drowned by the racket made by Nip and Nudge, who were trying to climb out of the window to savage Mr Tringle's elderly limping sheep-dog. 'Got to play the feudal baron,'

Jeremy said to me, as we gathered speed. 'It's a great bore but all the people round here are devoted to the family. We're the hub of their universe.' I looked back to see Mr Tringle waving his stick in rage with one hand while he clutched his chest with the other. 'A party. Hm. I think you've got something there. We could open up the ball-room.'

'We could have dancing!' I was getting excited. 'When's it to be?'

'I've asked people for Saturday.'

'Six days! We'll have to ring people up and tell them there's to be a party, organise the food, get in the booze and clean up the ballroom. It's not a great deal of time.'

'We'll have the scenery finished by then but there are the costumes. We need at least five more rehearsals. But the programmes are done. They came yesterday. Can you sew?'

'I once completed a traycloth. It took three terms, though.'

'Lalla's just as bad. I've got the Stinker crouched over the sewing-machine treadling away for dear life, running up a dress for Bess. The sailors can wear jerseys and gum boots but the Cobblestones, *père et fils*, need frock coats.'

'How did you get Miss Tinker to co-operate?'

'I promised her my father's army kit. I once found her in his dressing room, trying it on. He was a lieutenant-colonel in the war. He'll never notice it's gone.' I couldn't help laughing, though I felt sorry for poor Miss Tinker. 'I'd forgotten how much I enjoy hearing you laugh,' said Jeremy. 'It *is* fun to be together. All the other girls I know are either quarrelsome or want me to make love to them all the time. I suppose we shouldn't think again about getting married?'

'No. Really it wouldn't work. We aren't in love, whatever that is. Anyway I've decided that I want to be independent. I'm going to eschew men for several years at least.'

'Darling, that sounds terribly sad. For the men anyway. How long has this determination been twitching your synapses?'

'Since yesterday actually. My friend Tiffany, whom you

haven't met, announced her intention to be autonomous and I was greatly struck by the sense of this. Much too much time is spent by women fretting about men – or the lack of decent ones – instead of getting on with the job in hand.'

'And what are your jobs in hand?'

'Tiffany's going to set up a stall in the Portobello Road, selling her needlework, and I'm going to study seriously.'

When I explained about going to university Jeremy was inclined to mock but he desisted when he saw that I was in earnest. 'Seems a waste of a pretty girl to me but, then, you know I'm not made for stern endeavour.'

At that moment we turned into the park. From the gatehouse window I saw the baleful eye of Bowser staring out. A gibbet-like construction hung with the pelts of dead animals stood by his back door. 'I do think that that man is about the most unsympathetic character I ever met.'

'He was devoted to my grandmother. She taught him to read and write. My grandmother adored the underprivileged. She was a brute with us children when we came to stay, though. Obviously we weren't conspicuously downtrodden despite everything our father did to make our childhood hideous.'

'Like Mrs Jellyby in *Bleak House*.'

'Mm. Could be.' Jeremy was vague. 'Ah, here's Nicky. Shut up, you dogs!'

Nicky was running down the drive. When he saw us he grinned hugely, his large teeth flashing white in the sun. 'I got fed up with waiting at the house,' he panted. 'Hello, Viola. Shove up and then I can get in the front with you. I generally dig all day but I thought I'd take the afternoon off. I've arranged all my finds in my bedroom. Since I wrote last I've dug up the jaw-bone of a gigantic creature. I think it might be prehistoric. Perhaps a protoceratops. Or an ichthyosaur.'

'It's a horse, you clot.' Jeremy was squashing in an impersonal, big-brotherly way. 'One of Grandfather's hunters. I remember as a kid when they buried one up at the mausoleum. It took four men a day to dig a hole deep enough and lug the poor thing up the hill on a trailer. Grandfather whacked me because I cried.'

'Are all families as horrible as ours?' asked Nicky.

'Some are worse, I expect.'

Nicky looked depressed.

'I think from the sound of those triumphant yips Nip's found your nut chocolate,' I said.

I had brought not only chocolate but several bags of the exciting and colourful sweets from the jars in Mr Dring's window. Some had been there so long, alternately baking and freezing according to the seasons that Mr Dring had to take a screwdriver to the jar. He said anxiously, several times, that they might not be at their best and really he'd come to think of them as decoration since people these days preferred sweets ready-wrapped and didn't want the bother of having things weighed out in quarters, but I was convinced that there was more magic in a small paper bag of giant colour-changing gob-stoppers than in a tube of fruit pastilles.

It must be marvellous to be able to lavish expensive presents on one's friends but there is a peculiar pleasure, which has nothing to do with meanness, in being inventive with very little money. Mr Dring also had at the back of the shop an array of interestingly-shaped liqueur bottles of brilliant hue – things like yellow Chartreuse, Parfait D'Amour which is a zinging shade of violet, emerald crème de menthe and grenadine which I like to describe as Pozzuoli red. I settled for the improbable blue of Curaçao.

By the time Nicky had crawled into the back and rescued my bag of presents we had reached the Pekinese fountain. The valley cradled the house like sediment in a giant green cup and the onion domes gleamed like precious stones set in a burnished strip of sky. Waldemar stood by the open front door and dropped his huge jaw to give a sombre bark of greeting. Lalla came running down the steps. 'I'm so glad to see you. You're an *angel* to come. I'd almost decided to run away from home.'

'I'm thrilled to be back. I'd forgotten how lovely the house is.' I looked fondly at the marching elephants above the front door. 'And it's wonderful to see you all again. Giles particularly sends his love.'

This was perhaps an exaggeration. When I had telephoned him the day before to ask if I might desert my post for a week and go to Inskip he had said that if I could find someone to answer the telephone it would probably be all right. It being the end of July, things were slack anyway and he had been thinking of taking a few days off himself. Pierce had telephoned from America to say that he was on the point of returning home and was looking forward to being once more in the upright position, having spent two weeks lying horizontal, either on a sun-lounger by a pool or in bed on top of Mrs Vandermayling, which was becoming tedious.

I rang Stella Partington, my old flatmate, and offered her my week's wage to be receptionist for SCAB. Stella had a low boredom threshold, which prevented her from entering permanent employment, and she kept body and soul united by driving aged aunts to Biarritz, minding houses here and walking dogs there. As luck would have it she was free and delighted by the idea of a week's paid sunbathing on our balcony. When I telephoned Giles again to tell him what I had arranged he said to give his best wishes to everyone at Inskip and not to allow my brain to be turned by the prevailing madness of its inhabitants.

As I stepped into the hall I inhaled the familiar cocktail of dust and Glosso. But there was a missing ingredient. The buckets had gone, as had the black streaks and odour of damp. Now I could appreciate the full glory of the gilded scenes of turreted temples and flowing rivers on the crimson walls. The many-armed goddess smiled smugly from her niche, her cheeks free from rivulets of moisture and the grey-faced blackamoors held their golden palms aloft with what seemed to my imagination a sprightlier posture. Even the stuffed peacock had acquired in the lowering afternoon sun an iridescence of breast and tail, what was left of it.

'It *is* good to be back! Darling Fluffy!' I picked up the cat, who had strolled coolly up to me, winking with gooseberry-green eyes. 'I've got something for you. I brought the food I was going to eat this weekend – chicken for savoury *millefeuilles* and pork for a raised hot-water crust. There isn't a fridge at home so I didn't like to leave it. I'm trying to master pastry.' I thought sadly of Daniel who, before our starlit kiss, had been introducing me, via strict rules of cold hands, marble slabs and best quality butter, to the secrets of *pâte brisée*, *pâte frolle* and *pâte moulée*. The smallest speck of flour on the palms of my hands during the rubbing in had incurred a tremendous ticking off. We had got cross with each other over my failure to flour the rolling pin often enough. These hours of teasing and quarrelling and concentrated effort, which I had so enjoyed and from which I had learned so much, could never happen again.

'For heaven's sake, don't give it to the cat,' exclaimed Lalla. 'The new cook is appalling. Everything's either curried or devilled. I think it's because the ingredients are putrid. Chicken *millefeuilles* – ecstasy!'

'Come and see my exhibits,' urged Nicky.

'First come and look at the scenery and give me some ideas about the furniture for the first scene.' Jeremy put his arm through mine.

'Let's go on the terrace and have tea. I'm dying to talk to you,' pleaded Lalla.

I went first to view the exhibits. I must admit, to my shame, I generally find that looking into glass cases in museums to inspect virtually identical slivers of brown pottery, exhaustively labelled in fading typescript, is one of the dullest things I know. What makes it worse is that there is often a strong element of guesswork as to the original shape and colour of the pot or even if it *is* a pot and not an instrument for threshing corn, stripping hides or worshipping the gods. But Nicky's finds were interesting because one could pick them up and turn them over and they were all very different. I liked best the bits of painted china. There was at least half a blue-and-white plate, which Nicky was patiently assembling piece by piece, dropped perhaps by a Victorian Inskip picnicking with friends by the mausoleum. I imagined them looking down from the top of the hill to the house with its voguish wing just completed and gleaming with new bricks and fresh paint. When I had spent enough time discussing the bones, nails and shards to satisfy the budding archaeologist I went to find Jeremy. Nicky said he would come along later and give a hand with the painting but first he was going to watch the next episode of *The Man from U.N.C.L.E.* in the Hoggins caravan. 'They've got the biggest television you've ever seen and Mr Hoggins said I could come and watch it any time I liked. Now that Zed's always coming up to the house, the charcoal-burners are very nice to us. I quite like Mrs Hoggins. She makes mountains of chips all day long and we're allowed tomato ketchup with them. I don't like Zed, though.'

'Do those children still bother your mother? Looking in at the windows and things?'

'I don't know. Mummy's stopped coming down for dinner. Daddy thought it was better if she didn't.'

'Will you ask her if she'd like me to visit her?'

'I don't see her much. She stays in her room with the Stinker or goes for walks with Lalla.' Nicky had the abstracted look on his face which people have when they don't want to talk about something. 'I'd better go or I'll miss the beginning. I like Ilya Kuryakin best. I thought I might grow my hair the same. My ears wouldn't show so much. But my father likes me to be practically scalped at the barber's. Do you think you could speak to him about it?'

I promised to try but didn't hold out any hope. I found Jeremy in the theatre waving a paintbrush heavily impregnated with magenta paint.

'This is Wat.' He gestured in the direction of a broad back.

'Oi! This is me second best shirt! You've bin and gone and flipped some fucking paint on it.'

Wat was short and muscular with a broken nose, black hair oiled to a crest like a breaking wave and crenellated teeth, no doubt from fighting outside the pub. He appeared to have a cold for he wiped his nose frequently on the back of his hand.

'Hello,' I said, extending my own with secret reluctance as Jeremy introduced me. When I got close to I saw that the lobes of his ears were each tattooed with a swastika.

'Wotcha, Vi. Come to 'elp? That's good 'cuz I'm off now. My back's fucking breaking with painting this sodding stove. 'Ere you are.' He thrust a sticky paintbrush into my outstretched hand. 'Wendy don't like it if I'm late. She expects a good charvering in the back of the Capri before we nips down to the Dog and Bone.' He winked at me. 'Ta-ta, Jem, me old mate. See you tomorrah.'

'This is Zed. Viola Otway.'

'How do you do, Miss Otway? I trust your journey was agreeable.'

Zed had strolled out from the wings, the picture of an English gentleman at leisure in the country. He wore an old tweed coat out at the elbows, which I recognised as Jeremy's, and a pair of cavalry twills. He must have been terribly hot. Only when he turned his head slightly did I see the anachronous pony-tail neatly tied with black ribbon like a Georgian beau. It must be admitted that he was very striking in a rather frightening way. His small dark eyes were a little too close together and there was in them a calculating expression which seemed at odds with anything like good nature. His voice was refined to the point of silly ass-ishness.

'Thank you. It was all right.' I transferred the paintbrush and held out my hand. He took my fingers gracefully and dropped a kiss lightly on my knuckles.

'It's frightfully good of you to come and help us with our little show.'

'I shall love it.'

Zed's face broke into a smirk. 'Not bad eh?' he said in his normal voice. 'Wha'd'ya think? Sound like a lord, do I?'

'Identical, I should say.'

'Heydentical, hey should say,' repeated Zed, in an exaggerated imitation of my accent, which was infuriating.

'Do you want me to paint something?' I turned to Jeremy. 'Otherwise I'll go and have tea with Lalla. She's waiting for me.'

'Just come and look at the wave machine now we've got it painted up.'

It consisted of four strips of wood, like planks on their side, running the width of the stage. They were each attached at one end to a ratchet with a handle. The tops of the planks were cut into crests and troughs, and when you turned the handles as Jeremy showed me, the planks moved up and down. When all four were properly synchronised the effect from the auditorium was of a moving sea, tranquil or turbulent depending on the speed of turning. It required two people to work it. Now it was painted impressionistically with slashes of blue and emerald and white.

'It looks terrific. Do let me take one end in the storm scene. It would be such fun.'

'I was hoping you would. Everyone else is on stage during the storm or about to come on and we don't want people so out of puff that they can't speak their lines. Now, look at this lighthouse that Wat's made. Isn't it convincing?'

It was. Only the bottom part could be seen, painted in broad red and white horizontal stripes with a small diamond-paned lattice window, which stood open.

'From here Bess will look out and pray to the heavens to save her beloved. We copied it from a picture in a *Rupert Bear* annual. None of us could think what the bottom of a lighthouse looked like in detail.'

When I had eulogised sufficiently over all the arrangements, approved the choice of magenta for the walls of the Cobblestones' parlour and suggested the shell flowers under the glass dome from my bedroom as likely to lend a suitable touch of Victoriana, I said I would go and see Lalla.

'I'll stay on a bit.' Jeremy picked up a bit of wood. 'I've got to design HMS *Unity*. Really it will be a small model but its shadow – vastly magnified – will be projected against the backcloth. You'll see it gradually up-end and sink beneath the waves. Clever, eh?'

'Amazing! Honestly, Jeremy, I'm really impressed!'

'She's rally imprayersed,' said Zed. 'I'd like to imprayers you, Viola. What'd it take to imprayers such a chumming young leddy, I wonder?' Slowly he opened his mouth and showed me the tip of his tongue, which he wriggled suggestively.

'Give me a hand, Zed, would you?' asked Jeremy, who was standing with his back to us, fiddling with a lightbulb and a length of flex. 'You're wasting your time trying to chat up Viola. She's given up ordinary men. Unless you're a genius like Michelangelo you haven't a chance.'

'I'll like to see the wop that could organ-grind better'n me.'

Obviously for Zed there was only one arena of excellence.

CHAPTER 28

'I don't like him at all,' I said to Lalla five minutes later, when we were seated in ancient garden chairs on the terrace, looking across the park to the bridge. The poor leprous statues stood in their elaborate poses, animated by touches of sunlight. I imagined them playing that party game – the one where you have to stand absolutely still when the music stops and the first to move is out. I was tempted to hum something so that they would unfreeze and cavort about the little hedged squares. The thick grey trunks of the rosebushes, so unpromising in spring, had shot out an abundance of leaves and copper-coloured flowers and the air was exquisitely scented.

'Nor do I.' Lalla paused while pouring the tea and shuddered. 'He gives me the horrors. I can see why I was sexually attracted to him – partly it's the unknown quantity, isn't it? And I must say he was incredibly inventive and completely inexhaustible – but he's so mean. He doesn't care about anything, really, except himself. I prefer Wat any day. At least he's reasonably straightforward.'

'Then you aren't . . .' I hesitated, thinking how best to express it.

'Sleeping with Zed any more? No. He threatened to tell

the whole village what we'd been doing if I stopped but I decided to call his bluff.'

'That was brave!'

'Not really. It'll just make him sound rather stupid – boasting about his sexual conquests. Half of them won't believe him. Anyway, I don't care what they think. They've probably made up far worse things about me already. You know what villages are.'

'I don't, actually. It's rather disappointing. One imagines flower-decked cottages round the green with apple-cheeked girls and strong, silent men, all helping each other in times of sickness, sharing turnips in a hard winter, *Lark Rise to Candleford*, that kind of thing.'

'The reality is that they're hotbeds of malice, envy and small-mindedness. I really must get away from here before I become an embittered old spinster, only interested in triumphing over my neighbours. But what shall I do? I never passed that stupid shorthand exam. I shall have to look for another rich man.'

'You're meeting Hamish's train tomorrow?'

'I was hoping you'd come with me. In fact, if you don't come, I shan't go.'

'Oh – but I'd be so terribly in the way! Hamish would be furious!'

'I suppose I can go to the station with a friend if I choose? In the circumstances it seems a mere detail.'

'But why, Lalla? I don't understand.'

'I can't face a scene, that's all. Hamish will be angry and hurt and all that. I don't blame him. But I can't bear people spilling emotions about the place and expecting me to play my part. If you don't come with me then I shan't go.'

Lalla lit a cigarette and stared coldly down towards a family of ducks who were walking in a line towards the lake. Even though we were some distance away I could hear the mother duck talking all the time to the younger ones following. If only humans had these nurturing instincts how much happier everyone would be, I reflected, thinking of Lady Inskip and indeed almost all the mothers I knew, including my own. The only mother I could think of who seemed to have taken the job of rearing offspring properly in hand was Mab. I wondered if Giles was sufficiently appreciative.

'All right, then. I'll come. Anything rather than poor Hamish coming all that way to find nobody at the station.'

Lalla gave me a flash of her green eyes. 'That, I suppose, is a small thing compared with finding out that your betrothed has aborted another man's child. You've an oddly sentimental view of things, I think.'

I did not answer, as I might have done, that to me Lalla's perspective was heartbreakingly cynical.

After tea I went to see Lady Inskip. I had never been to her room before. It was large and shadowy and smelt of mothballs and scent. The curtains were drawn almost all the way across the windows but a pencil of sunlight pointed to the bed on which my hostess lay, fully dressed but for her shoes. Her bare feet were rigid, pointing straight up to the ceiling as though even in sleep she was unable to relax. Her head lolled sideways towards the door. She must have heard my footsteps for she opened her eyes.

'Is it Viola? Come here, my dear.' She held out her hand and I took it, sitting next to her on the bed. She looked, in the half-darkness, much younger and there was a prettiness in the roundness of the eyes and the full lips. 'Lalla said you were coming and I was so pleased. We always had such lovely talks, didn't we?'

'I'm sorry you aren't well enough to come downstairs.'

Lady Inskip rolled her eyes as though to deprecate the fuss. 'James thinks it best for me to be quiet. Francis comes to see me every evening and we play Scrabble. I beat him yesterday. Men hate that, don't they?' She giggled. 'I could tell he was cross. But he's a good brother to me. I feel much better when I'm with him. He still loves me.' Her eyes filled with tears, which sparkled in the beam of sunlight. 'I know the children don't love me any more. When Lalla was little she used to tiptoe into my room very early in the morning and creep into my bed like a mouse so as not to wake me. I called her Appley-Dapply. She loved my stories about all the little animals then. Later she got impatient. I know I'm a nuisance to everyone.'

I stroked her hand. 'I'm sure the children do still love you. Probably they don't know how much. I haven't much experience of families myself but, from what I've seen, people in them don't show each other their strongest feelings. I think it's generally taken for granted. I know Jeremy loves you. But men don't usually go on about how much they love their mothers. It would be . . . odd.'

'Odd. I see. That's what I can't tell about any more. When I think I'm behaving in an ordinary way, other people react as though I've said something peculiar. They look at each other, change the subject, tell me to go and lie down. I know I'm getting something wrong but I don't know what it is.'

'People often think I'm quite *absurd*. And they tell me so.'

Lady Inskip held my hand tighter. 'Do they? Do they really? But, you see, they don't tell *me* – that's the difference. It frightens me.'

'It's because you mind so much, I think. People sense that very quickly.'

'I'm too emotional, you mean. I know that's true. But I get desperate.' Lady Inskip pressed her free hand to her forehead. 'I feel excluded from the real world. Even the doctors talk to me as though I'm a troublesome child. They won't answer my questions. They only smile and say I need to rest. I've been resting for ten years! I feel so far away from other people.'

'If you could manage not to take things so much to heart,' I suggested. 'You know, really everyone's constantly being disappointed and wounded by chance remarks. We all want more love and more approval than we get.' It occurred to me that my eagerness to give advice was presumptuous. I knew nothing of mental illness. 'Lalla said in her last letter that you'd had a long walk together and you'd told her all about migrating birds.'

'So we did.' Lady Inskip smiled. 'I'd forgotten that. My mind's got into a track, you see, of remembering only the bad things. One doctor I saw said that was all that was wrong with me. He called it severe depression. He said that there was nothing else the matter but that made James very angry. I know what James thinks is wrong with me. But it terrifies me, the idea of being . . . you know.' She squeezed my hand convulsively. 'Then I don't know who I am. I remember myself as a young woman, so happy and hopeful. And this is what my life has become – a sick woman, useless, an irritant. I can't believe it's really me. When Lalla and Jeremy were born there was a little dip – I didn't feel quite myself, familiar things looked strange. But people said I was tired and I'd soon be myself again. It was natural with twins and a difficult birth. And they were right. I got over it, got back to normal. But after Nicky was born –' She closed her eyes tight suddenly and pressed both hands to her chest. 'No, I can't talk about it.'

I stroked her arm gently and after a while she opened her eyes again. 'Are you old enough, Viola, to understand what it's like to feel real fear? I don't mean a few seconds' panic, losing your balance or nearly getting run over crossing the road, but terror which turns your stomach to water and makes you shiver so badly that your muscles hurt? And it doesn't last a few seconds but goes on for hours, sometimes days.'

'No,' I said. 'I don't think I am. But, please, if it will help, tell me.'

She half sat up, leaned on her elbow and stared at me with huge, frightened eyes. 'I can trust you, Viola, can't I?'

'Well – yes. I hope so, anyway.'

'James hates me and he's quite right. I know usually it's wrong to hate people but in this case he's perfectly justified. You see I –'

'It's Miss Viola, isn't it?' Miss Tinker appeared at the other side of the bed with such suddenness that I jumped. When I thought about it I realised that she must have a bedroom adjoining Lady Inskip's but at the time the abruptness of her arrival made me think of catapults and trapdoors. 'I hope we aren't tiring Madam. She needs her rest.'

Her moustache seemed to have benefited from the long hot summer for it had a luxuriant gleam.

'I only wanted to ask Lady Inskip if she was coming down to dinner. We should all like it so much if she would.'

'I don't think that would be a very good idea.'

'No, Tinker. I can answer for myself. And I think it *would* be a good idea.' Lady Inskip spoke with a desperate gaiety. 'I should like it very much. I'm tired of being up here and Viola always makes me feel better.'

Miss Tinker gave me a glance loaded with dislike. Remembering my aunt's maid, Agnes, it occurred to me that her resentful attitude might be nothing more than a kind of jealousy, the craving for power over her mistress. But Sir James's behaviour to his wife I was convinced was much more sinister. At school when we weren't reading books like *Forever Amber* and *Katherine*, about country maidens being raped by aristocrats in fearfully scratchy armour, we read Gothic horror stories in which impecunious husbands tried to convince their rich wives that they were mad.

I met Sir James in the hall as I came downstairs after unpacking. He gave me a quick glance from his inflamed eyes, said, 'Good. We shall have some decent food, perhaps,' and walked off to the estate room.

Luckily my vanity was gratified by this praise of my earlier attempts at catering or I might have been annoyed to be mistaken for a replacement cook. I went to the kitchen, carrying the presents I had brought for the household, including the meat for the dogs and Fluffy. The blood from the pork had run into the chicken and altogether it was a rather disgusting sight.

'Was there anything you was wanting, miss?' The new cook looked just like Popeye's girlfriend, Olive Oyl, very tall and thin with dark hair in a bun, a large egg-shaped nose and enormous feet. She stood beside me with her arms folded across her none-too-clean apron.

'I'm afraid it got hot on the train, though I wrapped it in lots of damp newspaper. It smells a tiny bit off. But I don't think the animals will mind.'

Her glance moved from my face to the dogs' dishes and back again. 'Was there anything else?'

Although I was smiling at her, her expression was frozen with resistance. I was an intruder in her domain and she wanted me to know it. I had actually hoped for a biscuit or a piece of cake as I was absolutely starving and dinner would not be for another hour and a half but, confronted by her animosity, I did not dare to ask. In the passage that led to the dining room a painting of a tiger about to spring on a monkey, which was eating a banana, gave me such a pang of hunger that I determined not to be a feeble little coward and went back. The cook, whose name was Blanche Fry, which Jeremy said later was the only thing that remotely connected her to the culinary arts, was emptying my parcel of meat into a saucepan full of sizzling onions. While I was watching her, wondering whether to make my presence known, she added the bones from the dogs' bowls. Then she blew her nose heartily on her apron, wiped her hands on it and begun to cut up some muddy-looking carrots. I went away.

Nicky very generously shared his chocolate with us as Lalla professed to be faint with hunger. Jeremy appeared later, covered with paint, to declare a truce with the old cheese biscuits, which he had always scorned in the past. But there were none.

'The trouble is,' said Lalla, 'the cooks are given so much a week for feeding the household. There's no supervision, which means they can give us scrag-ends and mouldy potatoes and keep the rest of the money themselves. And this one drinks. Huddle's had to lock the cellar.'

'No one could call me fussy,' I said, 'but she does seem to have dirty habits.'

'Hand round the rest of those sweets, Nicky,' said Jeremy. 'That's if you don't want to lose a brother to starvation.'

'Those are called Purple Hearts,' I said, as Nicky rummaged through the supply I had brought him.

'Not really? Won't they make us very excited?'

'They're only sweets. Nothing to do with amphetamines.'

'They aren't at all purple.' Nicky sounded disappointed. 'Only pink like calamine lotion. They taste a bit like toothpaste. Of course they're jolly good,' he added quickly, so as not to hurt my feelings.

'I don't care. Give me the bag,' insisted Jeremy. He gobbled down several and then the rest of us ate quite a few despite their taste, which bore an undeniable resemblance to something from the bathroom cupboard.

Huddle hovered near with a tray of sherry.

'Hello, Huddle, how are you?' I said.

Huddle did an elaborate double-take. 'Bless my soul, it's Miss Hotwee, isn't it?' He fumbled for his spectacles. 'I mistook you for an elephant stool, madam. I'm as well as can be expected, madam, thank you. This spell of fine weather's made a difference to my arthuritis. Dry bedding, that's the secret. Only takes me twenty minutes these days to get out of bed.'

Lalla groaned.

I went upstairs to get Lady Inskip. She held on to me tightly as we entered the drawing room, like a blushing young girl coming down to grown-up dinner for the first time. I had forewarned Jeremy and Lalla. Lalla sat next to her mother on the sofa and allowed her hand to be held while Jeremy fetched Huddle back with the sherry and presented her with a piece of Nicky's chocolate.

'Sherry and chocolate! How original and nice!' Lady Inskip's voice was bravely gay.

'What's this?' Sir James came in, cigarette between his fingers, looking annoyed. 'What are you doing down here, Millie? I thought we agreed you were better being quiet upstairs.'

'Oh, but, James, I'm enjoying myself. It's so dull in my room and Tinker scolds me.'

'Well, don't blame me for the consequences. Where's the cursed sherry? Is it too much to expect a drink in this lunatic asylum?'

Lady Inskip looked utterly crushed and sat with drooping head, absent-mindedly finishing off the Purple Hearts.

Dinner was not, initially, a success. We tried to bring

Lady Inskip into the conversation but before her husband she was unable to achieve the precarious animation she had attained in his absence. Lalla, Jeremy and I attempted to talk among ourselves but it is hard to be spontaneous and convivial in the presence of someone silent and resolutely glum.

'What the blazes is this mess?' roared Sir James, interrupting Jeremy's monologue on the techniques of theatre lighting. 'Damn nearly took the roof off my mouth!'

'Devilled pheasant, sir,' answered Huddle.

'Pheasant? But it's July!'

Sir James made no further comment but stared about him from time to time with the wary curiosity of a man who finds himself adrift in a strange country.

'Where are Francis and Susan?' I asked, to fill the pause.

'They've gone to dinner with the Bishop,' said Lalla. 'Poor things! If you can believe such a thing possible the food's worse than here. Suet dumplings with everything. Last time *we* went Mrs Bishop managed to stretch one duck between eight of us. *And* there's an obligatory half-hour of the Bishop groaning on in prayer before you're allowed to spear so much as a lump of gristle. I only hope I'm not weak enough to relent on my death-bed and ask God to forgive me my sins. I should hate to spend eternity mewed up round the celestial throne with all those fearfully dull and stingy religious maniacs.'

'Perhaps, Arabella, you might refrain from blaspheming at the dinner table.' Sir James's nose looked particularly snoutish when he threw his head back, more than ever like the wretched Hog of Inskip hanging behind his chair. The Hog had gained nothing from being laved in sunlight. His mean little eyes seemed to drip red paint, his drawn-back lips were wet with spittle. But viewed from this new angle – I was now sitting on Lady Inskip's left – there was something about his expression that suggested vulnerability.

Lalla stuck out her tongue at her father when he wasn't looking. It was a rich purple. After that we poked our tongues out surreptitiously at one another to see if they were similarly dyed. Everyone had given up trying to eat the so-called pheasant so this was not as revolting as it sounds. It was extraordinary that such a silly thing had the power to cheer us up to the extent that we all became quite giggly. Lady Inskip seemed to find it particularly funny. I think it must have given her pleasure to be in league with her children against her husband as it must have seemed to her so often the other way round.

'What's so blasted amusing, I'd like to know?' Sir James had glanced up from burrowing among his potatoes and carrots to see Lalla laughing at Jeremy trying to view his own tongue. Sir James's wrath was deflected by the sight of his steward shuffling towards him. 'What the devil do you want now, Huddle? You can take this stuff away. If this is pheasant I'm the Duke of Wellington. What's more, there seems to be gravel in the sauce. I've damned near bust my plate. Tell the cook it's the worst dinner I've had since Anzio.'

'I'm afraid the cook is not available for comment, sir.'

'What? What the devil do you mean?'

'She is beyond the give-and-take of converse. She is at this moment laying on the kitchen floor with her head in the coal bucket.' Huddle's voice was grave but there was a spark in his rheumy eyes and I could see he was enjoying himself.

'Why? What? Bah!' Sir James's teeth took chunks out of the air with temper.

'The cook is inebriated, sir.'

'I told you to keep everything alcoholic under lock and key.'

'I have done so, sir, but I found this on the kitchen table.' He brandished my bottle of blue Curaçao. It was empty.

'I thought your father was quite decent about it, all things considered,' I said to Jeremy later that night as we lay in bed in my turret room, listening to the owls hooting in the balmy darkness through the open windows. In my absence Jeremy had adopted my former bedroom as his own and it seemed quite natural to be sharing it with him in our customary celibate way.

'That's because he thinks you'll feel morally obliged to cook for us for a week for free. And he can sack the cook without having to pay her notice. You will, won't you, my treasure?' He stroked my shoulder affectionately.

'Certainly I will. We could have *épaule de mouton à la boulangère*. That's very cheap but quite delicious. Lots of potatoes and onions and garlic roasted under a shoulder of lamb. Or *boeuf braisé à l'italienne*. That's stewing beef with tomatoes, red wine and mushrooms. I wonder if your father would like semolina *gnocchi*? Too foreign, do you think? Jeremy?'

In answer to my nudge Jeremy gave a little snore.

The next morning Lalla took me shopping in the Baby Austin. She insisted on wearing the blue beaded scarf I had given her though it didn't really go with her yellow sundress. Tiffany had found the scarf on a market-stall and had intended to cut off the beads but I had begged her to let me have it as I thought it was so pretty. I was delighted that Lalla approved my taste. In the matter of liking things as in everything else, she was incapable of pretence.

In the afternoon we had a rehearsal of *The Lighthouse Keeper's Daughter*. I was allowed to read my lines on this occasion though Jeremy told me sternly that by the same time tomorrow he would expect me to be word perfect.

'I don't think I can *keep* saying, "Alack! Alack! I fear I am falling into a swound,"' I protested. 'Of course it makes the lines easier to learn but isn't it rather dully repetitious? And what is a swound? Surely the word should be swoon?'

'No, it shouldn't, Miss Cleverdick. It's an archaism.'

'But this is eighteen eighty-something. Not even a hundred years ago. I think it sounds very odd.'

'Shut up, Viola, and don't argue. Now say it and throw yourself backwards into Zed's arms. Don't worry. He won't drop you.'

'No, I'll be sure not to do that,' said Zed, in a low voice, showing his lower teeth in a grin and cupping his hands into breast shapes.

'I think you ought to catch me round my waist,' I

returned in a cross whisper. 'No Victorian in his right mind would hold me like that.'

'For God's sake, stop muttering, you two, and let's get *on*.' Jeremy clutched his head.

I decided to speak to Jeremy about it later for I could see that my indignation was adding zest to the situation as far as Zed was concerned. Lalla stood with one hand on her hip most of the time, like a model in Dior rather than a rustic maid in dimity, and muttered her lines as though working her way through multiplication tables. I was sure this was to deter Zed, who took every opportunity to lay his hands on her that the script offered. I had to admit that Jeremy was right. Zed was good. You quite forgot that he was acting. And from a distance he looked every inch the romantic hero. You couldn't see how small and mean his eyes were.

Huddle was one of the drowning crew. He did not share Zed's natural acting ability. He made it clear that he was in the play under severe protest and, when not flinging up his arms with strange jerking movements like a monkey on a stick and groaning as though about to give birth, he was rubbing his limbs, wiping his eyes and holding his back in a display of one undergoing extreme refinements of torture.

Huddle's present had also been a success. I had not intended to bring him anything on the grounds that for one thing he would certainly not expect it and, for another, it might create difficulties with Bowser, Mrs Jukes and Mrs Tooth, who were not to receive my bounty. But when I saw the rubber galoshes in Mr Dring's back room, I could not resist, though they cost more than all the other things put together.

Huddle was as astonished and gratified as if I had presented him with a crock of gold. He got out his spectacles and examined the galoshes minutely holding them half an inch from his eyes, then stuck them over his boots and refused to take them off again, though now the stableyard was a petrified sea of baked mud. I tried to explain that they were really for outdoor wear but he was obdurate, merely remarking that it never did to get a cow in

385

calf so late in the year and Farmer Burden would find out the error of his ways soon enough.

After I had put the *boeuf braisé à l'italienne* into the oven to simmer for a few hours, Lalla and I left for the station. It was a fine warm evening. We drove through the countryside almost in silence and it wasn't until we reached the outskirts of Nottingham that Lalla referred to the object of our journey.

'I don't know how I can expect Hamish to forgive me when I can't forgive myself. I'm so ashamed. I don't suppose you've ever done anything that made you feel as though you could hardly bear to look at yourself in the mirror.' I thought about it and then decided that it had never quite come to that, though the folly and disloyalty of my feelings about Jack brought it pretty near. 'That madness with Francis I can more or less come to terms with,' Lalla went on. 'Since we talked about it in London I've thought about it a lot and though it was insane it didn't hurt anyone but me. But sleeping with Zed was cruel and destructive, even though Hamish didn't know. In a way I think I wanted him to find out. I wanted to behave badly and let him see what I was really like. Don't ask me why I do these stupid things because I honestly don't know. Now I feel I'd give anything not to have done it. If only I'd just married Hamish when he wanted me to we could have been so happy now. I've spoilt everything!'

'Look out!' I screamed, as we nearly knocked an old woman off her bicycle. Lalla drove like Jeremy, as though it was an elaborate game based on ninepins and not to be taken seriously. It occurred to me that I could learn to drive. Why had I never thought of this before? I really had no right to be angry with anyone for treating me like a helpless child.

'Ten minutes to wait,' moaned Lalla, as we strolled up and down the platform.

'Let's go and have a cup of tea and a doughnut,' I suggested.

'I couldn't eat a crumb. I can't even stand still. Oh, Viola!' She seized my arm. 'Let's go home. I'm going to be sick!'

'Nonsense! This isn't like you! You're always shamingly brave. This isn't something that can be ducked. You owe it to Hamish.' I was quite tempted to cut and run myself. Not only because I feared a horrible scene between Lalla and Hamish but also because I felt my presence to be embarrassingly superfluous. We walked up and down and stared without interest at the magazines on the bookstall.

'That's the bell for the London train. Oh, God, I *am* going to be sick!'

'Hold your breath and count to ten.'

I clung to Lalla's arm. I saw that tears were standing in her eyes and my own watered like mad in sympathy. The train came slowly in and at once doors flew open and people spilled on to the platform. They flowed to either side of us in a dash to the ticket barrier as though we were boulders in a river. Then I saw Hamish walking towards us, impeccably suited and standing out from the crowd because of it. He was carrying an attaché case in one hand and a suitcase in the other. He had not seen us. He looked tired and worried. It struck me then that I had rarely seen him looking serious. He seemed much older.

Then he saw Lalla. He walked up to us and put down his luggage, ignoring the hurrying crowds. He looked at Lalla, with an expression that was both troubled and speculative.

She tried to smile but I saw her mouth trembling. 'Oh, Hamish! I'm so very sorry!' Tears began to fall.

Hamish's face softened and he held out his arms. 'My poor girl! What a hopeless mess you've made of things! What have you been thinking of?'

CHAPTER 29

Despite Jeremy's protests Lalla and Hamish left for Scotland the next day. Hamish said that though he could probably forgive Lalla anything, he did not feel at all the same about Zed and rather than have a ridiculous and undignified scene it would be better to leave before Zed came to rehearse.

'Not that that gives you *carte blanche* to behave badly, my darling,' he added, looking severely at Lalla. 'I'm not saying that what you do doesn't matter and that I'm not cut to the quick just like any other man would be. It's just that I love you too much to make it a reason for casting you off.'

This was said in the kitchen as they helped me to fry mushrooms and bacon for breakfast. I could see that Lalla was ecstatically in love. Every time she looked at Hamish her eyes grew tender. I had taken Lalla a cup of tea that morning, as I had got into the habit of doing when staying at Inskip Park, and had barged in without knocking to find Hamish in bed beside her, looking rather sweet amidst the pink roses and organdie. Lalla was resting her head on his chest, which was smothered with blond silky hairs just like Pooh Bah's. I had carried it off quite well, I thought.

'Another glorious day. Shall I open the curtains? Do you mind sharing a cup? It's such miles to the kitchen.'

And Hamish had replied, 'Not a bit. Yes, do. Tea in bed! What luxury! You're a trooper, Viola my pet.'

Lalla just smiled, as though remote from mundane considerations.

I had to remind myself sternly now, as I saw them floating about the kitchen on some exclusive cloud of happiness, of my vow of emotional sequestration. Feelings were running high and it was catching. When it was time for them to leave we were scarcely able to speak because of the lumps in our throats.

'If you should happen to come across any Edinburgh rock,' said Nicky, as he stood on the steps to wave them off.

'If it really can't wait five days you'd better go with my blessing,' said Jeremy, still rather grumpy but trying not to be. 'Anyway, a dressmaker's dummy would put more into the part of Bess.'

'I'm sorry, darling.' Lalla hugged him. 'This is terribly important or I wouldn't let you down.'

'All right, you needn't strangle me. Have a good time. 'Bye, Hamish. Try and stay longer next time.'

Lady Inskip stood beside me, her arm through mine. 'I hate partings. So silly of me. I won't be upset. Goodbye, my dear children. Have fun.'

Lalla put her arms right round her mother and whispered in her ear. I couldn't help overhearing as we were standing so close. 'Now, do be good while I'm gone. Don't let Daddy and The Stinker bully you. I'm expecting you to stand up for yourself. Mind you do now, darling.' She kissed her mother's cheek.

'Oh, Lalla!' Lady Inskip caught my eye and pressed her lips tightly together.

When they had driven away Jeremy and I consulted each other as to how to save the play.

'You'll have to be Bess. You're not really strapping enough but we can pad you out and give you high heels.'

'But who will play Clorinda?'

'There's Mrs Hoggins. Though she's rather too fat for verisimilitude.'

'I don't want to be unkind but would there be room for anyone else on the stage? Besides, she's fifty if a day. What about Miss Tinker? Or Flo?'

'Neither a handlebar moustache nor cackling bare gums quite suggest a delicate Victorian miss forever dropping into a faint.'

Flo was Zed's sister. Jeremy had roped her in to be a sailor. With her hair pushed into a woollen cap and her sleeves rolled up to display her tattoos she made a convincing old salt.

'I've just had the most brilliant idea. I know someone who will be the perfect Bess. And she can learn lines in seconds. She's a professional actress. Well, understudy to one anyway. I'll call her at once.'

Jeremy practically led me by my ear to the telephone. I rang SCAB to be answered by Giles.

'Hello, Giles. How is everything? I need to get hold of

Tiffany urgently – mustn't lose a minute – but, as you know, there's no telephone at home – the play's this Saturday – the entire county's coming –'

This was actually true. As soon as word got round about the party, acceptances had been flooding in.

'Just a minute, Viola. I can't understand you if you gabble. Tiffany's on the balcony beneath layers of sun lotion. I'll get her.'

'Oh, what fun!' said Tiffany, as soon as I'd explained. 'I was just about to go home. Stella's asked her boyfriend over and they're practically raping each other under the awning. I was feeling not a little *de trop* and a tiny bit depressed. I'm dying to see the house and the charcoal-burners and everything. I'll catch a train this afternoon.'

We rehearsed on and off all day and when I wasn't learning my lines I was cooking. I loved being in the kitchen. Even the wooden spoons were well made and had aesthetic appeal, and the pans were a good shape, made from copper lined with tin. They were heavy to carry about but the heat spread evenly across the base and the range pumped out a fierce, sizzling temperature or a steady simmer depending on which section of the top you used. While I was stirring or whisking or waiting for something to boil I admired the blue and white tiles. Even the one with the snake curled round and round the branch was beautiful but my favourite was the fat, good-natured-looking leopard playing with her cubs, like a painting by Henriette Ronner-Knipp.

For lunch we ate scrambled eggs, ham and toast and, because I had discovered a large unopened tin of molasses, treacle tart afterwards. For tea I made gingerbread from a recipe in a cookery book I found in a cupboard. The receipts, as they were charmingly called, were written out by hand and dated from the early 1900s when prosperity and optimism still reigned at Inskip. It recommended that the gingerbread be eaten with a wedge of cheese. I had bought a pound of Cheddar that morning so, despite Huddle's expressive shuddering, I put some slices on the tray with the cake. It was a delicious combination.

'So man did eat angels' food,' said Jeremy, 'as the Prayer Book says. I used to think that angels dined on liquid silver and gold but now I know it was ginger cake and cheese. Yes, Huddle?'

'While you was in the the-ater, Miss Hotwee, a Miss Breadboard telephoned to say not to meet the train and that she is coming by carpet later.'

I thought I detected a glint of mischief before he shuffled away in his galoshes. 'Tiffany can't drive so someone must be giving her a lift. I do hope not Stella Partington. That reminds me, I must learn to drive.'

'I'll teach you,' said Jeremy.

'Thank you very much but your *à corps perdu* style is not for the beginner. Hello, Nicky. Have some tea. How was today's dig?'

'I found a complete rat skeleton. Look.'

It was not a particularly attractive sight but I made approving noises.

'For God's sake, take it away,' insisted Jeremy. 'It may be a perfect example of an early Georgian hamster but it smells of corruption.'

Nicky didn't seem offended. I reflected on the disadvantages of being an only child. Probably your brothers and sisters are the only people who ever tell you the truth. Your parents tell whoppers about how good you are at raffia baskets and kettle-holders, besides the more substantial untruths about your general attractiveness and intelligence potential, and the rest of the world shirks candour in favour of politeness. There had been no one in my life who could be relied upon to deliver a bold recital of fact and I felt the lack of it. Could I, I wondered, look forward to marriage as a revelation of my own character? Just as I was thinking about my parents and their unconventional relationship, Huddle came in with the afternoon post. There were two letters for me, forwarded from Tolgate Square. I recognised my father's tidy printed hand on one envelope.

Dearest Vi. Just to let you know that your ma has flitted. She has gone to Scotland to stay with some people in a castle there.

She says she is never going back to Peter and I believe her. Poor chap he came here after she had gone and talked to your aunt. He was my idea of a jiggolo decked with gold rings and chains like a Christmas tree but I could see that he suffered. I dont like to see a man howl. Not for his own self anyways. In my book its different if you cry for someone elses suffering like comrades in the war or a child hurt bad or even a horse as has to be shot. But in my view it isnt manly to cry because theres something you cant have. That notwithstanding it cut me up when she went as it always does but Im used now to her going and I know shell be back. Each time she comes back sooner. I hope you are well my buttercup dont you worry about your old dad hes fine and coping. You have a good time best comfort of my life. Im that proud of you I could bust. God bless. Jenkins.

'What's up, Viola? Not bad news?'

'Not really.' I searched for a handkerchief. 'Just my bloody mother's left my father again. He's the dearest, kindest, most honourable man you could ever meet. And I hate him to be hurt!' Jeremy came and sat on the arm of my chair and patted me until I had got my eyes and nose under control. I had another piece of cake which helped. 'It's happened about six times before so I expect he'll be all right. Darling Dad. I'll write to him this evening after dinner.'

I looked at the other envelope. It was from Daniel.

Dearest Girl [it began in Daniel's beautiful script],

It was good of you to let me know that you were going to your friends in Nottinghamshire. I hope that I have not, by the impetuosity of my feelings, driven you out of the house. Tolgate Square is your home as long as you wish it. But, I confess, I am pleased to regain the comfort of my own rooms and to see Josephine. For me it is hard to be away. It is part of that introversion and general crankiness which makes me an unfit mate for anyone and particularly for a young expectant girl of good hope.

I love you, my dear girl, and I do not regret this love. It is to me like that flower blooming in the wasteland. It is an unexpected beauty in the difficult terrain of my life. I shall not gather the blossom and shorten the natural span of its flowering.

My feeling for you has irradiated the gloom in which, like a Goth, I had grown accustomed to dwell and my recent absence has shown me in strong light how much I have that is good. My books, my music, my house and its inmates all so valued by me, good Mrs Shilling, the courageous and original Tiffany. And you. For a while, at least.

Come back, dearest girl, and I shall endeavour to be a true friend, perhaps a little stern in truth and too quick to admonish, but with a fixed love that cannot be swayed. Be not anxious, dear heart, all is very well. Daniel.

'You *are* in crying mode.' Jeremy resumed his patting and stroking.

'I always *like* getting letters,' said Nicky, rather thickly through cake and cheese. 'Unless they're from my godmother who sends me back *my* letters with spelling mistakes corrected. Once I sent back one of hers marked where she'd spelt "correspondence" and "conscientious" wrong – we get those practically every fortnight in our spelling tests – and she rang my father in a howling temper. She doesn't write nearly so often now.'

'I suppose it's unreasonable to expect that there are happy endings in real life,' I sniffed, 'but virtue *ought* to be rewarded. What's the point of everything if it's all just a hopeless, meaningless muddle?'

Jeremy laughed. 'Surely you don't expect such a simple scheme. Where would the virtue be if you knew it was certain of reward? It would cease to be virtue and become self-seeking.'

I detected a flaw in this argument but before I could put my finger on it Huddle came back to tell me that a Mrs Mad Fortress was on the telephone.

'Hello, Mab. How lovely to hear you. I'm in need of cheering up and you always do.'

'Oh dear, I was hoping to be cheered myself actually.'

'What happened?'

'I've just been to a Red Cross lunch – rather depressing anyway and I bought the most horrible draught-excluder shaped like a dachshund with ears and tail and button eyes just because one has to buy *something* – anyway, Deirdre Sutton-Smith, who chairs the committee, came up just as I was helping myself to some charlotte Russe – actually packet jelly, bought sponge fingers and powdered custard, *such* pretension – well, Deirdre asked me whether I'd met David Selkirk yet as she'd heard he'd moved into my area. She managed to imply some sort of descent on his part – she really is the most frightful bitch. "Ay thought ay ought to warn you" – her voice is so affected it sets one's teeth on edge – "he's terribly plausible and very good-looking, but he takes advantage of single women, especially widows and divorcees. Naturally, being lonely makes one vulnerable. Ay pity any middle-aged woman without a husband." That's because Anthony Sutton-Smith is having an affair with his secretary – it's common knowledge. "Actually, Deirdre," I said, "we spent a delightful evening at Covent Garden a few weeks ago and tonight he's taking me to La Tavola." That's the best Italian restaurant in Worthing and very expensive. I didn't tell her that we'd also had a cosy supper at home. As I've told you he's the perfect gentleman. Never more than a good night peck on the cheek. I was hoping that tonight – oh, damn it all. I *am* upset.'

'But what does he do? You haven't told me yet.' I was having trouble following what Mab was saying because she was speaking in a rush and taking great sucks on her cigarette at frequent intervals, which made her swallow her words.

'She said – the mean creature, I do hate her, she had the most pussy-cat smile on her face while she was talking – "You must not give him an inch, my dear. He has twice been taken to court for attempting to obtain money from women under false pretences. There's a rumour that he has actually served a prison sentence for bigamy." I said, "One can't believe everything one hears, Deirdre, as you, of all people, ought to know" – I know it was nasty of me, dear, but if you could have seen the pleasure she took in telling me all this. Anyway, she turned rather black then and said, "Ay can assure you, my dear Mab, that the man is an out and out confidence trickster. He finds out about single women who have money – who they were married to, that sort of thing – and then pretends to have known their husbands. He only claims the vaguest acquaintance so he can't be caught out but it's enough to make the woman feel it's safe to be friendly." Well, dear, as you know David told me he'd met Geoffrey in the navy and it did make me feel that he had some sort of claim on my friendship.'

'Poor, poor Mab. What are you going to do? Perhaps it isn't true. Perhaps she's jealous of you and has made it all up.'

'That occurred to me. But when you think about it, it would be a strange thing for someone to do. I see Deirdre half a dozen times a year at the most. I mean, why would she?'

'Who's paying for dinner tonight?'

'He is, I presume.'

'Well, what have you got to lose? You like being with him. Why not just go ahead and enjoy yourself? If he asks you for money, even as a loan, don't give it to him. He isn't going to steal your purse, I don't suppose. You're fore-warned and ready to defend yourself so you're quite safe.'

'Yes. I suppose I could. You're right. What harm can he do me? I knew you'd cheer me up. Though it has cast a shadow. I won't ask him in afterwards.'

'I don't suppose he's violent. Mrs Sutton-Smith would have been bound to tell you if he was. But perhaps to be on the safe side, better not. You could try probing him about his past. See if he gets shifty.'

'All right, dear, I'll do just as you say. Now that's enough of me. Why do *you* need cheering up?'

'I don't think I do now. Talking to you has pulled me out of it. And we're going to have a party here with dancing. I'm doing the food. I'm really excited about it. And there's the play.' I told Mab all there was to tell about *The Lighthouse Keeper's Daughter* and then about Lalla and Hamish. I had taken Mab's call in the kitchen as it was out of everyone's way and I liked sitting on the broad window-sill staring out at the sheep as they pottered idly about. As I talked, my eyes wandered from the park to the tiles on the walls and then to the shelves of cooking utensils. 'Oh, Mab,' I said, interrupting myself, 'I've just had an idea! I'll make it a jelly party!' I stared at the rows of jelly moulds of every size and shape. 'Won't that be original?'

'You mean, things in aspic?'

'Yes. Chicken and eggs and prawns and tomatoes all set in aspic with herbs. Think how pretty! I wish you could see the marvellous shapes of moulds there are here. My absolute favourites are the pewter ones. There's one shaped like a swan. There's a duck, a dove, a hen sitting in a basket, a bunch of asparagus, a basket of flowers and a pineapple. And fish-shaped ones for salmon mousse and a big beautiful one like a hare. I think I'll put ham mousse into that. I wouldn't like to cook a hare. Then there are lots of copper moulds like exotic sandcastles for puddings. And the beauty of it is there'll be no last-minute cooking. They'll just have to be turned out.'

'It sounds marvellous but killing. You must restrict yourself, Viola, or you'll be dead.'

We discussed jellies happily at length.

'I feel so much better, dear. Almost not minding about David. The trouble is he's the only attractive man I've met since Geoffrey died. Why *are* good-looking men such bastards?'

'They aren't all. Unless you've got much higher standards for looks than me. I think Jeremy and Daniel are violently attractive in quite different ways and *they* aren't bastards. Hamish isn't at all handsome but he's so nice you can't help being attracted. And think of Giles, after all. Quite the best-looking man I know and not in the least a bastard. Beneath the crust he's kind and thoughtful and sensitive and he makes me laugh.'

'Mm. Do you think so, dear? I can't tell, of course. As he's my son he's perfect in my eyes – well, nearly. I thought there was a time when you didn't get on so well.'

'I think – I hope – we're friends now. Of course, he's

much cleverer than I am and he thinks I'm completely deranged.'

'I wonder.'

Something in Mab's tone put me on the alert. 'Now, Mab, no match-making. Giles would go into a monastery rather than have me as a girlfriend. And anyway, I'm not getting involved with anyone for ages. Not until I'm much older and more experienced and know what I'm doing.'

'In that case, my dear girl, you'll die an old maid.'

I was wondering about this half an hour later as I stood on the Palladian bridge and gazed at my favourite view along the valley. Jeremy was rehearsing the second act with Zed and Wat and those villagers who, when accosted by Jeremy in the Dog and Bone, had been too slow-witted to think of a reason why they shouldn't be sailors. Nicky was prompt. Mrs Tooth's son, the local electrician, whose real name was Barry but who had been wittily nicknamed Buck by his chums, was doing the lights. I had put some pigeons *à la campagne* – that is, with bacon, mushrooms, onions and cider – into the oven to stew for dinner. As there was now no need to go to the station I had time on my hands so I had walked with Nip and Nudge to the bridge, intending to give thought to preparations for the party. Instead I brooded on the unfairness of life and how it was that two such essentially good people as my father and Daniel seemed doomed to sorrow in matters of love.

But I could not be unhappy for long surrounded by hills and woods shot to a vivid emerald by the curious amber light and divided by the waterfall like a string of sparkling silver. From far away came a low rumble of thunder, and the surface of the lake which, earlier, had been flaked with gold, turned grey and ruffled. The dogs ran along the edge of the lake in pursuit of a group of sheep headed by a defiant ram. I felt a drop of rain on my hand.

Someone came out of the drawing-room door and stood on the terrace. I could see a blur of blue and grey and a head with dark hair turned up to the sky. I watched idly as the figure, about the size of my little fingernail, strolled up and down, still looking up as though to gauge the likelihood of rain. Then it set off across the grass towards the Palladian bridge. He walked leisurely, hands in pockets, turning his head from side to side to admire the view. I screwed up my eyes and peered hard, thinking that if it was Zed I would go down and hide in the sluice room. When the figure was half-way between the house and the bridge I realised it wasn't Zed. It was Giles.

I was so surprised to see him there walking across the park at Inskip when I had imagined him to be in Pall Mall that I was overwhelmed by unexpected and extraordinary sensations. I leaned on my arms over the parapet of the bridge and, as he came gradually into focus, I tried to interpret them.

When I was very small my aunt had given me something called a Chinese water garden. It was a closed shell with a paper band round it. You had to cut the band and put it in a glass of water. I was enchanted when the shell opened and tiny balls of pink, yellow, purple and blue floated up, attached by cotton threads. Brilliantly coloured paper filaments unfurled on the surface of the water, like petals blossoming. In just that way the deepest, tenderest, most passionate feelings were floating slowly up from somewhere in the centre of my being, expanding to fill my heart, head and throat. My mouth was dry, my ears whistled, my eyes were dimmed by tears, my nose prickled. A hot, tight band round my chest and a weakness of the knees accompanied sensations of bliss. I loved him. When Giles came near enough for me to make out his face, I would not have been surprised if I had levitated several feet and drifted towards him across the lake, powered only by adrenaline. I stood in a daze of expectation until he strolled on to the bridge, the dogs following him.

'Hello, Viola! I didn't know you were here. I suppose you're sheltering from the rain.'

'Is it raining?' I asked, blushing, my voice squeaky from the banging of my heart.

'Well, I don't know what else you'd call it.' Giles came to stand next to me and pointed to the dimpling of the water.

His blue shirt had wet spots on the shoulders. 'It's going to get heavier, I think. We'll have to wait here for a bit.'

From this distance I could see the crinkles at the corners of his eyes and the infinitesimal growth of dark beard along his jaw. His eyes were somewhere between blue and grey, the colour of the darkest raincloud brooding over the combes and coppices across the lake. His nose was long and quite thin. It was a perfect nose, I thought. Quite the most beautiful nose I had ever seen. Now I noticed that there was a delicious little white scar on his chin. But while I acknowledged the flawless composition of his features I was aware that one cannot fall in love with a nose. I marvelled at the mystery of sexual attraction. What was it that made me feel that Giles was the most fascinating man in the world and that I wanted nothing more than to hold his body to mine in the closest possible proximity?

And why had I been so impervious to his conspicuous irresistibility before? The answer was, of course, that I hadn't been. The truth was that I had tried to protect myself by refusing to acknowledge it. When I first went to work at SCAB Giles had made it clear that he regarded me in the light of a wasp at a picnic, something tiresome, best ignored with the minimum of fuss. As Pierce's girlfriend inevitably I would be buzzing off before very long.

All the time that we had been growing better and better friends I had been delighted by evidence of his increasing tolerance of me, his willingness to spend time with me. Our visits to La Petite Sonnerie, our trip to Smith Square to the lunchtime concert, the talks we'd had, all these moments we had shared had been, I now admitted to myself, the sweetest thing in life.

I had liked him and been grateful to him but I had known him to be above my touch. Giles was clever, scholarly, cultivated – gifts I had come to admire above all others. I feared I was too ignorant and too immature to interest him very much. The shock of seeing him unexpectedly had revealed the extent of the physical desire I felt for him, which had been growing stronger and stronger as I knew him better.

Now I understood that my feelings for Daniel, for Jeremy and for Pierce, were very different from the love I felt for Giles. They sprang from my old childish longing to please. These men had wanted something from me and the novelty of finding myself in the position of having something to give had persuaded me to try to convince myself, in each case, that this might be the great love I sought.

But the feeling I had for Giles was quite selfish. I wanted him, emotionally and physically. I wanted to fix him to my side so that I could talk to him, listen to him, look at him, make love with him. I was completely and effortlessly in the grip of the emotion I had tried so hard to imagine and it was something so simple and so undeniable that it allowed no possibility of doubt.

'Looking at this incredible view one ought to be reciting Wordsworth.' Giles leant with both hands on the parapet.

> 'The sounding cataract
> Haunted me like a passion: the tall rock,
> The mountain, and the deep and gloomy wood,
> Their colours and their forms, were then to me
> An appetite.'

'What does it mean?'

'He's talking about the pleasure he took in Nature as a young man – his delight in it was instinctive and unthinking, whereas later, Nature becomes for Wordsworth a solace for pain and difficulty, a precept for human morality, perhaps even the physical embodiment of God. Wordsworth's philosophy is woolly and a great deal of the later stuff is banal but he sometimes hits it off exactly.'

I wanted to stand on that bridge with Giles for the rest of my life and to listen to him talking about all the things I longed to know. I could have moved my hand two inches and touched his. I might have rested my head on his shoulder and felt the warmth of his body. How would it feel to entwine my arms around his waist? I did not do any of these things but I took a step back and turned my head so that I could remember his face and the hills and the waterfall beyond it for ever. This was all my Paradise had lacked.

'Wilt thou forget
That on the banks of this delightful stream We stood together.'

Giles turned to look at me and smiled. I could have cried, 'Never! It was on this spot that I realised I was in love with you!' Luckily I didn't.

'What are you staring at?' he asked, as I continued to gaze at him.

'Sorry. I was just thinking . . . Never mind. I suppose you brought Tiffany? That was kind of you. Are you going to stay?'

'I can't.' I felt a blade-thrust of disappointment. 'I'm going on to Yorkshire to look at Pelshore Manor. It's a wonderful stone house, not large, with marvellous furniture. I really think we ought to take it on.'

'What period is it?' I asked, to be cordial, though I heartily wished Pelshore Manor and its contents at the bottom of the sea.

'Early seventeenth century. But I'm coming back for the play on Saturday. I've agreed to sell programmes. So I can give you a lift back to London the next day with Tiffany, if you like.'

'Thank you.' My spirits rose. 'There's going to be a party afterwards, you know.'

'Yes,' Giles made a face. 'According to Jeremy, the average age will be something over seventy and the main topics of interest will be the state of the harvest, the inquity of the Labour Party and the whereabouts of the first meet. Perhaps I'll sort some more books while it's going on.'

'Oh, but you must come! It's going to be marvellous. I'm doing the food. Don't look like that. I've improved dramatically since you last ate anything cooked by me. Daniel's been giving me lessons. He's the most meticulous teacher. Honestly I really can cook now.'

'No curried eggs, I hope. And what of Daniel? Did you find the right moment for declaring your intentions?'

'Oh.' I felt myself begin to blush. 'Yes. But – it wasn't – Now it all seems a terrible mistake. Anyway, Daniel is really too good for this world . . . I was stupid to think that I could make everything right. Some things are so badly wrong . . .'

I found myself getting hotter and hotter as I tried to explain.

'You don't have to tell me if you don't want to,' said Giles mildly. 'I thought you might want a sympathetic ear, that's all. I can guess what happened.'

'I'm sure you can't . . .' I was desperately anxious that he should not think that Daniel and I were having an affair.

'I bet I can. You very kindly intimated that you were ready to salve the wound and he declined to wield the knife at the throat of the sacrificial lamb.'

'How did you know?'

'You've told me a lot about him. I put myself in his place, that's all. If I were Daniel, I expect I'd indulge myself for a moment thinking that here was a delicious distraction from life's difficulties but a second's reflection would tell me I was only making trouble for myself.'

Delicious distraction? Was that particularly applicable to me or did Giles mean going to bed with anyone nubile and willing?

'Trouble?'

'The obvious incompatibilities of age and culture. And the moral question – that it would be taking callous advantage of your youth and inexperience. I don't imagine that he would lightly add to the burden of guilt he already carries. I assume one of the things he fell in love with was your youth and innocence – a *naïveté* that contrasted with the tainted, corrupted past. And you resemble his sister, a symbol for him of something that was pure and good. He would be unlikely to want to degrade that. It would be better to keep it ideal, untouched.'

'I'm not especially innocent,' I protested.

'Also there is the likelihood – the virtual certainty – that later on you'd fall in love with someone younger and more suitable. Perhaps more than anything, if I were Daniel I'd feel disinclined to take risks with whatever fragile equilibrium I'd achieved.'

'You're quite right. He did feel like that. All those things. It was stupid of me, wasn't it, to think that I could kiss it and make it better?'

'Perhaps it was. But it was also generous and sweet.'

Giles looked at me with a combination of amusement and something almost like tenderness. Then his expression became serious and very slowly he put up his hand to my face. My ankles became so weak I had to put my hand on the parapet to steady myself. I half closed my eyes and lifted my chin. 'Got it! This place must be full of spiders' nests.' He opened his cupped hand and a distressingly large spider ran over the balustrade and out of sight. 'What's the matter? I suppose you're terrified of spiders. Most girls are. That's why I didn't say anything when I saw it scuttling about in your hair. It was just about to launch itself from your forehead.'

'Like Cary Grant climbing down Mount Rushmore.'

I was pleased by the lightness of my tone, though I was so disappointed I could have screamed.

'Shall we go back? The rain's letting up a little. I must get on my way to Pelshore Manor. They're expecting me for dinner.'

We walked through the drizzle across the park towards the house. The ground was still hard from months of drought and the grass was slippery. Trees dripped icy drops on my face and down my neck. The dogs were soaking wet and diminished to half their normal size with legs like sticks. When we were half-way there the sky let down a torrent of water.

'Quick! We'll drown!' said Giles, and grabbed my hand. We ran after the dogs, jumping over tussocks, sliding down the steep bits. When we came to the parterre in front of the house we leaped the hedges like gazelles.

'I enjoyed that,' he said, when we reached the door into the drawing room. He was laughing and shaking the rain out of his hair. 'You look like Niobe, all tears. Much prettier, though. Niobe had something like fourteen children, didn't she? Probably she was past her best.'

Half an hour later Giles left for Yorkshire so I had to be content with that.

CHAPTER 30

The day that was to see the Inskip Strollers, as Jeremy now referred to us, give new meaning to the words 'smash' and 'hit' dawned in blazing heat. I opened my eyes to see Jeremy in a state of unusual wakefulness, leaning back on the pillows with his arms clasped behind his head.

'What do you think about cutting some of Simeon Stubbs's speech in the last act?'

I drew the fragments of my mind together. 'Good idea. There might be a chance of Bowser getting through it without a prompt if you make it only a sentence or two.'

'You're not thinking clearly, Viola. I only meant a line here and there. It's vital for the poignancy of the moment when Lord Cobblestone relents that Simeon should plead with him with some eloquence.'

'I think eloquence is asking rather a lot of someone whose voice could be mistaken for the bellowing of a stalled ox.'

Jeremy groaned. 'No director ever had to struggle before with such unevenness of acting ability.'

'You can say that again.'

'I wish I'd never started the thing. If I'd known what a great deal of work there'd be and what paucity of talent I'd have to work with I wouldn't have.' He turned his head on the pillow to look at me reproachfully.

Over breakfast Tiffany and I between us managed to cheer him a little.

'You're just experiencing first-night nerves,' said Tiffany. 'I think it's a really excellent amateur production. You'll see. The shortcomings of the supporting cast will be lost in the excitement of the performance.'

Tiffany continued to soothe Jeremy's apprehensions. She

had risen magnificently to the occasion, not only transforming the play by her commanding presence and real acting ability but also taking charge of the costumes. Within hours she and Jeremy had become the best of friends and I had gone to bed early the night before, leaving them on the terrace drinking Soul Kiss cocktails, deeply engrossed in thespian topics. In fact, she had been accepted into the household with astonishing ease.

She was very kind to Lady Inskip and had listened over dinner the night before, with every appearance of interest, to a detailed description of the moulting habits of speckled Sussex hens. She had not raised an eyebrow when Lady Inskip told her that St Pelagia had informed her of the most likely time in the year to see showers of meteorites.

Sir James seemed to find Tiffany rather attractive. I think he liked big, strong-looking women as a contrast to the fragility of his wife. When he discovered that Tiffany not only knew all the latest Test match scores but had played cricket for Roedean, he actually offered her a cigarette. Francis ignored her by and large. I suppose she was too much of an Amazon for his tastes. I saw that this made Tiffany popular with Susan and I realised that Susan was fearfully jealous of women her father liked. It was all very obvious, now I thought about it. All girls want their fathers' approval and if they don't get it they are apt to curdle inside. Poor Susan was positively coagulated with disappointment on this score.

Susan had only a small part in the play, that of Lady Cobblestone, consisting of three lines which she delivered with the phlegm of a cow in calf. Luckily the character of Lady C was not exciting. But when it came to the food she had been tremendously helpful. When I told her about the jelly party she had been at first incredulous then scornful, but after a while she began to come round to the idea and saw how useful it would be to have everything made several hours in advance. There would be only a few last-minute details – the dressing of some simple salads to counteract the richness of the savoury stuff and whipping cream for the puddings. Once Susan had made up her mind that the idea might work she hurled herself into it and it is true to say that without her the thing could not have been done. Together we scoured Little Whiddon for the freshest vegetables and fruit, fish, eggs and chickens and industrial quantities of gelatine. Because I couldn't face the poor little calves' feet necessary for proper aspic Susan made the chicken, ham and salmon mousses while I made things like haddock *suprêmes*, which were set by combining cream and egg whites then poaching them. I also made most of the puddings, which I much preferred.

All morning of the great day we rehearsed and in the afternoon we put planks across the billiard table and covered it with white cloths to serve as a buffet. Bowser had painted out the damp marks in the ballroom that had resisted the drought of summer. The doors and french windows which, according to Huddle, stuck fast even in the driest weather, were made to open with hammer and chisel. The dusty red plush-covered banquettes were beaten until they smoked like volcanoes. Mrs Jukes and Mrs Tooth debagged the chandeliers, made sticky arcs with their dusters and Glosso across the pier glasses and got up some of the worst of the dirt. It could not have been called clean but I do not think anyone notices details on such an occasion when rampant egotism – how does one look? who is there interesting to talk to? will anyone ask one to dance? what will be the nicest thing to eat? – is always to the fore. Jeremy and Buck Tooth spent the afternoon perfecting the lighting and scene changes, Huddle saw to the wine and Bowser decorated the centre of the billiard table with trailing vines, fig leaves and curiously repulsive warty gourds. Lady Inskip became excited and refused to go upstairs with Miss Tinker for her afternoon rest. She was very happy helping me to churn strawberries, sugar and cream in an antiquated ice-cream maker. When the mixture became granular we spooned it into fruit-shaped tin moulds and put them at once into the deep freeze.

I had made an appointment at the Snipping Scissors in Little Whiddon to have my hair washed. Lady Inskip was persuaded to put her feet up in the drawing room with a copy of *Fur and Feather* until my return. Susan agreed to take me into the village as she wanted to pick up some watercress. 'You'll have to come back on the bus. I'm too busy to wait. I don't know why you can't wash your own hair. I always do.'

Actually Susan's hair was no advertisement for do-it-yourself as it was as straight as a yardstick, the colour of wet straw and so thin that the pink tips of her ears always poked through like bald baby mice in a nest. I explained about the faucet in my bathroom. It would be impossible to wash my hair without either using all the hot water in the house or driving myself quite mad, turning the tap on and off with the spanner throughout the shampooing and rinsing procedures. I did not add that I wanted to look my very best because Giles was coming back that day. I was so longing to see him that I had been unable to eat or sleep properly or concentrate on anything for four days.

Mavis at the Snipping Scissors was admiring of my dark curls. She was a stout, middle-aged woman, very friendly and kind and dressed with flamboyance. Her drooping pink jersey was shot through with glittering metallic threads which, as she lathered my head energetically over the back basin, scratched my upturned nose until I cried out with pain. When I looked at myself in the mirror afterwards, my head rolled in a towel, I saw that the tip of my nose was as red as a glacé cherry. Mavis swept aside my suggestion that my hair should be blow-dried. Instead she wound it on to tiny rollers and pushed me under a hood dryer where I sat baking like china in a kiln. When I was released I quite expected my hair to drop off in little blackened sausages. My face was crimson and my hair was frizzy all over like Mrs Tooth's perm. Mavis sprayed it vigorously with cheap lacquer, which smelt like sick, and gave my hair the stiff stickiness of candy-floss. I stood waiting for the bus almost in tears.

'Hop on, Vi.' Wat drew up before me astride a huge, throbbing, black and silver motorbike. 'I'm on me way to the Park. Only don't let Wendy see yer. She gets fuckin' mad if I give other girls lifts on me bike. I'll tell her you're me Auntie Rube.'

I had seen Wat's Auntie Rube. A gargantuan woman with knees thicker than my waist. I pressed my face into Wat's leather jacket. There was a snarl of acceleration, the bike practically stood up on its back wheel like a rearing stallion and we were off. I would have screamed but when I opened my mouth a blast of air prevented any sound coming out. A sudden shower of rain and the howling wind of our passage transformed my hair into dripping rats' tails. As we roared up the drive sheep and cows galloped for the horizon.

Standing before the front door was Pierce's MGB. Wat applied his brakes with a racy burst of throttle so that we approached the portico sideways and slewed to a standstill, letting fly a blast of gravel at the car.

Pierce and Julia Sempill-Smith were standing in the hall.

'Hello, sweetie. How's the perfervid neophyte? My, you *have* gone Bohemian.'

They stared at my hair and then at Wat, clad in studded leather, his hair sticking up like a grimy question mark and his face very dirty apart from the two white patches where his goggles had been. Pierce kissed me on both cheeks. 'Who's the hayseed?' he murmured in my ear, giving my bottom a surreptitious squeeze. 'Aren't your tastes becoming just a touch depraved?'

'This is Wat. He's kindly given me a lift back from the village.'

Pierce extended a hand to Wat but as the latter was at that moment investigating the contents of a nostril Pierce put his hand quickly into his pocket and said breezily, 'What ho, Wat.' He turned to me. 'We've come to see the play. Our curiosities were aroused by Giles and Tiffany's talk. And Julia felt like a brief trip into the country. I take it they'll be able to put us up. One bed'll do. You know Julia, don't you?'

'Hello,' I said, waiting to see how Julia was going to react before putting any cordiality into my voice.

'Hello, Viola.' I found my ear being pressed against Julia's. 'Bliss to see you again.'

'Bliss,' I echoed, not wanting to be outdone in warmth.

'What do you think?' Julia held out her hand, on the third finger of which sparkled a large emerald and diamond ring. I noticed a bruise on her chin.

'What? You aren't . . . Oh, goodness, congratulations!'

Pierce raised his eyebrows and wrinkled his sharp nose in a sheepish way. He looked a little subdued.

'I'm so happy,' gushed Julia, and I believe she really was.

I took Pierce and Julia to Lalla's room, which was the only one available that I knew of and then went on to my turret for a bath as there would be no time later. While the water was running I tugged a comb through my hair. Getting out the knots made me screech but at least Mavis's efforts had been obliterated by the journey.

I took comfort in my dress. I had telephoned Aunt Pussy, asking her to send the most devastatingly seductive garment she possessed. I had imagined something scarlet and low-cut but my aunt's immaculate taste saved me from what would have been a mistake. The parcel had arrived that morning. The dress was a simple petticoat shape falling to just below the knee. It had thin straps and was bias-cut so that it clung to my waist, bosom and hips. It was made from dark cream slipper satin with a top layer of ivory Chantilly lace. Over one shoulder, snaking down to the opposite hip, was a garland of flowers and leaves made from silk ribbons and stitched with tiny pearls. It was the dress of a wood nymph, beautiful, subtle and enchanting. I imagined myself floating into the ballroom, striking the assembled company dumb by the resplendent beauty of my raiment. Giles would turn and catch sight of me – he would blanch and stand rooted to the spot, unable to speak or move, paralysed by surprise and desire. Very slowly he would gather his reeling senses, gain command of himself, walk towards me, take me in his arms and say – Well, I couldn't think quite what he might say in such circumstances that wasn't embarrassingly hackneyed. I could trust Giles to think of something suitable.

There had been, as yet, no sign of Giles. Supposing he was held up in Yorkshire? He had no inkling of the importance of the occasion. I almost bit a fingernail as I considered the possibility that he might not come.

Remembering what Agnes had always told me, I put the dress on a hanger and hung it over the bath so that the steam would get rid of any creases. While I waited for the tub to fill I manicured my nails and rubbed cucumber cream into my cheeks. After the play I would have to change fast in order to get downstairs again to start unmoulding the jellies. Luckily Aunt Pussy had also remembered to send shoes or I would have been clomping about in black snakeskin sandals, which were my only alternative to stout brown walking brogues. Thanks to her foresight I had shoes of ivory satin with pearl buckles. They were a little tight but nothing, short of having to cut off my toes, would have dissuaded me from wearing them. I ran down to the bathroom, feeling disturbing flutters of anticipation in the pit of my stomach, to find that my beautiful dress had fallen from the hanger and was floating on the surface of the water.

I snatched it out. It dripped sadly on to the linoleum. I felt very much like crying but instead I pondered the alternative ways of getting it dry by that evening. We had let out the stove to keep the kitchen cool and the aspic firmly set. There was no such thing as a tumble-dryer at Inskip and I did not dare to iron the lace. In the end I decided to hang the dress from my bedroom window where it fluttered like a pennant from a ship's mast.

In the billiard room Huddle and Susan had arranged plates, napkins and glasses. Despite its many inconveniences Inskip was plentifully equipped. There cannot be many houses which possess one hundred silver forks and spoons.

'Come on, you two!' Jeremy appeared in the doorway. 'Hurry up and dress. Viola, as you're on in the first act you must go to the head of the makeup queue.'

'Jeremy, you must come and see what I've dug up!' Nicky burst into the room and skidded to a standstill in front of us. He was muddy and dishevelled.

'Go and get cleaned up!' roared Jeremy. 'You've got to

play your fiddle piece. And you're supposed to be helping with the sound effects besides drowning.'

'Oh, but, Jeremy, it's important!' Nicky turned to me. 'Do come, Viola. I must show you.'

'I can't. I promise I will first thing tomorrow.'

Nicky ran out of the room without another word.

'Where's Buck? He should have been here by now,' Jeremy moaned. 'How can we have a play without lights? Huddle, you'd better start changing now as it takes you twenty minutes to put your trousers on. The Green Room's too small for everyone at once. Break a leg!'

'Break a leg, he says.' Huddle began to shuffle across the room in his galoshes. 'Most likely I will, the way this floor's been waxed. It's only these here glushies that's saving me measuring me length.' For once, Huddle's complaint was accurate. Mrs Jukes and Mrs Tooth had Glossoed the floor of the billiard room until it was like ice. 'Blessed if I haven't been a-washing up these last three hours,' said Huddle, shuffling slowly to the door. 'My skin's like a prune, it's that wrinkled. And bending over that sink's done for my back. My cartilage has slipped, I shouldn't wonder.'

Susan and I changed in silence. I was suddenly terrified and I think she felt the same. My face as I drew on black brows and bright red lips looked green with fright.

'Five minutes, beginners,' said Jeremy, who looked twitchy. I peeped through the curtain. There had been a gradual swelling of sound from something like pigeons cooing in a dovecote to a full-throated roaring of lions. The auditorium was filling with people wearing dinner jackets and long dresses, waving programmes, greeting acquaintances, looking for seats. I felt sick at the idea of appearing on the stage in front of them. I had never acted before. Aunt Pussy had discouraged me from being in any of my school plays out of consideration for Bert, who would have had to run me back and forth to rehearsals. I pressed the red baize curtain to my face and sniffed its comforting animal smell, like wet dog. I would pretend to myself that I was dancing.

The curtain drew back and the last murmurs from the audience died away. I rose, with a simpering transcendental look, from the *prie-dieu* on which I had been kneeling and, clutching my prayer book to my bosom, said to Zed, stunning in black velvet knickerbockers and a frock coat, 'Let us salute one another with an holy kiss.' Taken all in all, it was an appallingly bad play.

Twenty minutes later I was in the wings, my moment of greatness before the public gaze over. I donned, metaphorically speaking, the mantle of sound-effects operator. I looked through the curtain. Almost everyone in the front row was fast asleep. They lay like courtiers in *The Sleeping Beauty*, sprawled in their seats at diverse angles, some decorously with arms folded across their chests and heads bobbing forward, some rigidly upright but lower jaws agape, some frankly spreadeagled backwards over their seats, noses in the air, buzzing like Keats's innumerable bees.

'Where's Nicky?' hissed Jeremy. 'It's his cue for the Irish jig.' He thrust Nicky's violin and bow into my arms. 'You'll have to do it. Go on, play anything.'

Even 'anything' is asking too much from someone who has never held a musical instrument. I thrust the violin under my chin, grasped the bow and pushed it across the strings. A sound like a prairie wolf telling its plaint to the moon took me by surprise and made Zed, about to let the audience in on the secrets of his heart, falter. The wolf expired with a hideous shriek. Desperately I scraped the bow back and forth. The audience began to sit up and take interest. Could it be that the playwright of this ghastly Victorian love fable had got bored with the whole thing and someone was about to be stabbed in the shower? Jeremy took the violin firmly away.

On Nicky's behalf I stationed myself by the great wooden cleat around which was wound the rope that allowed the two halves of the curtain to descend gracefully across the stage. Nicky had practised letting it fall gradually so that Zed's poignant words on the subject of his love were uttered from the triangle of the closing curtains. It was much heavier than I expected and rushed through my hands, burning my fingers. The audience must have received quite a shock when Zed was suddenly blotted from view with a sound like 'woompf', his last words muffled by bouncing folds of red velvet.

There was a trickle of polite applause.

There was no time to apologise to Jeremy. We worked frantically to change the set to a village square with woods behind. I hung up the lantern in the window of the Bald-faced Stag Inn, stood upright the annoying bush that would keep falling on to its side and the curtain went up for the second act.

Tiffany made her entrance. From her first words there was a stir in the auditorium. She looked marvellous in a blue skirt, white blouse and black-laced bodice. Her beautiful hair hung over her shoulders and blazed Venetian red in the spotlight dextrously trained on her by Buck. I did my best to create sounds of birdsong, warbling trills of high notes on Nicky's recorder. Then I clattered coconut halves for Edwin Cobblestone's horse. This was tame stuff. I was saving myself for later.

By the end of the second act, at least half the audience had their eyes open. Tiffany had galvanised the spirit of the piece and everyone was acting better than they had ever done.

'Where's that wretched boy?' muttered Jeremy, biting his knuckles. 'Susan, you'll have to do sound-effects with Viola.'

'I can't do a seagull.' Susan was panicky. 'I don't know how!'

The curtain drew back for the third act. I took my place by the machinery of the storm.

I had to simulate the sound of waves crashing on the beach by shaking dried peas in a large box. I don't know how the Victorians managed to project the sound across the auditorium but we eschewed period authenticity and Buck had provided me with a microphone. I had put in some practice and was now able to make a very convincing so-o-o-sh-phe-e-e-w. Susan crouched over the microphone, making high mewing noises like an indignant kitten. Buck gave us a good flash of lightning against the backcloth and I shook my aluminium sheet gently to produce a menacing growl of thunder. Susan started to wind the wind machine. By varying the speed at which you turned the drum the wind could whisper or howl. The stage flashed dark and bright as the storm really got going. Then Mr Hoggins and I stationed ourselves at opposite ends of the wave machine and got to work. We turned the handles until sweat poured down our faces. From the back of the stage I could see a section of the audience, all of whom were upright in their seats, their eyes wide.

Suddenly Nicky, pale with laboured breath, was in the wings, poised beside the large brass bowl that usually stood in the estate room filled with old newspapers and Waldemar's half-chewed bones. He struck it expertly with rhythmic blows. The tocsin pealed with dreadful omen from the church steeple. At the height of the storm, when we had bounding seas, roaring winds, crackling thunder and lightning, Nicky lifted the model ship before a spotlight concealed in the wings and the shadow of HMS *Unity* descended dramatically into the deep. The audience began to clap and I heard cries of bravo. I gave them several terrific rolls of thunder with my metal sheet and another crash of waves. The wave-box flew open at one end and several pounds of dried peas cascaded on to the stage. I was horrified but the accident was providential. The drowning crew, who had been so distressingly wooden in rehearsal, came tumbling down like ninepins and inadvertently gave the performance of their lives as they fought to gain their feet and uttered yells of genuine suffering from banged elbows and broken heads.

By the time we came to the last affecting scene, when the storm had abated and the news of the deaths of the two young men was brought to their respective aged parents we had the audience in the palm of our hand. I saw one large hawk-nosed and moustached man in the front row hold his handkerchief to wet eyes. The curtain closed for the last time to a roar of applause. They gave the cast a standing ovation.

'Darling, you were *marvellous*!' Jeremy, flustered with

triumph, embraced everyone, even Mrs Hoggins, several times.

We were all intoxicated by success. All, that is, but Huddle, who was tenderly examining all parts of his anatomy. He went away to take up his post, serving pre-supper drinks in the ballroom, his brow dark with portent. The rest of the cast were gabbling to anyone who would listen how nervous they'd been and how good everyone was and how it was worth all the work for that sublime moment of complete identity with the audience – or variations on this. My own euphoria evaporated to be replaced by high tension as I wondered where Giles was.

I went upstairs to my room and began to plaster my face with cold cream. My hair had been considered too wild for a consumptive maiden so it had been screwed into a bun by Miss Tinker. It was not a style that suited me, I thought, gazing at myself in the glass. My face was too broad across the cheekbones and my chin too pointed. It made me seem all eyes. I fell into a reverie as I massaged the cream into my tarry brows. Was it the face that could enslave Giles until his (or my) dying day? He *had* once said I was decorative. What a pity that he rarely saw me without stripes of ink or blots of mud, rained upon or glistening with heat.

I went to the window and let out a bleat of dismay. My dress was not there. The entire window had fallen out again and my dress had gone down with it. I flew downstairs.

'Hello.' Giles stood in the hall. 'Are you looking for this?' Over his arm was my dress. 'I found it hanging from a tree. It seemed a strange place to keep it so I brought it in.'

I was torn between overwhelming relief at retrieving my dress and deep chagrin that instead of knocking him for six by the startling beauty of my ensemble as I sauntered into the ballroom, I was clad in a frock the colour of mould with my hair in a bun. 'I'm so grateful. How lovely to see you!' Careful, I said to myself, don't gush. 'I'm longing to hear about Pelshore Manor. But I've got to dash and get on with the supper.'

I took the dress, which he was holding out to me. On his face was an expression of something like . . . Well, it could only be called suppressed laughter. No doubt he thought it odd that I had left my dress draped over a tree but this was no time for explanations. I rushed towards the door where I caught sight of myself in the mirrored panels. I nearly screamed. I had forgotten about the cold cream I had rubbed so generously on to my face. A clown's mask, covered with white swirls in which were mixed streaks of black from my eyebrows and red from my lips, stared back at me like a portrait by Francis Bacon.

I may have sobbed a few times as I ran upstairs again. What chance was there that Giles would ever think of me as anything but a buffoon? I wiped the cream from my face and made up my lips and eyes properly, combed my hair and wriggled into my beautiful dress. It was still damp and there was a small tear near the hem, no doubt from its downward float, but otherwise it looked lovely and I was a little comforted. After all, the Paphians of Regency days had deliberately dampened their muslins so that they would cling all the better to their figures. I slipped on my pretty shoes, sprayed scent on my arms and neck and went downstairs at a deliberately slow pace to calm myself.

Susan was in the kitchen having changed into a grey silk dress. I had never seen her in anything so becoming and I was enthusiastic in its praise.

'Do I really look all right? I bought it in Nottingham the day before yesterday. I've never spent so much on clothes before. I went quite mad and bought these shoes to go with it.' Susan showed me the toe of a pair of silver pumps. Something about her manner told me that she also had been anticipating the party with eagerness. But for whom had the new dress and shoes been chosen?

We began to unmould the ham mousses, which had proved quite difficult to make. After rolling the aspic about inside the mould we had put in sprigs of parsley, slices of small mushroom, slivers of cucumber and tiny diamonds of tomato and set these with more aspic. Then the mousse preparation had been spooned carefully in. It had been terribly time-consuming. When we turned out the first mousse I knew that it was worth every exhausting moment.

A castellated edifice of the prettiest tea-rose pink, gleaming like something iced and studded with jewels, wobbled slightly on the plate. It was stupendous.

We set to with increased confidence and turned out fish-shaped salmon mousses, star-shaped haddock creams and chicken soufflés in the shape of hens. Susan had had the idea of filling the combs and wattles with little bits of chopped tomato and it had worked beautifully. Little egg darioles with scraps of olive and carrot as decoration nearly completed the colour range. In a moment of wild inspiration I had dyed some aspic with blue food colouring and the resulting gentian-coloured jelly we chopped up and piled around the fish mousses, like seas of sapphire.

While everyone was having drinks in the ballroom we placed our dishes on the converted billiard table. The effect of the finished assembly was magical. 'I've never seen anything like it,' said Susan, in some awe. 'All those glistening coloured castles – it's like fairyland.' Then, overcome, she put her arms around my neck and kissed me.

Compliments came fast as the company was invited in to eat. People exclaimed and praised and marvelled in the most satisfactory way. But where was the person whose approval mattered most? I fixed my eyes on the door. Perhaps he had gone to the library to sort books. If so he was the most aggravating man in the world and if I had not been so hopelessly in love with him I should absolutely give up –

'You look anxious. Are you expecting someone?'

Giles stood at my elbow. He must have come in through the french windows. My heart looped the loop at his delicious appearance in black tie, which suited his dark colouring to perfection. He smelt delicately of cologne and I noticed that he wore pearl studs in his plain dress shirt and a midnight blue silk cummerbund. I willed myself to take deep breaths and not look like a dog who has just spotted its favourite bone. Anyway Giles was staring at the table and not at me. 'This is astonishing! You said you'd learned to cook but this – well, congratulations. It's wonderful!' Giles moved to take a closer look and I tripped after him. 'I can't remember ever seeing anything so spectacular. It must have taken days to achieve this.'

'Susan did as much as me.' I felt bound to be honest, though my head sang with his praises. 'And it isn't difficult once you've done one or two.'

'The idea was inspired.' He looked at the table again and laughed. 'There's a touch of madness about it, which I like. I shall never again be able to eat salmon mayonnaise with any satisfaction.'

'I'm glad you approve. What did you think of the play?'

We moved to the doorway to make room for those who had come to inspect the supper table. The ballroom was filling fast. It looked rather grand and glittery. I saw Tiffany surrounded by a worshipping circle of men. I looked again at Giles. I noticed that he lifted one eyebrow up and down when he talked. It was a pity that all the noticing was entirely one way. Giles had barely glanced at me.

'I'm afraid I missed most of it. It seems to have been a _succès fou_. I met Nicky in the hall after you'd gone. He was in such a state of distress about something he'd dug up in the animal graveyard that I thought I ought to go and see. He wouldn't tell me what it was. He kept saying that it was probably something Jeremy had put there as a joke. It was obvious he was trying to convince himself.'

'What was it?'

Giles frowned. 'It was the skeleton of a baby.'

'You mean – human?'

Giles nodded.

'Oh, how terribly, terribly sad! Of course, children did die a lot in the past. It must have been just as awful for the parents, though.'

'The body wasn't very old. It still had remnants of skin and hair. I'm not an expert, of course, but it was probably buried in the last twenty years.'

I was silent as I considered the implications of this. I saw Lady Inskip by the window, talking to the man with the big nose and moustache who had been so moved by our performance. She was smiling and sipping at her glass. I had never seen her look so relaxed and well.

'What does it mean?' I asked Giles at last.

'The grave was unmarked. The body was wrapped up in a cloth. No coffin. It's probably a police matter.'

I spilled some of the wine from my glass. 'You think – Oh, how horrible. Someone's child died and they buried it there thinking it was consecrated ground and not wanting anyone to know. Some poor girl from the village, perhaps, an unmarried mother. Or perhaps it was a little baby charcoal-burner.'

'Possibly. I can't decide what I ought to do. It seems a shame to rake up someone's unhappiness, doesn't it? But supposing the baby didn't die of natural causes?'

'You mean someone might have murdered it?'

'It happens all the time. Stepfathers, jealous boyfriends, even the mother herself occasionally.'

'Oh, Giles, no. I feel sure that's not what happened.'

'Why not?'

I had no immediate answer. 'I suppose . . . if you really think that someone killed this baby and is walking around, scot-free, then perhaps . . . Oh, no, I'm sure it was some poor girl who thinks she's got away with it.'

'This isn't the Victorian age. Girls aren't kicked out of the house, these days, because they're pregnant.'

'Why not speak to Sir James? It's on his land. Or Jeremy. Where *is* Jeremy?'

I had expected to see Jeremy prominently on view, bathing in the glory of audience appreciation. But I hadn't seen him since the end of the play. Sir James stood before the fireplace, his legs apart, talking to a circle of men, all middle-aged with large stomachs, and whatever he said must have been amusing for they guffawed in unison. Sir James's little red eyes gleamed with self-satisfaction. It occurred to me for the first time that Sir James was probably very lonely at Inskip. His wife was afraid of him, his children avoided him, his brother-in-law despised him. Only Susan treated him with respect and seemed to like him.

Then I caught the eye of Francis. He was standing with a middle-aged woman who was talking to him with great animation. But Francis was looking at me and there was on his face a look of – well, anger. It frightened me.

'Aha! Giles and Clorinda!' Pierce was already slightly drunk. Beneath his dinner jacket he was wearing a lurid waistcoat with bare-breasted mermaids on it. 'What a turn-up for the books this evening's been! I never knew the country could be so exciting without anything to shoot. Loved the play, doxy – oops, shouldn't call you that now my troth is plighted. Old Sempill-Smith's got me bound and buckled. A hundred thousand a year but I can't get my hands on the capital. And joint signatures on the cheques.'

'What are you talking about, darlings?' Julia came rolling up to us, her glossy chestnut hair sizzling beneath the chandeliers.

'I was just saying that your father – oh, never mind.'

'Felicitations are due, Giles.' Julia shot him a glance from beneath her lashes which might have meant anything – lust, triumph, regret, I couldn't tell.

'You mean you two are engaged?' Giles could be endearingly obtuse sometimes, I thought. 'Well, certainly I congratulate you both. I'm extremely pleased.' And he looked it.

'Let's dance, my angel,' said Julia, seizing Pierce by the arm, as the strains of music filtered through the noise of conversation, 'and then we can have some more of that yummy food. It's a wonderful party. I've been talking to an absolute pet of a brigadier. A hundred if a day. He was teetering about on his sticks, trying to look down the front of my dress.'

We all stared at Julia's *décolletage*. Her technique for drawing attention to herself was much better than mine. Pierce allowed himself to be led away. Giles looked reflectively after them.

'Probably they'll be happy enough. If any woman could enjoy being knocked about it's Julia. Poor girl. It's a great relief for me, though. What are we going to do about Nicky's unlucky discovery? It isn't our business, after all. Perhaps I'd better ring the police and let them handle it.'

'That is a most ravishing dress, Viola.' Francis had

walked up behind me and his voice in my ear made me jump. 'It's easy to see that you've inherited your aunt's taste.' Giles looked at my dress for the first time. Francis, who noticed everything, looked from Giles's face to mine with an expression of amusement. Suddenly I was afraid he knew my secret. 'Come and dance with me,' Francis said, resting his hand gently on my arm. He must have sensed my reluctance for he tightened his hold. 'Come on. I want to talk to you.'

CHAPTER 31

'Do you know you're looking perfectly enchanting? There isn't a girl in the room who can hold a candle to you. How like your mother you are! But her nose was a fraction too short for perfect beauty.'

Francis danced lightly and expertly despite his *embonpoint*. We managed a very passable quick foxtrot. Solly's Stompers' four tunes were all torch songs about the pangs of unrequited longings, painfully appropriate in my own case. At that moment we were stepping out to 'I'm Gonna Cry You Out Of My Heart'. I remembered listening to Ella Fitzgerald singing it when I was a schoolgirl and languishing for Jack.

'And you can dance!' continued Francis. 'A rare accomplishment among young women, these days.' I could not help but be pleased by this praise, even though I disliked and distrusted Francis. 'I know you don't like me,' he went on. The man was a thought-reader. 'You know, it's as hard for a man to face the fact that he's getting old as it is for a woman. Of course, he doesn't generally set the same store by his appearance. We don't shudder at the encroaching wrinkle or thickening waist.' Just as well in your case, I thought, unkindly. 'But what we find difficult to accept is the depletion of energy and excitement. People don't get wiser as they grow older. Rather, they cease to find temptation irresistible. I can't drink much now because of gout. I don't put money on horses because I know the elation of winning is no longer greater than the unpleasantness of not being able to pay bills. And though you are entrancing, I shall not seduce you because now the thrill of conquest does not equal the trouble of dealing with emotionally demanding young women. I prefer a ripe creature who knows the game, is content with a little pleasurable sex and does not expect me to write poetry to her or sit up late into the night discussing her id.'

'No one could accuse your id of being in anything but the rudest health, anyway.'

'You think I couldn't seduce you?' Francis looked down at me and smiled. He seemed to have forgotten that he had tried during my last visit. 'There is hardly a woman in the world who does not fall half in love with any man who tells her how passionately he adores her. There is nothing so sweet as the incense of the worshipper. He tells her she is divine – flawless – peerless. At once she perceives that this man, though he is perhaps stupid, ugly and married to her best friend, has powers of perception that set him quite apart from the common run. He has succeeded in his first object. She will always be aware of him in the crowd. His strategy of pursuit will vary according to her character. You, I imagine, being of the soft, sentimental kind, would feel increasing pity for the poor supplicant. Compassion would, sooner or later, drive you into my – I should have said his – arms.'

'How horrible you make relationships between men and women seem! Calculating and cynical.'

'But accurate?'

'I don't know. Perhaps, sometimes. I'm not very experienced at those kinds of games.'

'I'm glad anyway that you haven't bothered to try to refute it. That shows you are as quick-witted as I surmised.'

'It's not very intelligent of you to pay me a compliment, having shown men to be false and women to be fools.'

Francis laughed. 'All right. Instead I'll tell you why I wanted to talk to you. I suppose Nicky's dug up that child.'

'Oh!' I was shocked by his casual manner of referring to it. 'How did you know?'

'I wondered if he would, ever since he started this crazy hobby. But the area was so large and then children are apt to give things up before very long.'

'Nicky's unusually persevering.'

'When I saw him so upset this evening I was practically certain. I offered to go with the boy but he said he wouldn't trouble me to walk so far. He closed up like a wall to my questions. I watched him going up to the mausoleum with Fordyce. Then I saw you two in cahoots, obviously disturbed. I was sure then.'

'You know who buried the baby there?'

'I did.' A couple danced past us at speed, creating an eddy of dynamism among the other more sedate dancers. It was Tiffany and the hawk-nosed man. They seemed to be enjoying themselves. I stared up at Francis, wondering what pitiful tale he was about to disclose. 'Not quite unaided, I should add. Bowser dug the hole and filled it in again while I recited the appropriate prayers. You needn't look at me as though I were all the sons of Belial rolled into one. It's what I complain of in you young girls. You're so extreme, so black and white in your views. When you're my age you'll have learned that almost no one is good but neither are many wholly bad. You think me a monster but I assure you my part in this was, in its intention anyway, benevolent. Let me tell you a story.'

Francis saw a temporary space on the dance floor and steered us towards it, where a refreshing breeze blew in through the open french windows. The sky was darkening now and I saw the first stars above the horizon.

'Imagine a young woman, very pretty and endowed with enough simple goodness to make any man happy. If she has a fault it is that she is a little nervous, inclined to be fanciful, easily upset. She marries just the kind of husband her parents prescribe for her – of good family, a respectable career, a country seat, a little money, sound views on Church and state. She bears him twin children. Their birth brings on a brief depressive illness but, with drugs and

423

nursing, she makes a full recovery. All goes well until the third child is born. Everyone knows about post-natal depression but few people understand it. This time the despair is too profound to be alleviated by tranquillisers and rest. Her doctor, her husband, her brother are all in ignorance of the extent of her suffering because she has been brought up to make light of her own maladies. Because the baby thrives no questions are asked.

'One morning, very early, she wakes, convinced of the impossibility of enduring one more hour of torment. She takes the sleeping baby from his cot in the nursery and walks through the garden to the lake. As the sun rises she walks into the water, kissing her baby perhaps, telling him – what shall we guess? – that he is too precious for life's struggles, that together they will go to a better place, or at least oblivion. But the nurse wakes, sees the crib empty, runs to her mistress's room, observes a letter addressed in her mistress's hand on the dressing-table, puts two and two together and wakes her master. He calls his steward, who runs to rouse the head gardener. They search the house and grounds.

'Tracks in the dew are discovered leading to the lake. Minutes later two bodies are dragged from the water. One, the mother, is brought back from the very edge of drowning. The baby is dead. Now if you cry,' Francis looked severely at me, as we circled slowly in a corner by a painting of a mildly hoggish Inskip in Victorian kit, 'you will attract attention. I can assure you that I have not gone through all this to have some silly girl betray me.' He squeezed my right hand, which he held in his left, until I winced with pain. 'Control yourself. Remember, you are an Otway.'

There was no record of an Otway being conspicuous for anything that might remotely be called self-control that I knew of but I recognised the need for discretion.

'I'm sorry. I'm so sorry – Poor La–'

'Sh! For goodness sake! Remember we are not alone!'

I did not need to be reminded of this as more and more people were taking to the floor and Solly's Stompers were playing at a pace and volume quite unsuitable for their adopted genre in order to be heard above the chatter of the guests.

'Yes – yes, all right. I – I'm better now. Go on.'

'One more tear and I have done with you.' Francis looked at me very coldly. I held my breath and blinked hard. 'Where were we? Ah, yes. The mother and the body of the dead child are taken back to the house. The husband is distraught. A weak-headed, unimaginative man, he does what has become a habit with him when dealing with his wife. He sends for his brother-in-law.

'The brother finds mayhem. His sister is now conscious but is in a highly confused state. She babbles of talking to the ducks on the lake and having fallen in. She does not remember the baby. He has to decide what is best to be done. He can, of course, send for doctors, for the police. There will be an inquest. The questioning, the police, doctors, the scandal may push his sister, already at the point of nervous collapse, into insanity. For her sake he decides to take a great risk. He instructs the nurse, the gardener and the steward to say nothing of what they know. Miss Tinker, for that is the nurse's name, is ready to comply. Her mistress is sweet-natured and tolerant of the nurse's oddities. The steward is devoted to his master. The gardener, like his father before him, has worked on the estate since a boy. They none of them can visualise a life for themselves apart from the family.

'The brother and the gardener bury the body of the child that night in the grounds of the mausoleum. Now the brother knows of another baby, also a boy, of the same age, give or take a few weeks, as the drowned child. The governors of the village school have dismissed the baby's mother from her post as headmistress for she is unmarried. The brother offers her a substantial sum to part with her baby if she will make her life elsewhere. She is jobless, penniless, disgraced. Her baby will be brought up in the first family in the county. Can she deny her child this opportunity?'

'I think she ought to have done! Poor woman! It was very wrong of the school governors to dismiss her. Couldn't you have stopped them? Surely it's more important that a baby should be brought up by its own –'

'Oh, for heaven's sake! Be quiet or I'll shake you! Youth today has no idea of what's important. A generation of self-indulgent sentimentalists! Of course I *could* have influenced them. I happen to be chairman of the board of governors. The final decision rested with me.'

'Well! I see that it suited you! Our generation may be sentimental and self-indulgent but we aren't hypocrites!'

'Thank you.' Francis was sarcastic. 'Well, contrary to your views, the schoolmistress *did* consider it better for the child. She handed the baby over and went away with an income for life – if sensibly invested.' I made a 'tst' sound and put all the contempt I could into my eyes. Francis looked wrathfully at me but when I said nothing he went on, 'The substitution was made and no one was any the wiser. One baby, after all, looks much like another. The brother knew that his greatest difficulty would be to persuade the mother to accept the baby as hers. Shock had, fortuitously, driven all memory of the attempted suicide from her mind. I believe it's not uncommon. For a while it was touch and go as to whether she would ever be rational again. But as time passed she grew stronger and more composed. When she was well enough – after several months – to have the child with her she accepted the baby as her own.'

'It's the most preposterous thing I ever heard!' My indignation was so great that I could be quiet no longer. 'It's like something Jacintha Plumbe might have written. How could you allow yourself to play with other people's lives as though nothing mattered but suppressing a scandal! What about Nick–'

'If you continue to make a fuss you will be responsible for the unhappiness of a great many people.' Francis held me so tightly that I squealed.

'And what about the baby's father? Supposing he wanted to have some say in his son's future?'

'You're forgetting that the child has been brought up as a member of the ruling class with every possible advantage.

Can you honestly tell me that it would have been better for him to be the bastard of a destitute nobody? As to the father,' Francis paused and chuckled, 'I think I may safely say that he was entirely in favour of the deception.' The complacent spark in his eye conveyed the dreadful truth. 'Of course, like the one that was drowned, he has the Ashton nose. That was providential.' Francis's handsome mouth took on a self-satisfied twist.

'Did you ever hear of anything so bad?' I said to Giles later.

We were eating jelly and ice-cream by candlelight on the terrace. The air was warm and rose-scented. The light from the ballroom gilded the white hand of a statue and the blanched flowers in her hair. On the horizon lightning flickered prettily, very far away. We were sitting at a table by ourselves. Almost all the other guests were either dancing smoochily to the tune of 'Stormy Weather' or befuddling their brains with cheap fizz mixed with brandy in the billiard room. The respectable element of the party, the dowagers, generals, clergymen and Justices of the Peace, had departed for Ovaltine and the late-night news on the World Service. That left everyone aged less than forty and two Members of Parliament. Tiffany and the hawk-nosed man were still circling but slowly now, gazing into each other's eyes. As he was six inches taller than she, they seemed like giants among midgets. His sandiness perfectly complemented her tawny magnificence.

'It was very convenient for Francis,' said Giles, blowing a cloud of cigar smoke into the night sky. 'His mistress was paid off and his illegitimate child neatly disposed of. But who's to say his first concern wasn't his sister? If it had come out it would pretty well have ruined her life, wouldn't it? The thing is, as you say, very bad but it's worked all right for ten years. A woman who could sell her own child isn't perhaps the ideal mother. Nicky has been brought up by his uncle and aunt, which is a common enough thing.'

'I know. But it's the lies. Oh dear. Perhaps I'm being ridiculous. Naïve, Francis would say. Obviously you think we should let sleeping dogs lie.'

'Don't you?'

'Mm.' I thought about it. 'I can't bear the idea of poor Lady Inskip finding out what she did. She's seemed so much happier these last few days. But you can't help seeing that her recovery is precarious. It's the sort of thing that might drive anyone over the edge.'

'She does seem, well, more sensible. We had quite a reasonable conversation while you were dancing with Francis, about Cobbett's *Rural Rides*. She is a great admirer and quoted that poem by G.K. Chesterton about him. You know "The Horseman of the Apocalypse, the Rider of the Shires".'

I did not know and felt automatically for my notebook but there were no pockets in my beautiful dress. 'So do we decide to say nothing?' Giles's profile, sharp against the violet blue of the sky, was serene. I examined with pleasure the length of his upper lip.

'What about Jeremy and Lalla? I think they ought to be told.'

'Oh, yes! After all, our finding out about it first was just an accident. But I haven't seen Jeremy all evening.'

'No, nor have I. It was a good party. It's a shame he's missed it.'

'It isn't over yet.'

'It is for me. I promised Nicky I'd take him up some food and play a game of chess. He was miserable at being sent to bed.'

'Oh.' I was mortified that I had not thought of it myself. My preoccupations had all been selfish. Perhaps I could visit Nicky, too. But a third at chess could only be superfluous.

'Care for a spin, Vi?'

Wat, striking in black tie and a bright-pink, frilled dress shirt, stood swaying in front of me.

'Good night, then.' Giles got up, a smile in his eyes, his mouth serious. 'I'm glad to leave you in such capable hands.'

Wat and I followed him into the ballroom. I saw him go into the billiard room and emerge, after a minute, bearing two plates laden with food. He left through the far door.

'Ouch!' I said, as Wat trod hard on my foot.

'Sorry, mate. I ain't much of a prancer. If you'd give half a mind to what we're about we might get on better. It don't look like he's coming back so you may as well.'

'Sorry.' I felt too crushed to attempt a denial. We rocked on the spot until the band struck a definite beat. Wat then set off with the precision of a marching platoon. I ran alongside, trying to keep up.

'Lovely party, isn't it?' I said, with what breath I had left for we were traversing the ballroom at speed.

'All right, I suppose, if you like this sorta thing. I've only stopped to show Wendy.'

'Show her what?'

'That she can't boss me abaht. She was that mad I was coming.'

'Why didn't you say? We could have asked her too. I wish I'd thought of it!'

'’S too late now. She said if I stood her up down the Dog and Bone to come to a fucking toff's party she'd never speak to me n'more. Well, I couldn't 'ave that, could I?' Wat's eyes, crossed with too much to drink, were appealing.

'I don't know. I would have been tempted to give in for the sake of peace.'

'Ah, but that's it, i'nt it? Give in once and you got no peace ever after.'

I could only concede that Wat's experience was greater than mine and that he probably knew best. We were on our third circuit of the perimeter of the ballroom and I was, anyway, too puffed and hot to argue. Tiffany and her partner were the compass foot to our circle.

'Who is that man?' I asked Wat, when I had the breath.

'The geezer with the snoz? That's Lord Bognor's son and hair. Called Beaky on account of it. Not a bad bloke for a toff. Once gave me a lift back from the races. We shared a cigar. The Bognors are all mad as 'atters and Beaky's madder than the rest. But loaded. Your mucker's on to a good thing there if she can stand the pace.'

I contemplated Beaky with interest. Now they were dancing practically nose to nose.

'It's a bummer, life, sometimes,' said Wat, waxing

philosophical suddenly. 'I wish Wendy weren't such a quarrelsome bint. Life's a fucking arsehole.'

'Yes.' I looked through the open window to the now deserted table where Giles and I had been sitting. The candle still burned like a star. An evening of glamorous alchemy, seductive surroundings, achingly coquettish music, the loveliest dress in the world and an oh! so willing girl in it – and he had not once danced with me. 'As you say, it's a fucking arsehole.'

A woman, quickstepping nearby, looked at me with surprise. I tossed my head and Wat and I cantered away.

I opened my eyes the following morning and saw with relief that I was safe in my own beloved turret. I had dreamed that I was in some low seafaring haunt being tattooed on my earlobes with the words 'love' and 'Giles'. It would have been a hideous mistake. I lay still, allowing the breeze from the missing window to cool my hot cheeks and restore me to a sense of reality. But where was Jeremy? This was the first night I had spent alone at Inskip. I sat up.

Pinned to my pillow, which was spotted with blood, no doubt from the aforementioned lobes, was a piece of paper. I had missed seeing it when I had flung myself into bed the night before, exhausted and despondent at the failure of all my plans. I unpinned it, pricking my finger as I did so and adding yet another red blob to my pillowcase. It was a particularly sharp and malevolent pin.

Darling Viola, I'm going away. I haven't told anyone else. You can tell them, if anyone asks. Doing the play made me realise how useless my life has been up till now. I *have* to get away from Inskip or I'm done for. Zed wants to go to RADA. I really think he could get somewhere. I'm going to try to get into stage managing. Of course I want to produce but I can't expect that all at once. We're leaving tonight in the Armstrong Siddeley. Can't quite see the Land Rover in Piccadilly. Square that with the old man if you can. [I really had little hope of success with this but I felt duty bound to try so I made a mental note.] All that's for public consumption but this is for you alone, my dearest girl and I know I can trust you. Zed and I became lovers last night. It was a revelation. I still can't quite believe how wonderful it was. I never guessed that was the problem. Well, that's not true. I suspected but I couldn't face up to it. Of course, there were episodes at school but we all assumed that when there were girls around we'd give it up. And then, when I was sixteen, Francis and I . . . oh dear, I find I can't write about it, even to you. You can probably guess. It was the formative experience of my youth, as they say. Francis laughed at me afterwards and said I shouldn't take it seriously, that for the Greeks it was the answer to long wet evenings in. That hurt more than anything, that it wasn't supposed to matter. I thought I must conquer my unnatural desires or be damned for ever. Zed showed me that it needn't be shameful or adolescent. He was extraordinary. I've honestly never felt so close to anyone before. I know you don't like him. You must just believe me when I tell you that just now he means more to me than any other person in the world. As you can imagine I'm still in a state of shock. We're going to stay temporarily with a mate of mine in Notting Hill. I'll telephone SCAB and the minute you get back let's meet. I do want to make you see that this is all right. It's the best thing that could have happened – finding out who and what I really am. Thanks for all your help with the play. We did have a good time, didn't we? Your loving Jeremy.

I read the letter again, twice more. I ought to have realised that Jeremy was homosexual. But it had never occurred to me. I knew so little about it that I had a very unclear picture of what love-making between men might involve. R.D. had once described a man of his acquaintance as a 'faggot' in a tone of absolute disgust, and Aunt Pussy had explained to me later that this was a man who preferred other men for sexual purposes. That was the full extent of my education on this subject.

Would Jeremy's euphoria last? As I asked myself this I knew at once that the answer was no. Not because he was homosexual but because he had chosen Zed as his sexual mentor. That man was untrustworthy and fickle and bad.

431

I bathed and dressed in low spirits. Although it was late, nearly ten o'clock, I could not make myself hurry. After all the excitement and hard work of the day before I felt flat and apathetic. If Giles had been unmoved on such a romantic occasion and when I had been looking my very best, the chances were that he would never find me desirable. I stood before the missing window brushing my hair. The day was overcast and there were stormclouds above the mausoleum. My attention was caught by movement on the periphery of my gaze. A car was travelling at speed down the drive and towards the gatehouse. It was Giles's Bentley.

The dining-table looked like a modern version of those satirical engravings by artists like Rowlandson and Hogarth. This was Idleness to a tee. Chairs stood at angles to the table, a cornflake packet displayed its crumpled innards next to several jampots holding sticky spoons. There was a bowl on its side, its brim resting on a mound of sugar. Fluffy was crouching in the middle of all this, her nose deep in the milk jug. I put Fluffy on the floor with a saucer of milk and cleared a place for myself among the dirty plates and cups. From the smooth, lustrous appearance of the butter I guessed it had been Fluffy's first port of call. I helped myself to some lukewarm coffee. I was in such a profound state of depression that several minutes passed before I noticed that there were two notes addressed to me propped against the epergne.

Dearest Viola, Forgive dashing off without saying goodbye! Mummy rang this morning to say my aunt (hateful but has all the family jewels) insists on my lunching with her today at Claridges to discuss the wedding! Mummy wants her diamonds for the big day! Shatteringly heavenly party, too original for words! Have quite lost my heart to Huddle! Isn't he a ducky dear? Thanks for everything! Mummy will send you an invite for engagement party drinks. Mind you come! Chow! Julia.

I unfolded the second.

Dearest Viola, Thought I had better take the lift when offered as train expensive and art gallery exhibition opens tomorrow. Thanks for the most marvellous time, the play was terrific fun and the party – wow! I now understand what it is about the house you like so much. Its beauty is so fantastical and quite different from anything I've ever seen before. I'm being nagged to get a move on. Must just add that Beaky has asked me to have dinner with him tomorrow night. He says he's coming to my show and then we'll go to Wilton's. He's quite mad but awfully funny. I hope you don't despise me after all I said about giving up men. [How could I when my own period of temperance had been even briefer?] Got to go. See you soon. Best love, Tiff.

I stirred several spoonfuls of sugar into my coffee, now completely cold. I was glad that the evening had created happiness for someone. Giles had not even cared enough to remember that he had promised to give me a lift. I scrubbed at some marmalade, which had transferred itself in a mysterious way to my elbow. It felt very lonely without the others. I would think of something enjoyable to do with Nicky and forget my own misery in giving someone else pleasure. Aunt Pussy had always encouraged this as a sound precept.

'Morning, Miss Hotwee.' Huddle came in, his oyster eyes more than usually baggy. His hands had a marked tremor. 'I'll clear the table if you've finished. We're all at sixes and sevens today. The master hasn't stirred from his bed yet, no more has Madam. Them blancmanges were very tasty but they've played hell with my arthuritis. Scarcely a wink all night and stiff! My joints is seized like a rusty machine. Them others left earlier. Not before time, I might add. The young lady, Miss Simply-Pist, was still under the influence, if you ask me. I haven't never been kissed by a guest of Sir James's in forty years and I don't intend to start that sort of thing at my age.'

He looked at me sternly.

'I promise I won't kiss you, Huddle, if it upsets you.'

'Thank you, madam.'

'I'll come and give you a hand in the kitchen in a minute.'

'The band, madam? Well, it's not for me to criticise Master Jeremy's choice but to my way of thinking a little variety doesn't go amiss. And what's wrong with a haircut, I'd like to know? Like performing chimpanzees, more like.'

'They were rather hairy.'

'Fairies, you say? Ah, that'll account for it.'

I left Huddle clearing away. I would go and do some washing up later when I had managed to cheer myself up. There was no sign of Nicky. The house was silent but for the ticking of the clocks and that faint susurration, like trickling water which I had heard before. I felt wretched. I would go into the library, which was the room I most associated with Giles, and unburden my heart with the shedding of a few secret tears.

It still smelt faintly of the cologne he used. I sniffed hard as I walked over to the desk, picked up one of the sheets of paper covered with his writing and kissed it. Unrequited love was humiliating. What was I doing, slobbering over lists of books, my pulse set galloping at a whiff of Dior Pour Hommes?

'Damn! Blast! Bloody hell!' I said loudly, and stamped my foot.

'You seem in a bad mood. What's happened to upset you?' said a voice above my head.

I turned quickly. Standing at the top of the library steps, with a book in one hand and a magnifying-glass in the other, was Giles.

CHAPTER 32

'I decided to take another day to finish sorting the books. I've just found these old estate maps. Look at the quality of the draughtsmanship. Those are the original ground plans.'

Giles pointed to the sheets of paper lying on the desk. While I admired them I glanced covertly at him. He was looking refreshed and alert and particularly handsome in a pale yellow shirt I hadn't seen before. Because I thought he had gone I had put on my oldest jeans and a jersey with a hole in it. I reminded myself that it hardly mattered as he wouldn't notice anyway.

'We'll go back to London in the MGB tomorrow. Pierce has taken the Bentley because Tiffany needed to get back today. What are you grinning about?'

'I didn't know I was. I was just thinking what a nice day it was going to be. The play having been such a success and everything. Oh, there is something, though, that's rather bothering.'

I told Giles about Jeremy's flight with Zed. Giles was inclined to take a positive view. 'The implication is that they're lovers, isn't it? Otherwise it's all too secretive and sudden.' When I didn't say anything he went on, 'All right, if I'm not supposed to know, I won't. It's what I thought about Jeremy, that he was probably bisexual, I mean. In fact, if it weren't for his fling with you I should have said he was decidedly homosexual.'

'Well,' I said, feeling very self-conscious, 'we never did make love. It was all just playing about.'

'Oh.' Giles looked at me consideringly for a moment. I hoped he was revising his former view of me as a woman of unbridled lusts. 'It's none of my business, anyway. As for Zed, I doubt if he's fussy about such refinements as sexual orientation. He's the sort of man who's always on the make. It won't be a bad thing if he encourages Jeremy to do a little making of his own. He'll probably hurt Jeremy but who hasn't been hurt? It's what teaches you the most valuable lessons. Don't worry. You can keep a motherly eye on him now he's in London.'

This was a robust masculine view but one with which Jeremy himself would probably have agreed. I decided to adopt it as nearly as possible, though I could not be indifferent about Jeremy being unhappy, however instructive it was for him.

'And what about Nicky?' I said. 'It's not a good thing for him to be here alone.'

'Hardly alone.'

'Not physically, I know. But Sir James and Lady Inskip aren't exactly suitable companions, are they?'

'It's no good thinking that this is a perfectible world. There are children being far worse treated in every town, probably in every village in England. In other countries he could be begging in the street. Nicky's being fed and sheltered and educated, and no one beats him. I agree the situation is far from ideal. But you can't bind up every wound. If you think you ought to, you'll become neurotic. One of my aunts rescues flies from spiders' webs. She doesn't think about the spider going without lunch.' I tried not to look guilty as more than once I had done the same thing myself. 'All right, don't look so mortified. I've no right to lecture you. I know that one can't practise the hard-headedness one preaches when the sufferer's someone you know. But, in Nicky's case, what's the alternative?'

'We might take him to London with us. Just till the end of the holidays. He could sit on the balcony at SCAB and read and things.'

'That doesn't sound much fun. Where would he sleep?'

'I suppose you couldn't –'

'Have him at my flat? Oh, Viola! I might have known. Well, yes, it's possible. But it isn't a suitable place for a young boy.'

'What's it like?' I was eager to visualise Giles's chosen setting.

'Well, there are rather too many things – furniture and paintings and silver – that I've collected over the years. In fact, it's appallingly overcrowded. I'm thinking of moving though it's an attractive set of rooms. Good cornices and architraves and a Venetian window I particularly like. And there's the garden – small but very charming with a pool and a fountain. Anyway, I'm wandering from the point. I think Nicky would be better off here. I'm not saying that because I don't want him. But at least at Inskip he can run about and be free to do his digging –'

'What about the baby's body?' I interrupted. 'I'd forgotten about that.'

'I told Bowser to fill in the grave this morning. Nicky's gone off to compose a service to be read over the grave to mark its reburial. We're going to do that this afternoon.'

'What did you tell him?'

'I just said that Francis knew all about it and that the person whose baby it was had gone away and it was better to leave matters as they stood. I think he was happy with that. We're going to mark it with a cross, which Bowser's making. I thought it would be better for Nicky's sake to have some kind of ceremony. He's an unusually sensitive boy and he might have nightmares.'

'Oh, Giles, and *you* tell *me* that it isn't a perfectible world. Beneath that elegant, intellectual exterior, you're quite as soft-hearted as anyone I know.'

Giles frowned. 'If you're going to chatter you may as well be useful. Write down the titles of that pile over there, will you?'

I spent an hour helping Giles to sort books, then I went to do some washing up and see about lunch. As soon as I walked into the kitchen the telephone rang.

'Hello, Mab. I'm so pleased it's you. I've been wondering how your evening at La Tavola went.'

'It's good of you to take an interest in the affairs of a dull, middle-aged woman like me.'

'Oh dear. It went badly, then.'

'You could say that. The food was excellent, though. And we had champagne, which always makes me feel, at the time anyway, as though nothing can be too awful. David was sweet, terribly complimentary and very amusing. By the time we got to the *zabaglione* I was triumphing meanly over poor Deirdre Sutton-Smith's dog-in-the-manger jealousy. We were waiting for coffee to be brought and I was holding my cigarette for David to light when he said, "How lovely you're looking tonight, Mab. It's nothing to do with the champagne or the candlelight. There's a sort of glow about you, as though you're completely relaxed and happy. I should like to think I may be good for you."

' "I think you are," I said. "I wonder if I'm good for you?"

' "If it comes to that," he said, "there *is* something you could do for me, which would be of the most enormous help. But I hardly dare to ask it." Well, dear, when he said that a little warning bell went off in my mind. I didn't say anything, just tried to look interested and friendly so that he'd go on talking. But all the good effects of the champagne started to disappear.

' "I've got a chance to invest in a particularly promising venture," he said. "Absolutely cast-iron-guaranteed safe. If I can raise the wind they'll ask me to go on the board of directors. That'll mean a very nice little salary for several years to come. I could do with some extra funds to be frank. But I'm a few hundred short of the full amount. You'd get the interest, of course. It's as safe as houses. I don't mind telling you, I'm putting in three thousand myself. If you could let me have – just for a while, you know – another thousand, it'd mean a lot to me." Quite honestly, Viola, I could have burst into tears. "I'll think about it," I said. "Let me have the name of the company and I'll ask my stock-broker to look into it."

' "Dear Mab," he said. I think he took my hand at this point. Anyway he got very smiling and confidential. "This company hasn't been floated as yet. It's all very hush-hush. That's why it's a chance not to be missed. You mustn't say anything to anyone about it for the moment. What a soft little hand you've got." Then he kissed me on the inside of my wrist. No one's ever done that before in my whole life. Giles's father would sooner have thought of kissing Dodo's paw. "Let's drink to our future together." Well, I did – what was left of it. "Darling Mab," he said, "have I the right to call you that? Is there to be what used to be called 'an understanding'?"

' "I think I understand you," I said. "Now, I'd like to go home." I could see that he felt very triumphant when I said that. He practically skipped all the way to my front door. "Dare I ask to come in for a nightcap?" he said, oh-so-smoothly. "I know you're not the kind of woman who entertains men casually. I respect that. A woman with all the feminine assets of beauty, charm and wit has to be very careful not to be taken advantage of."

'"Yes," I said. "And even we plain, dull ones have desirable assets, don't we, David?"

'"What do you mean by that?" He looked so taken aback I almost felt sorry for him.

'"I'm afraid your investment in opera tickets and dinners was wasted. You'll have to look elsewhere for your nice little salary. Thank you so much for a lovely evening. Good night." Then I closed the door in his face, went upstairs, threw myself on my bed and howled my eyes out.'

'Oh, Mab, what a dreadful shame! But how brilliantly you handled it. I'd like to have seen his face.'

'Do you know, even then when I was crying my heart out, a tiny bit of my mind wondered if his story about the shares might have been genuine? What fools women are! That happened on Thursday night. The newsagent told me this morning that David's done a bunk without paying his rent and leaving debts in all the local shops.'

'Mab! I can't believe it! Even worse than we thought! Not a gentleman confidence trickster but a common criminal! Thank goodness you weren't taken in!'

'I'm afraid it's all due to that cow Deirdre. Otherwise I should probably have lent him the money and not thought very much about it. I mean, you do, don't you, if you're in love with someone? You're only too keen to show them how much you care about them.'

I knew I would have lent the seven pounds and 40p left in my savings account to Giles like a shot if he had wanted it.

'What a lesson for us all. Poor Mab! How horribly disappointing. Why don't you cheer yourself up and come up to London for the day? We could meet for lunch – perhaps Fortnum's, that's where my aunt likes to go – and you could do some shopping. Spend the thousand you might have given him on some gorgeous clothes.'

'Lunch would be lovely. But I think I'd rather give the money to Giles. There's no point in my spending money on my appearance. I've done with men. They're such beasts.'

I smiled to myself as I heard this, knowing, as I had reason to, that there was every chance that Mab would change her mind. 'Yes,' I said. 'But some beasts are very attractive.'

'Indeed they are. I've decided I'm going to get another dog. A beast of a superior kind.'

No sooner had I finished my conversation with Mab than the telephone rang again. 'Lalla! How are you? How's Hamish? We're all missing you. The play was a triumph! You'll never guess how well it went in the end – despite my making a few blunders.'

'I'd miss you too, darling,' said Lalla, 'if I weren't so exquisitely happy. Hamish and I were married this morning.'

'Lalla!' I felt tears rush into my eyes. 'Well done! Oh, I'm so glad! Put Hamish on, will you, a second?'

'Hello, Viola.'

'I just wanted to say that you're a genius. If ever anyone is happy ever after, you two will be. Now give me back to Lalla, will you?'

'Thanks, dear girl. Let's have dinner, the three of us, next week when we're in London. I'll take you both to the Savoy and I'll be the proudest man in England. Bye for now.'

'And,' said Lalla, 'I want to have lunch just the two of us so I can tell you how Hamish swept me off my feet that last night at Inskip. I didn't know whether he was going to ravish me or kill me. It was the most romantic thing – Shut up, darling,' this evidently to Hamish, 'of course we tell each other these kind of things. I've written to Mummy about our being married,' Lalla continued. She spoke quickly and with energy, her voice transformed by her new-found happiness. 'We can have a drinks party or something at home if she wants. I don't honestly think she'll mind not having had a proper wedding with me waddling about in yards of white like a fairy doll. Very vulgar, I've always thought. Hamish's mother is the most marvellous woman, paints and breeds goats.'

'Paints the goats?'

'No, silly. She paints mountains. She's the kindest,

440

funniest woman you ever met. We haven't stopped laughing since we got here.'

'What about Hamish's father?'

'Been dead for years. Sibyl, Hamish's mother, hates men and says she's much happier with goats. Of course she dotes on Hamish.'

'I don't blame her.'

'For hating men or doting on Hamish?'

'Both sentiments get the popular vote. But, Lalla, I must talk to you seriously for a minute. Hang on.'

I ran to check that all the doors were closed and that Mrs Jukes and Mrs Tooth were not within earshot. Then I told Lalla all about Nicky's discovery and Francis's explanation of the mystery.

'I'm stunned! Do you mean to say that all this time – good God! But poor Mummy, how terrible! It's like making a fool of her, isn't it? How I hate lies! Now I feel I don't ever want to come home. It's all pretending and misery. And Nicky! Poor little tyke! I feel so sorry for him. I suppose that's why my father had it in for him, even more than for us.'

'I'm worried about Nicky. Now that you and Jeremy have gone –' Lalla made me stop and tell her about Jeremy. I censored the bit about Zed, as instructed. 'You see there's no one left to be a companion for Nicky. We thought he could come with us and stay in Giles's flat. I'd have him at Tolgate Square but he can't very well share my bed and there isn't so much as a sofa –'

'No. I've got a much better idea. He can come to us. He and Hamish get on brilliantly and it'll be my chance to make it up to him for having been a selfish bitch. Do you know, I really long to do that? It's strange how being happy has made me look at things differently. Sibyl's mad about children and he's just the sort of boy she approves of – bookish and brainy. That's if he'll come. I've been a pig to him so often but, please, if you can persuade him . . .'

'Hold on, you can persuade him yourself. Here, Nicky.'

Nicky had just come in and was hovering about the

biscuit tin, which contained nothing but a broken bourbon and a dusty gingernut, as I knew to the cost of my waist-line. I gave him the receiver. Lalla's voice buzzed, inaudibly to me, for at least a minute.

'It's okay, really, it is,' said Nicky from time to time. 'Were you? I didn't really notice. Honestly, yes, of course, I do, you fathead.' He listened a bit more then his voice changed. 'Scotland? Do you mean it? . . . Would I! You're not joking? . . . Hello, Hamish . . . It's very kind of you. Are you sure I wouldn't be in the way? . . . Wow! If you really don't think Lalla will be fed up with me . . . I'll bring lots of books . . . Yes, I'll tell her, okay. Thanks a million!' He handed the receiver back to me, his green eyes spherical with joy. 'Hamish'll tell you about trains. Gee whiz! Jiggerty-jig! I'm going to pack!'

'Hamish, if you could see how happy he is, you'd cry.'

'Perhaps not quite that. You know how we chaps keep our upper lips in solutions of starch. But, really, I'm delighted he's coming. He's such a good kid. Can you find a way to get him on to the sleeper at Newark tonight and we'll pick him up in Edinburgh tomorrow morning?'

'A sleeper? His cup will be full. That'll be all right. Giles is here. I'll ring the station at once.'

While I made lunch – the remains of the last night's egg mousses, which I cheered up with a salad of bacon lardons, olives and lettuce – I thought a great deal about Lalla and Hamish. There, at least, was a happy ending. My intuition told me that this was so. I must not become cynical and take notice only of the disappointments. And perhaps even those might have compensations. Dad had his hopes. I wouldn't have been at all surprised if my father weren't actually happier living in a condition of expectation. By all accounts, even the best marriages had their pricks and stings. Being in tandem with my mother must be like being smeared with honey and dropped into a bear-pit.

And there was Daniel. Perhaps I should believe him when he said that all was well. Giles had seemed to understand it clearly enough. Daniel had chosen his solitary state. It seemed that guilt and sorrow were an intrinsic part of him, like flesh and bone, and that he could not, by volition alone, relinquish them.

I realised that my idea of a happy ending was drawn from popular culture, the only desirable result being that men and women should find the machinery of true love oiled and running smooth and straight to the end. This was trite and unoriginal but not unreasonable. But there were those who had lived the single life creatively and it was perhaps as agreeable to them as the conjugal way to the rest of us. As for myself, I was in no doubt that if Giles could not be brought to love me, I should die broken-hearted and regrettably young.

After lunch Giles, Nicky and I planted the cross on the baby's grave. We said a prayer and each of us read a poem aloud. I chose one by Yeats, which I had learned at school. It always makes me tearful because it is so beautiful.

Come away, O human child!
To the waters and the wild
With a faery, hand in hand,
For the world's more full of weeping than you can understand.

Giles read the famous passage from 'Endymion' by Keats.

A thing of beauty is a joy for ever:
Its loveliness increases: it will never
Pass into nothingness: but still will keep
A bower quiet for us, and a sleep
Full of sweet dreams, and health and quiet breathing.

Nicky read the Belloc poem about Henry King whose chief defect was chewing little bits of string because, he explained, it always made him laugh. I was reassured by the soundness of this reasoning.

There was another burst of rain as we threw rose petals on to the newly turned mound. 'Summer's going.' I looked down towards the house. 'The trees are turning yellow already.'

'Because it's been so dry the trees are going to shed their

leaves early. See the marks of ridge and furrow down there?' Giles pointed to the left of the house by the road that led to the farm. 'There must have been a medieval village. The drought makes the lines show up particularly well. If you dig there, Nicky, you might find some Saxon things for your collection. And you can see the full extent of the Victorian flowerbeds in front of the house. More than twice as much as there is now. I expect they were a blaze of begonias and alyssum. Those long straight lines coming in along the drive and right up to the Victorian wing are probably drainage tunnels. They haven't shown up until now. The water table must be very low.'

We walked back to the house. Nicky said he was going to spend the afternoon watching television in the Hoggins caravan in case Hamish's mother didn't have one. Giles was going back to the library and I intended to help clear up in the ballroom. I found Huddle laboriously shuffling back and forth in his galoshes carrying dirty glasses on a tray the size of a postcard. He was marking off on a sheet of paper, the various sets.

'I darsen't carry any more, madam,' he said, when I remonstrated with him. 'The floor's got a sheen on it like glass after all that dancing. And them tarnation doors is stuck again. I've got to go the long ways round. My corns are playing up but there's no help for it.'

He was right. The doors were stuck fast, however much I pushed. 'It must be damp. No, how can it be? Oh, well, bother! All right, I'll give you a hand.' I picked up the pencil to strike six hollow-stemmed champagne glasses from the list.

'Can I help?' Lady Inskip came in. 'I don't want to rest. Tinker bullies me so much and I feel so well. The party was *such* fun. I haven't danced for years.' She came and kissed me. 'Thank you, darling. You worked so hard. I told St Margaret of Antioch all about it this morning and she said that you were sent.'

'St Margaret of – Oh, you mean a chicken. It was clever of her to know that. Well, I suppose it's very clever of a chicken to talk at all. Sent where?' I was getting confused.

Lady Inskip laughed. 'Don't be silly, Viola! How could a hen talk?' She looked at me with an expression of gentle reproach. I felt embarrassed at having been detected in condescension. 'She communicates in hen language, which I understand. She said that you were sent to make us better and happier.'

'How nice that would be if it were true. That I'd done something to help, I mean.'

'Of course you have. And now let me help you in some little way.'

'You could carry some glasses to the kitchen, but be careful, the floor's so slippery.' I looked at her kid slippers. 'You ought to have rubber-soled shoes on.'

'And all that horrible soot's come down the chimney again.' Lady Inskip looked with vexation at the fireplace, where a great mound of soot had slid forward in front of the grate. She stood and stared at it. 'Do you know, I've the strangest dizzy feeling? The room seems to be moving away from me.' She put her hand to her head. 'It must be my pills. Or perhaps I had too much to drink last night. Oh, Viola!' She put out her hand towards me.

'It isn't your pills. You *are* sliding backwards.'

I took hold of her hand and grabbed her, dropping my pencil. It rolled rapidly down to the far corner of the room. 'It's this floor. It's quite crooked.'

We laughed though Lady Inskip looked shaken. 'I really thought things were swimming. I'll take my shoes off. I'll manage better in bare feet.'

'Look how filthy everywhere is.' I looked with puzzlement at the pier tables, which were so thick with dust that you could have written your name in it if you really had nothing better to do. And the marble chimney-piece was grey with every bulge of carving positively grimy. Yet the fire had not been lit. 'I never knew such a room for –'

I stopped. Lady Inskip was gripping my hand. She was absolutely white but for two streaks of rouge on her cheeks. 'Do you hear it? That awful noise?'

'I can't hear anything – Wait a minute. Yes, I've heard it

445

several times before. A sort of soft rustling, like running water. There it is – it's getting louder.'

We listened, hand in hand. 'I don't think it's anything to be afraid of –'

'Oh, hush! Hush!' Lady Inskip put her finger to her lips and her eyes widened in terror. There was the faintest tinkling sound, very high-pitched, like the chiming of a thousand glass bells. It was pretty but eerie. 'Look!' whispered Lady Inskip. She pointed up towards the ceiling.

The chandeliers, all six of them, were shivering as if stirred by a strong current of air, though all the windows were closed. As we stared up at them they began to jangle angrily, as though possessed by some malignant spirit. Some of the glass lustres fell to the floor and shattered. I felt the hairs on my scalp stand up. Lady Inskip began to whimper.

'It's all right, really it is,' I said, putting my arms around her, though my own heart was beating uncomfortably fast. 'It's something to do with the electricity. I expect Buck's here, playing about with the lights.'

The chinking and jangling paused. There was a moment's absolute silence and then a groan, such as I had heard once before, expressive of intense agony of body or mind, came up from beneath the ground. With a violent detonation one of the pier glasses split in two. Lady Inskip put her hands over her ears. 'He's coming for me! Oh, my God!' She opened her reddened lips and screamed so loudly that my ears hurt.

I held her close though she struggled to be free. 'Please! Stop! Stop screaming!' But she went on and on until her voice was cracked and she was breathless, while the beast that lay beneath the floor of the house groaned and howled until I was on the point of screaming myself.

'What is it? What's the matter?' Giles prised Lady Inskip out of my arms, shook her and when that failed to stop her, he slapped her face hard. She gasped but it worked. She no longer screamed but sobbed with every breath, like a terrified child, her hands hanging by her sides, her mouth open. Giles pulled up a chair and pushed her on to it. I stood over her, stroking her hair. I felt quite incoherent myself. As suddenly as it had started, the bellowing from beneath the floorboards stopped.

'What the devil's that racket? I could hear you screaming from the estate room.' It was Sir James, his teeth bared, his jowls trembling with annoyance.

'It was him! The Hog! He's calling for me! It's that terrible, terrible curse!' Lady Inskip hiccuped through her tears. 'Help me! Please, James, help me!'

'Oh, not again, Millie! Please, not that again!' Sir James flung his cigarette into the grate where it sparked amid the sooty heaps. 'I tell you these phantoms don't exist. And if they did they'd have better things to do than come howling after you. I've had enough! I'm going to telephone Dr Gordon –'

'But I heard it, too!' I said, as Sir James turned to go, ignoring his wife's outstretched hand. 'It was terrifying! There is someone down there!'

'If this is some cruel game, young lady, making fun of me and my poor deluded wife –'

'I heard it as well,' said Giles, 'and I think I know what it was.'

Lady Inskip fell from her chair on to her knees and clutched at Giles's trouser leg. 'Oh, thank God! Tell him! Tell him you believe me!' She shuffled, still on her knees, over to her husband. 'I'm sorry! So sorry! I know how good you've been! You've put up with so much. Of course you hate me! I deserve it, I know. But I'm so frightened!'

The roughest, hardest, most unsympathetic man in the world could not have failed to be moved by her pleading face, makeup streaked into grotesque lines, her mouth an arc of woe. Sir James put down his hand and patted his wife clumsily on the top of her head. 'Of course I don't hate you. Get a grip on yourself, Millie, and stop talking nonsense.'

Lady Inskip gave a sigh that was wrenched out of her soul. 'Yes, yes! You do and I don't blame you! He was such a sweet dear boy, such a darling, and I loved him so much! Too much, don't you see? He was my baby and I killed him because I didn't want him to suffer as I was suffering. It was wrong of me, I know that now, but before God I wanted to

447

save him from pain!' Lady Inskip bent her head until it rested on Sir James's foot.

'Oh, my God!' Sir James's face was working with emotion. Then he turned and left the room. Lady Inskip, her forehead bowed to the ground, wept.

'Can you look after her?' Giles said to me. 'I've got to look at something. Here, take this.' He thrust his handkerchief into my hand and followed Sir James.

I sat on the floor and took Lady Inskip by the shoulders, pulling her gently until her head rested on my knee. 'Poor little boy,' I said. 'Poor Nicholas. I know you loved him.'

'I would have given my life to save my darling from pain,' she sobbed. 'Oh, my baby!'

For a while we sat like that, and while Lady Inskip cried, I made soothing murmurs. When her tears were more or less exhausted she sat up and I dabbed at her face with the handkerchief. She began to talk, in a soft, strained voice. 'I was confused, you see. Sometimes I heard voices in my head telling me that the world was wicked and sinful and that it wasn't a safe place for a child. They went on and on, these voices, they never left me alone, I couldn't get away because they were inside me – Oh, no, that's silly isn't it? They couldn't be. It was my imagination. But at the time I couldn't be sure. I tried to drown us both because I couldn't go on living in this terrible world. I've been punished for being a coward – I shall be punished to the end of my days.'

'There's no such thing as that kind of punishment. Who would exact it?'

'I've longed to go down to the lake again and finish it but I'm never alone. Tinker, Francis, James, they watch me all the time. Part of the punishment is that we never speak about it. I see it in their faces when they look at me, remembering what I've done. At first I tried to confess but they gave me pills, made me drink things, told me not to talk. I was almost always asleep . . . and the confusion got worse. And then Francis put into my arms this stranger, a baby with eyes that saw through me, that knew me for a cheat and a liar and a . . . something worse. Of course, it wasn't mine. Only a man could imagine that a woman

448

doesn't know her own child. But who was I to cavil at the deception? Francis smiled when I held the baby and called him Nicholas. Above his poor little head, we exchanged looks, agreeing to deceive each other and the world.' She allowed her eyes to meet mine and my heart was wrung by the fearful sorrow I saw in them. 'Do you hate me, Viola?'

'No! Not the tiniest bit!' I kissed her. 'You weren't well. I know that you did it out of love.'

'Yes! Out of love! I often feel that I don't understand things as well as other people,' she went on. 'I can't seem to be hopeful – to find excuses for what people do. It seems to me that everything in the human world is ugly and wrong. But I suppose it can't be.'

'We all feel like that when we hear of something dreadful. When I read about terrible things in the newspapers I'm furious with everyone. But there are also deeds of heroism and love, acts of charity. And men make things that are beautiful.' I thought of Raphael's *Madonna della Sedia*. A species that could produce such a painting couldn't be entirely beyond hope.

'Listen to me.' Giles was back. He squatted down beside us and took hold of Lady Inskip's hand. 'Those noises we heard have nothing whatsoever to do with ghosts or legends or anything incorporeal. This part of the house is built over the old gypsum mine. I've been looking at the estate maps. The foundations have been gradually subsiding as the shafts have fallen in. Don't you remember, Viola, we saw the lines running up to the wall of the house? I thought they must be drainage conduits but they were mining tunnels. My guess is that the dry summer has caused the shoring to shrink. That's why the noises have been more frequent.'

'And that's why the doors were always stuck, and everywhere full of dust, because the room is sinking.'

A groan came up from the floorboards as Giles finished speaking. Despite my conviction that Giles was right, it did sound frighteningly human.

'Come on,' he said, taking Lady Inskip's arm. 'I don't suppose it will go all at once but we ought to get out of here.'

She did not seem to have understood that the danger to her was physical rather than supernatural. She looked dazed and clung to us both as though she might be swept away by vengeful spirits.

'What's happening?' Francis came panting into the room. 'James telephoned. What's up, Millie? My goodness, your face! You are in a state. Now, I'm sure there's nothing to get upset about.' He looked at Giles. 'What's going on, Fordyce?'

'Oh, Francis.' Lady Inskip put out her hand to touch his sleeve timidly. 'I'm so very sorry. But I don't think I can go on pretending any more.'

CHAPTER 33

After Francis had driven off with Lady Inskip for a quiet hotel by the sea in Scarborough, Giles and I loaded the boot of the MGB with the books he was arranging to sell on Sir James's behalf.

'I wonder if she'll be better now she doesn't have to pretend any more,' I said, staggering out on to the drive with a volume of Clarendon in my arms.

'I haven't the faintest idea. But I think it'll help to be away from here. Francis told me that he was arranging with his curate to be absent for three months if necessary.'

'And what about the house? Will the insurance company pay to have the foundations shored up?'

'Highly unlikely. They usually cover themselves against that sort of thing. Probably the whole wing will have to be demolished.'

'Not Jeremy's theatre?'

'Possibly. It would cost a huge amount to make it into a separate building. Besides, for all we know, there are workings under that too. The maps get very vague at that point. The Inskips would probably do better to sell up.'

'After all these years? What a pity!'

I looked up at the marching elephants and the domes and wondered how the Inskips would feel, driving away for the last time. Even Lalla, who professed to dislike it, would surely be sad. I would be extremely sorry myself not to be able to visit it again.

'By comparison with some houses this is a mere infant at less than two hundred years. Of course it would be a shame but, anyway, it's useless to speculate. Whatever you do, don't drop that book. It's much older than the house. Put it very carefully between the blankets.'

'I think I'll just be able to squeeze my suitcase in behind the seats.' I looked doubtfully beneath the hood. 'It's a very small car, isn't it?'

'That's because it's meant to be a tool of seduction not a conveyor of parcels. It says something about the man who drives it – virile, dangerous, a rakehell.' Giles flashed his teeth and growled in an absurd parody. 'But don't worry. I shall drive as though it were an Austin Princess on its way to church and you my maiden aunt about to be shriven.'

'Oh,' I said, not quite able to keep the disappointment out of my voice.

I went into the kitchen to make sandwiches for Nicky to take on the train and for Giles and me to have when we got back from the station. The speed with which one tires of leftovers is inconvenient. I already felt that anything vaguely gelatinous would be repulsive. I made a plate of cheese and tomato sandwiches with walnuts and spring onions, and another of chicken, watercress and mayonnaise. I packed some of them in a box with biscuits, apples and a bottle of lemonade. I had inspected Nicky's suitcase, which he said he had finished packing and added clean socks, pants, a thick jersey, pyjamas and toothbrush to the string, sieve, magnifying-glass, trowel, specimen boxes and books.

We left for Newark in the Land Rover, which was the only remaining vehicle large enough for three. There was a little argument about whether or not we should take Nip and Nudge, which I won. We sent Nicky in to say goodbye to his father. He came out again almost immediately. 'He gave me this and told me to run along,' said Nicky, showing us a pound note. 'He's never given me so much money before. He actually smiled.' Then his face fell. 'It's probably because he's glad I'm going. Never mind, I'm not going to let anything spoil my first ever journey on a sleeper. I've decided to stay awake all night so as not to miss anything.'

At the station Giles bought him comics and chocolate and we put him in the care of the guard.

'I'll send you a postcard.' Nicky leaned out of the window as the whistle blew and doors were slammed. 'Thanks for the lift and everything.'

'Give our love to Lalla and Hamish. Have a wonderful holiday.'

A porter came to check that his door was properly closed. 'Mind you keep your head in, sir, once the train's in motion,' he said to Nicky, and touched his cap.

Nicky's face grew serious suddenly. He was clearly struck by his own importance in travelling alone, proud occupier of a couchette, all the way to Edinburgh. As the train drew out of the station I had a last glimpse of him sitting very upright in his seat and waving solemnly like an archduke departing the capital on a peace-making mission.

'What is there to cry about?' asked Giles, with something of exasperation in his voice as we walked back to the station car park. 'He's going to have a marvellous time.'

'Don't you ever cry because something touches you deeply? It doesn't have to be sad. Anyway, I don't call slightly damp eyes crying. I love Nicky. Perhaps they'll let me adopt him.'

'You'd adopt the whole world if – Oh, bloody hell!'

We stared at the Land Rover. Nip and Nudge, who had been a perfect nuisance every step of the journey, launching themselves with ferocious barks at every car that passed, had chewed up the driving seat. They screamed a welcome when they saw us, their muzzles bearded with little pieces of foam. 'I know what you mean now about wanting to cry because something has touched you deeply. How am I to explain this to Sir James?'

It rained all the way home from the station and the heater in the Land Rover was not working. I said what a good thing we'd brought the dogs as their panting warmed up the atmosphere beautifully. Giles said that he would prefer to be cold than have his neck washed by a tongue like a rasp and now he knew how a nutmeg felt. I moved fractionally closer to him, envious of the liberties dogs can take without anyone thinking them brazen.

'I can't change gear if you put your knees there.'

Susan was in the kitchen when we got back. She was making soup out of ham bones and peas.

'How good that smells! I'm so cold and hungry.'

'I've made plenty.'

'I'll swop some soup for sandwiches.'

'Walnuts? What a very odd thing to think of putting in. You are a funny girl.'

'Try one.' I was never offended now by Susan's sharpness. I knew it was just a habit of self-protection.

'Actually, it's quite a good combination.' Susan ate two more sandwiches quite quickly. 'I don't think James will like it, though. Nuts get under his plate. He's very fond of soup. Now she's gone I'm going to give him all the things he likes and never gets.' Susan had about her an air of satisfaction. I noticed that she was wearing lipstick and earrings. 'I've lit the fire in the estate room. He usually only has a smelly oil stove. I thought we'd have a cosy supper in there. You won't mind, will you?'

'Mind?'

'Us not joining you for supper. James has had a tiring day with one thing and another. He needs a little pampering.' I could have as easily imagined pampering an enraged bull. But Susan's incomprehensible desire to closet herself with her uncle gave me an idea. I began to make my own plans. 'Can I trust you?' Susan went on. 'There's something I've never told anyone.'

'I hope you can.' So far I had not stumbled beneath the burden of secrets I carried, though this was largely, I suspected, because I was the repository of so many confidences that I had already forgotten a great many of them.

'I know you don't like James . . .' Susan paused and

blushed to her eyebrows '. . .but he's always been so good to me. When I was a kid he used to stick up for me. My father . . . well, you know what he's like. He's ashamed of me because I'm not pretty and I can't make people like me. I was ten when my mother died. My father wallowed in regret, probably because they'd quarrelled a lot. I expect it was because of his affairs. Mummy was so pretty and kind. Everyone loved her. After she died he never bothered to think what her death might mean to me. Aunt Millie gave me a new dress for the funeral – very frilly. I looked hideous in it, like a suet pudding wrapped in lace. James found me sitting alone in the drawing room after the service. He patted my arm.' Susan stroked her own forearm with an intent look on her face. 'He said, "Poor little Susan. Poor little girl." Then I started to cry – you know how it is when people are sympathetic and no one had been, just brisk and avoiding the subject – and James sat down and took me on his knee and stroked me. That was all. He didn't say anything but I felt the kindness in him that he couldn't articulate. After that we sort of looked out for each other. When my father was particularly sarcastic James would trumpet and look angry. He was no match for my father when it came to words but it helped to know that there was somebody who was on my side. I saw how James suffered from Aunt Millie's bouts of illness. Even before Nicky was born she was unstable. You know she tried to drown him? It was all hushed up but there was gossip. Poor James! He was so miserable. Millie was no good to him after that. A man has to have outlets. It was then that we became lovers. I was twenty-five. I knew what I was doing,' she added, perhaps seeing the surprise on my face, which I tried to hide. 'He wept in my arms. It was the closest I've ever been to another person. He's got . . . tetchy, you might say, and unsociable with the years, but who can blame him? He'll never divorce Millie. He says that they married for good or ill before God and a man's word ought to mean something. I think that's very fine, don't you? There can't be many men who'd put up with her.'

'Poor Lady Inskip. I'm very fond of her.'

'That's because you always sympathise with the under-dog. But James suffers too. He just doesn't let it be seen. I admire that.'

I thought about this afterwards as I put candles in the conservatory and found a cloth for the table and cushions for the chairs. It had not occurred to me to feel sorry for Sir James. I had simply put him down in my mind as an unfeeling bore. But Susan had seen other things in him, and she was right. Susan did not judge by superficialities, did not care that he was ugly and without charm. I felt ashamed of my lack of insight. He must be twenty years older than she. It was almost impossible to imagine them as lovers, sighing sweet endearments in each other's arms. I blanked out the prurient images at once. Anyway, they would be happy for a while now.

I went out on to the rain-soaked terrace and picked a handful of roses for the table. Raindrops and insects tumbled from the blooms as soon as I had arranged them but I thought men probably didn't notice these things. I heated the soup and brought two plates of it, together with a tower of sandwiches into the conservatory. I opened a bottle of wine left over from the party, put the gramophone needle on to 'Love Is The Sweetest Thing', then went to fetch Giles from the library where he had been sorting the maps and a cache of letters – between the Inskip who had built the old part of the house and his architect – into some kind of order.

'This is very elegant,' said Giles, sitting down at the table. 'I'll pour the wine, shall I? I'm hungrier than I thought. This soup looks good.' Giles paused, his spoon full of soup, to look up to the cast-iron rafters clad in creepers. 'There can't be many conservatories of this height. You know, I'm coming round to this High Victoriana. The billiard room and the ballroom are beyond hope. But I think we ought to try to preserve this.'

'I'm so pleased to hear you say so. I love this house. I love all the things that are wrong with it, just as much as the things that are right. It's like loving a person. You have to

455

love even the things that annoy you most about them because that's a vital part of them.'

'That would be a love well worth having. I'm afraid it's probably quite rare. Look at these little black things swimming about in the soup. This one keeps getting out of lane. All the others are streaking like mad for the finishing line. I'd better eat the maverick.' He drank a spoonful of soup and snapped his teeth together. 'Um, deliciously crisp!'

'Oh, don't! Poor thing! It must be horrible to be eaten alive.' Then I saw by the smile on Giles's face that he was teasing me. 'Oh, you mean thing! You didn't eat it.'

'It seems I can't win either way. You have him, if you're so concerned about his fate.' He spooned the struggling insect on to the rim of my plate where it lay, wriggling its legs in the air. 'I'll have a sandwich, I think. I hope these crunchy things aren't spiders.'

'They're walnuts. Isn't this a lovely song?'

'Mm. Who is this week's essay about? Or did you get special dispensation?'

'It was to have been "Correggio – A New Sensuality?" Julian said I could make notes instead, just this once, but he wants an extra good essay next week about Titian. Do you remember dancing in here when we first came to Inskip?'

'So we did. I made an idiot of myself over Lalla. But I suppose it's good to make a fool of yourself occasionally. I've got a useful book about the Venetian painters I must lend you. I remember seeing Titian's *Danaë* at the Prado. The technique is extraordinary, almost impressionistic. The light falls on her face like molten gold.'

'I must go and see it. I don't think you made a fool of yourself at all.'

'Thank you, that's very charitable. Do you know Madrid? I wish I'd put on my coat. It's cold in here. I'd better get back to the library.'

'But I've made coffee. I know what will warm you up. Dance with me.'

'What, now?'

'Yes, why not?'

'Just the two of us? Won't we look rather silly? And I've got to finish everything tonight if we're leaving first thing.'

'Oh, do shut up and come on.'

'Oh, all right.' As he took me in his arms for the first time, I turned my face away in case my expression was ridiculously gleeful. There was a pause. 'Well, at least you feel warm.'

'I put on an extra jersey. Won't it be sad to leave?'

'Perhaps. In a way. But we might come back.'

'It won't be the same now that Lalla and Jeremy have gone.'

'No. I'd forgotten that you can dance.' Another, longer pause. 'Did you put something in my wine? Apart from insects. I feel quite light-headed.'

'Do you? So do I.'

Another pause.

'I didn't know you could sing. Yet another talent.'

'I'd call it humming. I suppose anyone can hum.'

'I can't. Completely tone-deaf. Listen.'

'So you are. Were you really trying?'

'Absolutely. It sounded fine to me but other people always complain.'

'I think it's rather sweet.'

'You don't surprise me. I expect you'd think Hitler and Lucrezia Borgia were rather sweet if you met them.'

'Probably I would.' Another, very long, pause. 'Are you warmer now?'

'Yes. Suddenly quite hot in fact. Viola –'

'What?'

'Nothing. Sorry. I think I've had too much to drink. This music is heady stuff.'

'Yes.'

'Do you know something? I hadn't realised before how very much . . . how very, very much you –'

'Yes?'

'Don't laugh at me, Viola – but I really think I'm in danger . . . of . . .'

'Here you are, Fordyce.' Sir James stood in the entrance to the conservatory. In the candlelight his eyes gleamed pink

457

like an albino rabbit's. His stocky figure was embraced by a yellow waistcoat on which there were dark splashes, probably soup. 'Deuced cold in here. I must get Bowser to clean the flue first thing tomorrow and light the stove. I don't want to lose what few precious plants I've got left. Look here, Fordyce, I'm trying to make sense of the insurance policy and I'm buggered if I can make head nor tail of it. Will you be good enough to cast an eye?'

It was the first time I had heard Sir James make a request rather than deliver an order. Perhaps the cosy supper with Susan had softened him. It was difficult to be sympathetic. He had interrupted Giles just at the moment when he had stopped dancing and was looking down at me with an expression in his eyes that made my heart try to climb out of my chest.

'All right.' He was half-way out of the door after Sir James when he turned round. 'I don't expect I'll be long. Will you wait for me?'

'Yes.' I cleared my throat. 'Yes, of course.'

And I did wait. I rushed through the washing up and brought the coffee pot and two cups back into the conservatory. After half an hour I was very cold. I would be as constant as the northern star but there was every chance that when Giles came back he would find me rigid and unkissable due to glaciation. The stove and its basket of kindling and firewood became ever present in my thoughts. Eventually I decided to light it myself and save Bowser a job. The twigs blazed immediately. In minutes there was a hearty glow. I drew my chair near and settled to luxuriate in its heat.

I stretched my limbs and exulted. I was almost sure that Giles had been on the point of recognising that I might be more to him than a colleague of limited usefulness, or someone with whom it was amusing to have lunch occasionally, a child to be humoured and teased. I closed my eyes and tried to imagine what would have happened if we had not been interrupted. The scent of the ferns and the jasmine was tantalisingly exotic. If the night had been warmer we could have danced out from the conservatory into the moonlit garden, among the statues and stone baskets of pineapples.

Under the moon, as we swayed among them, the crouching leopards and tigers seemed alive. Their eyes glistened and their tails twitched. I was unsurprised when a silver snake with emerald eyes coiled itself round a branch of the deodar and flicked his tongue at us as we floated effortlessly just above the ground, skimming the tops of the parterre with the soles of our shoes. Giles's eyes were tender with passion. 'Viola! You are brighter than the sun, lovelier than the moon, more brilliant than the stars, more blustery than the wind –' Blustery? Just a minute. Something was wrong –

'Viola! Wake up! It's after one o'clock.' Giles was shaking me. I had a crick in my neck from lying sideways in the wicker chair and my mouth was so dry that I was miserably certain I had been sleeping with it open, perhaps, horrible thought, actually snoring. 'I'm sorry I was so long. It was difficult to get Sir James to understand that the insurance people won't give him anything. You must go to bed.' Giles pulled me from my chair. 'Come on.'

'The coffee's cold.'

'It's much too late for coffee. Can you walk now?' I staggered along in front of him while he chivvied my faltering steps like Nip and Nudge after a sheep. 'All right?' he said, at the door to his room.

'Yes, thank you,' I murmured dozily. Damn! I thought afterwards, as I pulled off my clothes and threw myself into bed without washing and with only the most cursory brushing of teeth. Could I possibly have asked him to help me undress? Giles, I thought, was the kind of man who liked to do the running but perhaps an obvious pass would have stirred his senses to the point . . . when . . . I was fast asleep before I could bring the scene to any kind of exciting conclusion.

I woke just as dawn was breaking. Fluffy had jumped on the bed and was pressing a nose like an ice cube to mine. Through the missing window the sky was a wavering glow of light. I closed my eyes again and thought of the scene in the conservatory. I had just got to the point in memory when we began to dance together when my eyes sprang open again and fixed themselves on the sky. Why was it shimmering red and gold and what was that terrible scorching smell? I leaped from my bed and thrust my head out of the window. If I had not been too terrified to utter a sound I would have screamed. Inskip Park was on fire.

CHAPTER 34

Black plumes of smoke rose into the sky. Gouts of bloody-orange splashed from the windows of the ballroom and dissolved into gold flashes. There was a sound like an explosion and flames began to leap through the roof of the conservatory.

I picked up Fluffy and ran so fast down the spiral staircase that I bruised both arms against the walls and fell the last few steps. Fluffy wriggled from my grasp and shot away down the corridor. I opened the door of Giles's room and practically threw myself on the bed. 'Giles! Giles! Wake up!'

'What's the matter?'

'The house is on fire!'

Giles was out of bed almost before I had finished speaking. 'Who else is in the house?'

'Only Sir James and the dogs. And Fluffy. Huddle sleeps over the cowshed.'

'You wake Sir James. I'll telephone for the fire brigade. Then get out of the house. Don't do anything stupid like trying to find the animals. Promise me!'

'Oh, but – all right, I promise.'

I ran down to the landing where Sir James slept, calling Fluffy's name. There was no sign of fire in the old part of the house but the smell of burning was everywhere. I banged on the door. This was no time for good manners. I threw it open and turned on the light.

'What on earth – Viola? What's the matter?' Susan sat up in an enormous four-poster bed. Beside her Sir James lay on his back in deep sleep.

'Fire! In the ballroom! And the conservatory! Giles is ringing for fire engines. We must find the dogs!'

Waldemar lifted his head from the pillow on the other side of Sir James and gave a brief bark of recognition.

'Jimmy! Jimmy, darling! Wake up!' Susan shook Sir James and Waldemar growled in protest. Sir James snorted and turned on his face, flinging his arm round the dog. 'Too much whisky last night.' Susan leaned across him and grabbed the glass that contained her lover's teeth. These she extracted before flinging the contents of the glass over Sir James's head.

'Ha! Hoo! Hell! What the blazes is going on?'

Sir James sat up, gobbling indignantly. I left them to it. I took the back stairs down to the kitchen. I knew that Nip and Nudge slept in the boiler room. It was as quick as going down the main stairs so I was not breaking my promise to Giles. With every step I called Fluffy's name. I opened the door into the service passages but the rolling smoke that began to pour into the kitchen forced me to close it again. I could hear the dogs whining. The boiler-room window looked on to the scullery yard. I grabbed a meat-tenderising mallet and smashed the glass. The moment I got the window open Nip and Nudge jumped out and ran round me in a frenzy of barking. There was no sign of Fluffy.

A gate in the wall of the yard brought us out on to the farm road. I turned the corner and saw that the whole of the Victorian wing was burning. The flames leaped forty feet high, a melting mass of brilliant red, orange and copper, and though I was many yards away the heat was intense. Smoke scorched the back of my throat and stung my eyes. The sound, a terrifying roar punctuated by the cracking of glass, made my flesh come out in goose bumps. Nip and Nudge had disappeared. I ran as fast as I could round to the front of the house.

'Where the hell have you been?' Giles, looking furious, was standing outside on the drive with Sir James, Susan and

Waldemar, who kept up a low growl despite his master's threats. 'I was about to go back in and look for you.'

'I only went to let Nip and Nudge out. They've run off somewhere. And I've lost Fluffy.'

'They'll be all right. They've got more sense than silly little girls. Remind me later to tell you what I think about people who make promises and don't keep them.'

'I pray God they'll come before it reaches the main house.' Sir James, in striped pyjamas, stood staring at the façade, which was dark but surrounded by a brilliant aureole. 'Lord help us! The dear old house.'

I saw tears running down his cheeks which he rubbed away with the back of his hand. My eyes were wet also. I could not think of the house as mere bricks and mortar. As I heard the timbers crashing it seemed to me that something vital was enduring death pangs.

'They'll be here any minute.' Susan spoke soothingly. 'Here, I brought your teeth.' She removed them from the pocket of her dressing-gown, handed them to her lover and put her arm through his.

'Oh, Lor'! Oh, Lor'!' Huddle came running towards us, his white hair on end, his overcoat over his pyjamas, galoshes flapping on bare feet. 'Oh, sir! That I should have lived to see this! All lost, everything gone! This is the end!'

Sir James put his arm round the old man, who was sobbing and knuckling his eyes. 'All right, old chap. The main house is untouched as yet. We'll pull through. Stand to it, like a man.'

They might have been preparing to go over the top together. I was so touched by the loyalty of the one and the instinctive mastery of the other that I cried more than ever. Giles put his arm round me and I pressed my face into the sleeve of his dressing-gown for comfort.

'Don't cry. The fire engine will be here any minute and everyone's safe.'

'I don't know where Fluffy is! I was carrying her and she ran off!'

'She'll keep away from the smoke. Cats are very clever. Don't worry.'

At that moment we heard the sound of sirens and then saw lights coming down the drive. Four fire engines rushed upon us with deafening noise and throbbing blue flashes. Sir James became a man of action, directing them to the mains water supply, ordering the dogs to be put on leads, telling Susan and me to take the Land Rover and wait at the Rectory. Once there were troops to be commanded he was sure of himself. He wanted to organise a party of men to start bringing out the furniture but the chief fireman was adamant about not letting any of us into the house. Clearly he would have liked to banish Sir James to the Rectory with the women but didn't quite dare.

'Will you look out for Fluffy?' I asked Giles, as Susan went to get the Land Rover. I had Nip and Nudge tied to each end of his dressing-gown cord. I was wearing only a nightdress. Shock had prevented me from feeling cold at first but now I was shivering.

'All right. You'd better have this.' He took off his dressing-gown and put it round my bare shoulders. We had a little argument about it which Giles won, threatening to wind it tightly around my neck if I did not do as I was told, for once. He pushed me into the Land Rover after the dogs.

Susan and I drove in silence. Now we were away from it we began to comprehend the extent of the disaster. The sky was just beginning to pale. It was far earlier than I had supposed. The fire must have begun in the middle of the night. Supposing Fluffy had not woken me! It was only a mile to the Rectory but during that mile I gave some thought to what might have started the fire.

'Come in.' Susan unlocked the front door and led the way with Waldemar. I unfastened Nip and Nudge, who immediately roared round the hall and disappeared up the stairs barking at the tops of their voices. This was the first time I had seen the Rectory. It was a square, uncompromising stone building, not without dignity, and with a very little effort it could have been charming. It was furnished in the Arts and Crafts style with more than a few touches of *art nouveau*. I had learned to recognise this from one of the booklets SCAB was producing, on styles of interior decoration. Sturdy oak, beaten copper and coloured glass abounded. 'Come into the study.' Susan bent to unfasten her dressing-gown cord from Waldemar's collar. 'It's the most comfortable room.'

I saw at once that this was Francis's room. A large desk, leather armchair, footstool, books and newspapers, a tray with bottles of sherry and whisky, a humidor, all spoke of masculine occupation. 'You have the chair. Go on. You look exhausted.'

Susan put me gently into it and began to lay kindling in the grate. The clock on the chimney-piece said ten past five. Susan went away, saying she was going to make some tea. Waldemar lay down in front of the fire and rested his head on my foot. Nip and Nudge came in and settled themselves against his great flank. On the table beside my chair was a piece of writing-paper covered with a feminine hand in violet ink. 'Francis, my darling, how could you be so cruel –' I read, before I recollected myself and averted my eyes. Outside the sky was changing from pink to ivory. When I shut my eyes I saw again the gusting smoke and fierce orange flags of flame.

'Here we are.' Susan put the tray on the table, picked up the letter, read the first few words and threw it into the fire with an expression of disgust. 'Hot tea. Just what we need for shock. Lots of sugar.' Susan seemed, like Sir James, to be in her element when her capacity for organisation was called upon. She gave me my tea, even stirring it for me, and sat on the footstool, prodding the fire with a poker and pushing back her hair behind her ears every time it fell forwards. She wore a sensible camel dressing-gown and brown fur-lined sheepskin slippers of which the toes were almost poked through. The tea made my blood sing and I did begin to feel better.

'Poor Sir James.' I was the first to break the silence. 'It must be the most dreadful thing that could have happened to him, to have his house burn down.'

'I don't know.' Susan continued to stir the coals. 'He told me last night about Nicky. He had to tell someone, he was dreadfully upset. I never guessed, you know. The baby was always in the nursery. I don't suppose I saw it more than twice in six months.' Susan looked savagely at the poker. 'My God, what could be worse than living year after year with a woman who has murdered your son? And then to find out that she was only pretending not to know what she'd done!'

'She was so ill,' I said, wounded on Lady Inskip's behalf. 'And then, afterwards, she didn't say that she knew because she thought it was what they wanted. It was all done out of love, that's the great pity of it.'

Susan was silent for a moment. 'I know,' she said at last. 'It's just – you must see – of course, I'm jealous of her,' she finished in a burst. 'I know it's wicked to be jealous of a poor, feeble, sick creature like that but she had him all the time. Now, for a while anyway, he's mine. I can make life pleasant for him. I want him to be happy again.' I saw tears standing in Susan's small, fierce eyes.

I put my hand on her arm. 'Perhaps she won't want to come back after all that's happened. She might be happier away from the house and all its memories.'

'But he's so loyal, you see. He thinks it's his duty to stand by her, no matter what. He thinks divorce is ungodly.' Susan smiled. 'He told me last night – that I was the best thing in his life. The only thing that made it possible for him to go on. He was rather drunk but I believe he meant it.'

'I'm quite certain that he did.'

Waldemar lifted his head, and in a second Nip and Nudge were racing to the front door.

'All right, all right, get down, you dogs! Down, sir! Down!' Sir James stood in the hall with Huddle.

Giles came in last, carrying an indignant Fluffy. His hands were streaked with blood. 'Here you are,' he said crossly. 'My career as a concert pianist is in ruins. I never met a more disobedient, unco-operative creature. Bar one,' he added, looking at me severely, so I knew I was not forgiven.

I chided and kissed Fluffy simultaneously and took her away to the kitchen where I fed her with milk and pâté, which was all I could find in the fridge. She did a cursory search of the kitchen for things she ought to know about, then settled on her haunches to breakfast.

'I'm going to make more tea. Will you scramble some eggs?' asked Susan, coming in. 'Oh, I'm glad they found the cat. Hello, Fluffy. What's that you're eating? Father's *foie gras*. Good. It was a present from his latest flirt. Revolting stuff but it wouldn't do to waste it.'

'Will you be able to look after Fluffy? I suppose you and Sir James will stay here for the time being.' I was anxious to settle at least one of the questions, which were worrying me. 'I'd take her back to London but my landlord has a monkey and I don't think they'd get on.'

'I'll take care of her. She's a nice little thing. Yes, we'll stay here and Huddle can come too. It's not suitable for a man of his age to live in a cow-byre, whatever feudal notions he entertains.' It was evident to me that Susan was actually enjoying the change of circumstances. She meant to rule and I had no doubt that she would do it competently. 'And, of course, we'll have Waldemar. But I draw the line at those two sheep-dogs.'

'Oh, but they're adorable! I'd give anything to be able to have them. They're so friendly and intelligent and funny.'

'And mad,' said Susan darkly. 'No. I'm putting my foot down. You're letting the eggs stick.'

I stirred diligently and made toast while Susan got out trays and knives and forks.

'This is the stuff.' Sir James looked up from his tray across the room to where Susan sat. His face was soft with gratitude. 'We've come through not too badly on the whole. The old part of the house is pretty much untouched by the fire. They've made a devil of a mess with the hoses but we shall get it to rights, by and by. The new wing is quite gone.'

I thought with sadness of Jeremy's theatre. I would ring him the minute I got to London and break the news myself. It was quite beyond Sir James to understand what it would mean to his elder son.

'My lungs'll never be the same again, that's for sure,'

Huddle confided to his eggs. 'I've swallowed that much smoke as'd make a factory chimney cough.'

'Do they have any idea what started the fire?' asked Susan.

'They're investigating now.' Sir James spoke through a mouthful of toast. 'The whole place is roped off. I wasn't even allowed to get my cigarettes. You wouldn't think it was my own house. Apparently no one can go in until it's declared safe and that won't be until late this afternoon at the earliest.'

'We'll get some cigarettes from Little Whiddon,' said Susan. 'You can wear some of Father's things.'

'They'd better let us back into the house,' said Giles. 'I refuse to drive all the way to London in my pyjamas.'

An hour later Giles came downstairs wearing Francis's coat, shirt, trousers and socks, which were much too big for him. 'Don't laugh,' he said to me, in a low voice, through clenched teeth, 'until you've seen yourself.'

I was wearing Susan's church-going coat and skirt which, she explained, due to her wardrobe being so meagre, were the only things she could manage without for a few days. They were fawn gabardine and the kind of thing that a Methodist missionary who was also a temperance worker would have rejected instantly as being too dowdy. Because her feet were much smaller than mine I wore a pair of sling-backed sandals with the straps undone.

'My, I hadn't realised how hideous that suit is,' said Susan critically. 'You needn't bother to send it back. Now Father's away I shan't be going to church. Just donate it to the Salvation Army.'

Privately I thought even they might refuse it on the grounds that anyone down and out would be brought to the brink of suicide by being required to wear it.

'You're not suggesting for one moment,' said Giles threateningly, as I appeared by the side of the MGB with Nip and Nudge refastened to the ends of his dressing-gown cord, 'that we are travelling even as far as the gate with those two hooligans?'

'They'll be good if I watch them.' I put a coaxing note into my voice. 'We can't leave them here. Susan doesn't want them. Sir James suggested giving them to Bowser to look after. I wouldn't put it past him to kill them and skin them.'

'Viola! Do you remember what they did to the Land Rover? I'm responsible for this car. Besides, what about when we get to London? I thought you said you weren't allowed pets.'

'Well . . . that's true . . .'

'Oh, no! Absolutely not! No, no, no!'

'Only until you can get them down to your mother.'

'My mother? What has she to do with it?'

'I happen to know that she wants a dog. In fact, I was talking to her about it only yesterday.'

Several minutes later, and after much bitter vituperation on both sides, I put Nip and Nudge into the tiny space behind the seats next to my suitcase, while Giles sat in the driving seat staring straight ahead with the expression of an early-Christian martyr about to have his brushwood lit.

We travelled the first forty miles in silence apart from the snapping of teeth about our ears while Nip and Nudge tried to bring the passing traffic to order. A pathetic sun attempted to cheer a section of sky like grey worsted. I thought about Susan. She had kissed me on parting and said that she would write and let me know how they were getting on. I hoped that now she would have her heart's desire. I thought about Lalla and Jeremy and Nicky, and wished the same for them. Then I thought about the fire.

'What I really don't understand,' said Giles suddenly, making me jump, 'is how you could have formed this apparently intimate relationship with my mother without my knowing. Of course I don't mind – it isn't any of my business – but it seems peculiar. I shall never understand women.'

'No,' I said. 'I don't suppose you will. In my experience men don't understand women nor other men either. I expect because they can't be bothered to make the effort.'

I meant to provoke Giles because I preferred him angry to

silent and contemptuous. To my surprise, he laughed. 'You could very well be right. But do stop sulking. There's a long way to go.'

'I like that! When you're the one – Oh, well, you're quite right. It's silly to quarrel. Anyway, I'm very fond of your mother and, you know, she's rather lonely. Naturally, she adores you.'

'I understand women well enough to know that you're about to bully me into going down to see her. All right. I admit I haven't been lately. I'll go and spend the night there and take her out to dinner. Though what she'll say when I appear with these two mohawks, I can't begin to guess.'

'Giles . . . changing the subject for a minute, what do *you* think caused the fire?'

'I haven't the least idea. Probably we'll never know. Faulty wiring, a cigarette, soot in a chimney – what's the matter?'

'*I* started it!' I burst out, unable to keep quiet. 'I'm so careless, I'm worse than useless! I've virtually brought ruin on the Inskips. I opened the sluice and flooded the valley. I left the conservatory door open and killed all Sir James's plants. I broke the lamp and smashed the window. And now I've burned their house down! I lit the stove in the conservatory last night and it was only this morning when I thought about it that I remembered that Sir James said he was going to tell Bowser to sweep the flue first!' I began to cry again, overwhelmed by the enormity of what I had done.

Giles drew the car in to the side of the road. 'Stop crying!' He turned towards me and put his hands on my shoulders and shook me gently.

'I can't! It's so terrible! I've destroyed their lives practically. How could I have been so stupid! I didn't think. But I ought to have done!'

'You haven't destroyed their lives. As it happens you've done them a tremendously good turn. Don't you see, you idiot? The insurance wouldn't pay for damage due to subsidence. But they'll pay for damage caused by a fire. Enough for the Inskips to repair the house to a much higher

469

standard than they can ever have dreamed of. That fire was absolutely providential. What do they want with a library or a ballroom? Wonderful to have, of course, but for a family with a wretchedly small income, something they can't afford. It would have been a crime to demolish them but as it's happened accidentally it honestly is the best thing. Far from wrecking their lives, you've ensured that they can go on living there, better than SCAB could ever have done.'

'Really?' I longed to believe him.

Giles was holding my hand now, alas! in a manner wholly brotherly but still very kind. With his other he fished for his handkerchief. 'Damn! Of course, these are Francis's trousers. You'll have to sniff. Better now?'

'Much better.'

'We'll get on, then. We should get as far as Northampton by lunchtime. There's a good restaurant there where I once had an excellent fish soup. The cook comes from Provence. Does that sound all right?'

'Yes,' I said, suddenly almost happy.

We stopped at La Salamandre in good time for lunch and Giles ordered a bottle of what he said was a rare and beautiful wine. He explained to me how to taste it and what to look for. 'I've had nothing but piss and vinegar since I left London. The Pelshore people were charmingly hospitable but the food was indescribable and the wine worse.'

I listened with interest as Giles told me about the house. 'The end result is that it needs much more money spent on it than SCAB can afford. We ought to apply for government funds. I've been asked to write a series of articles for the *Architectural Times*. I'm going to use it as a platform to focus attention on what's needed. It's a wonderful opportunity.' Giles talked quickly. I loved that expression of happy absorption that made him look quite boyish, the way he gestured with his hands as he sought the exact words he wanted. 'I've also been asked to give three lectures at the Institute. I could get something in there about the need for more serious conservation. But I mustn't neglect SCAB's interests.'

'Might you give up working for SCAB?'

'I don't want to. I like the freedom of it. I don't want to be an academic or work in a museum again. SCAB is engagingly eccentric in the way it operates.'

'You'll have to get a new girl Friday when I go to university next year.'

'So we shall.' Giles frowned. 'I hadn't thought of that.'

'You can have someone who can really type and who knows how to do long division.'

If I hoped to hear protestations that it would be impossible to find an adequate replacement I was destined to be disappointed for Giles only laughed. 'And a good thing, too. Stop fishing, Viola. As secretaries go you are entirely deficient in all important areas. But you are not without some rarer talents, which partly compensate.'

I blushed and found I could not meet his eye.

'I was thinking as we drove here . . . you know, you've made a difference to those people's lives, quite apart from burning down their superfluous accommodation. Tiffany talked to me about Lalla and what a good friend you've been to her. She was very mysterious and dramatically discreet and as a result I was able to guess pretty much everything. You've made Lalla see sense.'

'Lalla did that herself, I think.'

'Yes, but she needed someone to point out to her what an ass she was being. And you taught her to think about other people. You have a real talent for friendship and that's unusual. Nicky, Jeremy, Susan – all their lives will be changed because of you.'

'I can't bear this.' I felt myself glowing like an electric element. 'I wanted you to say nice things about me and now you are I could hang myself. It's much too embarrassing. You can kill with kindness, you know.'

'All right. But I thought I ought to say it because you so clearly lack self-confidence and that's a pity. I don't know anything about your life except the most recent past but it's easy to see that you've always had to give in to other people's demands. So you've chosen men who conform to the same pattern. Take Pierce, for example. Intelligent, interesting, amusing, all that I freely grant. But you'd have to be much tougher to make him behave properly. And Jeremy. Well, we all like him but he's hopelessly self-centred. He won't be able to be with Zed, that's one thing. And Daniel. Potentially a wound for ever needing to be bound. What you need is a man who can see beyond the obvious charms of your appearance and is interested in you as an intelligent, imaginative, generous woman. With any luck, when you go to university you'll find him. What's the matter? What have I said?'

'Nothing. You've been more than kind. Don't you think we'd better go and see why Nip and Nudge are barking?'

It turned out to be nothing more than the restaurant cat who was sitting with her back to the car, displaying cool indifference to their menaces. We drove towards London through the most dreary drizzle, which accorded with my mood. Giles drove with silent concentration. I stole glances at him and felt the pain of imminent parting like a severe burn. We reached the outskirts of London, despite all my prayers to the contrary. Gradually familiar landmarks began to register on my lovelorn consciousness. My throat was tight with misery.

'Damn! There's definitely something wrong with the clutch.' Giles changed down and up a few times. 'She's starting to slip badly. I thought so, a few miles back. I'd better pull into this garage.'

Reprieve. So desperate was I not to lose him that I was content to sit in the forecourt of an evil-smelling petrol station just so that I could feast my eyes on his profile. A mechanic prodded beneath the bonnet and then got under the car. Giles walked up and down impatiently, the collar of Francis's coat turned up against the rain. Though everything he wore was at least four sizes too large, such is the power of love that I thought he looked godlike. Eventually he tapped on my window. 'We'll have to leave the car here. Apparently the clutch cable is quite worn through and they'll have to order a replacement. We'll get a taxi.'

No taxi would stop for us once they spotted Nip and Nudge. Several times Giles hailed one only to have it accelerate away as soon as I advanced to the pavement's edge with Nip and Nudge straining like leashed tigers on the ends of the cord.

'This is all we needed.' Giles began to grind his teeth. 'We'd better walk to your house and then ring for a mini-cab.'

'We haven't a telephone. But I'll run round to the box on the corner.'

'Oh, God!' was all Giles said.

It was quite a long way to Tolgate Square and the rain came down in earnest. We got many odd looks in our strange ensembles. Nip and Nudge wanted to chase everything from small boys on tricycles to the large red buses that invoked their most intense rage. In the end they were unmanageable on the same piece of cord and Giles had to sacrifice his belt to Nudge and walk along holding him with one hand and keeping his trousers up with the other. He was furious. 'Why is it that when I'm with you I'm generally embarrassed and uncomfortable and at some ridiculous pass?'

He seemed to have forgotten all about my intelligence, imagination and generosity. We reached Tolgate Square very wet and exhausted.

'Come in and I'll find some string so you can have your belt back,' I suggested. 'Just wait a minute while I shut Josephine in the kitchen.'

When I let Giles in his annoyance evaporated like smoke. 'This is a wonderful house! Why didn't you tell me you lived in such a beautiful place?'

'Didn't I? I thought I had mentioned it.'

Giles walked around the hall, looking at the panelling, the looking-glass, the porcelain, the long-case clock.

'Would you like to see the rest of it? Here's your belt back. I could show you my room.' This was not as brazen as it sounds. I had absolutely lost heart. I fastened the string to Nudge's collar.

'I'd like to see it but not now. I must change into something dry and get rid of these two.' He smiled, picking up and examining one of the silver chamber-sticks. 'I might have expected you'd choose somewhere like this to live. No, don't bother to come out again. I'll find the call-box. You ought to go and change. I'll go down to Worthing tonight, I think. Goodbye, Viola. I'm sorry I was cross. It wasn't your fault.'

'It's quite all right.'

'We're friends?'

'Of course.'

I put up my cheek to be kissed but at the last moment I turned my face and his mouth met mine. The next moment we were in each other's arms and kissing as though we were never to be parted again.

'I feel as though I've been concussed!' said Giles, as we clung together in shock and confusion. 'I don't know what made me do that – exhaustion. Our nerves must be all to pieces after the fire –' He pushed me away from him. 'Look. I'll go – I must get back – goodbye.' He grabbed the dogs' leads and turned to look at me. 'Viola, I'm sorry.' He fumbled with the lock, opened the front door and almost ran down the steps.

I rushed to the window. Giles was walking down the street, his arms spread wide by the opposing forces of Nip and Nudge. He walked fast and then stopped abruptly. Nip and Nudge catapulted ahead but he resisted them. He seemed to be deep in thought. I held my breath. Then he set off again much faster, across the square. I ran up the stairs, two at a time.

'Sorry to burst in without knocking,' I said to Tiffany, who was looking at me in surprise, 'but – oh dear, I'm *so* miserable – I've got to see him go.'

I went to her window.

'Who? Giles?' When I nodded dumbly, she said, 'Aha! I thought so. When I saw you both at Inskip I was struck by how perfect you looked together – as though you belonged. You can tell very quickly when two people are very interested in each other. And in character, from what little I know of Giles, though you're very different I think you complement each other beautifully.'

'Were you? Do we? Really? Oh, but, Tiff – he's going! Why can't people love the people who love them and be

474

happy ever after? He's nearly reached the corner now. Downstairs he kissed me without meaning to and now he'll always be on his guard against me. I'm much too frivolous and he's tried that and knows it isn't what he wants. He's looking for George Eliot, only prettier, of course, or Madame du Châtelet or someone quite brilliant. Oh, damn, damn, damn! He's nearly reached the corner – no, wait a minute, he's stopped! He's – he's thinking hard, he's turning round – he's staring at the house – oh, Tiffany! He's coming back! He's walking very fast! Can he really be – Oh, Tiff, supposing he's just forgotten something – I can't bear the suspense – What if there is such a thing as a happy ending?'

'Stop blithering and go and let him in.'

I crossed the room in two bounds and descended the stairs in large arabesques. I opened the front door just as Giles reached the top step. He was propelled into the hall by Nip and Nudge, who were desperate to get back into the house. He let go of them and took hold of my hands. 'Viola, I've just come to my senses – I can't do without you – I've been such a fool! When we kissed just now, I realised it was what I've been wanting to do for such a long time. I fell in love with you weeks ago – I think probably that first time at La Petite Sonnerie – but I wouldn't let myself admit it – Could you? Is it possible –?' He must have seen the answer clearly on my face for he took me in his arms. 'Oh, my dearest, darling girl! I'm an idiot –'

'I know you are,' I said, as I lifted my face to kiss him. 'That's why I love you.'